Daughter of Mystery

Heather Rose Jones

Bella
BOOKS

2014

Bella Books, Inc.
P.O. Box 10543
Tallahassee, FL 32302

Printed in the United States of America on acid-free paper.

First Bella Books Edition 2014

Editor: Katherine V. Forrest
Cover Designed by: KIARO Creative Ltd.

ISBN: 978-1-59493-380-6

About the Author

Heather Rose Jones is a manufacturing discrepancy investigator for a major San Francisco Bay Area pharmaceutical company and has a PhD from U.C. Berkeley in Linguistics, specializing in the semantics of Medieval Welsh prepositions. She has previously published a number of short stories, including the "Skin Singer" series in Marion Zimmer Bradley's *Sword and Sorceress* anthologies, as well as non-fiction publications on topics ranging from biotech to historic costume to naming practices.

Dedicated in loving memory to Phyllis G. Jones
and Judy Gerjuoy

Acknowledgments

I would like to thank my test-readers and subject matter experts, whose advice and feedback were endlessly helpful: Adrien S., Allison T., Chris L., Connie S., Cordelia S., Cyn M., Judy G., Laurel L., Lauri W., Mary Anne S., Sara U., Sharon K., and Ursula W.

Author's Note on Pronunciation

For interested readers, there are three basic rules for Alpennian pronunciation. Names are stressed on the first syllable. The letter "z" is pronounced "ts" as in German. The combination "ch" is pronounced as "k." Non-Alpennian names follow the rules for their language of origin.

CHAPTER ONE

Prelude

Baron Saveze nodded almost imperceptibly to the waiting footman who removed a silver cover from the dish of *chapon à la Provençale* and slipped it deftly onto the table before him. He prodded the capon delicately with his fork, sliced off a morsel then paused with the fork halfway to his mouth to announce, "We shall be going out this evening."

If the baron were less rich or less powerful, he would have been called an Eccentric, but Alpennian society didn't use that word of a man like the baron. As he was the only person sitting to dinner, and as it was neither one of his eccentricities to explain his plans to the lower servants nor to presume such exalted rank as to speak in the royal plural, the target of this remark appeared to be the motionless figure standing precisely one step behind and to the right of his chair.

The baron turned his head the smallest fraction that would enable him to catch any reaction as he continued, "We shall be going to a ball."

His auditor gratified him with a startled shift in stance.

Another dinner guest—had there been another dinner guest—would have been able to place that figure's position in the household with some certainty, up to a point. That the coat and breeches were in the archaic mode indicated a position in the household staff. That they were of costly fabric spoke of valued talents. That a narrow-bladed sword hung at the waist—even here at a simple homely dinner—gave the profession as *armin*, a formal bodyguard, indeed as a duelist. That the body wearing those clothes and that sword was slim and muscular argued a seriousness to the position that went beyond the longstanding fashion in Rotenek for armed shadows. And that this slim, muscular body was also curved was…unexpected. But that *was* one of the baron's eccentricities.

CHAPTER TWO

Barbara

Barbara knew the game they played and maintained her stance of attentive but disinterested readiness as the baron turned more substantially toward her and said, "I should like you to wear the bottle-green satin tonight. My goddaughter is being introduced to society and I must make an appearance. I should like to make a good show."

"As you wish," she responded, in a tone that acknowledged that no reply had been needed.

He finally completed the path of the capon to his mouth and chewed thoughtfully for a few moments. "I do hope she's grown more personable since I spoke with her last. She insisted on conversing with me in Latin! Said she needed the practice. But what does a fashionable young lady need with Latin conversation, I ask you?"

When his grumbling had died into silence, Barbara murmured, "May I speak?" in a tone slightly less formal than before. It had the light fluidity of a polite formula and she didn't continue until a raised hand gestured his assent.

"What need, after all, has an armin for Latin conversation? Or for Italian? Or—"

"But that was different. Back when I set you to studying, I had no notion what use I might want to make of you. Margerit's path has been fixed since the day she first set foot on it. A pleasant face, the usual social graces, a brilliant season and the best marriage her dowry can buy. A pity her father had the poor taste to follow his wife to the grave or she might have a bit more to bargain with."

Again, the pause. Again, "May I speak?" Again, the nod. "You are a wealthy man and her godfather. Might you not—"

"Oh, certainly, certainly. Why else did they offer me that honor except in the hope of some return on the investment? And every penny I spend on her escapes the grasp of that nephew of mine. At least he hasn't followed us out to this godforsaken town yet or he'd be tying bells on my purse strings to know every coin that slips out of his expectations."

Barbara watched in concern as he took a second bite of the capon then sighed and pushed the plate away. The nearest footman whisked it back to the kitchen, following the path previously traveled by the trout and the *galantine de veau*. "Nothing tastes right any more." He sighed again. "What's the point of hiring a cook all the way from Paris if everything I put in my mouth tastes like pap?" From the aroma as each cover was lifted, Barbara knew the dinner had been among Guillaumin's best. He shifted in his seat to rise and a second footman appeared to draw back the chair—pausing just in time when he sat back heavily with a hand pressed to his chest.

Barbara took a quick step forward in alarm. "Mesner, you're ill. Don't go to this ball; you should rest."

The baron's head snapped up. "You forget your place!"

She dropped to one knee beside him as if felled by an ax. There were no murmured politenesses this time.

He patted her gently on the shoulder, then gripped it firmly, using the action to mask how heavily he leaned on her as she helped him rise to his feet. "Your job is to protect me against the rest of the world, not against myself. That would be a task beyond even your skills." He moved now with no sign of weakness. "Be ready in an hour," he added from the doorway.

An hour might have been just barely sufficient for the baron's meticulous preparations. In a quarter of that time, Barbara had changed clothes and was cooling her heels in the library with a copy of Fortunatus's *De Mysteriis et Misteriis*. But translating Fortunatus failed to distract her this time. The green satin. That meant tonight was just for show and she hated being used for show. In the city, even a friendly ball might lead to— Her mind shied away from the events of the last month. That was real. That was sure. But this…this was an incongruous mix of frivolity and intrigue, of curious stares and blind obliviousness. The only thing that could redeem such an evening was the certainty of her duty and the satisfaction of performing it. But tonight she would be no more than a mark of the baron's status, no different from the crest on his coach door or the number of footmen that waited to usher him to it for the brief trip through darkening streets.

* * *

There had been no chance to examine the venue in advance. The family of Margerit Sovitre, the baron's goddaughter, was evidently of sufficient birth that the guest list was extensive but not of sufficient wealth that their own house could contain it. In Rotenek, it was the other way round: the oldest and wealthiest families hired the public *salle* for the entertainments their narrow mansions couldn't contain while the new money, on the outskirts, had room for private ballrooms. But here in the country the titled kept expansive properties and those of lesser means hired public rooms in the civic hall. It occurred to her, seeing the rows of carriages lining the neighboring streets, that the most practical gift the baron might have given his goddaughter for her coming out would have been the loan of his house to host it. The ballroom would have been more than sufficient and currently it saw no greater use than her morning fencing practices. But no, this event would have been in train since long before the baron had abruptly moved his household from the city. And even simply housing the event would have been more strain than she'd wish on him at the moment.

There was no trace of his earlier weakness now as they entered into the noise and bustle of the foyer on the heels of a family dressed in the height of provincial fashion. A tall man in an elegantly sober suit hurriedly broke away from the preceding party and approached. He didn't aspire to the heights of fashion that she was accustomed to in Rotenek but he would have done well enough if his sweeping side-whiskers weren't so badly swallowed by the high stiff collar of his shirt. It gave the impression of a tortoise. He had the look of a man accustomed to the respect and obedience of those around him, but he bowed to the baron in a manner that stopped just short of obsequious.

"Mesner, you do my niece great honor by your presence. Would you care to—"

The baron interrupted him. "I would care to find some quiet place to sit down, Fulpi. And then you may bring my goddaughter to me."

"Of course, Mesner." He bowed once more and looked around searchingly. "There is a small sitting room behind the stairs and to the right." He gestured in the general direction. "Your, ah…" Barbara felt his eyes fall on her disapprovingly. "Your attendant may wait downstairs, if you please." He gave a nervous laugh. "After all, this is hardly Rotenek, where one might expect assassins behind every curtain."

The baron waved his hand dismissively, but not in her direction so she remained fixed in place behind him. "I do not please. Indulge an old man's affectations," he said. "I never go out in public without my duelist, even in such quiet places as this." He made the word "quiet" convey the sense that little of any interest—either good or bad—could be expected to happen in a town like Chalanz. Barbara prayed that it would prove true.

By habit and reflex she looked around as they were led to the small blue-upholstered room. A grand arching staircase led up to the main ballroom. She was grateful that the baron wouldn't be asked to climb it. Music and laughter and the sounds of dancing drifted down from the upper rooms.

The tall man disappeared as the baron settled himself carefully at one end of a damask-covered settee and Barbara took her post one step and to the side of the curving armrest. "Niece," the host had said. She recalled the baron mentioning something about dead parents. And yet the girl's presentation didn't seem to lack for much. Still, no doubt there were cousins to be brought out as well. A brief splash, a push to accept the first decent offer and an uncle satisfied to have completed his duty and have her off his hands. She might have been stirred to sympathy, but they were like figures in one of the tapestries on the wall, living out their lives in sight but in no way touching her own.

CHAPTER THREE

Margerit

As Margerit moved through the figures of the minuet, Laurint leaned in closely to ask, "Is your coming-out ball everything you ever dreamed it would be?"

Aunt Honurat, during that afternoon's instructions, had strongly emphasized the value of dissembling, so she smiled and nodded. Was there anyone here tonight who would believe that she'd never spent a single moment dreaming about her coming-out ball? Sister Petrunel would have understood. Her governess was the only person with whom she'd shared her closest secrets. The Sisters of Saint Orisul were among the few who thought that, for a girl, devotion to learning could be only slightly less important than devotion to God. She'd certainly learned the value of dissembling on that topic very young. The only time she could recall her uncle beating her was the year Sister Petrunel had first joined them and she'd excitedly proclaimed that when she grew up she and Petra were going to run away to the university in Rotenek together. No, she'd learned to keep those dreams secret.

Laurint smiled encouragingly at her as their hands met in the next figure. The hall buzzed with conversation over the thin sound of the musicians. He'd said something she couldn't hear, so she merely smiled back. One season, Uncle Mauriz had said. One season done right and properly. Two, only if absolutely necessary. He'd set it out for her as if it had been one of his business contracts. If she would undertake to do her part, he would see that she wore the right clothes and went to the right parties and met the right young men. Of course, in the end it was Aunt Honurat who saw to the clothes and Aunt Bertrut who knew which were the right parties. And all of them together couldn't quite agree on just who were the right young men, so they invited everyone of sufficient birth, along with their sisters and mothers. Laurint was a "right young man" by anyone's standards, with a pleasing face and manner and expectations of a very comfortable income. He was also as good as engaged to Mari Faikrimek with the announcement delayed only due to her grandmother's recent death. In her opinion, this made him an ideal dance partner, for he was charming and entertaining— and a fair enough dancer—but there was no worry that he'd mistake her enjoyment for encouragement. The truth was that while the making of a good match was the acknowledged purpose of her season, it was a goal hard to envision.

One season as part of society's parade of eligible young women. Not as young as most—that had been part of the bargain as well. Her cousin Sofi would come out in a few years at seventeen and have her dancing seasons before being expected to settle down to the serious business of match-making. But she herself only had that narrow span between too young to marry and on the shelf. One season done right and properly. A second, if needed, with fewer new gowns and no grand ball. After that—after she had come of age and her bloom was considered to be fading—a last chance at the balls and parties, escorting Sofi on her own rounds. Uncle Mauriz might then look for some minor business alliance he could use her to cement. And if no match were forthcoming still, she could look forward to taking her own turn as governess to little cousin Iulien and companion to Aunt Bertrut and so on, stretching out down the years.

Aunt Bertrut had argued for a dancing season. Her two guardians had butted heads over that as over so many things. Bertrut Sovitre might be her father's sister, but Mauriz Fulpi claimed authority as her closest male relative, her mother's brother. Bertrut had taken her part countless times, often it seemed as much out of contrariness as sympathy. But Uncle Mauriz held the purse strings. The gowns and parties were at his expense. Her own resources were to be hoarded for her dowry. And Margerit knew, though she had never been told in as many words, that Bertrut lived as comfortably as she did because the shared guardianship gave her an excuse to live in the Fulpi household. Her own funds would never have stretched to bringing out a debutante.

In any event, she hadn't wanted a dancing season. She'd been immersed in her studies: drinking in every scrap of the classics that Sister Petrunel could pour out for her, wheedling books to borrow from her uncle's friends or from her cousin Nikule when he came home from the university. Coming out had spelled the end of all that. But tonight there were more immediate matters on her mind. There were names and relationships to remember, new faces to place. She must remember the movements of dances she'd only previously practiced at family parties. Aunt Honurat had drilled her in the need to keep moving, to speak to everyone and linger with no one. Each time she was presented with a new partner she sighed silently in relief.

The music ended. Laurint bowed and she curtsied and then that refuge was gone for now. Her uncle stepped into the gap just as Aunt Bertrut was descending on her with another *grande dame* to be charmed.

"Margerit, your godfather is here to see you," he said in a low rushed voice. "Bertrut, why didn't you tell me Baron Saveze was in residence?"

Aunt Bertrut looked just as flustered as he did. "How could I tell you when I didn't know myself? Let me look at you child," she said turning to pat a curl here and arrange a ribbon there. "Go. You mustn't keep him waiting."

* * *

As far back as Margerit could remember, the coming of spring was marked, not only by the snowdrops and daffodils giving way to more robust blooms, but by the town gossip over which of the great lords would take up residence in Chalanz for the summer. The city's season ended when Rotenek lay stifling in the heat, bringing the risk of fever and the sureness of tedium but in Chalanz the season was only just beginning. The only one of the great lords who held any interest for her was Baron Saveze who, for reasons of very distant kinship and hope of patronage, had been named her godfather. His attention to her spiritual development had been nonexistent and for the most part he seemed to forget about her entirely. But in those seasons when he took residence in Chalanz there were presents and trinkets and the hope of being given glimpses of his larger world. At certain key turns of her life he had been appealed to for some more substantial support. But of the man himself she really knew very little. That he had deigned to attend her ball was promising. That he was in town at all was startling. The social calendar in Rotenek ran past Eastertide and that was quite some time away.

It had been three years since she'd last seen her godfather up close. He was much as she remembered him, though greatly shrunken with the years. Just as she was on the point of making her curtsy, the baron waved a hand at her uncle and said, "Thank you for bringing her to me. You may go and we shall have a nice comfortable little chat."

Margerit was shocked to hear someone speak so dismissively to her uncle and she felt him tense with irritation but he merely bowed wordlessly, turned and left.

Now she made her curtsy and raised her gloved hand for the baron to take and press lightly with his fingers. Some salutation seemed called for and she fumbled through, "You do me great honor—that is…oh, Godfather, I'm so glad you came. We had no idea that you were in town or my aunt would have sent you an invitation, of course."

Even if he weren't so high above her own birth, she wouldn't have expected the same full gallantry shown by the young men upstairs, with their near-kisses and deep bows. But she was surprised that he made no move to rise in greeting. She raised her eyes as he released her hand and only then did she notice the second elegantly-dressed person standing nearby. She stepped forward into another, smaller curtsy and raised her hand once more, saying, "I'm sure we've been introduced earlier but I'm being so stupid with names tonight—there are so many new people." Her words trailed off as the figure remained motionless except for a quick darting glance toward the baron.

"No, no, my dear," the latter said with an amused chuckle. "It's quite unlikely that anyone has introduced you to my duelist."

"Oh," she said, feeling her cheeks redden in confusion. Her mind raced through her aunt's teachings. What was the social place of that most elite rank of armin? Here in Chalanz such a thing was unheard of except among the visiting nobility. Most armins were mere hirelings but she had heard that in the capitol the young cousins of great men might serve as duelist for a time. And then she exclaimed, "Oh!" again when she saw the second mistake she'd made. What she'd taken for cropped curls were only unruly wisps of tawny hair that had escaped from their pins. This was no youth but a woman, the satin breeches displaying her trim figure to immodest advantage. Margerit expected to see mockery of her error in the woman's gaze but those pale blue eyes rested on her with no reaction.

"Never mind," the baron said. "Come sit here beside me and let us talk for a bit. You're looking very pretty tonight."

"Oh no," Margerit replied shyly. "I know I'm not pretty but the dress is and that helps."

"Never contradict a man when he says you're pretty," the old man chided. "We don't like women who argue with us."

"Have you been in Chalanz long?" Margerit asked quickly. Flirtatious talk made her uncomfortable even when it was so clearly meaningless. "You told me last time we spoke that you never leave Rotenek before the roses bloom, but we've barely started seeing the crocuses just last week."

"My exile," he said heavily, "is of fairly recent date. We only arrived on Tuesday last and I haven't yet settled in enough to be paying social calls."

"Exile? Oh, you're teasing me," she said hesitantly.

He sighed. "There was…an incident. Barbara killed a man, it seems." He looked back over his shoulder at the duelist. She stared straight ahead, but Margerit saw her face take on a stricken cast. The baron continued, "Oh it was all legal and proper. He'd threatened and insulted me there in the public square. But it seems he was one of Princess Elisebet's favorites. It would have been wiser to have settled the matter without blood. Instead we are sent here, to Chalanz, until it please Elisebet to forget the matter."

"But I'm sure it wasn't…" Margerit began. "That is…" There was nothing to say that wouldn't sound like reproach, but it seemed monstrously unfair to her that the duelist should be blamed for doing her job well.

The baron followed the direction of her glance and frowned. "Barbara, perhaps you could go fetch my goddaughter a glass of whatever it is they allow young women to drink at these affairs. And brandy for me."

Barbara bowed and left the room silently. Margerit's curiosity overcame caution, now that politeness didn't forbid it. "I've never heard of a woman armin before. How did you come to hire her?"

In any other man his expression might have been called mischievous. He leaned forward and whispered conspiratorially, "I didn't, I bought her." He seemed to enjoy the shock this caused. "Her father sold her to me as an infant. But that's a story for another day. I'm told that it has been my duty to see you properly educated. Tell me, have I done so?"

It might have been a joke but Margerit wasn't certain enough to laugh. "You sent one of the *Orisules*—one of the teaching Sisters—to be my governess and I can't think of anything you could have done that would have been better. Uncle Fulpi thought it was a mistake to hire her, but he didn't want to go against your wishes. He thought I should be learning watercolors and singing and the harp rather than geometry and Latin and philosophy, but I'm so glad you wanted me to have a classical education."

"Did I? I don't recall saying anything of the sort. What a peculiar woman she must have been. What was her name again? I can't say that I remember sending you a governess at all."

Margerit's heart sank. He didn't remember? All her life her greatest joy had been knowing that her godfather valued the same things she loved. Had it all been a misunderstanding? "Her name was Sister Petrunel. She showed me the letter you sent asking for a teacher. You wrote that you wanted the best they could provide."

He thought for a moment. "I suppose I must have, in that case."

"Then you didn't…that is…I thought you sent her because you meant me to be a scholar." She couldn't keep the disappointment out of her voice.

Unexpectedly, he laughed out loud. "Well that, I suppose, accounts for your strange enthusiasm for Latin conversation! You're a odd child, but I suppose it hasn't done you any harm."

Margerit floundered in confusion but was saved from making a stammering reply by Barbara's return. She offered a tray with two glasses to the baron first. He waved it over to her before taking his own glass. He swirled the very small amount of the liquid around in the glass and frowned up at his armin but said nothing.

Barbara asked softly, "May I speak?" At the baron's consent she continued, "Maistir Fulpi is waiting outside. He asked me to inquire when the young lady might be able to return to her other guests."

Having delivered this not-quite-a-question, she took her place once more, two steps to the baron's side, staring at nothing and watching everything.

"Well I suppose I must give you back, my dear," the baron said, handing her up from the sofa but remaining seated. "Perhaps we shall see more of each other soon."

Margerit's head was spinning but she seemed required to do no more than smile and bob yet another curtsy as she left the room.

Uncle Mauriz was, indeed, waiting just at the other side of the doors. He questioned her mercilessly as he escorted her back up to the ballroom: What had the baron said? What had he wanted? Why had he come to Chalanz so early? What had he offered? Would he use his influence to see her well launched in society?

"We talked about...I don't know. Unimportant things." She weathered his scorn, knowing answers would only lead to more pointed questions. When she thought on it, the conversation had been very odd. Her uncle would pick it to pieces, looking for meaning, for usefulness. Instead he berated her for her unworldliness. What was the point in having ties to such an important man if you didn't make proper use of him?

But the avowed purpose of the night was dancing and so when they reached the crowded hall she could escape him by doing her duty. It felt more and more like a duty as the night wore on. Did other women really enjoy this? The endless stream of insincere pleasantries, the touch of hands in the dance figures—all either clammy and sweating or hot and lingering. She kept trying to imagine marriage to any of the young men presented as eligible and felt nothing but a faint panic. And Aunt Bertrut was determined that the ball be a success, so there was no release until dawn began lightening the sky.

CHAPTER FOUR

Barbara

The hesitant tapping on the door had Barbara not merely awake but on her feet and slamming the door open before she even remembered what she feared. The previous evening's excursion had not ended well. After the girl had left, the baron had sat quietly cradling his glass of brandy for long enough that Barbara began weighing whether she was being punished with a test of patience. Or perhaps there had been some disturbing topic in the conversation she'd missed that must be pondered immediately. At last he broke the silence. "Barbara, find one of the servants who knows this place. Have my carriage taken to some discreet back door and then have my footmen come here to me. I think I shall need to be carried out and I don't care to become a spectacle for all the town."

She had arranged it all, then returned to hover over him as he was bundled out through a deliveryman's door to the carriage and then from carriage to bed. It had been late indeed when she had been free to seek her own sleep. And now, on being woken, her first thought was of further disaster.

The housemaid who had tapped on the door stepped back quickly with her eyes wide. "The…the fencing master is here. Mefro Charsintek sent me up to fetch you."

Barbara took a deep breath and rubbed at her eyes. "Damn." Ordinarily she would have woken at dawn. "Tell him I'll be down in—" She made a quick calculation, balancing the man's reputation for short temper with the need to look somewhat presentable. "—ten minutes." She was there in five by virtue of tying her long tawny hair back in an uncombed mass and forgoing a neckcloth.

He was waiting for her in the grand hall, a room currently bare except for several lumps of muslin-draped furniture in one corner. The curtains had been pulled open all along the south side of the room to spill light across the floorboards. The fencing master was a wiry Italian, just barely taller than she was herself. She preferred Perret, her teacher back in Rotenek, not least for the fact that his reach and height more closely matched those of her likely opponents. But he was a man of established reputation and could hardly be expected to abandon his school to follow one pupil into the country, no matter how generous her patron.

Signore Donati had the primary virtue that he was willing to take a female student when the better-known Chauten had refused her entrance to his academy. Barbara had needed only five minutes to convince him that she was no fashionable dilettante, playing at learning a few passes with her skirts kilted up. Keeping him waiting was not the way to maintain that evaluation.

"I do beg your pardon, Signore. It was a late evening. The baron had a ball to attend—" She yawned, adding support to the explanation.

"Balls will always be late at night. You must be sharp in the morning nonetheless. Sleep some other time than during your lessons. Now begin."

They moved briskly from drills to sparring to theory. If it came to bright blades in dark alleys, Barbara had few doubts of her ability to keep the baron safe. He had seen to that in his choice of her first teacher. But to be a duelist was to be an actor on the courtly stage and there were no end of nuances to learn.

Donati surprised her with the sudden question, "Do you dance?"

She continued moving through the figure pondering the intent of the question.

"You go to balls; do you dance?" He saluted to signal a break in the action.

Barbara shook her head. "I go to balls in my office. Dancing is for the guests." There had, of course, been dancing lessons in the past. There were very few arts of gentle living that she hadn't been given a taste of at some point. But there had never been any occasion to put the knowledge to regular use.

"You should dance. Dancing, fighting, it is the same. You think too much on how you move, what you do." It was the same criticism Perret made regularly. "Thinking, moving, they should work like two horses in harness. You must be able to carry on while disputing philosophy or reciting poetry or making love. It's better to learn this while dancing—safer."

Barbara's lips thinned in annoyance. *And who would dance with me?* But aloud she said only, "I will consider it."

She had begun the lesson nearly exhausted but in the end the exercise substituted for the lost hours of sleep. The desire to seek her bed again had faded by the time she'd washed and changed afterward.

The baron's valet, quizzed in the kitchen over a late breakfast of bread and tea, allowed that his master was awake, if not yet up. That would be sufficient for arranging the duties of the day. Barbara tapped on the door and entered on a faint assent. At first she thought she must have imagined his response and that he still slept, but then his eyes opened and turned in her direction.

"Pray pardon for disturbing you. May I speak?"

"You usually do in the end." His voice was thin and querulous. Barbara waited silently. "Yes, yes, what is it?"

"I thought I might take the bay mare out for some exercise this afternoon…unless you'll have need of me."

"Do I look like I plan to go gallivanting about the town? No, do as you please until the afternoon. I may not get up until supper, so there's no sense in you kicking your heels here."

Barbara hesitated. When he became snappish it meant he was feeling truly unwell. "Perhaps you'd like me to read to you?"

"No, be off with you. I only need to rest and I can do that by myself. But if you see Ponivin, make sure that he's sent that letter off to Maistir LeFevre."

Does he mean to increase the girl's dowry after all? But no, LeFevre had already planned to follow them to Chalanz. This was just the baron's impatience at work. "I'll see to it."

The butler, of course, had sent the letter days before and was more than a little piqued at the suggestion he might need a reminder. "For it isn't as if he could be here any sooner. And with a storm coming it may well be later."

But the storm—if it existed anywhere other than the butler's arthritic joints—was nowhere to be seen at the moment and the crisp air was perfect for shaking the fidgets out of the mare.

* * *

The town of Chalanz filled the circle of land where the Esikon River bent westward and spilled out onto the opposite bank across a bridge said to have been built in Roman times. To the right of the bridge, on the site of the old Axian Palace, stretched a long grassy park dotted with ruined walls and mysterious hollows. It was there that the energetic and the fashionable paraded on horseback or in carriages or even on foot, along pathways interlacing the riverside, thickly planted with flowers and hedges.

Barbara cantered the mare twice up and down the outermost road where such speed was allowed, up to the broad parade ground where the local militia was practicing, then back to the park gate. After that she reined back to a more sedate walk along a middling path that meandered back and forth among the scattered trees, now drawing near the riverbank, now falling back to touch the carriageway. On previous days she hadn't paid much attention to the other park-goers as individuals, noting them only to stay out of their way. But now, as she neared one of the walking paths, she recognized the girl from the evening before. The baron's goddaughter had left little impression the night before. She'd seen a hundred girls in their first season. They all looked much the same and none of them fell within the scope of her duties. But here in the open air she looked different. What was it the girl had said? *I know I'm not pretty but the dress is and that helps.* It wasn't true, though. The gown had been a hindrance if anything, drowning her heart-shaped face in a sea of lace and ruffles. The deep blue of her pelisse suited her coloring far better than a debutante's pastels and the chill air of the park had left roses in her cheeks and teased a few chestnut-colored curls out to escape from her bonnet. In the moment that Barbara noticed her, she glanced up and their eyes met across the grassy span. The girl leaned toward the older woman at her side and said something rapidly. Then just as Barbara would have turned away, she beckoned, hesitantly at first and then more surely.

Curious, Barbara dismounted and led the mare across the strip of lawn separating the two graveled paths. "How may I serve you, Maisetra?" she asked with a carefully calculated bow.

"I was wondering…that is, I thought it would be proper to call on my godfather. But my aunt," she laid a hand gently on the other woman's arm, "thought that perhaps he wasn't receiving visitors, since he hasn't sent cards around."

Barbara acknowledged the other woman with a briefer bow. She hardly looked old enough to be Margerit's aunt. A timid-looking, willowy creature, but dressed in elegant style, not the edge of fashion that spoke of the brute force of money, rather one that stemmed from a foundation of taste and a trained eye.

"But I thought perhaps you would know what would be best," Margerit continued. "And so I could know to leave him in peace, if that's what he wants. But then perhaps he doesn't expect me to stand on ceremony and would be insulted if he hears nothing." Her words trailed off with a trace of a frown.

"I think the baron would be very glad to see you," Barbara began. "Not today—he's resting today—but soon."

Margerit's frown deepened. "I hope he isn't unwell."

Barbara drew a breath to answer and unexpectedly felt it catch in her throat. "He's dying," she blurted, then drew another more ragged breath trying to regain control. It was the first time she had admitted it even to herself.

"Oh!" said Margerit.

The older woman nervously interjected, "Then we shouldn't disturb him. I told you, Margerit, you aren't to be a bother to him."

"No!" Barbara protested, then hurriedly softened her words. "That is, I know he would be pleased to see you. As the poet says, *In the autumn of a man's life, the days grow short—*"

"*—and the leaves fall suddenly,*" Margerit finished. Her face brightened with sudden pleasure. "So you know Pertulif? I've never liked his melancholy works, but do you know his *Song of the Mountain*?"

Barbara seized on the distraction to keep her voice from breaking and nodded. "Pertulif was born near Saveze, you know. His mountains are old friends of mine."

"Margerit, this is unseemly!" her aunt said sharply. So…not quite as timid as she seemed.

Barbara looked away, trying to become invisible, as Margerit blushed at the admonition. The mare felt her tension and began tossing its head. She took the excuse. "The horse is still fresh—I shouldn't keep it standing." She mounted without waiting for leave. She owed no obedience to strangers. But she turned back at the last and urged, "Do come to see him. Tomorrow." At Margerit's promise, she pushed the mare into a trot, leaving them behind.

The path blurred in and out. She blinked rapidly, trusting the mare not to run anyone down. He was dying. Surely she'd known it since last summer—long before that unlucky duel had chased them from Rotenek. And wasn't it lucky instead? Here he could spend his remaining days quietly, without demanding relatives, scheming courtiers and needy supplicants. She would miss him. No, that was too weak. The solid foundation of her world would be ripped away. He had promised—little throwaway promises accumulating over the years—that when he was gone she would be her own woman. That he would see her established in the world. And more than that, there would be a name. A name to give to her parents and to take for her own if she chose. But outside those things lay a gray curtain. She had never given thought to what lay beyond and now it frightened her. A prayer formed on her lips that he be granted many more years but it felt selfish to give voice to it.

* * *

The moment Barbara set foot in the house she sensed the heightened bustle that accompanied a visitor. She stopped one of the footmen as he hurried past her in the back corridor. "Who?"

He rolled his eyes. "The nephew, who else?" If he'd been out of doors, he would have spat at the mention. Her position might be an anomaly in the servants' hierarchy, but on this topic she was one with them in conspiracy.

"When?" she continued hurriedly. "Is he up with—"

"For the last quarter hour at least. And if you can dislodge him, it's more than himself seems able to do."

Barbara took the stairs at a run and paused outside the half-cracked door more to catch her breath than to overhear.

"You've no call to pinch pennies with me, Uncle. What are you saving them for now? If you want to be rid of me quickly, you know how."

Then the older man's voice, sharp with scorn. "And what is the excuse this time? A new pair of horses? More gambling debts? Perhaps you've been more inventive this time—is your mistress with child?"

Barbara took the pause as her cue to push the door open and enter. She feigned surprise. "Ah, forgive me for the interruption! You had asked to see me when I returned from riding."

The baron gave her a sharp look at this blatant lie. Estefen gave her a much sharper one and said, "We don't need you here. I haven't rushed to my uncle's bedside to be interrupted by the likes of you."

Barbara ignored him and slipped into her silent waiting stance just inside the door. Estefen certainly didn't look as if he had ridden in haste all the way from Rotenek. Those black locks meticulously dressed *a la Titus* might appear in careless disarray, but it was a barber's hand and not nature that had tousled them. And the starched frill of his shirtfront had spent no time stuffed into a saddlebag. No, he had set out at leisure some days before. The concern was pure playacting.

"My dear nephew," the baron said in a milder tone than before. "Any *requests* you have to make of me can be made tonight over dinner. I have no taste for being harangued in my own bedchamber. And you show no taste in doing so."

Estefen sneered. "There was a day when everyone in Alpennia quaked at your displeasure, but that day is long past. You're a tired old man, Uncle. You've lost the royal favor. And the only further use you can be to the family is in backing my career. You know it as well as I."

The baron closed his eyes with a sigh. "You don't have a career—you have a drunken stagger. You have no concept of what it took to build what I hold and it will slip through your fingers like smoke. You are a stupid, greedy little boy and *I want you out of my chamber!*"

When his voice shifted into steely hardness, Barbara threw off her waiting pose and slipped sideways to herd Estefen toward the open doorway. When he balked, she slid her fingers around the grip of her sword. Not drawn—not even a fraction of an inch. Estefen hesitated. "You wouldn't, Uncle."

"That was what your friend Iohenrik thought, didn't he?"

Barbara took a deliberate half step forward and Estefen chose to preserve his dignity by turning for the door. Once past the sill he turned and hissed at her, "Someday soon you'll need a new patron. Don't think I'll have forgotten." But he had no opportunity to see whether he'd hit the mark for the door was closed firmly in his face.

Barbara closed her eyes briefly and willed herself to relax. She was a bow—drawn but not loosed—and it took a moment for her mind to unbend. At the baron's word, she would have done what he might later regret. That was their balance: his the regret and hers the guilt. The law might forgive a death as falling within the scope of her employment, but this went beyond law. Estefen and his uncle were one step away from the edge of the cliff and the baron was not yet ready to let himself be pushed into the abyss. They all knew—without it ever said aloud—that the dead man in Rotenek had been Estefen's proxy. Yet the fiction of family unity must be maintained on all sides.

Her reverie was broken by a tired voice. "If you would, pull the bell. I should like some tea. And then you will read to me."

"Do you want me to change from my riding clothes?" she asked as she summoned a waiting servant.

He waved a hand vaguely. "I'd rather keep you close for now."

Barbara showed her teeth. "He was quite the vulture today. I worry—" No, she didn't want to share that worry.

The baron reached out and gripped her hand. "I am beyond his reach already. And you, my dear, will be taken care of. Something will be arranged." But he frowned, releasing his grip weakly, as if he hadn't figured out quite what, yet.

"Don't worry about me," Barbara reassured him. "I'll manage well enough on my own."

Estefen had not only backed off from the confrontation, it seemed, but had left the field entirely for the moment. The maid who brought up the tray responded to her whispered question that he'd left the house in a foul temper and given the butler the name of an inn where communications might be sent. Even the pretense of family feeling didn't extend to either of the men being willing to share a roof, despite the array of empty rooms that Fonten House boasted.

When the tray had been settled across the baron's lap, Barbara picked up the heavy volume that lay ready on a bedside table.

"Not yet," he said. "Talk to me for now."

That request always felt like the opening of a gate to a garden. It was one of the few occasions with him when she needn't guard her tongue and hedge every word. But then, when he asked her to talk to him, he didn't care much what was said, only that it distracted him from his cares.

She described the crisp clarity of the morning. The play of light and shadow among the old stone walls where patches of snow lingered. The mare's impatience and promise. "And I met your goddaughter on the path near the fountain," she continued. "She asked whether you'd be at home to visitors and I confess I encouraged her to call tomorrow. I hope that was right."

The baron roused himself to closer attention. "Did you, now? And what do you make of her?"

The gate to the garden slammed shut again. "It's not for me to say, Mesner."

He looked sideways at her and sighed. "No, I suppose not. And yet, I'd like to know."

Barbara shifted uneasily on the bedside stool. "She seems...very well-educated. *Where ancient pens trace paths within memory, wisdom follows.*"

The baron snorted in laughter, ending in a cough. "Yes, indeed. You wouldn't count that a fault, of course, but I suspect her uncle does." A thoughtful look came over his face. "Yes, let her come visit. I'd like that. And I'd like to see how the two of you get on. My two favorite goddaughters—what a pair! Now you may read to me."

Barbara was grateful for the command. She was never comfortable when the baron's mood turned to teasing. It felt like he was setting traps for her, though they were never sprung. She opened the book that still lay across her lap and caressed the pages as she found her place at the *Life and Mysteries of Saint Marzin*. The saint hadn't even reached the point of slicing up his clothing before the baron was sleeping comfortably.

CHAPTER FIVE

Margerit

Aunt Honurat had made it clear what she thought of visiting the baron uninvited—the duelist's plea hardly counted in her eyes as an invitation—so Margerit approached Aunt Bertrut. She thought it an excellent idea for her own reasons. "It never hurts to keep yourself in the thoughts of rich friends. And if he's feeling poorly, then any small kindness will be more warmly remembered."

So it was Bertrut who accompanied her that next afternoon when they approached Fonten House up its long curving drive. It wasn't too far to walk for those accustomed to country rambles. No need to beg Uncle Mauriz for the carriage and risk Honurat forbidding the visit outright.

The baron's house on Fonten Street showed a broad stone face on approach, shadowed both by the northern orientation and the row of ancient trees flanking the drive. Margerit could see that the back side of the house would be more pleasant. The ground fell away down toward the river, and all the spring sunshine, when it came, would fall on whatever gardens and terraces were hidden there out of sight. It wasn't an ancient house—no older than a century or so—built when Chalanz had first become a fashionable retreat from the capital. It was relatively newly come into the baron's hands, she recalled. His titled estate was farther south, at the foot of the mountains, so it was no wonder he preferred Fonten House when the cold still lingered.

It seemed their visit had been anticipated, for when Aunt Bertrut offered her card to the footman, a more significant-looking figure appeared instantly at her side to receive it, nodding at them with, "Welcome, Maisetra Margerit," and, after glancing at the card, "Maisetra Sovitre. If you will wait here a moment, I'll see if the baron is able to receive you." There was no polite fiction about whether he was at home.

Soon they were led upstairs to the baron's bedchamber. Aunt Bertrut wasn't the least disconcerted so Margerit took it for the manners of the older generation or perhaps simply his failing health. If the baron had escaped looking frail at the ball, he now embodied Barbara's judgment of the day before. He was dying; he knew it and did not attempt to conceal it. Margerit curtsied and then, at his gesture, took the stool at his bedside.

"You should never have come the other night. I hate thinking that my little party has—"

He cut her off in a voice that still commanded. "No one has ever forced me to anything I didn't care to do. You may rest easy on that. And if I hadn't come to your affair, you wouldn't be visiting me now, would you?"

At that, Margerit had to smile and that seemed to please the old man. He dismissed her aunt summarily and if Bertrut had any qualms about leaving her alone with him, she must have suppressed them. In some trepidation Margerit watched the door close behind her. What did one say on such a visit? To hide her discomfort, she idly picked up a thick volume that sat in easy reach on a bedside table. "Bartholomeus' *Lives and Mysteries of the Saints*. Sister Petrunel nearly had me memorize the entire thing. The important parts, anyway. I suppose it's a great comfort to you at this—" She faltered, realizing that it was probably impolite to bring up a man's impending death.

He snorted. "Comfort! Goodness no. It's the most stultifying text I own. When I have trouble sleeping—which is most days—I have Barbara read to me out of it. Works like a charm." He laughed again. "A better charm than any of the verses in it. I never did learn the trick of making them work. So that governess of yours had you working mysteries?"

"No, she felt that—" Petrunel had never quite put it in words and Margerit reached for an explanation. "She felt that too much petitioning of the saints distracted from the worship of God. But she had me study mysteries for the logic. How did they use the formulas?

For what purpose? When do you speak prayers and when are they written? What petitions need the power of a relic and when is it enough to use an image? It was a bit like studying Latin verbs: the patterns are there, but incomplete and unpredictable. But you'd know all that," she ended self-consciously. "They say that at one time you meant to become a priest."

He raised his eyebrows at that. "Where did you hear that old gossip? A priest? By God, they meant me to become a bishop—a cardinal even. But then my brother had the poor taste to get himself killed in the French Wars and they released me to take up the title. But I? No, I never meant to become a priest." He seemed to stare back through the years. "Mihail never did have any sense of timing. He died too soon yet far too late."

Margerit was saved from finding a response by a soft tapping at the door. At the baron's "Enter!" Barbara stepped in, wearing the riding clothes Margerit had seen her in the day before.

"Mesner, I wondered if you needed anything." She glanced over briefly but whatever message she intended was unclear.

"If I need something, you can be sure I'll ring for it," the baron said impatiently. "Go away." And then when the door had closed again, "She worries over me like a mother hen." Margerit felt his sharp glance. "If you have something to say, out with it." She shook her head and his mouth twisted as if she'd failed some test. "I hear you share Barbara's fondness for poetry. What do you think of my armin?"

"She...interests me." How to express the idea that in the duelist she sensed a kindred spirit, as out of tune with what everyone expected of her as she felt?

"I promised you her story, didn't I," he said. "It's not a tale I tell often. People get the strangest ideas when you tell them you own a young woman. People are mostly fools."

Margerit could feel her cheeks burning when she realized what sorts of strange ideas he meant.

"Barbara's birth is as good as your own—better even. But her father, he was one of those who have the need to hazard chance as a fire in the blood and it never goes out until the blood is cold. Not just a hand of cards and the occasional horserace. Deep play of the kind that loses a man everything. He hid his debts for a long time. The properties were all quietly mortgaged. He had squeezed as much as he could out of his own relatives. Barbara's mother was married to him for the sake of his...name and her family paid dearly for the connection. But her fortune was a sponge to sop up a river. When her family found out the true state of affairs, they were wise enough to cut her off. Cruel, but wise." He'd closed his eyes and spoke as if he'd forgotten she were there.

"She never asked them for anything again after that. His family had already lost everything of value, even the honor of their name. So they abandoned it to try to build new lives: drifted away, found patrons or professions, no longer recognized by their former friends. So it happens in such cases, as if the line had never been. At the last, the pair were thrown into debtor's prison. Or he was, and she followed him because she was too proud and too hurt to beg charity from old friends." His voice quavered and Margerit thought he must have been one of those old friends.

"But there was also the child. Did you know that Barbara too is a godchild of mine?" The baron had opened his eyes again and addressed her directly. Margerit shook her head. "When her mother fell ill in prison, at last she sent word to me and begged me to take Barbara into my care. It was an impossible request. There I was, a bachelor. What should I do with a child? But how could I say no? And then, that…viper of a husband forbade it. He wouldn't ask for me—out of charity—to care for his daughter. But he would sell her to me. He named a sum. It was outrageous, but it could supply a few comforts for them in that place: fuel to keep warm, medicines and charms for her illness, the guarantee of a priest at the end. I ordered the gaoler to bring ink and paper and drew up the contract then and there. In two days, I had found a nurse and made the other necessary arrangements. When I returned to take the child, he was dicing away her price with the guards. Barbara's mother gave up after that. I saw her twice more in the following weeks and then she was dead. I think he lived a few more years. It meant nothing to me so I didn't keep track of his passing."

When he finished, the silence stretched between them. Margerit had listened to the tale with growing dismay and knew she couldn't entirely keep it from her face. How must it feel, to know that about your father? And to know that the baron…When he'd made that sly comment the night of her ball, she'd assumed Barbara must have been a foundling or some peasant's bastard, handed over for the hope of a better life. But this?

"Don't be mealy-mouthed girl," he challenged. "Tell me what you think of me."

Aunt Bertrut's advice rang uselessly in her ears. Be tactful. Dissemble. Play the game until you get what you want. Margerit stood, expecting to be dismissed afterward. "I only wonder what Barbara's mother would think of you. She might have expected better from an old friend!" There, she'd let her words run ahead of wisdom again. No doubt she'd ruined her chances for any further generosity. She could only hope her guardians wouldn't learn of it.

The baron's mouth twitched in an odd smile. "I wondered if there were any steel in you. Well, my reasons were my own and I won't be explaining them to you or anyone." He closed his eyes with a sigh and an awkward silence stretched out.

"Perhaps I should leave," Margerit ventured.

"Perhaps you should," he replied and fumbled for the bell rope. Margerit pulled it for him. The maid must have been waiting in the hallway for she opened the door before Margerit had crossed to it.

The baron was nothing like how she'd imagined him. Some of that she attributed to his frail health but she'd always seen him as a benevolent—if distant—figure. Close up, she thought "capricious" might be a better word. One expected great men to be self-serving, but every move he made seemed to be directed by a hidden plan.

He had maneuvered her into asking about Barbara's history and therefore he had wanted her to know it. But why? Why had it felt like he was testing her? And had she passed the test?

Aunt Bertrut broke into her reverie as they walked the long blocks back home. "Was he pleased to have you come, do you think? Will he sweeten the pot of your dowry?"

"Aunt!" Margerit protested. "It would be unseemly for me to ask."

"Of course it would! But there are ways of hinting and wheedling. You should be sharpening your skills in that regard for your husband."

Dread clenched her stomach as it always did when they talked of marriage in such practical terms. She had few romantic expectations but surely her future could be more than a campaign of managing and working around and making do. That felt too much like her life so far.

"Margerit," Aunt Bertrut said more softly. "Have a care. Seize your chances now. Some day you'll find they've all slipped away."

Was that what had happened to her? It wasn't often that Margerit looked at her aunt and wondered what her girlhood had been like. Familiarity made it hard to see her clearly. Gossip said she'd been acclaimed a beauty in the bloom of her youth, but none of her features had been strong enough to retain that title in middle age. The chestnut hair that matched Margerit's own was streaked with gray now and though her cheeks had retained a pleasant glow, pleasant was as far as one might honestly go. What chances had fate brought her that she'd failed to seize before they were gone? Aunt Bertrut seemed content enough in her life now, but surely there were other choices.

CHAPTER SIX

Barbara

The only member of the baron's household who was glad of Estefen's visits was Monsieur Guillaumin, the chef, who had despaired of his talents being appreciated in this exile until his employer's nephew arrived. Barbara knew Ponivin and the rest of the staff were feeling the strain of enforcing the baron's scheduled truce as Estefen tested the limits, dropping by at odd hours only to be denied with the implausible response that the baron was not at home.

The baron was always at home. He left his bed only for those hoarded hours of strength when Estefen was allowed to join him at table. There the truce ended and Barbara was hard put to stand silent as he pecked at the edges of the baron's peace. Though, for his part, the baron delighted in baiting him in return.

"Whatever are you still hanging around here for," he challenged as the port was brought in at the conclusion of the meal. It was his habit to provoke a quarrel when it was time for Estefen to leave.

Barbara almost had brief flashes of sympathy for Estefen. The two men were closely matched in pride and arrogance. The difference, she thought, was that the baron had earned the right to his while Estefen had merely assumed it. And was that entirely his fault? They said his father had been so struck by the realization that he'd sired the heir to a barony—and he could hardly have expected it, given that he'd married a woman with two living brothers—that Estefen had been raised as if he already bore the title. By the time Mesner Chazillen was gone and the baron might have stood in place of a father, he and Estefen were already constantly at daggers drawn. And there her sympathy ended, even apart from her own grudge.

"Is it so impossible, dear uncle, that I might be concerned for your health?" Estefen answered blandly. "Here you are, all alone, with none but servants to care for you."

The baron appeared to consider the idea for a moment then shook his head. "No. Impossible."

"Then let us say that I feel the need to look out for the family's interests."

"Good heavens," the baron exclaimed in mock surprise. "Do you think you might be disinherited?"

"Don't be absurd," Estefen scoffed, but there was a flash of doubt in his eyes.

The baron saw it too and couldn't resist exploring the chink in his facade. "After all, by law I can leave the title where I may. All it takes is the prince's consent to my choice, just as it only takes the council's assent to his own choice of heir."

Estefen shook his head. "You're joking. There's no one else left in the Lumbeirt line within seven degrees. He'd never break tradition to go outside that, not when his own succession is under dispute."

"There's always your sister," the baron said, toying idly with the stem of his glass.

Estefen let loose a bark of laughter. "Antuniet? Over a male heir?" But his dismissal sounded less certain than before. It would be outside tradition but not outside law. And there was precedent within living memory.

The baron echoed his laugh more softly. "No, I suppose I have no grudge against her sufficient to set you at her throat. You may remain secure in your hopes. But if you think to find me generous of my purse because of that, you're wasting your time."

At last their fencing match came to an end, but with the door safely closed on Estefen's heels it was an hour before the baron could summon the strength to be helped again to his bed.

* * *

Sleep came more easily for him now; harder for her. After seeing him settled, she moved restlessly from room to room, too uneasy to rest, too anxious to find useful employment. She found herself eventually in the library, returning to the study of *De Mysteriis*. Her tutor—back when there had been tutors—had insisted that anyone who aspired to study Fortunatus must work their own translations. She suspected this longstanding scholarly custom came not so much from respect for the difficulty of the text but was simply a favorite dodge of lazy instructors, disinclined to navigate the competing schools of interpretation. Perhaps it was both. This was the third time she'd worked through the text and each time she came to a different conclusion regarding Fortunatus's position on the nature of miracles.

It was strange to think that his work had been dangerously revolutionary in his day. His views on the nature of God were of the most orthodox. And his study touched not at all on those mysteries that belonged to the sacraments or were the prerogative of ordained clergy. Yet there was a lingering unease around his position that the celebration of mysteries to petition the saints—and any miracles granted in response—could be understood and not simply accepted. That was what drew her back time and again to the text: that quest for understanding. The chance of grasping the complexity as a whole, both seen and unseen, and comprehending its workings and consequences, if only for a fleeting instant.

She put her pen aside at last and glanced at the windows. The last traces of dusk had faded hours ago. From a distant corner of the house she heard a clock chiming midnight. Morning would come too soon, but perhaps now she could sleep.

* * *

The days still carried ghosts of normal routine. Up at dawn to meet Donati for sword practice. Taking one of the horses out for exercise in Axian Park. She would have foregone that except that the baron commanded it directly. And Estefen kept to fashionable hours, so even at his worst there was no chance of him assailing Fonten House's defenses before noon. The illusion of a normal routine required consultation with the baron before she rode out, to know his plans for the day.

"No, I won't be rising before dinner," he acknowledged in a tired voice. "Is there word when LeFevre will be here?"

He'd asked the question several times each day. This time she was able to answer, "Mefro Charsintek ordered the maids to prepare his room so there must have been news that he's arriving today."

"Good. That's good," he responded. "And why hasn't that goddaughter of mine visited again?"

The answer seemed obvious. "May I speak?" At a faint gesture that could be interpreted as assent she continued, "She knows you're ill. I expect she fears to tire you."

"More likely she thinks she offended me last time."

That was a surprising idea. Margerit Sovitre hadn't seemed likely to offend a mouse. But perhaps she had hidden depths.

"Invite her. A formal invitation. I want to see her one more time. Be sure."

Be sure she comes? A formal invitation would certainly accomplish that, whatever her qualms. For an offhand instruction, the request entailed complex protocol. It was one thing to encounter the girl casually in a park, but that wouldn't do even if she could rely on a second such meeting. LeFevre wasn't available yet to act as secretary, but she could pen the note herself. The formal phrases were familiar enough. There must be another visit to the baron's bedchamber to seal the missive with the signet ring that never left his possession. For the delivery, the question must be pondered of front door or back. In Rotenek, she would have been understood as a formal emissary, entitled to the front door in the baron's name. But country towns and country manners took a different view and she decided to play it safer by taking the role of ordinary messenger and bringing the note to the back entrance.

An hour later she arrived at a modest house on Chaturik Square in the southern quarter of town. Modest—well, that was a matter of perspective. Not in the newest style, meaning the family's money was old enough to be respectable. But neither the sort of crumbling edifice that spoke of ancient lineages and failing finances. As she waited for the response she had a glimpse of a finicky tidiness that told of roots not too far removed from the merchant class. An absence of excess or ostentation. All quite the opposite of the baron's household. Perhaps that was the amusement he found in Margerit's visit: the theater of an ordinary *burfro* life without the hazards and dramas of the court.

Word quickly came back from the mistress of the house. "Maisetra Fulpi sends word to Baron Saveze that Maisetra Margerit will attend on him tomorrow as requested." The messenger looked her up and down with an expression Barbara found all too familiar. It made her tired, dealing with the unbending propriety of his sort. She returned him a look that said, *I speak for Baron Saveze and you will give me his due respect.* But aloud she said only, "I will take Maisetra Fulpi's response to the baron."

CHAPTER SEVEN

Margerit

Margerit's first visit to Fonten Street had been an impulsive affair, done quietly to avoid Aunt Honurat's qualms. But a formal invitation to visit, that was a different matter and there was no question of disapproval this time. There was a barely concealed excitement among her guardians at the thought that the baron was taking a personal interest in her at last.

"For it only stands to reason that he didn't pay you much mind as a schoolroom girl. Now that you're coming out into society his attention will do you nothing but good." Aunt Bertrut was fussing over a choice of dresses, urging her to an ever more elaborate ensemble. Honurat cut the matter short by stating quietly that an ordinary day visit called for nothing more formal than the blue merino.

Margerit was less certain that the baron's request reflected an interest in her welfare but she saw no point to raising her doubts before her aunts. The invitation meant he'd forgiven her pertness and perhaps he was simply bored. At this time of year, Chalanz society must be far smaller than he was accustomed to, even without being shut in.

When they arrived, the baron had been closeted half the morning with his estate manager and couldn't see them immediately. Margerit thought they would leave a card and return the next day but Aunt Bertrut was more tenacious.

"We can wait on his excellency's convenience," she told the apologetic butler. And though he frowned discouragingly, evidently he had no orders to turn them away.

Tea was provided and they were shown into a cozy room opening off the front entryway, a place lined with bookshelves and furnished with a warm fire and a few chairs, ranging from the stiff and practical to a throne of overstuffed comfort that Bertrut instantly commanded. The next time Margerit looked back at her, she had nodded off to sleep.

The baron's library was a thing of wonder. And these were only the books he felt should grace a house by default, Margerit thought, and those he particularly cared to carry with him from place to place. What must his house in Rotenek hold? She sat at one of the chairs next to a small round table and ran her finger over the red-bound volume that lay open on it. Several ribbons marked places in the text and there were sheets of closely-written paper inserted haphazardly throughout. She carefully marked the place where it had been open and turned to the front to examine the title page. *Fortunatus!* Her heart jumped and she leafed through the first pages of the introduction to make sure. For all that she'd read summaries and citations, she'd sometimes wondered if the book were only a legend. Sister Petrunel had discounted the work as idle sophistry but those glimpses had left her hungry for more.

She turned to the first set of inserted papers and spread them out across the table. Someone had been working through a translation, interspersed with commentary and underlined questions. It was the cramped, rapid script of someone writing only for their own reference and Margerit was so engrossed in deciphering it that she didn't notice the door open and close. A faint but deliberate cough brought her back to the room and she looked up to see Barbara standing close.

"Oh! Is my godfather finished?"

"No, Maisetra, not yet." There was an awkward pause and then, "I don't mean to intrude but I came for the book." She gestured to the open volume.

"Is it yours?" Margerit asked eagerly.

The other woman flinched slightly. "The baron permits me—"

"No, I mean, are these your notes? Is it your translation? My governess only gave me a few extracts and I had more questions when I finished than when I began. But maybe you know." The armin's stiffness eased and a wary curiosity sprang up in those pale eyes. Margerit turned the pages quickly but gently back to the section she'd been examining *On the Manifestation of Miracles.* "Sister Petrunel always insisted that all miracles come only from God. That when we celebrate the mysteries of the saints, the saints are only intercessors and have no power of their own to grant what we ask."

Barbara pulled a second chair up to the table and followed along on the passage in question, her slim muscular hands taking over the task of turning the pages.

Margerit continued, "But Fortunatus makes all these distinctions between the greater miracles and the lesser, between objective miracles and subjective ones, and he seems to claim that some come from God and some from the saints and that some come from the celebrant himself."

Barbara pointed to a phrase where the glosses in the margins ran several layers thick. "He doesn't exactly claim that. Remember that he was constantly dodging accusations of heresy, so he wrote in such a way that nothing he said could be pinned onto his own beliefs. Everywhere it's 'were this the case' and 'it emerges in consequence' and 'it would need to be concluded that.' I think there's one entire chapter where every single verb is in the subjunctive. But what he says here is that if you observe the nature of miracles and that if logic is applied to those observations, then if it were the case that God's laws for miraculous events are not capricious and arbitrary and that God has not chosen to garb a capricious and arbitrary world in the garments of law and logic, then certain patterns regarding the nature and manifestation of miracles emerge."

Margerit puzzled over that for a few moments. "It seems a dreadfully complicated way of saying that's what he thinks."

"Dread probably had something to do with it," Barbara said with dry humor. "We'd be a lot poorer today if he'd been less cautious and more dead."

It was hard to grasp that level of caution. Thaumaturgy had been an accepted field of theology for centuries. She looked to see if Barbara were teasing her but the armin's lean face was animated only with interest. Margerit turned a few more pages. "There was a question I had once…about the relationship of miraculous visions and the visual manifestation of mysteries. Sister Petrunel didn't think it was an important distinction but there was a hint in that bit of Fortunatus she gave me that he—"

Barbara took the heavy volume from her and cradled it easily in one arm, turning to a section marked by one of the scarlet silk ribbons.

"This may be what you're thinking of." She read a bit of the Latin aloud and then skipped through the next page, summarizing in translation.

"Yes, that was it," Margerit said. "Because he seems to be saying that a miraculous vision is extrinsic—that it comes from God or the saints and you may see it or not as it pleases them—but that there are some who possess an intrinsic ability to perceive...*things*...I'm not sure how to describe it. Something that *exists* for everyone but that not everyone can *perceive*. Like a sound that some people are deaf to."

Barbara smiled slightly. "And that's the sort of thing that got him in trouble: the Mechanistic Heresy. His student Pezzulin did end up getting executed for it. He summed it up that there were Doers and Seers—*actors* and *vidators*—more traditionally, those whose prayers the saints heed and act on and those who could tell which people's prayers were heeded. And he thought that if only the two could be harnessed together, then in celebrating the right mysteries we could create reliable miracles at will. But it doesn't much matter whether miracles are unreliable because God works by His own laws or because we have no reliable way to distinguish between the true miracles and the lucky chance of a charlatan."

Margerit had been watching the other woman closely as she talked. The impassive stillness she had found so daunting at their first meeting was entirely gone. Here was a mind and a curiosity that matched hers step for step. She frowned slightly and sighed. "It just seems so unfair."

Barbara grinned. "What? That logic alone can't explain the universe?"

"No, that...that all your learning and philosophy is wasted." She saw Barbara's face twist in a frown and scrambled to find words for what she meant. "We might have been sisters when we were born, but fortune has made such a difference between us. Why should you be punished for what your father did?"

Barbara reacted as if she had been struck. "He told you. Everything." Her tone was flat and expressionless. She stood up to leave, then turned on her angrily. "How dare you think to pity me! The only difference between us is that you will be owned by a husband instead. And what will your philosophy and learning mean then if all he wants you for is to breed his children? Or for the price of your dowry," she added bitterly. She pulled the book away roughly and closed it with a clap. "I have been given permission to keep this book with me, if you please," she said stiffly and left before Margerit could answer.

Aunt Bertrut had started awake at the snap of the book and as the door closed she said, "What did that peculiar creature want? I think it's outrageous the way the baron keeps her. If he wants to have his mistress close, that's one thing, but to parade her around in breeches—"

"You don't understand anything," Margerit said sharply and then hurried out into the hall, quaking at her own impertinence. She was always having to apologize for her quick tongue, which was strange because it seemed as if she rarely had the nerve to answer back at all. She accosted the footman by the front door. "Did you see where Barbara went? I need to speak with her."

"I'm sure I couldn't say, Maisetra," he said, although his eyes darted toward the stairs. Further comment was cut off by the sound of a carriage in the drive. At what he saw from the window beside the door he hastily jerked three times on a bell-pull saying, "Pardon me, Maisetra." A tone sounded somewhere deep in the house.

The doors were opened just as a fashionable young man was climbing the steps. Margerit stepped back into the shadows by the library door hoping to avoid his notice. How Nikule would envy the cut of that coat! With his dark brooding features and careless manner she recognized here the sort of image for which her cousin strove.

"Is my uncle at home?" the visitor barked at the footman. "What's that you say? He's not at home? How convenient for—" Margerit tried not to shrink as his eyes fell on her. "And how curious that he seems to be at home for everyone except me."

The butler had joined them in the entry hall, no doubt summoned by that distant bell. "I'm afraid the baron is currently engaged with Maistir LeFevre. I expect he will be finished shortly, however there are other visitors before you." He nodded vaguely in her direction so she had no choice but to step forward and curtsy in greeting.

"But how charming," the stranger said, shrugging off his greatcoat for the footman to catch and turning toward her. His manner had turned abruptly from temper to an oily smoothness. "My uncle has become quite the connoisseur." Margerit knew she was being mocked but she also thought she might have been insulted. She let him take her hand and raise it to his lips. "Will no one introduce me to this ravishing creature?" he said to the room at large.

Margerit heard her aunt come out of the library behind her and felt acutely embarrassed to be caught in such a position. From halfway up the stairs came Barbara's voice, sharp and cold. "She's your uncle's goddaughter, Estefen, not a toy for your little games." Margerit noticed in some puzzlement that Barbara was now wearing her blade. She hadn't worn it before in the library.

Estefen laughed and pressed her hand with his fingers. "Enchanted! But come, that's hardly a proper introduction."

"It's not my place to make introductions," Barbara said, descending the rest of the way to the hall. "That wasn't an introduction, it was a warning."

Estefen turned to confront her and Margerit managed to pull her hand free and slipped back a few paces. His voice turned ever more silky. "You exceed your mandate, Babs. There's no threat to the baron here. You can't slice me open just for being friendly to his guests."

Barbara pretended to ignore him and addressed her. "The baron has finished with his business and is ready to see you."

Estefen said, "Ah, then I shall escort her up." He took her hand again and tucked it under his arm but Barbara blocked his way to the stairs.

"*I* shall escort her up," she said stonily and Estefen laughed as if it had all been a game as he released her arm.

Margerit slipped past Barbara up the stairs and waited for her at the landing. "I wanted to apologize for what I said earlier," she began, but Barbara wouldn't meet her eyes.

"There's nothing for you to be sorry for, Maisetra," she said flatly. "I spoke too freely. It is I who should apologize."

When they reached the door of the baron's chamber, Barbara touched her arm to pause her for a moment. "He finished with LeFevre some time ago. I hoped to let him rest a while, but…" She glanced back toward the stairs and Margerit realized it had been a deliberate rescue and no coincidence. "Don't stay long today. He's tired. From arranging business. If he hadn't commanded it…" The apologetic tone was gone. This was the baron's armin speaking. Margerit nodded silently.

* * *

He was pale—very pale. And his hand shook slightly when he raised it in greeting. Impulsively, Margerit knelt at his bedside and pressed the chill fingers to her lips.

"You should rest," she murmured. "I can come another day." Whatever she might think of his motives, her heart melted at the old man's condition.

"No, no, stay," he replied. "There will not be many more days. Come, sit here and talk to me. Tell me about something pleasant."

She was bewildered but willing and spoke admiringly of his library. It was the pleasantest thing that came immediately to mind. From there, when he urged her to continue, she recounted the discussion with Barbara over the nature of miracles, saving only the quarrel at the end.

"Ha!" he exclaimed. "I thought you might suit each other." And in the next moment he ordered, "Leave me now. Come back some other day."

She went to the door, wondering if she should call someone. In the passage, Barbara was waiting and stopped her as she headed for the stairs, but this time she was deferential. "Would you be willing to engage in a small deception?"

Margerit frowned. "I don't understand."

"Estefen—the baron's nephew—is…a stubborn man. But if he thinks you're still with the baron, he won't try to press the matter. It will give him a little more time undisturbed. Would you be willing to leave by another way? I'll have someone fetch your aunt."

"Of course," Margerit said hurriedly.

She waited in a back hallway, enduring curious stares from several passing servants until Aunt Bertrut was escorted to her by a distinguished middle-aged man she hadn't seen before.

"Margerit, what on earth is this about?" she asked sharply. "This…this Mefroi LeFevre only told me to come with him and say nothing."

Margerit briefly explained the subterfuge.

The man nodded and said, "I do apologize for spoiling your visit. I'm afraid there were business matters that couldn't wait."

The estate manager, Margerit concluded, for he looked bookish, with thick spectacles perched in the middle of a round good-natured face. He gazed at her overlong with frank curiosity, as if she were a puzzle he was trying to work out. She felt herself blushing and when he saw that he apologized again. Aunt Bertrut took it amiss, muttering about impertinent clerks who were no better than they should be, and dragged her away before she could wonder further.

* * *

Margerit's evening was claimed by a small dinner party. Uncle Mauriz's business associates had the attraction of a son several years older than her and a daughter also newly out in society. There would be no dancing, but the promise of music and cards made an excuse to lure other young people. Margerit had known most of the guests since girlhood and had yet to find a one with whom she could enter into any serious sympathy. Yet one of these men would shape her future.

It was just a light informal supper—nothing elaborate—but the protocols of seating still ruled, so Margerit found herself between Maistir Palmir, an elderly bachelor, on her left and Cheristien, the son of her hosts, on her right. The older man had no conversation when it came to debutantes. He offered a remark on the weather then turned to more serious matters on his other side.

Cheristien had never previously considered her worthy of notice, for which she forgave him. A man just at the start of making his own name needed to distance himself from the company of mere children. And it was amusing to see him pretend to have suddenly noticed her maturity—as if she were now years older than when they'd last crossed paths. He asked whether she'd enjoyed her coming-out ball, whether she'd been invited to many parties yet and what she'd found to amuse herself lately, given that the weather was still so dreary.

In a spirit of mischief, Margerit answered, "I had the most entertaining conversation today at my godfather's house, about the distinction Fortunatus makes between intrinsic and extrinsic miraculous visions."

He stared at her blankly for a moment then burst into such loud laughter that heads turned half the table away. "Oh, but that's droll! Have you been rehearsing that line all day in hopes of a chance to use it? Who told you to say that?" He gestured across the table to his sister. "Helen, I think I must forbid you to go out walking with Maisetra Sovitre or she'll teach you to talk like a bluestocking or an eccentric and you'll scare away all your suitors!"

Margerit stared down at her plate, torn between embarrassment and anger. Yes, she'd said it to provoke him, but how dare he treat scholarship as a party trick? Or rather, treat a woman's scholarship as such.

"Now, now," he said more kindly. "You've had your fun and I've had mine. No offense taken or intended."

But for the rest of the meal she answered his conversation in monosyllables until he grew tired of it and confined himself to his other dinner partner. And though the company was pleasant, as such things go, she was hard put to pretend enjoyment. When the evening had run its course and they were private in the carriage going home, there was a long scold to endure from both aunts and an even more terrible stony silence from her uncle. And the worst part of it was that they meant it kindly. They were right that it was no way to attract a husband. And that was the bargain after all.

* * *

Aunt Bertrut would have returned to the baron's house the next day but Margerit protested that, despite what he had said, he should be allowed a rest before being pestered by company again. Her aunt hadn't seen how frail he looked. They compromised on sending a footman to inquire discreetly and he returned with the information that his excellency was unwell and could not see visitors.

"But surely that isn't meant for you, Margerit," Bertrut said.

"Aunt, have pity. He's ill and may be dying."

"Then all the more reason to fix his interest in you while you still can," she said.

Margerit was appalled but held her tongue. *She means well,* she thought. *She didn't intend it to sound so selfish. Perhaps in a few days when he's stronger.*

* * *

He never was stronger. A carefully accidental pass by Fonten Street a few days later discovered that straw had been laid down in the street to quiet the wheels of passing carriages so as not to disturb the invalid. And the next morning the cook hurried back from the morning marketing with the news that the old baron had died.

"And they say he's to be buried here at Saint Andire's and not back in Rotenek or at Saveze," came the gossip from the kitchen. "It should be quite the spectacle."

The cook was mistaken. The funeral was a quick and quiet affair. Rumor said it was attended only by his household—that even his nephew had been left in ignorance until he was in the grave. So for the desired spectacle the gossips of Chalanz were forced to wait for the reading of the will. If he had been half as wealthy as common report had it, the simple listing of his bequests could provide speculation for a year. And even more than the funeral, it was curious that he had specified that the reading was to be held here in town and not in the capital.

Margerit wasn't surprised to receive an invitation to the reading. Bertrut was eager to know if she would receive more than a token bequest but Uncle Mauriz squashed expectations. "He's hardly taken notice of you before. Pray he leaves you something of value and not a useless memento."

For her own part, Margerit's thoughts turned to Barbara. Did she mourn the old man? Would she return to Rotenek? Would they ever have another chance to discuss Fortunatus or what poets they both admired beyond Pertulif? She looked for the duelist when walking in Axian Park, but if she still rode out it was not at the hours for fashionable exercise.

CHAPTER EIGHT

Barbara

LeFevre had hired a room at the civic hall for the reading of the baron's will. Barbara couldn't help but recall the last time she had entered it, at the baron's side and watching the signs of his final failing. Her eyes followed each set of arrivals. That instinct would long survive the baron. Ponivin and Charsintek and a handful of the other upper servants had come to represent the staff and were enjoying the novelty of being served rather than serving. Barbara watched out the window to see the arrival of a scattering of local notables who had received invitations indicating that they were remembered in some way. They wouldn't expect anything substantial—a token to ensure their presence so they could bear witness in any ensuing disputes. The prince's magistrate was in attendance for the same reason, although the token left to the crown was traditionally more substantial. It served the purpose of ensuring enforcement of the will's provisions, as it would be forfeit if they were broken. Of course there were other recipients who could not attend due to the distance. A whole scattering of connections and relations back in Rotenek. Of those, only Estefen could be expected to show.

There was Margerit, dressed in a deeper mourning than was properly called for. Perhaps the gown had been made for a different loss and was being reused. She was surrounded by a cloud of relatives. Barbara recognized the uncle from the ball, his mouth pursed as if in perpetual distaste, arm in arm with the delicate woman from the riverside park. At his other side, a girl who—from the resemblance to the woman—must be a daughter and so Margerit's cousin. And there was the other aunt—the cheerful-looking woman who had accompanied Margerit's visits. LeFevre greeted them enthusiastically as they entered, showing them to seats near the front of the room. No one was ready to settle yet, with the reading scheduled for noon. The newly-arrived party dispersed among their neighbors, sharing greetings and the news of the day.

Barbara had turned back to the window, watching for one particular arrival. LeFevre had sought her out that morning with an unexpected request. "I fear that Estefen will be trouble," he'd said. Barbara expected the same—not knowing the details of what form his disappointment would take, but of course LeFevre wasn't free to elaborate yet. "You would do me a favor if you would…stand prepared for any unpleasantness."

Barbara had raised an eyebrow at that. "Are you asking me to come armed? I had license to bear a sword in the baron's name. Legally, I suppose I'm still in his service, but—"

LeFevre had assured her that he would stand surety for her. "But in any case, it shouldn't cause comment. And I hope I'm being over-cautious. He's unlikely to make serious trouble at such a solemn event and with the magistrate in attendance."

Barbara was less sure on that last point. And here it felt odd to stand ready, her senses keyed to action, without that axis around which her duty had always revolved. A step behind her made her turn sharply.

Margerit flinched back, saying, "I'm sorry I startled you."

Barbara bowed silently in apology.

"I've been looking for you, to tell you how sorry I am for your loss."

Barbara felt awkward in answering. "There was no need, Maisetra. My loss is no greater than yours." She retreated into a verse from Tanfrit. "*All come at last to serve and solve the final mystery.*"

"But surely you—" Margerit hesitated, as if uncertain of her ground.

Barbara didn't offer any guidance. There was genuine sorrow in the girl's brown eyes, but her own wound was too raw and too deep and she had no intention of displaying it to the crowd of strangers here.

"What will you do now?"

The question was so sincerely concerned that she bent a little. "Whatever I choose, now that I'll be free to do so. I'll have some time to decide. I have reason to believe that the baron will have remembered me sufficiently to give me some choices. He always said he meant to do that."

"I'm glad for you. What a thing it must be to see all manner of roads stretching before you and only need to choose!" Her voice turned from wistful to tired. "I'm not even sure why I'm here. Uncle Fulpi would have taken care of all the details, but Maistir LeFevre insisted that I come."

"I believe," Barbara said carefully, "that the baron meant to leave you a sum to increase your dowry. I wasn't in his confidence, of course, but—" She looked past Margerit and stiffened. While she had been turned away from the window to speak to the girl she'd missed Estefen's arrival. Now here he was, striding into the room as if he were the awaited guest of honor. He took a seat directly facing LeFevre's desk.

"What is it?" Margerit whispered.

"I think things will be starting soon," Barbara said. "You should find your seat." She moved away to position herself in a place where she could watch carefully…and move if necessary. Estefen threw her one sharp glance and then studiously ignored her.

LeFevre, sensing his audience's mood, moved to take his place behind the desk and unlocked a document case with a small brass key. The rest took that cue to finish their conversations and find places: chairs for the greater, a place to stand around the back of the room for the lesser. He spread the sheaf of papers before him and cleared his throat. Someone unacquainted with his mannerisms might have thought him nervous. "Please understand that this will is in Baron Saveze's own voice and words. And as you know, he was a man of firm opinions."

"Get to it, man," Estefen interrupted impatiently.

LeFevre shrugged and bent his head to the papers. "I, Marziel Lumbeirt, Baron Saveze," the legal formulas that LeFevre himself must have insisted on rolled on for several lines. "Being of sound mind and having consulted deeply on the law—" An odd phrase, Barbara thought, but she had only once before heard the reading of a will. "—set forth my will concerning the disposition of my worldly wealth." LeFevre's voice took on some of the cadence and tone of his late employer. "As my nephew Estefen Chazillen is doubtless anxious to come into his inheritance, I shall break with custom and begin by easing his mind."

Estefen snorted at that but stirred in his chair uneasily. Normally the will would begin with the litany of small bequests and token gifts and work slowly toward the more substantial transactions.

"From my family, I inherited the estate of Saveze and with it the title of Baron. Thanks to the profligacy of my forebears, in particular my brother Mihail, the estate was greatly encumbered."

LeFevre cleared his throat again and his voice dropped back to its normal tone. "Pray have patience. I told him there was no need to include ancient history in the will, but he insisted."

He rustled the papers and took on the baron's tone again. "Through my own efforts, I not only lifted the debts on my ancestral lands but amassed a considerable fortune and added several other properties to my holdings. And though my relations have been disdainful of the industry that made this possible, they have lived in the expectation of benefiting from the profits. My nephew Estefen—the heir-default to the title and estate of Saveze—has in particular been living for years on the expectations of his inheritance. It is now time for him to reap his just reward."

Estefen frowned at the word "just."

"Estefen Chazillen, the eldest son of my sister Iosifin, will receive—with the grace and permission of Prince Aukust, should he choose to grant it—the ancestral lands of Saveze, with all their rents, revenues, incomes and debts, and I wish him the joy of the title of baron."

It would be startling indeed, Barbara thought, should the title not be confirmed, but the common formula bowed to the prince's right.

"He will find," LeFevre continued, "when he reviews the accounts of his property, that every penny he has begged, wheedled and extorted from me over the years has derived from the revenues of that property that is now his. If he had lived a careful and frugal life, he would now be a wealthy man. However as his financial demands have frequently exceeded the income of the estate, he will find that it once again bears mortgages, though not nearly as heavy as when I first received it. May he enjoy the fruits of his labors both past and present."

Barbara saw LeFevre raise his eyes to meet Estefen's, not in challenge but with confidence. "The baron consulted the best doctors of law concerning inheritance of titular land. The legacy is sound. If you contest it, you will spend your own substance to no return."

Estefen pushed up from his chair. "I have friends higher than your doctors of law. I will have what is due me. And you—"

When Estefen stepped toward LeFevre, Barbara shifted her stance. There was no motion toward her sword, just enough movement to catch his eye and remind him of her presence. His mouth curled in a snarl. "You will be sorry you stood by him in this charade!"

He strode from the room, pushing through the people standing closest to the door. Barbara didn't relax until she heard him shouting distantly for his horse to be fetched.

LeFevre accepted a glass of wine from one of the waiting attendants and once again cleared his throat. "Please forgive the interruption. I fear the young man has suffered a disappointment." With a repetition becoming ritual, he once again shuffled the papers before him and continued reading.

Now the document fell into the usual pattern. The servants were remembered. Distant relations and absent friends received gifts or keepsakes. The local notables were granted their tokens. A sum to the cathedral in Rotenek and another to the village church at Saveze for Masses to be said. It continued for several pages, as the baron's circles had been extensive and eclectic and reflected long years of tightly woven webs of relationships. LeFevre sipped at the wine again and began a new section.

"To my goddaughter, Margerit Sovitre, in token of the love I bear for her, I leave the remainder of my properties, holdings, goods and monies, as will be detailed in the attached inventories, with the sole exception of the manor of Firumai and the sum of ten thousand crowns, which I commend to Prince Aukust in true loyalty and in the certainty of his justice."

There was an uncomprehending silence for a moment then a gasp ran through the room as people contemplated the baron's rumored wealth and calculated what that "remainder" might entail. Barbara allowed herself the hint of a smile. She knew he had intended to thwart Estefen's smug expectations but thought the church would figure more prominently in the strategy. This—this was a slap in the face above and beyond a social death knell. Estefen's debts were crippling, though small enough compared to his former expectations. The baronial estate, encumbered as it was, would provide little but the requirement of upholding his new station. He couldn't even sell it, as it was bound to the title. She spared some pity for Margerit's situation: she had inherited a fortune and along with it the deep enmity of a man with powerful friends.

Margerit herself looked confused. Her uncle looked stunned, with a rapidly growing awareness lighting him from within. It was only when Barbara turned back to LeFevre and saw him gazing at her with a worried look that it occurred to her what she had not yet heard in the will.

LeFevre raised his hand for silence and continued, "—with one stipulation that will be detailed below. Regarding the woman known as Barbara who has served me well and faithfully as my duelist. It had always been my intent to see her established in her chosen course of life and it is to my sorrow that I could not live long enough to accomplish that goal. I would not see her cast out alone and friendless into the world, without protection or support. Therefore the woman Barbara is to be included in that portion of my possessions that I leave to my goddaughter Margerit and—"

Barbara thought at first that she hadn't heard correctly—and no wonder, given the roaring in her ears that drowned out the burst of startled exclamations among the crowd. They meant nothing. The world had narrowed to her and LeFevre and the treacherous papers in his hands. She approached the desk slowly, her voice husky with disbelief. "He promised I would be free! You were there—you heard him!"

LeFevre glanced up at her briefly then looked back at the papers as if unwilling to meet her gaze and said, "If the will were silent on this matter, then a verbal statement might be taken into consideration. But the document is very clear." And low, so only they two could hear, "Barbara, my hands are tied."

She slammed a palm against the desk. The baron had been many things, but he had always been a man of his word. "He *promised*!" The swift descent from dark amusement to despair had left her light-headed. Someone—she didn't know who—laid a hand roughly on her arm and she instinctively spun away, breaking the hold and falling into a crouch with her back to the windows and her blade drawn. A woman screamed. Around the room chairs scraped the floor as people came to their feet.

Barbara's anger was washed away by a flood of panic at what she'd done. There was no law that would back her. No excuse that would stand. She saw the shocked look on LeFevre's face. It had never occurred to him not to trust her and she'd failed that trust. Even as she edged backward to keep everyone in sight, she wondered if flight were possible. In an eyeblink her imagination took her out the window, had her stealing a horse, fleeing into the mountains, then…what? In two more minutes someone would have run to fetch help and there would be more weapons in the room and she would need to kill a man…or be killed…or both.

CHAPTER NINE

Margerit

The remainder of my properties. There had been no time to think seriously on what that meant in the chaos that followed. And then Barbara was backing slowly toward the edge of the room with her sword out and her eyes darting wildly. Margerit knew how it must look but she'd seen Barbara's face when she spun around. In that brief instant there had been no anger, no murderous intent, no emotion at all. Only afterward had she realized what she'd done. And now the room felt like the moment between the lightning flash and the crack of the thunder.

Without any thought or plan Margerit rose and walked slowly toward her, stretching her hand out in entreaty. Her heart was pounding. When she came within inches of the blade's point she hesitated. Barbara backed up another step and then the tip of her sword wavered and dipped toward the floor. She seemed paralyzed. Margerit closed the distance in two short steps and reached out to touch her lightly on the wrist. She closed her other hand around the base of the blade. Quietly, so that only the two of them could hear, she said, "Barbara, you're frightening them—I'm afraid someone will do you an injury."

"Don't...please," Barbara pleaded. "It's sharp."

"I know," Margerit answered. She could feel the edge against her palm but she held firm. "Give me the sword. Let go. Please!"

So gently that the steel moved not a hairsbreadth, Barbara released her grip. Margerit took the hilt in her other hand and held the weapon lightly, tucked into the folds of her skirts. Her palm stung and she clenched it into a hidden fist.

The moment she stepped back, there was a rush of some of the bolder men. Margerit tried to protest as they seized Barbara by the arms and forced her to her knees but no one paid her any mind in their haste to make up for their former timidity. She raised her voice, hating how it quavered. "Maistir LeFevre, I think we can solve this problem simply enough. If Barbara has been given to me, then *I* will free her."

LeFevre held up his hand to stop her. "I think it would be best if I finished reading this clause." He wiped his balding forehead with a kerchief and took up the papers again. "'And to ensure that my wishes in this matter are carried out, it is stipulated that Margerit is to take and maintain the woman Barbara in her own household and Barbara is to serve her as armin until such time as both of them shall have attained their majority. And if these conditions are not met, then my legacy to both Margerit and the crown is forfeit, save that each will be given five thousand crowns, and the residue of my estate will be given instead to the Convent of Saint Orisul, for the benefit of my soul.'"

The gathered crowd again erupted in noisy comment and speculation. Margerit heard her uncle begin to speak and raised her voice over them all. It was her one chance to see it through before she lost courage entirely. "Please, Uncle, let me speak." From the look he returned her she knew there would be a price to pay later. Her voice was shaking even more now but she continued. "When I came here today, I had no expectation of being remembered with anything more than a token. Instead, I've been left a fortune beyond what I can imagine. Five thousand crowns is still far more generous than anything I had a reason to expect. What is the harm to me if I forfeit an inheritance that I've never touched in order to see justice done? Give Barbara her freedom and let the convent have its fortune. I will be content." In the back of her mind, a voice whispered, *Is this worth the price?* And the answer, *Let her be what I can't: free.*

LeFevre was watching her with a startled and bemused expression but just as he might have spoken, Uncle Fulpi's voice cut through the room. He had pushed his way to her side and looked as if he wanted to shake her. "You will do no such thing! You may be too foolish to see what you're throwing away, but that's why you have guardians. You have no power to alienate any part of your inheritance if I forbid it."

"I'm afraid it's true, Maisetra Sovitre," LeFevre confirmed.

For the first time the magistrate spoke up, adding, "I believe that Prince Aukust will also have some opinion on any action that would greatly reduce his gift."

Her uncle's voice turned harder. "You needn't concern yourself with this matter further, Margerit. I have no intention of allowing this," he glanced at Barbara with an expression of distaste, "this unwomanly freak into my house. There are only two years until the conditions of the will are fulfilled. Something will be arranged."

The moment was slipping away. If she couldn't give Barbara her freedom, she could at least try to keep her safely close by. Her uncle's looming presence was daunting but an unfamiliar strength flowed into her from her clenched fists—one on the hilt of the sword still half-hidden in her skirts and the other in a white-knuckled ball. She looked over at LeFevre and asked, "Could you read that last part again? I'm not certain I understood it perfectly."

A small smile quirked the corner of his mouth as he bent over the sheaf of papers with a faint cough. "And to ensure that my wishes in this matter are carried out, it is stipulated that Margerit is to take and maintain the woman Barbara in her own household and—"

"Uncle," Margerit interrupted. "I'm afraid the will is clear. If I'm not to forfeit, then nothing different can be arranged." Before he could respond, she turned and took two quick steps over to where Barbara still knelt. In a quiet but firm voice she asked, "Barbara, do you promise to serve me as well and faithfully as you served my godfather?"

Barbara hesitated and Margerit thought she could see the reflection of all those other roads that had briefly stretched before her. "I promise," she said.

In the impulse of the moment, Margerit stretched out her hand to her—still clenched tightly—and glared at the men holding Barbara with what she hoped was a commanding gaze. They loosed their grip and Barbara reached out to take the hand and press it to her lips. Margerit winced slightly as her fingers relaxed and saw the faint smear of red left on Barbara's fingertips. Barbara had seen it too and jerked her gaze up in concern. Margerit locked eyes with her and shook her head almost imperceptibly. Barbara nodded just as faintly then rose to her feet as Margerit handed back her sword and she returned it home. As Margerit turned back to LeFevre's desk, she saw Barbara step into the same post she had always taken with the baron: one step behind and to the right. She glanced back briefly. Barbara's expression was relaxed now—as if the world had returned to spinning on its true axis. The rest of the room was staring and whispering but she paid them no mind.

LeFevre once more shuffled his sheaf of papers, bringing all eyes back to him. "That's all there is of note. There are the inventories and lists but they needn't be included in the public reading. Maistir Fulpi, perhaps Maisetra Sovitre's guardians could meet with me in the next day or two to begin on the details."

And then, it seemed, the reading was over. In the milling confusion of the exodus, Barbara stuck to her as if they had been harnessed together. There was a delay at the carriages for Uncle Fulpi, who had stayed to make further arrangements. Then a brief argument when he returned to find the new armin ensconced inseparably at her side in the smaller chaise. She had hoped for a respite at least until they returned home, but he joined her for the ride, first shouting, then cold and cutting and at last retreating into a stony silence. It took no dissembling, when they arrived, to plead a headache and retreat for her room. Barbara mounted a rear-guard action against her aunts' sudden solicitude as they pursued her with insistent offers of tea and cold compresses. She answered Barbara's continual questioning looks with a steadfast shake of the head until she finally was able to close the door behind them and turn the key in the lock. Released at last from the need for control, Margerit sat on the edge of her bed, her hands still clenched in her lap. Abruptly she began crying in deep tearing gasps.

It took some time for the storm to abate. She became aware of Barbara once more when she ventured, "Maisetra, should I call someone?"

"No!" She hadn't meant to be so forceful. She saw Barbara stiffen into her waiting pose as if rebuked. When her voice again could resolve itself into words, she said, "He was so angry. So angry. I'm frightened. What will he do?"

"Estefen?" Barbara inquired crisply.

Margerit looked up at her in confusion. "Uncle Fulpi. I've never defied him like that before. I never…he was so angry." His shouting in the carriage still rang in her ears. "I've never…I don't know how I could…and even so I failed." That was what filled her with despair: that she had risked all to defy him and won nothing from it.

Barbara took a tentative step forward. "May I speak?"

Margerit was startled. She had been talking mostly to herself. When she said nothing, Barbara repeated, "May I speak?"

"Yes. Yes, of course."

Barbara knelt down at the bedside, but it seemed more an intimate gesture than a servile one. "You were magnificent. You were like Penthesilia on the plains of Troy. Defeat is not dishonor. And I will never forget what you tried to do for me. What you offered to give up."

Margerit blinked at her. She followed the sense of the words but not their meaning. But the silence had been broken and Barbara pressed further. "Let me see your hand." She touched the back of her fist and Margerit finally unclenched it and stared at her palm where she had grasped the sword. The cut was the barest scratch; it had long since stopped bleeding. She felt like a small child about to be scolded for rough play as Barbara found a small cloth on the dresser, moistened it from the water pitcher and carefully cleaned off the smear of blood. "Do you want me to bind it up?"

Margerit looked down at her hand and shook her head. "No, then someone would ask questions. It was a stupid thing to do. I didn't know what else to try. You looked so wild."

Barbara flushed deeply. "Forgive me, Maisetra."

"No, you had every right to be angry. It's outrageous. I don't know what he was thinking. He...he told me the story, how you came to him." She felt embarrassed now, to have been told something so private. "Why should you be punished for your father's debts? He could have raised you as a daughter, not as a...a servant."

Barbara pressed her lips tightly together and Margerit couldn't tell what she was withholding, whether contradiction or assent. She must have had the same questions through the years. But all she said was, "Shall I have them bring you tea now?"

Margerit managed a weak smile. "It's the remedy for everything, isn't it?"

CHAPTER TEN

Barbara

What an odd homecoming, that the first protection she lent was against Margerit's own family. Was the uncle truly that much of an ogre? She had seen his tirade in the carriage but both that and Margerit's response could be blamed on the strangeness of the day. It seemed too soon to test Margerit's fragile calm so she applied all her diplomatic skills to fending off the lurking aunts who accompanied the housemaid bringing up the tea tray. But when the rituals of pouring and sipping had been accomplished, she moved on to more practical concerns. "May I speak?"

Margerit frowned at her. "You don't need to ask like that."

Uncertainly, Barbara explained, "The baron preferred that I—"

"I'm not the baron," Margerit said briskly, "and if I have to approve every word out of your mouth, it will drive me mad."

The implications of that statement nibbled at the back of her mind but she let them be for the moment. "If I am to join this household, there are things I'll need to collect from the baron's—that is, from Fonten House. It's your house now, of course."

"It is? That mansion?"

Barbara stifled the laughter from her voice, but not from her eyes. "Maisetra, you're rich now. Very rich. Fonten House is only the smallest part."

Margerit looked frightened again. "How much—no, leave that for later. Yes, your clothes and belongings. And the housekeeper will need to find you a place in the servants' rooms. I don't know what needs to be done. What were the arrangements when you served my godfather?"

Barbara glanced around Margerit's small chamber and compared it to the room she'd occupied in Fonten House. "It doesn't matter. As you said, you are not the baron and this is not the baron's house. I must follow the customs of this one."

* * *

When Margerit was ready to face her aunts, and when the matter of her own presence in the house had been acknowledged by them as inevitable, Barbara placed herself in the care of the maid who returned for the tea things, to be taken downstairs to see what needed to be done. As it happened, LeFevre had foreseen the matter. When she descended to the understairs, a pair of familiar trunks were nearly blocking the passageway in from the back entrance.

Mefro Lozenek, the housekeeper, was a tall, forbidding woman of the sort who could keep a staff in line with only a glance. She looked Barbara up and down as if she were a street urchin applying to scrub pots. "We run a traditional household here," she intoned briskly. "I'm in charge of all the female staff. Except, of course, for the kitchen help." She made that omission sound as if it bordered on anarchy. "You will be assigned to share a bedroom based on your station. Meals are eaten here in the lower hall. As you won't be serving at table, you will eat with the rest of us—no keeping a plate warm, no special meals from the kitchen. Seating at table is by rank too. There will be no gadding about. Unless you're sent out on errands, you're expected to stay indoors. Unless you're attending on the family when they go to Mass, you go with the rest of us to Saint Mari-Mirikur. There is to be no skulking in private. Bedrooms are for sleeping and dressing, not for lazing around. At the times when Maisetra Margerit doesn't require your presence, you will be given useful occupation."

Barbara briefly contemplated taking the willow path for the moment and bending until matters could be cleared up later, but that would only put the burden on Margerit's back. And protecting Margerit was now her first task. She drew herself up and looked the housekeeper in the eyes. "I respect your authority over the servants of this house, but I answer only to Maisetra Margerit. I take orders only from her. If she gives me leave, I will come and go as I choose. I will follow the rules of the household regarding bed and board but beyond that I do not answer to you."

The housekeeper stared at her with her mouth open like a dead fish. She shut it with a snap then said, "We'll see about that. You must excuse us, we've never had a *duelist* in service before." She gave the word a peevish tone that made it clear she considered the very occupation an affectation. "And what, pray tell, is the rank and station of a *duelist* in relation to a parlormaid?"

Barbara's stomach clenched. Did the woman not know how matters stood? Had the understairs gossip not reached that detail? Or was she taking petty revenge by making her say it aloud with all manner of others listening in? "Only a nobleman may keep a duelist," she said carefully. "I serve the maisetra merely as armin, as her bodyguard. An armin may rank high or low, but since it matters here, you may count me among the least in the house."

Mefro Lozenek frowned impatiently. "Don't play games with me and tell me what I may do and may not do. Tell me plainly, what is your station?"

Barbara's voice became flat and expressionless. "The late baron left me to Maisetra Margerit in his will. What do you think my station is? I am her possession." She dared the woman to make mock over it.

There was a brief flash of triumph in the housekeeper's eyes before she turned to rebuke a cluster of maids who had stopped their work to gawk. "Fetch Aggy and Luzza from the kitchen." When the two girls were brought out, it was clear that their position entailed little higher than scrubbing pots and cleaning the stove. "Aggy, Luzza, this is the new girl Barbara. She will be sharing your room. One of you show her where to take her things."

Barbara gave a silent sigh as the girl identified as Aggy gaped at her and started babbling, "Oh no, ma'am! I can't, ma'am! They say she killed a man—we'll be murdered in our beds for sure!" The one called Luzza added to the rising hysteria with, "My mum will have a fit. She'll call me home if she hears I'm sharing a bed with…with…" Her vocabulary failed to rise to the occasion of what she believed the objection would be.

The housekeeper gave each of the girls a quick slap and said they'd do as they were told, but one of the footmen who had been loitering at the back of the room interjected, "You weren't thinking to fit those two big trunks into Luz and Aggy's room were you?"

Mefro Lozenek peered around the corner to examine the offending luggage and threw up her hands. "It can't be done. There aren't any free rooms and it would be beyond what is allowable to turn anyone else out for your sake."

"Put her in my room," came a voice. Barbara recognized Maitelen, the young woman who had brought up Margerit's tea. Her clothing marked her as an upper parlor maid, well toward the top of the hierarchy. "Since Gaita took the end room with Ferlint, I've had it to myself. And there's that odd corner behind the chimney where the trunks would fit. And *I'm* not afraid of being murdered in my bed. Come on," she said to Barbara, heading for the stairs without waiting for the housekeeper to approve.

A few minutes later she surveyed the cramped but adequate space that Maitelen showed her as the trunks were stowed away. "It was kind of you to make the offer."

Maitelen snorted. "Kindness don't get you on in the world."

Her speech habits betrayed her as a country girl, one step removed from the dairy and chickens. That she had climbed as high as she had, Barbara thought, was a tribute either to her shrewdness or to the unavailability of more refined servants in a town like Chalanz.

"Here's the deal," Maitelen continued. "Maisetra Margerit—she'll be wanting her own lady's maid now, not just making do with help from Gaita who knows how to dress and do hair on the side. And when she comes to choose someone, I want to be the one she thinks of. I don't care if you're a slave or the Queen of Sheba, suddenly you're the one the young maisetra wants at her side. So you're my new best friend."

Barbara admired the girl's honesty and straight talk. They would deal together well enough, she thought. And if she weren't yet ready to provide an enthusiastic reference, then sharing a room would give her a basis for judgment.

When Maitelen had left, Barbara looked around the room. The width was barely enough for space to walk between the bedsteads on either side. At the far end from the door stood a low dresser and washstand on the left side. The right side was blocked by a wide brick chimney, passing through from the family rooms below to the roof above. Maitelen thought that made it a choice bedroom for it was never cold. But an architect who cared more about symmetry than practicality had positioned the room's only window behind the brick column and it was in this slight hidden bay that her trunks had been deposited, in a space not useful for a third bed.

She went to sit on the edge of the nearer trunk where she could see out the window. Dusk was falling but she could make out the lines of a small paved yard and then a carriage house opening onto the lane behind. That was where she'd entered last time when delivering the baron's invitation. She was startled by a tear that blurred her vision and threatened to fall. She tilted her head back and blinked until it retreated and could be denied. If it could be denied it didn't need to be explained.

Through the walls she heard the chiming of the tall clock in the hall downstairs and jumped up. Best not to add further antagonism by being late to her first meal. Almost as an afterthought she unbuckled her swordbelt and laid the weapon inside the trunk she'd been sitting on.

* * *

With the ordeal of the first understairs dinner endured, her goal was to speak to Margerit again that evening—to know what to expect in the morning. Morning. Her lessons with Signore Donati. Would anyone have thought to send a message around to him? It was nothing that could be mended at the moment. Maybe once things had settled down. Did Margerit go out in the mornings? They had met that one afternoon in the park, but she had no idea what a well-born young lady's daily schedule might be.

She was hesitant to wander into the family areas of the house without permission. Maitelen had promised to let her know when Margerit went upstairs to change for bed; that would be the best time to ask questions. The enforced idleness was maddening. She had no books, no occupation, not even the relief of solitude as she didn't care to flout too many rules on the first evening. It was almost a relief when one of the footmen—still liveried from serving at dinner—came to tell her the master wanted to see her in his office.

With Mefro Lozenek, she had chosen to draw a line from the beginning. Margerit's uncle was a different matter. He might not technically command *her*, but he did command Margerit. Any trouble would rebound there. So she followed the footman up. With every path through the house, she picked up more bearings but she itched to explore it thoroughly—to know every turn and corner as well as she knew all the baron's properties.

The man was sitting before the fire examining some papers on a side table. He didn't react as she entered and bowed silently. The minutes stretched out. If he thought to rattle her he'd chosen the wrong tactic, Barbara thought as she settled into her watchful stance. The baron had been a master at that game.

A quarter of an hour passed before he pushed the papers aside and looked up. "The clothing will need to change."

Barbara stole a moment to choose her response carefully. "I will, of course, dress as the maisetra commands me. But there are garments that can make my work easier or harder."

"Do you seriously think that my niece requires an armin, much less a professional duelist?"

The question made it clear what he thought of the idea, but she answered as if it had been sincere. "If we were in Rotenek, there would be no question. Every year you hear a story of an heiress snatched and forced into marriage. Some of them may be complicit in their own abductions, of course, but not all. Two years ago there was a young woman from a good family—rich, but with enemies. She was affianced to a promising young man. The brigands who took her claimed they wanted money for her safe return but the rumor was that it was for revenge on her father. She escaped on her own but the whispers started. She swore she was untouched and yet the young man broke off their engagement. In the end, she hanged herself." She paused to see if he believed her. "It's possible that here in Chalanz a young unmarried heiress can come and go about town without fear of seducers and abductions. You are more familiar with this place than I am."

She could tell that the image had hit home. The sardonic look had left his face and he leaned toward her. "You have begun to persuade me that Margerit should be guarded. You have yet to persuade me that I should trust you to guard her. That...scene this afternoon."

Barbara could feel the heat rising in her face. There was no answer she could give—that she *would* give. She had abased herself to Margerit; she would not do so to this man. "My honor lies in keeping your niece safe. But all I can promise is that I shall do what she commands."

His frown deepened. "What *she* commands."

She nodded ever so slightly, acknowledging the unspoken addendum: *not what I command*. Would it help to explain to him about Estefen? But not before she had warned Margerit. That felt too much like disloyalty.

He sighed. "We shall see. But for the moment, I'll inform Margerit that she is not to leave the house unless you accompany her. You may go."

Barbara noticed that the subject of her clothing had become unimportant.

As she opened the door to the hallway, she nearly collided with Margerit, hovering indecisively by the door.

"Is...is there a problem?" Margerit asked anxiously.

Barbara closed the door behind her. "No, I think we've come to an understanding for the moment. But Maisetra, I need to speak with you. There are," she waved her hand vaguely, "matters to arrange."

Margerit nodded vigorously. "Come to me in my room. I'll send for you after I've spoken to my uncle."

CHAPTER ELEVEN

Margerit

Dinner had, as always, been calm, dignified and formal. It gave her no reassurance that her defiance of the afternoon had been forgiven. Hiding in her room could only provide a temporary respite and she had long ago discovered that it was better to face her uncle immediately and take the consequences. Aunt Honurat could never steel herself to do so and would spend a month in slowly grinding anxiety rather than face ten minutes of her husband's direct disapproval. Aunt Bertrut was free of any direct obligation to him and on those occasions when she found it unpleasant to live under his roof, she was quite content to visit friends about the countryside until the growing disorder in the household forced him to send his wife as an unacknowledged ambassadress to beg her return.

But Margerit had no such haven nor was her happiness essential to the smooth operation of her uncle's house. And so she slipped into the room and made a vague and general apology for the events of the afternoon that she hoped would cover all possible transgressions.

He received it with a mild frown but said merely, "I would expect a girl of your age to know how to control servants properly. Maisetra Fulpi seems to have been remiss in that part of your education. You will be mistress of your own household soon enough and then you will learn what lax standards can lead to." He shifted back in his chair and put on a more friendly expression. "I'm glad you came to speak with me. I imagine you're feeling quite dizzy with today's change of fortune."

A change indeed if it absolved her of her sins! But she was grateful for the respite. "I had no idea. I didn't think—that is, when he spoke to me at the ball, it seemed as if he'd almost forgotten me. And when I visited, there was no hint." She hesitated, recalling the curious stare from LeFevre. He must have known. No doubt that was what they'd spent the morning arranging.

"Well, it seems that you must have impressed him favorably in that last week." He tented his hands together and spoke with the fatherly tone that had always unsettled her for its rarity. "This will mean a great many changes in your life, naturally. It's fortunate that you haven't been out long enough to have formed any attachment yet. You'll be able to look much higher for a husband than you might have dreamed. I wouldn't recommend that you be in any hurry to encourage the particular attentions of any man."

"Don't worry, Uncle," she assured him in a rush. "I'm in no hurry to be married yet. In fact—" She bit her tongue. No need to confess that she had never been in any hurry to be married.

"Well, that's settled then."

What was settled? She felt as if she'd missed some essential question.

"I was thinking that it might be a good idea to spend a part of the fall season in Rotenek. The best prospects are unlikely to come to you here. It would be too awkward to expect anything to come of it this year, but you would have a chance to meet the right people, make the right connections. And then the year after...why, who can say what might happen."

When the prize mare wins a race, you don't sell her at the local village market. But to go to Rotenek! That was something they could agree on. The suggestion had planted a seed that she hardly dared to contemplate. "That would be very nice," she said.

Now her uncle's face pulled sideways in distaste. "There are a few less pleasant things to consider now. I don't want to be indelicate—I leave that for your Aunt Sovitre—but you will find that a great many unsavory people may come buzzing about you. I don't speak of the ordinary run of social climbers—"

Like you, Uncle? she thought. But no, that was unfair. He was ambitious, but he had rather old-fashioned notions of keeping to one's place. It was only that her place had now changed in his eyes.

"—I mean fortune hunters intent on fixing your interest. You must become very circumspect and behave with the greatest propriety to avoid gossip. The matches we can contemplate will expect an unsullied reputation. Don't take to conversing with dashing army officers or fashionable do-nothings. Be seen with no one to whom you haven't been properly introduced."

At this Margerit was hard put not to laugh out loud. "But Uncle, when have I ever shown any interest in men in bright uniforms or garish waistcoats? And I've already been introduced to anyone I'll be meeting about town."

"This isn't a frivolous matter, Margerit! With great fortune come dangers that you couldn't possibly imagine—for which I'm grateful. That woman Barbara has opened my eyes to things I wouldn't care to have you subject to. Since fate has given you the services of an armin, for the moment I would prefer that you be in her company whenever you leave the house. Promise me that, Margerit."

With relief, she promised what he asked. And to think she had been in agonies that he would find some way around the will and would send Barbara away! As for those unspoken dangers she couldn't imagine, she had some idea who could enlighten her on that end.

* * *

Barbara was waiting for her upstairs, standing somewhat uneasily beside the narrow window that looked out over the square by daylight. Maitelen had brought her and stayed to lay out her nightclothes and see that the fire was set for the night. It was more attention than she was usually paid unasked. Margerit recalled her uncle's caution about flatterers. Did it start this close to home?

"Maitelen, that will do very well for now."

The maid bobbed a curtsy. "Will you want me to help you undress?"

That confirmed it. Well, why not? No doubt she could afford her own lady's maid now and Maitelen was a familiar face. It occurred to her that she knew very little of what lay between "I can afford it" and the reality of hiring away her uncle's servants under his own roof. "Come back in," she considered the hour she had last heard struck on the case clock in the hall, "half an hour?"

When they were alone, Margerit sat on the edge of her bed as she had earlier that afternoon. Someone had smoothed away the traces of disorder in the coverlet.

"Please sit," she told Barbara. There was a single chair in the room, tucked into the window-nook, but the other woman settled herself gingerly on the foot of the bed. She had changed out of the strict mourning that had begun the day, trading it for the informality of a plain linen shirt and fawn breeches. The only reminder was a simple black ribbon tied around her arm. Her hair hung loose in an unruly wave as if she had been interrupted in the act of braiding it for the night. Uncertainty lurked in her pale eyes.

"May I sp—"

"Why did—"

They both stopped, then Barbara dropped her eyes and made a gesture of surrender.

"Why did he do it?" Margerit finished. "Why did he leave…all that to me?"

Barbara hesitated so long in answering that Margerit thought she hadn't quite understood. But at last she said, "Why you? I don't know. I wasn't in his confidence. Obviously," she added bitterly. "But why leave it to someone? To spite Estefen, his nephew. You heard what he thought of him. Estefen spent his entire life in expectation of being the baron's sole heir. He traded on it. He borrowed against it. The baron didn't just want to disappoint him, he wanted to torment him. You will need to beware of Estefen. But I think that's why he didn't simply leave the whole to the church. That could have been explained away. But to leave it to someone like you—with only the faintest connection—that would be an unmistakable slap to his family."

Margerit swallowed heavily, trying to fight back tears. "Just like my governess."

"What?" Barbara asked in confusion but Margerit found herself unable to explain. "I know he felt some affection for you," Barbara continued. "He didn't choose randomly."

"But it wasn't for *me*. He didn't give me all this because he had plans for *me*."

"Maybe it's better that way," Barbara said softly.

"What?" Now it was she who was confused.

"If he didn't have any grand plan in making you his heir, then you're free to do with it what you like."

Margerit tried the idea on for size. It wasn't at all as simple as doing what she liked, of course. But maybe there was something in the idea. Because she had fallen in love with learning, she had clung fiercely to the notion that the baron wanted her to be a scholar. Did it matter, now, that it had been based on a lie? Her uncle wanted her to go to Rotenek; it was almost a sign. Dare she follow that road simply because *she* wanted to?

Barbara broke into her reverie. "May I speak?"

The question grated on her but it was clearly a habit that would take some time to break. She nodded.

Barbara leaned forward and spoke briskly. "If I'm to accompany you when you go out, it will help if I know what your habits are—what you normally do with your days."

Margerit thought a moment. "In the late morning or afternoon I might go walking in the park if the weather is nice. In the afternoons I might have errands or go visiting with one of my aunts or I might be needed for something at home. It's hard to say. And then of course there are dinners in the evenings sometimes and after Easter there will be balls again—oh, will you accompany me to those as well? That could be strange."

Barbara shrugged. "In Rotenek it raises no comment to have armins at a ball. They hang out in the galleries, leaning against the pillars where they can watch everyone and scowl at each other. At dinners… the baron always had me attend him at table when he dined out but he was an eccentric and did it to shock. I think you're too young to be an eccentric."

"It's a pity," Margerit sighed. "If I were, I could do what I pleased, like old Maisetra Rivier."

Barbara turned serious again. "What do you plan for tomorrow?" She explained hurriedly, "I only ask because there are matters I need to take care of—arrangements to make. And if you didn't need me, I thought…"

The answer came to her in sudden resolution. "Tomorrow morning I should like to speak with Maistir LeFevre. No doubt my uncle will be seeing him, but I should like to know for myself just what has come to me and how my business stands." Her voice faltered. "But I suppose I would need an appointment. And I don't even know where to go."

Barbara grinned. "That's the simplest part—he's staying at Fonten House. And as for an appointment, I think you needn't stand on ceremony. In one sense, he works for you now, just as he worked for your godfather."

"Then I'd like to go in the morning. After breakfast, perhaps ten o'clock?" She saw Barbara waiting expectantly and made it a statement. "Ten o'clock. And…if anyone asks, we're going for a walk." It wasn't in her nature to be deceitful, but she had learned that there were better and worse ways to avoid her uncle's scrutiny.

Barbara looked affronted. "Maisetra, it isn't my place to discuss your affairs with anyone else."

It was an odd feeling, Margerit thought later when Barbara had left and Maitelen had come and gone and her private prayers were complete. An odd feeling that there was even one person in the world whose first loyalty was to her, Margerit, and who professed herself bound to follow her orders above any others. She shivered a little with the intoxication. It wasn't with cold. For once, this evening, her fire was well-set for the night with no skimping on fuel. That too was an odd feeling. Not that she had ever lacked for anything she truly needed. But no one had thought her worth exerting effort to please before—not the servants and certainly not her relatives. Already today things had shifted and she expected little would be the same again.

CHAPTER TWELVE

Barbara

Barbara had wondered how difficult it might be for Margerit to slip all other chaperonage but the under stairs gossip was that Maisetra Sovitre was closeted with a sick headache. That left Maisetra Fulpi to manage the household tasks alone—which evidently strained the limits of her abilities. And with the excuse of a walk there was no need to worry about a coachman carrying tales; the distance to Fonten Street was no further than Axian Park along the river would have been. They set a brisk pace and for several blocks a companionable quiet lay between them until she ventured, "May I—I'm sorry, you asked me not to do that, but I don't know how else to begin."

"You could begin with 'Margerit'," came the teasing answer.

For only a moment Barbara envisioned a world in which that would be possible. But only a moment. "No, Maisetra. That wouldn't be right." A higher wall stood between them now than had existed when they were near-strangers.

"Then if you must, Maisetra Sovitre," she said. "Everyone here still treats me as a child with 'Maisetra Margerit' all the time. If I'm to be a grand lady now, I think I should be Maisetra Sovitre."

Barbara responded to the earlier teasing tone by pausing in mid-stride to sketch an overblown bow and say grandly, "Maisetra Sovitre."

She took it in good part with a laugh. "But it does seem unfair, if you're going to 'Maisetra' me, for me to use only your Christian name."

Barbara shrugged. "You know how things stand."

"But even the scullery maid is Mefro Lutild on Sundays."

Barbara stiffened. She tried to hide the response but Margerit asked, "I'm sorry. How did I offend you?"

In a low but even voice she said, "Whoever he may have been, my father was no common M'froi Iannik." And then more warmly, seeing Margerit's chagrin, "I'm content to be called only by the one name I know I have a right to." They continued on for another block until Barbara broke the silence that had fallen. "Maisetra, we can't be friends. You can't make it work. It would be too easy for me to forget myself. Let me do my duty to you and let it be enough."

This time it was Margerit who broke step and paused. "It isn't fair." Once again, Barbara shrugged but this time remained silent. She'd never had the luxury of expecting the world to be fair.

* * *

For the first time, she came to the house on Fonten Street as if a stranger. As if it were no longer home. And what must Margerit be thinking as she came to the top of the steps and looked up at the carved stonework looming over her? Barbara saw her hesitate and raise her gloved hand to lift the knocker.

"You needn't knock, Maisetra," she said quietly. "It's your house." She reached past her to try the knob and pushed it open. It should have already been opened for them. Footsteps heralded a startled footman rushing into place. Margerit shrank a little before his curious stare and Barbara touched her arm lightly for reassurance. "Maisetra Sovitre would like to see Maistir LeFevre," she said firmly. "If you would let him know."

"Yes. Yes, of course," he stammered. He gave Margerit a quick bow, almost as an afterthought, murmuring, "Maisetra!" and turned to hurry back down the hallway.

Margerit drew a deep breath. Barbara repeated, "It's your house. These are your people now. Don't be afraid."

With a brief nod, perhaps to convince herself, Margerit followed the servant down the corridor. LeFevre met them at the door to his office, bowing curtly with a quizzical expression. "Luzek, if you please!" He signaled the footman to take her coat and bonnet. "Maisetra, I wasn't expecting you until this afternoon. Your uncle should have sent a message with the change. I'm afraid I'm not entirely prepared…"

"I didn't…that is, my uncle hasn't shared his plans with me," Margerit said. "I'm here on my own account." Barbara saw LeFevre shoot her a questioning glance but she gave the faintest of shrugs. It wasn't for her to explain. Margerit continued, "If it's convenient for you, I would like to know more about my inheritance and…and everything." Her voice trailed off as confidence faltered once more.

"But of course!" he replied promptly, as if it were utterly expected, but he glanced behind him with a frown at the paper-strewn desk. "Perhaps…could you give me, oh, half an hour to set things in order? Barbara could show you over the house. I think you've only seen the smallest part of it. I'll have tea brought in and—will you be staying for luncheon?"

Margerit shook her head. "Oh, I shouldn't. I don't want to cause a fuss. You weren't expecting me."

Barbara cleared her throat and softly repeated, "Your house."

"It's no trouble at all," LeFevre said kindly. "I think the staff would be insulted if you were here and gone so quickly. And Monsieur Guillaumin would be in complete despair if you give him no chance to exhibit his skills. But perhaps you have another engagement?"

"No. That is, if you think it would be proper, I'd be happy to stay. And," she looked questioningly back over her shoulder as if looking for guidance, "perhaps it would be best to begin by meeting the housekeeper and the butler. That is, I've met Mefroi Ponivin, but not in a formal way. Do you think…?"

"If you wish," Barbara said, with a nod of approval.

The footman had returned from disposing of the coats and was sent ahead to warn the downstairs. On arriving in the servants' common room they found two dozen or more liveried figures arrayed in near-military order at the sides of the room and into the kitchen at the far end. If Margerit were daunted, she hid it well. Barbara could tell she was struggling to fill her role but Ponivin stepped in to make the introductions and eased the way. The butler had shed the stiff formality the baron had preferred and put on a warmer avuncular face. It was still a mask for now, she knew. Ponivin had grown old in Saveze's service and his heart would not be so quickly re-given. From the common room Barbara led Margerit all through the house, ending up in the corridor running past the baron's rooms. "You've seen these, of course. They haven't started clearing things out yet. With no guests, we've really only used the south wing this season—it makes things easier for the housekeeper. When there are visitors, they normally go into the north wing, but the rooms are all in covers at the moment. Maistir LeFevre has a room off the office that he uses. He never lets the baron—let the baron put him in the guest wing."

"But this is a charming room!" Margerit exclaimed as they passed an open door at the end of the corridor. "I thought you said there were no guests?"

Barbara hesitated. "This room…that is, the baron being ill, it was necessary, in case he should need me. He has permitted me to use this room." It wasn't entirely a lie—only by implication. The room, of course, had been hers as long as she could remember. But she saw it in a new light, comparing the tall ceilings and rich bed hangings to the cramped simplicity of Margerit's own chamber. To cover the awkwardness she crossed to the open wardrobe and began tidying the drawers so they would close, quoting, "*The changing season scatters blooms across the meadow.* I apologize for the mess. Maistir LeFevre had some of my things sent over to Chaturik Square last night. He had no idea what…how long…"

As she shoved a group of hanging garments aside, Margerit leaned in past her to draw out a gown of a sky-blue silk. "How beautiful! But is this yours?" she asked doubtfully.

Barbara flushed. "I don't always wear breeches, you know," she said quickly. Then she reddened further and said, "Forgive me, Maisetra. I spoke out of place."

Margerit let the skirt fall. "It's all so strange."

Barbara closed the wardrobe doors and turned the latch. "I think Maistir LeFevre will be ready for you now, if you please."

CHAPTER THIRTEEN

Margerit

LeFevre had cleared the desk of papers, but instead of ensconcing himself behind that fortress he had moved two chairs near the small hearth. A tea tray sat on the low table between them and was crowded on either side by rolled parchments and bundles of documents, all tied up in scarlet ribbons. Margerit settled gratefully into the cushions and LeFevre pulled his own seat a little closer while Barbara poured two cups of tea and then stood back in silence.

"What is it that you wish to know?" LeFevre began. "I'm sure you have a great many questions."

Margerit took a deep breath and folded her hands in her lap. They were shaking too much for her to dare the teacup yet. "I would like to know what my inheritance is. What properties do I own? What are their incomes? What are their expenses? How are they managed and by whom? Who are the people? What are my responsibilities to them, by law and by custom? What other incomes are there and how will they change with my godfather's death? And…well, that will do to begin."

She dared to look up when she had finished. LeFevre was frowning at her, the teacup untouched in his hand. He pursed his lips and thought a while before answering. "You know, Maisetra Sovitre, that all this will be managed by me and by your guardians until you are of age. You needn't fear that you'll be pestered by accounts and clerks."

Another deep breath. She hated how her speech turned stiff and formal, betraying her discomfort. "Maistir LeFevre, all my life my aunts have instructed me in the importance of managing a household. In knowing how to do sums and accounts. How to make a quarter's income cover the bills so that my husband will neither want for the pleasant things in life nor be importuned by creditors and tradesmen seeking payment. I know this is no basis for managing a great estate but how could the management of great things be less important than the management of small ones?" She pretended to more confidence than she felt by picking up the china cup and lifting it to her lips briefly. "I know my uncle will be happy to see to all of my business matters but I wish to know what they are and to understand them." When she dared to look over at LeFevre, she saw a smile so broad it was nearly a grin.

"You surprise me at every turn. Perhaps the late baron was not— well never mind. I think we shall deal together very comfortably, Maisetra," he said. "Now, let us begin with the properties." He rose briefly to bring a bundle of papers and a ledger book from the desk and handed items to her one at a time as he listed them. "There is, of course, this house. And Tiporsel, the house in Rotenek. At the moment, they share a staff for the most part—long-time employees of the late baron. I think it would be good for you to keep both properties, for now. There is the estate at Zortun. It's a purchased estate, separate from what went with the title. It supplied a good deal of the late baron's table—definitely to be retained—and his cellar as well. The family that manages it are trustworthy people. You needn't concern yourself with that one.

"There are several other properties that you may want to sell. A hunting lodge on the lake at Feniz. A townhouse and several warehouses in Genoa. And that brings us to—" He opened the ledger. "You own two ships that operate out of Genoa. These you should sell—offer them to their current captains first. The late baron had a talent for choosing cargos and destinations. Without that talent, you might as well be betting on horse races. I know I don't have the talent.

"Now there are another six ships in which you have a silent interest—your partners are responsible for the management. Keep those: the income is not enormous, but it's as steady as any and your agent in Genoa will see to your interests.

"The majority of your income will be from investments and a number of smaller properties. The baron had instructed me to do a certain amount of consolidation lately. His affairs were much more complicated five years ago. Most of your funds are with Escaferd's, which is secure as long as the peace continues to last. A certain amount is scattered in foreign holdings for at least some protection in that regard. There are several other minor sources. I'll draw up a list for you but there are no decisions to be made on that score at the moment.

"Obligations…there are a number of institutions and individuals for whom the late baron was a patron. Some you may wish to continue, some you may not. We can review them in detail at a future time. He provided substantial support to the convent of Saint Orisul which is located adjacent to the Saveze title-lands. I believe you have some connection with that establishment yourself?"

Margerit frowned in thought. "My governess, Sister Petrunel. She was from Saint Orisul's. But I think—that is, I was told my mother attended the convent school there for a while."

LeFevre nodded and smiled. "Then I'll assume you'll be continuing the patronage. It's not as if the new baron is likely to do so. There is also a school for orphans in Rotenek that the baron was generous to."

He ran his finger down a list in the ledger. "Several artists: two painters and a sculptor that he made gifts to on occasion, although I believe he supported them more in sending commissions their way. A banquet given every feast of Saint Perinerd for the…but no, that had its own bequest so you needn't concern yourself. This one—" Unexpectedly he blushed. "Your godfather was the patron of an opera dancer, but of course that connection won't be continued."

Margerit found herself giggling, although it was more from embarrassment at imagining…no, it wasn't to be pursued.

A discreet cough brought her attention back. "I've drawn up a list of once-given charities from the past several years. There wouldn't be the slightest expectation for you to revisit them unless you choose."

He closed the ledger and passed it over to her. Margerit left it lying in her lap. "There's a great deal to consider," she said. She wanted to ask about Rotenek—about the plan that had only just begun to form in her mind—but she wasn't sure how.

"Well, it's much too soon to settle anything today. If you're interested—truly interested—we can work on the details together over the next several weeks. If your guardians permit, of course, although the final decisions are in my hands. If you find that your curiosity is satisfied by this much, then you can leave it to me. And if I have interpreted Ponivin's look from the doorway correctly, then lunch is ready to be served."

* * *

The table was spread in a small parlor overlooking the gardens. When the weather warmed a bit more, the beds would explode with blooms. It was as if the house had been designed for a private audience at the coming of spring. The main public rooms had no particular vistas. The best views all seemed to be from cozy spaces like this one.

There were three places set at the table and Margerit wondered momentarily if her uncle had arrived early. "Ah," said LeFevre, catching her confusion. "It was sometimes the late baron's habit—when dining informally in private—to include Barbara at his table. Since I am joining you, the kitchen may have assumed…"

Barbara broke in, "I'll go and tell them."

"No," Margerit said quickly. "Please—if my godfather thought it proper, then I see no harm. That is, I'd like you to join us." Barbara looked for a moment as if she might demur, but then relented. Margerit thought back to their conversation on the walk over. Had she once again asked Barbara to cross a line she'd prefer to preserve? Would she get a true answer later?

Margerit knew enough of the workings of a kitchen to know that the baron's chef had worked a small miracle to set the table before them. It had been barely more than an hour since she'd arrived on the doorstep yet he'd turned out a bit of ham in a delicate *ragout de champignons*, a fricassee from a fowl that must have been boiled for a different purpose entirely, a clear soup with spring herbs and some crisp apple fritters. By the time they had come to the *crème de marrons*, Margerit had found the courage to pursue what she'd fallen short of before. "I wondered," she asked in as casual a tone as she could manage, "what I may and may not do with my inheritance."

LeFevre cocked his head to one side as if amused. "Well, as you learned yesterday, you may not give it away without your guardian's permission. But I suspect you had something smaller in mind?"

Margerit bit her lip thoughtfully. Smaller in expense, perhaps, but how much would that mean? Best to test the waters with something trivial. "What if I wanted to hire my own lady's maid? Could I do that?"

LeFevre looked surprised. "You don't have your own maid? But… I'm sorry. I don't know how these things are done in—" He faltered, clearly looking for a tactful way to say "ordinary households."

Margerit shook her head. "No, it wasn't thought necessary." The word covered so many things left unsaid. "Could I hire one?"

Now it was LeFevre's turn to frown thoughtfully. "Well, of course—in fact, it should be arranged soon. But I think it would be best to leave that to your aunt or to her housekeeper perhaps. Unless you mean to set up your own household, which would be a different matter. But a maid of your own, that would be more than reasonable."

Margerit thought about following up on the household idea but it seemed too large a jump. What sort of extravagance might give him pause. "What if I wanted to order a dozen new gowns and," he hadn't reacted, "and a new carriage and—"

He threw up a hand to stop the tumult of images. "I would remind you that you already own a carriage. Several, in fact: a traveling coach and a town chaise, and in Rotenek there's a light landau better suited to the narrow streets. I'm sure that your guardians will consider a new wardrobe to be entirely suitable. I'll set up an account for your everyday expenses. Your guardians can administer it for you. Or you could simply have the bills sent to me." He cleared his throat softly. "I would, however, suggest that you defer to Maisetra Fulpi in matters of dress. She'll know the difference between what you can afford and what it's suitable for you to wear."

Margerit felt her face burning. This wasn't at all the direction she had meant to go, sounding as if she cared only for silks and carriages. Her frustration showed in her voice at last. "You speak of what is reasonable and what is suitable. What if I wanted to do something entirely unreasonable and unsuitable? What are the boundaries of what I could do if my guardians didn't approve?"

LeFevre seemed to wake up at last to the serious intent of her questions and answered very carefully. "So long as you are under age, those boundaries are small indeed. When you come of age, then it's a question of what you're willing to give up to do it. The baron's will gives you complete control of your fortune on that day."

Margerit's heart leapt when she heard that. She'd expected her inheritance to be tied up for years or until she married.

He continued, "But the law isn't the only matter you need to consider. I can't really give you an answer unless I know what you plan to do. An unsuitable marriage? Foreign travel? The case may not be as dire as you think. Again, I'd need to know more." He stopped short of asking directly.

Margerit was still uncertain how far he would go beyond amused curiosity. The next question tumbled out before she knew she wanted the answer. "Whose man are you?"

LeFevre blinked slowly but not, it seemed, in astonishment. His face had gone very still and bland. "I beg your pardon?" he asked softly.

Margerit scrambled for the question she thought she was trying to ask. "Who are you…to me? Another guardian? A property manager? Or a clerk? Do you answer to me or I to you? Or do you answer to my guardians? What were you to my godfather? Do you answer to him still?"

A light kindled in LeFevre's eyes that told her that at least some of the questions had been the right ones. His answer was as careful and precise as the previous one had been. "In matters concerning the late baron's will—in all senses—I am his man, both by contract and by oath. Some of those matters involve you; some do not. All of those matters come before anything else I might do.

"However, one part of the baron's will is that I shall manage the inheritance he left to you until the specified term is fulfilled. In that, I answer not to your guardians, nor to you, nor—I should point out—to any husband you may acquire, but only to my understanding of good and prudent management. Management of monies and properties, that is. It isn't my business to manage any other part of your life. However," he repeated, this time with quiet intensity, "whatever is left to me of discretion and loyalty, when all else is done, I am free to offer to you, if you would have it."

It was a gift carefully hedged about and bound up but Margerit thought it more valuable for that. In return she offered him her dream. "I want to study philosophy and theology at the university in Rotenek."

He nodded without speaking and steepled his fingers before his face in a few minutes of quiet consideration. "Is this a plan of long standing?" he asked at length.

"How could it be?" she replied with a smothered laugh. "Before yesterday I might as well have wanted to…to become empress of Russia! I know that women are allowed to enter the lectures and libraries—my cousin Nikule told me—even though they can't take a degree. He seemed to think it wasn't quite the thing but he thinks that about a lot of things. Is it really something that is done? Could I do it?"

LeFevre quirked one corner of his mouth in a half-grin. "You'd do better to ask Barbara about that. She could tell you far more than I can."

Margerit looked over at Barbara where she had been sitting silently throughout the conversation. She nodded. "I've attended some lectures—when it was convenient for the baron, of course. There are difficulties, but none that can't be overcome."

"There are, in general, three types of women who attend university lectures," LeFevre continued. "There are the poor-scholars, who attend under scholarship to become teachers and learn what is allowed them of a clerkly trade. Needless to say, that wouldn't do at all for you. There are the Eccentrics." His tone made it more of a title than a description. "They have the money to buy a place, the time to indulge their interests and the social standing to do as they please. If you had been born to the nobility, you could claim a place as an Eccentric. To be sure, they're mostly older single women: widows, those who failed to marry or never cared to. There are a few matrons who achieved Eccentricity after marriage but none, I think, who achieved marriage after Eccentricity. But what they all have in common is a position in society that can't be taken from them and there you are at a disadvantage. Fortune can open the doors of society to you but only if you're careful to play the game. I don't think your guardians would allow you to behave in a way that closed those doors again.

"But there's a third case," he added hastily as her face fell. "It's a fashion among certain silly young ladies to play at being scholars. They attend the lectures in academic robes of satin and lace, flirt flagrantly but safely with the ordinary scholars, mingle more freely than otherwise with the well-born dabblers and generally grow bored with the whole exercise after a few terms. The *dozzures* put up with them because their parents pay outrageously for the privilege. The serious students despise them as a distraction. But society considers it as harmless a diversion as riding to the hunt or playing piquet. So a serious young woman might find entrance both to society and scholarhood by disguising herself as a silly dilettante. If it happened that your uncle approved of you living in Rotenek, then there might be the opportunity…" He let the suggestion trail off and sink in.

As if summoned, Margerit heard her uncle's voice distantly through the halls. She looked anxiously over at LeFevre and said, "Don't tell him."

He frowned a little, but nodded. Barbara hurriedly pushed her chair back and stood as the footman came in to notify them that Maistir Fulpi was waiting in the office.

* * *

Margerit could tell he was startled to see her but he didn't seem angry. Was he only concealing it for policy's sake? How much had changed in their relationship? How much was yet to change?

"Does your aunt know you're here?" he asked sharply.

"I told her I was going out," Margerit answered, which was no answer.

LeFevre rescued her by adding, "We've been having a very pleasant discussion about the generalities of the baron's will. You and I can move on to the details." He turned back to her with a polite bow. "It has been a lovely morning and I hope to see you again soon." And then a nod to Barbara as he addressed her: "I had almost forgotten— Donati came by this morning. I told him to expect his regular fee while matters are being settled, but perhaps you could send him word about new arrangements for your practices."

Barbara murmured, "I don't yet know what might be arranged."

"Easy enough," LeFevre replied.

Margerit saw what seemed to be a warning glance from Barbara, but LeFevre ignored it as he turned to her uncle. "Arrangements will need to be made for Barbara's practice sessions with her fencing master. Is there a large enough space in your house? If needed she could continue them here. Some convenient transportation could be arranged."

"That will not be necessary," he said shortly. And when LeFevre seemed confused as to which part of his question was being answered he continued, "In keeping with His Excellency's will, that woman may keep the title of armin, but I think I will be making other arrangements for my niece's necessary protection."

"Then you're a fool," LeFevre said in an even voice, as if merely commenting on the weather. But he escorted them out of the room and closed the door before continuing in inaudible tones.

CHAPTER FOURTEEN

Barbara

Whatever arguments LeFevre made, they must have bent Maistir Fulpi's objections. For while no space for her practice could be found at Chaturik Square, allowance was made for her to stable the bay mare there. Not only could she slip out more easily for her lessons but there was more freedom in the hours when Margerit received visitors at her aunt's side. Or the endless hours with the dressmaker.

Over the next days, things settled into a routine that passed for normal. Barbara was amused at the narrowed scope of her duties. Though she trained and practiced as if her potential opponents still worked at the highest levels, her everyday chores were more that of a governess or hired chaperone. The potential hazards she had sketched out that first evening might have been exaggerated, but there were everyday pitfalls to navigate, even in those first weeks.

The visits to Fonten Street and lessons in the management of properties became more common than walks in the park. Margerit claimed the time as private. The aunts might oversee her social visits, but they had no patience for sitting through LeFevre's detailed explanations. Her uncle didn't take her interest in the estate seriously enough to pay it any heed. But at least one person had noted that her midday walks to Fonten House were unaccompanied by any of her guardians. From the promptness with which the man fell in beside them one morning, Barbara concluded that he had been loitering for the purpose. He touched his hat and addressed Margerit with, "It isn't right for a lady to go walking out unescorted," as he offered his arm to her.

Margerit paused, appearing to flounder for a response. And yet she clearly recognized the man and Barbara could see he was a respectable gentleman, perhaps a colleague of her uncle? This was not someone to be warned off with a hand on the hilt and a menacing glare. Barbara cleared her throat and sought a safe middle ground. "Maistir, she is not unescorted."

He blinked at her as if he had only then noticed her existence. "Hmm. Yes. As you say." He turned back to Margerit. "Would you grant me the honor of accompanying you on your errand?"

Margerit threw her a flustered look but this was her lead to take. "Maistir Palmir, I thank you for your kind offer, but there is no need."

"Of course not, my dear." He smiled. "But it would be my pleasure."

With that "my dear," Barbara concluded, he had stepped across the line. She took a step closer to Margerit and said in the most deferential tone she could manage, "If the gentleman wishes to walk out with you, Maisetra, it would be best if he called at your home and spoke with Maistir Fulpi first." Although she addressed Margerit, her eyes were fixed on the stranger.

The surest confirmation of his transgression was the promptness with which he demurred, "As you say. As you say." He tipped his hat once more and strolled in the opposite direction with the self-conscious casualness of a cat.

Margerit stifled a laugh as they continued on. "Do you think he really will speak to my uncle?" she wondered.

Barbara considered it unlikely. He didn't have the marks of high birth, and mere money wouldn't be considered sufficient attraction now. But he might not have the sense to realize that. He'd lacked the sense to guess how few personal charms a fifty-year-old man might hold for a girl of eighteen.

There were two other approaches in those first weeks, as clumsy and as easily deflected as Maistir Palmir's. The serious suitors would take their time and employ more subtlety.

* * *

It seemed that no sooner had the Fulpi household settled into its new routine than it was broken again by the advent of Saint Chertrut's day. They followed the old custom of traveling to the countryside, to the home village of their family, to celebrate the saint's mystery and decorate the churches with flowering boughs. Barbara could faintly remember honoring the patroness of gardens and orchards in the village church at Saveze. That was before the baron had begun taking her with him to Rotenek. The festival fell too early in the year to return south for no other reason.

Evidently Maistir Fulpi's people lived too far away for the trip to be practical but his wife's family had a manor near Mintun and the entire household was to go. For that, several carriages were required, and even with one of Margerit's new acquisitions pressed into service, space was tight. At first Barbara was grateful that her duties gave her a seat outside, up with the coachman. Another pair of sharp eyes was always useful, though any lurking highwaymen would be better addressed with the coachman's musket than her sword. But even the one-day's journey stretched out well after dark. At dusk a bitter wind sprang up, reminding her that Saint Chertrut's Day brought only the promise of spring, not the season itself. And when Margerit noticed that at every pause she stamped around briskly to loosen up her frozen muscles she insisted that she join the rest in the interior.

Barbara squeezed into one side, between Margerit and the door, with the girl Sofi on Margerit's far side and Maisetra Fulpi, a nurse and little Iulien ranged opposite them. The children had long since dropped to sleep and Margerit herself was yawning constantly although she had the excuse of a late dinner party the night before. Finally she gave up and leaned against her saying, "I hope you don't mind," as she closed her eyes. Barbara shifted enough to get her arm free and draped it across Margerit's shoulders to help steady her against the lurching of the road. Margerit sighed again and leaned in closer, her breathing soon falling into the slow rhythm of sleep.

It should have been an awkward arrangement but Barbara found herself relaxing as the miles rolled by. Margerit's warm presence against her body seemed to belong there like one of her own limbs. She hadn't expected to become resigned to her fate so quickly, much less to become comfortable. Her duties themselves were both easier and more complex than they had been under the baron but they were beginning to untangle themselves. If Margerit convinced her uncle to let her go to Rotenek—or more likely, let him believe he'd convinced her to go—even the work of protecting her would be easier. There were more watching eyes in the city. Accidents would be more difficult to arrange and she knew the players more intimately. If she could see her safe past a year's cycle of university terms and balls...two years? It occurred to her that she didn't know the precise date when the conditions of the will would be complete and she would be free. And would she?

To be sure, the baron's will had no power to enforce what happened afterward, but if Margerit had been willing to forego her inheritance entirely to see justice done, why doubt that she would do right when the terms were fulfilled and it would cost her nothing? In the meantime, one must serve someone, after all. Though her service was constrained, there was still pride and honor in doing the job well. Loyalty—that was in her own gift and it had been earned in that first afternoon. Loyalty and more. To the baron, she had been like a hunting dog or a fine sword—a tool to be employed to his ends. But with Margerit she felt more like a cloak to protect her from the wind or a hawk mantling over her chick. She smiled at how the image matched their posture.

Barbara had been staring out through the glass window of the carriage door, catching glimpses of the landscape as the moonlight allowed. But as they passed through a long patch of darker road, the reflection of Maisetra Fulpi's pale face, lit by the wan carriage lamp, replaced the silvered fields. The woman was staring at her with a blend of fear and disgust. Barbara froze. That look had not been meant for her eyes and she tried to give no sign acknowledging it. She knew Margerit's aunt had been far from happy about her presence in the household but what had inspired this? Margerit sighed in her sleep again and snuggled closer. The aunt's look grew sharper. Realization ran coldly through her veins. Did she think...? Did it look...?

It was the masculine clothing, in part—it put curious ideas in people's minds. There had been men at the court who found it exciting to flirt with a boy-girl. Even if the hazards hadn't been so great, they'd sparked no interest in her. But there had also been a few women who played the same game. And for a brief time, intrigued and flattered by the interest and starved for the human touch that she was denied in the ordinary way, she had let things go further than had been wise. Her cheeks still burned at remembering that glorious imprudence.

Was *that* what Maisetra Fulpi suspected of her? With that thought lodged in her brain, Barbara became exquisitely aware of every inch of contact between Margerit's body and hers. Of the alternating heat and cold where Margerit's breath caressed her wrist between the glove and the sleeve. Of the way their breathing had fallen into synchrony. No, it was madness. She sealed the matter away in the corner of her heart that was reserved for the impossible.

Only five more miles lay between them and the crossroads at Mintun. It was an eternity and heartbreakingly short.

CHAPTER FIFTEEN

Margerit

At the barking of dogs and the rattle of carriage wheels over stones in the yard Margerit woke with a start. In the first moment she couldn't quite place whose arm would be holding her so closely. Then she breathed in the mixed aroma of leather and lavender that she had come to associate with Barbara's working clothes. She pulled herself upright, feeling strangely self-conscious.

The chaos of unloading passengers and baggage was cut though by the brisk efficiency of Maisetra Saldirenk, pulling her guests into the common hall where a bright fire and food waited. They were not the only group of cousins who came to Mintun for Saint Chertrut's feast-day pleasures, so the arrangements were cramped and cozy. A group of dairymaids had been evicted temporarily from their shared dormitory by the kitchen to make way for the girls. Margerit didn't mind being lumped in with the children one more time but she pointed out, "We're going to be dreadfully snug this year," looking from the two beds to the people—augmented by one—who would share the room.

Aunt Honurat gave her an odd look but Barbara said, "Find me a pallet for the floor and I'll do well enough."

The worst part of the arrangements, Margerit realized, was the loss of any hope of sleeping late. Sofi was a restful bedmate but little Iuli was up with the sun, chattering with her nurse until led away to the kitchen to break her fast. Even so, the bustle of the kitchen and yard leaked in easily. It was supposed to be part of the charm of Chertrut's Day—the return to country habits and schedules. The charm had lost a little of its luster for her over the years given its way of turning schedules topsy-turvy.

Those who planned to keep wake through the night would normally take the excuse for indolence and a nap before dinner. The rest would be content to be woken before dawn the next morning to go out to the hills to celebrate the mysteries and take in the Mass afterward in the village church. Margerit would have been glad to be one of the latter but Aunt Honurat took her aside to ask whether she would be one of the celebrants in the mystery. "If you're going to be spending all that time reading books, you might as well put it to some use."

It was a flattering request despite the wording, more so given that she was related to the hosts only by marriage and participation was usually saved for daughters of the house. But there had been an underlying edge in Honurat's voice that belied the kindness of the offer.

"Aunt Fulpi," Margerit asked hesitantly. "Have I offended you?" Her overt displeasure was rare and not to be ignored.

Her aunt pressed her lips together and looked around briefly as if worried who might be listening. "I'm concerned about…that woman."

"About Barbara?" Margerit asked.

She nodded and seemed to make a decision. "There are things it isn't appropriate for a young woman—a decent young woman—to know about. But I think you should be warned. That woman has led a very irregular life. While I'm sure the baron was a respectable man, still a girl growing up in that sort of household, allowed to run wild and to fall into habits of depravity—"

"How can you say that?" Margerit protested hotly.

"Margerit, open your eyes. You're not a child. She takes the part of a man in her dress, in her duties. Who's to say she doesn't take a man's part in…in private, as well? And that will reflect on you and your reputation if you aren't careful."

It took her some moments even to begin to imagine what that might mean. "But how could…what…?"

"Never you mind. Just consider: while she's guarding you from the intentions of unscrupulous men, who's guarding you from her?"

To her surprise, she felt not embarrassed but angry. "Anyone who thinks that has an evil mind! Barbara would never…I trust her with my life!"

Aunt Honurat shrugged. "What do you know about her really? What can we ever know about what goes on in servants' minds? But you'll do as you please, now that you're rich. All I can ask is that you don't allow her to practice indecencies under my roof."

It was the most forthright speech Margerit had heard from her aunt—at least for anything outside of manners—and she was startled by how much venom it contained. The confusion lingered long after Aunt Honurat's demeanor had returned to its accustomed calm. What had she meant about "playing the man's part in private?" At the time, she'd reacted to the tone of the accusation; now the substance exercised her imagination.

It still teased at her that afternoon when it was time to catch some sleep before dinner. Margerit claimed the tiny room from her cousins, and Barbara—hesitant to leave her unattended in a strange place—settled a comfortable chair across the doorway to be able to rest and guard at the same time.

Sleep eluded her at first as her aunt's words echoed in her mind. Of course she knew the ways of men and women. She might have been sheltered but you couldn't read widely in the classics and remain ignorant. That was a different matter than thinking what it might mean to her personally. How would a woman kiss when playing a man's part? Differently? She looked over at Barbara obliquely and imagined what it might be like to kiss her, to be kissed by her. It had never occurred to her to imagine kissing any of her prospective suitors. She'd simply accepted that it would happen in its own time.

Margerit had danced with girls—one did, after all, at family parties when no thought for careful balance had been taken. It was different dancing with men who saw you as a potential wife. There was a possessiveness in their hands, an assumption of control in the way they guided you through the figures. What might it be like to dance with a woman who danced as a man? Who treated it not as a pastime but as the allegory for a further act? And how…? What…? In her mind, she offered her hand to Barbara and led her out onto the floor as the music began.

Barbara noticed her intent stare and rose. "Is something wrong?"

Margerit looked away guiltily and shook her head. Barbara sat on the edge of the bed, frowning at her in concern. "Are you sure?" She raised a hand tentatively, paused, then reached out to tuck in a hairpin that had come loose.

Margerit shivered at the unexpected touch and two thoughts came simultaneously into her mind. *I could find out what it's like. I could command her to kiss me and she would.* But then: *She would be blamed, if someone discovered us. She would get the censure and punishment. Because of who she is and what she does. And for what? To satisfy my curiosity?* She knew her duty and responsibility better than that. She sighed and said, "I'm too tired to sleep, that's all. And it's so hard in the daytime, even when I know I'll be up all night."

Barbara picked up the copy of the *Life and Mysteries of Saint Chertrut* that Margerit had left at the bedside. "Would you like me to read to you? The baron always said it helped him sleep."

Margerit giggled unexpectedly. "He told me that improving texts were the best for the purpose!" The two shared a grin as she settled back against the pillows and closed her eyes. Barbara's voice followed her deep into her dreams.

CHAPTER SIXTEEN

Barbara

Dinner was a plain affair: the fast before tomorrow's feast—such as it was for a feast day that inevitably fell during Lent. But what passed for a simple country meal among the propertied families still stretched out to several courses. Barbara had been wary of the crowd of strangers at first but none of them were strangers to Margerit. It was safe enough to leave her in their company for a time. There was no chance that she'd ever be alone. The day still had an hour of light and she took the opportunity to have one of the stable boys show her up to the shrine where the mysteries would be held at dawn. It might not be necessary—more a matter of staying in practice—but to someone accustomed to the hazards of city alleys and palace corridors, it was difficult to predict what sorts of dangers could lurk in the open countryside.

The shrine was a small stone building set against the hill where a stream sprang forth from the rocks. It was placed to catch the very beginnings of the spring sunlight and at some early date the clearing in front of it had been planted with wild plum and sour cherry trees— the sorts known to bloom earliest. It was considered the greatest of luck if the trees were blooming for Chertrut's feast and flower-laden branches could be brought down to adorn the altar for the Mass. But though the buds were swollen fat and showing promise of color, it seemed unlikely that this would be a lucky year.

Mintun lay just at the edge of the hills and it was one of those crisp, clear days when the entire Tupe valley spread out below like a carpet pattern. The silvery thread of the river rushed in spring torrent down to where it would join the Rotein. From the rise where the shrine stood, she could see the black and gray slate roofs of the village, wreathed about with tendrils of blue smoke. Chalanz was well out of sight around a curve of the hills behind her but in the other direction, to the south, she could see all the way to where the mountains rose, snowcapped, on the southeastern border of Alpennia, guarding the roads to Switzerland and places beyond. She could almost pretend to spot the white speck at their base where the convent of Saint Orisul stood in the Saveze lands that had been home until a month ago. The lines from Pertulif ran through her mind: *Our fortress walls, frost-capped, white, first watch against what lies without.* A faint cough behind her broke the reverie. It was an honest cough from the sharpness of the air but her guide looked mortified that she might think him impatient. "It's enough," she said and let him lead the way back down the hill.

* * *

She was glad of the advance scouting when dawn neared and the celebrants set out. In the dark, with only lanterns to chase the shadows back, the shrine was a very different place. The evening's music and games had gradually sobered to quieter activities through the night hours until finally it was time to gather up the younger or less dedicated from their beds and tumble into the carriages for the short ride up to the shrine.

This sort of informal family rite was barely familiar. Like most of the nobility, the baron had belonged to several mystery guilds: those it was politic or expedient to join. Their ceremonies—at least the ones she had been allowed to witness—were stiff and formal affairs, barely different in tone from the cathedral Mass that followed them. This celebration of Saint Chertrut had almost a carnival atmosphere and she suspected that some parts of the rite might have been addressed, in ancient days, to an entirely different listener. Each celebrant, from the aged grandmother down to Margerit, took her turn to lead the *Pater* and the *Ave* and then to recite the prayers addressed specifically to the saint.

Some spoke by rote in a singsong chant. Some closed their eyes as if in private meditation. One read her lines from a book, stumbling over the bits of Latin in her text. The whole assembly chimed in on the common prayers. By the time Margerit's turn came around the day was brightening, although the first edge of the sun wouldn't top the mountains for some time yet. Margerit looked older, more mature as she stepped into her role. Her voice came clear and sweet, telling the lines she had worked to learn by heart the previous day.

"Bless us, Saint Chertrut, with the new corn in the field. Bless us with the gentle soft rain. Bless us with the warm soft breeze of spring that wakens all creation..."

Barbara felt the hair stand up on her neck and it wasn't only in response to the air moving lightly down the hillside. She looked around but couldn't tell if anyone else had noticed.

Margerit raised her arms, as the others had, at the concluding lines and their echoing responses from the crowd, then crossed herself to signal the finish. As if in answer, a swirl of breeze picked up, knocking a dusting of pink and white petals off the trees to fall among the assembly. The children squealed in delight and danced around gathering them up to keep for luck.

Did no one else question it? For nine out of ten, the mysteries were a simple act of devotion. To one among the ten, the saint might hearken and answer. And to one in ten of *those*, that answer might take tangible form. No wonder Margerit was such an avid scholar if her studies had been encouraged by such notice! The others seemed to take the finish as a pleasant coincidence, one pulling out a small knife to cut a few of the flowering twigs to take with them. But Barbara had seen those buds still tightly closed only the evening before.

Soon afterward they returned to the carriages and made their way down to the village church, already filled to overflowing with neighbors, the town square crowded with farm carts and market wagons. The Saldirenk family were of sufficient prominence to push their way through to their accustomed places, but Margerit became separated from them in the press and Barbara drew her back. "Perhaps you would be more comfortable out here?" In truth, *she* would be more comfortable to avoid the suffocating crowd of strangers. But an armin didn't say that to her charge.

"Even here?" Margerit asked. "Do I have to be so careful everywhere?"

It wasn't quite the message she'd meant to convey but her goal was accomplished and they retreated to the comfort and shelter of the carriage. They were not the only ones giving up on entering the church itself who had to make do with what bits of the Mass came out through the doors and tall windows.

A couple of minutes passed in silence as the opening notes of the choir drifted across the square, then Barbara asked, "May I speak?"

Margerit frowned at her saying, "I thought I—"

"May I ask something?" she clarified. At a nod, she continued. "Does that happen often when you participate in mysteries?"

Margerit looked confused. "You mean not just as part of the congregation? I've never really been a formal celebrant before. Not like this. Sister Petrunel taught me theory but she didn't really encourage practice. She thought prayers were better than petitions, especially to God but even to the saints."

"Did she know? That the saints heard you?"

The confusion lingered. "Isn't that the purpose? I know you shouldn't pray over trivial matters, but—"

Barbara was hard-pressed not to burst into laughter, fearing it would be taken amiss. "Do you think the saint opens the buds before their time for everyone who asks? Did you see many other families bringing in boughs of blossoms to deck the altar? Do the saints always hearken and answer you?"

Margerit shook her head, looking startled. "I don't know. Sometimes I…I don't…What does it mean? Does it mean I should become a nun?"

Now Barbara couldn't suppress a laugh. "Goodness no! It doesn't even mean you're more pious than the next, although that helps, I've heard. At least the baron always seemed to think so. But some people are…are blessed with the ear of the saints. And study and devotion can make a difference. I thought that was why you wanted to study at the university—because you had the gift and wanted to increase it."

"I just—" Margerit shook her head. "I want to know things, to understand. It's…when I read through an argument or a puzzle and I see all the parts fall into place and everything just—" Words seemed to fail her and she gestured vaguely with both hands. "Everything just feels so *right*, as if the world came into balance. Most of life isn't like that. At the mystery this morning it was like the world shifted just a little to be in line or as if a fiddler tuned one string just a little to bring the instrument all into tune. I—" She paused breathlessly, her eyes shining in excitement.

Barbara dared to reach out and take her hand. "Go to Rotenek. Study. It's what you were born for."

Their eyes locked for longer than was comfortable. Barbara snatched her hand back muttering, "Forgive me." Without asking leave she swung down out of the carriage and spent the remainder of the wait prowling from one side of the carriage to the other as if expecting assassins at any moment as the sound of the organ rolled out in a swelling chorus.

CHAPTER SEVENTEEN

Margerit

The experience at Mintun was still in her mind as the services for Holy Week began. There had been a time—she must have been not much more than seven because she thought it was that first summer after the red fever struck, when she was still learning the rules of Uncle Mauriz's house—that Aunt Honurat had taken her to Saint Andire's, not to the smaller church nearer Chaturik Square. It probably hadn't been her first time there but perhaps the first time on a brilliant summer day when the sun poured in through the rose window, casting flecks of crimson and lapis across the tiles.

Aunt Honurat later told her she must have imagined it: that the Virgin rose up from the scattered light, clothed in a blue mantle and rose-colored gown and shining so brightly her face couldn't be seen. Margerit remembered she'd laughed in delight and pointed, only to be hushed and have her hand slapped. That year she'd learned that you don't stare around at the other worshippers to see the play of lights. You watched the priest and learned your responses. She'd assumed it was part of growing up; it had never occurred to her that other people weren't distracted by strange sights in church because they saw nothing. And so she learned not to notice, in the same way you learned not to notice the crippled beggars who had once been soldiers.

Sister Petrunel might have been able to explain some of it but for her the mysteries were for devotion, not experimentation. Petra's inquisitive mind had led her into the groves of learning but never touched that particular fruit. She tried to remember how much she'd told her governess about the visions. When had she ceased to take note of them? If it hadn't been for Barbara's questions she wouldn't have given the blossoming boughs a second thought. She tried to look with new eyes again as the services rose to the triumphant celebration of the resurrection, staring so hard at the candles and the beams of light filtering through the tinted glass that they swirled and swam before her eyes. Was what she saw of God or of the world? There were no answers, only questions.

* * *

With the release from the strictures of Lent she was thrust once more into the round of dances and musical evenings. Margerit had had been prepared for Chalanz society to envy her sudden fortune and turn jealous, but once the families in the Fulpis's circle had overcome the shock of her luck they seemed happy to claim her as their own triumph. If the riches the baron had left her had been smaller—if they had fallen within the scope of ordinary comprehension—people might have resented it more. Any sign of change in her life would have been food for criticism. But as it was, in being snatched up so high above her expectations, it seemed she was now beyond comment. The trappings that accompanied her new position were swiftly accepted and forgiven.

One shadow of doubt regarding her fortune was lifted with LeFevre's return from a trip to the city. "The courts have closed for the summer," he explained to her after a long morning closeted with her Uncle Fulpi. "The new Baron Saveze has been unsuccessful in having his challenge heard."

Margerit knew he'd sworn to challenge the will but lawsuits could drag on for years. "Is it entirely over then?"

LeFevre shrugged. "As a nobleman he will have taken his petition directly to the prince's court. Decisions come more quickly there. It wasn't that the case was heard and judged against him, the prince simply declined to take it up. In one sense, it leaves the matter undecided, but in another, it signals that the challenge was found to have no merit at all. That's fortunate for you. An open case in court could have proven awkward for you when you go to Rotenek."

When. There had been no further discussions on that point with her uncle. There was time. The university term wouldn't start until late in September and the Rotenek season would be well begun by then. There would be no need to mention her plans to him at all until they had already arrived. She could wait, hard as it was.

* * *

If the better families of Chalanz had been eager to adopt her as their favorite daughter, the first sign that the larger world had noticed the change in her fortunes came with the annual tide of Rotenek nobility exchanging the city's unhealthy air for the countryside. Count Oriez, whose title-lands lay just north of Chalanz, claimed the right to the first ball of the summer. And from nowhere—for Uncle Mauriz had no dealings with him that she knew of—Margerit received an invitation.

It was as if a sudden storm swept through the household. The days teemed with lectures and admonishments: how she was to behave, who to speak to, who to give which courtesies, what to beware. And then there was the dress.

When it came to matters of fashion and taste, Aunt Honurat was rarely challenged within the household. Her family having climbed to prominence more recently, she took more conscious care for such things than Bertrut's relaxed attitude. But the elderly widow who had served Aunt Honurat's dressmaking needs for years had been proclaimed insufficiently up to the current mode. Bertrut had recruited a more fashionable modiste and rival gowns had been created. Margerit was dreading the moment when she could no longer remain neutral in the standoff and would need to instruct Maitelen to dress her in one or the other.

She fled to Fonten Street as often as she could in the afternoons, simply to spend time reading or sitting quietly in the gardens. She had been right about the gardens: they had exploded in a riot of color and when the sun was hot the breeze spread a perfume of roses and heliotrope through the paths.

"I wish the ball were over," she complained to Barbara as they returned home.

"It'll be over soon enough," came the answer. "And then there will be another ball. It's never over. You'll get used to them."

"I don't want to get used to them!" Margerit said irritably.

"And yet," Barbara pointed out, "the only acceptable reason to go to Rotenek is to dance at balls."

"I just know I'm going to do something gauche. I'll step on some duke's foot—"

"I don't believe there will be any dukes in attendance."

"—or drink from a flower vase—"

"Then it would be the fault of the servant who handed it to you."

"—and I'll never remember anyone's name."

"You shouldn't be speaking to anyone without introduction."

In spite of herself, Margerit laughed. "You sound almost like Aunt Fulpi! She thinks I'm foolish to be in such a state too."

"Not foolish, Maisetra," Barbara said more formally. "But it's only a ball. There are more daunting matters than dancing ahead of you."

It was only a ball—nothing to do with her plans for the future. But it was hard not to be infected by the importance everyone around her placed on it.

* * *

The night before, as had become their daily habit, Barbara escorted her to her room when she retired and asked, with the comfort of ritual, "Will you be needing me tomorrow?"

"Not until the evening. Aunt Fulpi never wants me to go out when there's a ball. She thinks it shows a want of proper frailty. And in the morning there's one last fitting."

Barbara glanced at the ruffled confection in pale yellow that lay spread across the bedside chair. "I thought…?"

Margerit sighed. "That's Aunt Fulpi's choice. She still hasn't given up." Abruptly she gathered up the gown and handed it to Maitelen to put away. "Wait until you see what Mefro Teres has made for me. Tomorrow. She's still finishing the trimming." As Maitelen returned to help her into her nightgown she asked, "And what will you wear that's splendid enough for a count's ball? The green satin that you wore to my coming-out?" How elegant she'd looked with the old-fashioned skirted coat hugging her slim body! And how very daring. She turned questioningly when Barbara hesitated over answering.

"If you wish it," she said at last.

"That means you don't think you should." Margerit despaired of breaking that habit: her avoidance of saying no outright. One had to listen for the refusals in the pauses and silences.

Barbara's response was careful. "When I served as the baron's duelist, I dressed to ornament his station."

"And my station is not as high as his," Margerit concluded for her.

"It isn't only that." But as soon as she said it, Barbara looked as if she'd wished she kept silent.

"What?"

"That night—that was just for show. There was no possible danger to the baron at your ball."

The implication sank in. "Do you think I'll be in danger?"

"No!" The answer was swift. "Never when I'm there with you!"

And then, as if embarrassed by the fierceness of her response, Barbara bowed formally and bade her good-night.

CHAPTER EIGHTEEN

Barbara

The invitation to Count Oriez's ball thrust her back into a more familiar role. The world of the Fulpis was an alien land where people hired guards only for highway journeys and a young woman's companion carried a parasol, not a sword. Barbara knew she bewildered them and found them bewildering in turn. Count Oriez lived in a more familiar world where certain things were understood and had their own rules. Where the symbols and rituals of an outmoded age still held sway. Barbara knew the name and habits of his duelist as well as she knew the streets of Rotenek. A note sent around procured an appointment to review the layout of the count's ballroom and the other public areas. A copy of the guest list was formally requested and just as formally denied. Barbara had relaxed into the rhythm of the preparations even as Margerit grew more anxious.

Maistir Fulpi had determined that the honor of the occasion called for his personal attendance though he was content to allow the ladies the task of chaperoning Margerit at ordinary parties. It was clear he didn't choose to miss this opportunity to mix with his more important neighbors. He led the way when Margerit's carriage took its turn in the queue disgorging brightly-colored ladies and their more sober escorts into the portico of Count Oriez's entryway. Barbara kept close at their tail as they ascended the steps and were passed along to the majordomo who announced their names to the hall. Only then did she slip off to the right along the colonnaded walk that ran down the side of the ballroom under the gallery. The gallery itself would have a better view of the room but with less means of intervention, should it be necessary. The colonnade was a between-space, inhabited by hurrying servants and loitering armins, crossed by the guests only to reach the doors to the terrace and the garden beyond.

Barbara strolled down the row, looking for the best vantage point. That point was already inhabited by Amund, the count's duelist, unconsciously embodying the description she had once given by leaning against a pillar and scowling. He acknowledged her greeting with the barest of nods. Only five or six other guests so far had considered it necessary to be attended by armins and those had taken similar stances along the colonnade. Barbara found a place some distance away from the others and looked out into the ballroom to locate her charge.

Margerit was first led into the dance by a gawky young man. It was not the best of choices to put her at ease, but her next partner was more skilled and coaxed her into forgetting to be self-conscious. Then a return to her aunts, a bit of refreshment, a new introduction and the round began again.

In watching, Barbara thought back on what Signore Donati had said about dancing. As with sword work, it wasn't about knowing all the steps in their proper order. It was the way the movements flowed together when you ceased to think of them separately. The way a skilled dancer could guide a partner—or opponent—into the flow of the dance. The baron hadn't danced, of course, so her attention had never been drawn to it when attending him. Now she imagined how it would feel to move in concert with a partner, putting that sureness of movement into the service of bringing out their best, not with the goal of finding a weakness or forcing a fault. Perhaps it wouldn't be a bad idea to return to dancing lessons after all. Not, of course, that she would make use of it on the ballroom floor. But that didn't stop her from watching Margerit with measuring eyes, envisioning herself in the place of each partner in turn. Wincing when they made her stumble. Heartened when they made her laugh.

That reverie was broken by the majordomo announcing, "His excellency, Estefen Chazillen, Baron Saveze." Barbara's heart dropped and her eyes turned instantly to the door. Here? Now? He had no valid business in Chalanz. And if he were a close friend of Oriez, this was the first she'd heard of it. He meant trouble and he had journeyed all the way from Rotenek for the purpose.

He stood paused in the entrance, well aware of the impression he would make as he scanned the room from under lowering brows, his mouth twisted in something just short of a sneer. At one step behind he was followed by a young man whose posture declared him an armin. Evidently Estefen's new position demanded proper attendance, rather than relying on the company of friends. She recognized the man as a local, from Chauten's fencing school. In a previous generation he might have found scope for his moderate talents in a regiment, but the French Wars had marked the end of the age of valiant cavalry charges and flashing blades. War was a business now and he would have done better to take up the rifle than the sword. In the next generation, even the post of armin might become obsolete. For now the best positions required either skill or connections and this boy had neither. Estefen had likely been able to hire him for little more than pride of place and the dream of romantic adventure. She searched her memory. Perzin, that was his name.

Barbara's eyes darted back and forth from Margerit to Estefen to Perzin. The latter made his way around to the colonnade and stood awkwardly looking around. She could almost feel sorry for him. Amund took him aside and leaned closely to speak to him. They both glanced in her direction. The count's man shook his head in an emphatic negative and the boy moved off toward the far end of the colonnade.

For some long time Estefen pretended to no pointed purpose in coming, beyond what enjoyment anyone might seek. He disappeared into the card rooms for a while then stood in conversation at the far end of the room. She lost sight of him for a few minutes in turning her attention back to the dancers. Then, between the blink of an eye, he was there at Margerit's side, being introduced to her and leading her out toward a forming set.

Barbara's stomach clenched and she took a step forward, but there was nothing to respond to. Margerit might be hesitant, but she went willingly enough to the dance. And what harm could he do in the middle of a ballroom surrounded by a hundred others? The figures of the dance brought them apart and together. With every approach Estefen would lean close and say something that brought a stumble to her foot and a blush to her cheek. Once, Barbara thought Margerit tried to catch her eyes but other dancers came between them and the moment passed.

After an eternity, the dance was over. They remained on the floor, Estefen still holding the tips of Margerit's fingers from the final reverence. Only the closest observation could discern the small movements she made to free her hand. Barbara realized she had taken several steps out from the shelter of the gallery when Estefen's armin stepped in front of her. He looked terrified. Reflex drove her hand to the hilt of her weapon, but thought stopped her from drawing it. Amund drawled in affected laziness at her shoulder, "I would beg you not to make fools of yourselves at my master's party. You know the law. There has been no threat, no provocation, no insult given."

"There's threat and threat," Barbara snarled. "I have eyes to see with." But she stepped back behind the invisible wall marked by the line of the gallery. When she looked out again, Margerit had escaped and Estefen was looking in her direction with a mocking smile.

Seeing that look, Perzin cleared his throat and said to her, "My master the baron sends a message for you. Tomorrow you will find your position changed and you would do well to tread cautiously."

She sneered. "Tomorrow you can go back to playing at tin soldiers. Don't take up with Saveze unless you're up to the task." She pointedly turned away from him to scan the ballroom. She'd taken his measure and had no fears from that end.

Margerit was deep in conversation with her Aunt Fulpi by the windows where the older women loitered, fulfilling their duties as *vizeinos*, the chaperones necessary when any unmarried woman ventured out in formal society. Her aunt's normally timid expression was tight-lipped and frowning. She shook her head repeatedly and sharply to whatever Margerit was saying. Finally she took Margerit's chin in her hand and said something emphatic. Margerit straightened her shoulders and stretched her mouth in a weak smile. And shortly thereafter the round began again with another introduction, another dance.

Estefen had disappeared back to the upper rooms where gambling ruled the evening. If she could, she would have relaxed at that knowledge, but there were other hazards, no less worrisome for being smaller. As the evening wore on, Margerit looked more flustered and uncertain. When a dance partner began leading her casually through the colonnade toward the terrace, Barbara closed the distance with a few long strides and passed through the door before it had closed on their heels.

She took a position in the man's line of sight, too close to be ignored. He bristled, then—recognizing her profession—blanched and muttered, "Forgive my error," as he turned back toward the door alone.

"You need to be more careful," she chided Margerit in a quiet voice. "You know what they say: a walk in the garden is as good as a betrothal." And then, at a sudden catch in the other's breath, "Hush, don't cry! I'm sorry." She pressed a handkerchief into Margerit's hand while turning to shield her from any curious eyes.

"I didn't know how to refuse without being rude. One moment I was at the punch bowl and the next we were out here."

"Never mind. That's why I'm here—to be rude for you."

"Barbara—he said he's going to come speak to my uncle tomorrow." No need to say which "he" they were talking about now. "What can I do?"

Barbara looked around hastily. "Not here; not now."

"I want to go home." There was a shake in Margerit's voice but it might have been the cold. It might be nearly summer, but the evening was still too brisk for lingering outside in a light ballgown. No doubt her former escort had hoped for an excuse to remedy the chill himself. Barbara put an arm around her shoulders only long enough to draw her closer to the building and out of the breeze.

"What did your aunt say?"

"That we couldn't possibly leave until they go in for supper, but that we might leave then without dining. How can I face him if I see him again?"

Barbara shook her head—the gesture meant only for herself. Margerit needed more of the steel she'd shown at the reading of the baron's will. This wouldn't do. Her instinct was to comfort but instead she said, "And how will you face the men students at the university when they tell you to return to the drawing room where you belong? How will you face the gossipmongers who will be ready to cut up your reputation at any sign of weakness? I know what you want, but a fortune alone won't buy it for you if you aren't strong enough to reach out and take it."

This had the desired effect: Margerit glared at her in outrage. Barbara pressed the point home. "Did you think your uncle was the only gate you need to pass? If you can't face the stares of a few neighbors in a ballroom, you'll come running home after a week in Rotenek."

She was relieved to see Margerit stiffen, but saw she was staring behind her and turned.

"What are you doing out here, Margerit?" her uncle asked sharply.

Abandoning her previous tone, Barbara leapt to her defense. "Maistir, she was only feeling a little warm—I've been with her the whole time."

He gave her an annoyed glance but accepted the answer. "Be that as it may, come back in. You shouldn't be out here."

"Yes, Uncle," Margerit answered, following him back toward the door. In the pause as the footman opened it for them, Margerit passed the crumpled handkerchief back to her and pressed it into her hand with a squeeze.

In the end, they stayed through the supper after all. Estefen made no further appearance. And by whatever means the adventurers among the male guests communicated among themselves, the word passed that Margerit Sovitre might be a naïve little nobody of an heiress but she was well looked after and not to be plucked easily.

* * *

There was no chance to speak again until they were home and Margerit was preparing for bed. Her Aunt Bertrut pressed her for a tête-à-tête but Margerit pleaded a headache and exhaustion and begged her to wait for the morning.

"If that's the case," her aunt said, "don't let me find that you've been up to all hours talking to the servants." Barbara caught her meaningful glance.

"You heard your aunt, I mustn't stay long," she cautioned when Bertrut had left.

"Don't go yet," Margerit answered, holding her tongue further until Maitelen had finished her duties and been dismissed. When they were private she said, "He wants to talk to my uncle. If it were anyone else, I'd know what that means. But why?"

She wondered how far Margerit had thought it through. "I assume he plans to ask your uncle for permission to pay court to you. Or maybe just for permission to marry you. It depends on how subtle he thinks he will need to be."

Margerit nodded. "That was what I thought. He didn't say it in as many words, but…" She sat slumped on the edge of her bed and looked miserable again, but as Barbara watched she hardened her expression. "What should I do? No, I don't mean about marrying him—I won't do it. But how can I convince Uncle Fulpi? I need more than just a refusal. He's a baron; I don't think even uncle thought to look that high."

Barbara knelt beside the bed to avoid looming over her. "Your uncle may think a title is a fine thing to have in the family, but the title is the only thing Estefen is offering you. Remember, he thinks your inheritance should be his by right. Submit to him and he will feel no gratitude—not to you nor to your family. If his ring goes on your finger, your property goes into his control. Oh, not until you're of age, to be sure, but that's only two years away. When that day comes, your cousins will never see a *teneir's* benefit. If your uncle thinks they will all rise in society on the hem of your skirts, he's mistaken. For that matter, don't expect that you would be welcomed by Estefen's family and friends. You would be a convenience only. And entirely in his power. And if something…unfortunate happened to you, once that property was his, who would there be to ask questions?"

Margerit had grown so pale that Barbara wondered if she might faint. "But he wouldn't…you don't think…"

This wasn't the time to soften the dangers. "He tried to have the baron killed, you know. That duel I had, just before we left Rotenek. Everyone knew it, though it couldn't have been proven. Why would he hesitate over you?" Perhaps that was too far; she meant to caution her, not terrify her. "But the baron had me to guard him and you have me too. So long as I'm allowed to be at your side, he can't harm you."

Margerit clutched at her hands and held them tightly. "Promise me that you'll always be there. Uncle wants what's best for me, but best to him is a good match, a good family, a chance for advancement. You're the only one I can really trust, the only one on my side."

Barbara wished she could deserve what she was being offered, but it lay in her stomach like a stone. She pulled her hands free and stepped back away from the bed. "No, you can't. You can't trust me."

Margerit looked at her narrowly. "What do you mean?"

Barbara's answer was precise and mechanical. "Did you think I have no fears of my own? Estefen hates me. You—he's simply indifferent to you. You're a road to the baron's money. But I—"

No, Margerit didn't need to hear that story yet. "I've been a thorn in his side for years. If you consent to marry him, you put me in his power. He sent me a personal warning about that this evening. Do you think that doesn't affect what advice I give you?"

Unexpectedly, a smile replaced the anxiety in Margerit's face. "Ah, but you'll tell me *why* I shouldn't trust you. And that's why I trust you." She shook her head. "No it isn't sensible, but it's enough." She sighed, stood and turned the covers back on the bed. "I wish I could ask you to stay at my door tonight. I don't think I'll sleep a wink. But you need your rest as much as I do."

When Barbara had closed the door behind her, she contemplated standing guard there until dawn, but what would it avail? In truth, if Margerit weren't safe in her uncle's house, no mere blade could protect her. A secret vigil wouldn't put Margerit's mind at rest and an open one would only fret her. And though Barbara longed to place her body between Margerit's and all dangers...her thoughts shied away. That road led nowhere.

CHAPTER NINETEEN

Margerit

Margerit sought her uncle out after breakfast, before there could be any possibility of visitors. *Tomorrow.* That could be at any time and she needed to speak first. Her heart shrank under his impatiently curious silence as she fumbled for the right words. There was nothing in her etiquette lessons that covered how to refuse an offer that hadn't yet been made.

"Uncle…at the ball last night. You know that the new Baron Saveze was there? He spoke to me, after the dancing. He asked…he said that he planned to speak to you." He still waited silently for her to finish. He must know something—Aunt Honurat would have told him. "Uncle Mauriz, I don't want to marry him," she finished in a rush.

He frowned, but not at her, she thought. "Don't think so much of yourself," he said in a dampening tone. "He hasn't made any offers yet and I think your fancy runs ahead of the truth. Not every man who dances with you is going to make you an offer of marriage. Your aunt said that you were put all out of countenance by something he said. You need to learn to keep your composure better. If you spend a season in Rotenek you'll be mixing more with the noble families. You can't become flustered every time a man with a title dances with you."

She tried once more. "Uncle, he told me very plainly that he meant to speak to you. What else would it concern? You warned me to beware of fortune hunters. And Barbara thinks—" She closed her mouth abruptly. If he thought this was coming from Barbara it wouldn't help her cause.

His expression had turned more thoughtful. "It would be a great honor, you know. I hope you don't have any childish dreams of making a love match. If your fortune could buy you a title…"

"No, Uncle." She thought about telling him that all it would buy would be a death sentence, but he'd think she was being melodramatic. Better to base the argument on sound business. "I don't expect a love match but if you want to buy me a title I suspect there are better values to be had. You heard what my godfather thought of him. He collected an estate's worth of debt before he even came to the title. How long would my fortune last in his hands? And what value would I be to him when it was gone?" It occurred to her that it was Barbara's story all over again.

The idea seemed to settle into her uncle's mind. With luck, he'd conclude it was his own. "Perhaps you're right. I'm not saying I think he'll make an offer. But should he mention anything of the sort I think it would be best to discourage the matter. Wealth is not the same as birth, niece. You're more likely to make a successful match among our own kind." He looked as if he might say something more but then thought better of it.

That his reasons ran parallel to her own arguments didn't prevent her from feeling that he'd dismissed her concerns as childish fantasies. Still, it was a reassurance greater than she had hoped for.

* * *

Barbara was waiting in the corridor when she left him at last. "Will he support you?" she asked urgently.

Margerit shrugged. "I think so. He didn't really believe me. Oh, I want to go out somewhere! Anywhere."

Barbara nodded, but in the hesitant way she used when she disapproved.

"What?" Margerit asked.

"It would, perhaps, be unwise to risk meeting Estefen on the street before his interview with your uncle."

"But I can't bear just sitting here waiting. I'll go mad. He might not even come today. He might not come at all. Maybe it was just a threat."

She paced one way and then the other. She wanted to hide in her room but then there would be no way to know if he came. She wanted to keep watch from the front parlor windows but that might be where her uncle would receive him. She wanted to hear what was said but without being seen. She twisted like a fish caught in a net and jumped when Barbara touched her lightly on the shoulder.

"This does you no good, Maisetra. Spend the time with your aunts and cousins in the drawing room. You'll know if anyone comes."

It turned out to be an excruciating morning filled with domestic needlework and palpable tension. Aunt Honurat was still out of sorts with her and was clearly unhappy that Barbara refused to take the hint and absent herself. Her young cousins were caught up in it as well. Sofi fretted over her stitches, not daring to ask what the adults were not talking about. And Iulien chattered away obliviously until her mother could stand it no more and sent her back to the nursery. And around about the time that Aunt Bertrut began putting things away in preparation for luncheon, they heard a muffled knock at the front door, the sound of men's voices and footsteps in the hall. Aunt Honurat gave her a sharp glance but it seemed she guessed something of what was going on for she remained seated and distracted Sofi with a new task.

Margerit stood and moved restlessly around the room. There was no hope of overhearing any of what was said. The long minutes stretched out to fill the better part of an hour. She wondered if her uncle were allowing himself to be persuaded after all. Then footsteps again. They paused outside the drawing room door and Margerit saw Barbara tense until they moved on. A few minutes later Uncle Mauriz came in and summoned her with a look.

"It seems you were right," he said, when they were both private together. "I hope you're quite certain that you don't care to be a baroness because he was very unhappy at my refusal. I doubt he would extend the offer a second time."

Margerit took a deep breath and answered, "Quite certain."

* * *

Life returned to what passed for normal. As the year turned toward summer, garden parties were added to the schedule and offers of carriage rides along the lanes of Axian Park or out to scenic points in the countryside. Margerit was relieved when Aunt Honurat systematically declined the carriage expeditions.

"That's too particular an attention," she explained. "Even in a larger party, people would talk. You aren't ready to give anyone that kind of expectation."

If the close confines of a carriage were too particular, other venues seemed too open to all. The warming weather turned her favored walking paths along the river from a matter of brisk exercise to a more leisurely promenade that invited chance meetings and conversation. In sharper weather, Aunt Bertrut had been content to entrust her to Barbara's sole care but now she claimed a place at her side when she walked out. Margerit could hardly protest that she preferred the faster pace and the wide-ranging conversation that she and Barbara enjoyed. And when Bertrut pointed out that she was well-employed engaging with the near-endless stream of acquaintances that flocked around each time they set out, Margerit refrained from pointing out that Barbara managed to fend off unwanted suitors with a mere look. But if too particular an attention was to be avoided, Margerit knew that too pointed a disdain would also cause trouble. So Bertrut became a fixture on her afternoon walks and only Fonten House remained as a refuge of solitude.

CHAPTER TWENTY

Barbara

Estefen was still in Chalanz. Barbara hadn't pinned down which of the great houses he was visiting but she'd seen him twice at a distance. She hadn't told Margerit—no need to worry her. It might be only to save face. He could hardly admit that he'd come all this way to offer marriage to a *burfro* girl who then refused him. But she kept her eyes open and her nerves were stretched thin until even Margerit noticed and she had to fumble for an explanation. The fine weather only made the job more difficult. She found herself wishing for an unseasonable storm—one that would keep visiting indoors and all travel in carriages. A week passed, then two, and she saw nothing further of him and began to relax.

They had walked along the river wall nearly to the end of Axian Park when Barbara heard the sound. As she turned, she briefly considered and discarded the possibility that the hoofbeats heralded an impromptu race, heedless of the strict conventions of the promenade. Time slowed as she took in and interpreted what she saw. Two men. Their faces masked by scarves. The farther a bold and competent rider, the nearer on a horse wild-eyed and barely under control. No weapons in hand, so it was a snatch and run, not a killing. Her memory searched the area for a barrier, anything to slow or prevent access. The marble bench on the opposite side of the pathway from the river wall, not three steps away.

"Margerit!" she shouted, grabbing her by the arm and pushing her toward the bench. "Behind! Now! Stay there!"

The elder Maisetra Sovitre could fend for herself. She wasn't the target. But she did carry a useful weapon. Barbara grabbed the daffodil-yellow parasol carried by the older woman and ran toward the oncoming horse, thrusting the bright fabric into its face as she dodged aside. The horse shied violently against the river wall, lost its footing and slipped, throwing the rider over and into the flood with a shout. As the horse scrambled to its feet she turned toward the second man. She heard him curse as he overshot the mark, passing the bench where Margerit crouched and where her aunt stood by, open-mouthed.

He pulled the horse up and turned back toward them. A professional would have continued on, counting the quarry as lost. A desperate man would have ridden her down. Instead he swung down from his mount and drew his blade. His stance spoke of good training but little experience. Barbara met him with her own weapon, simultaneously testing him and working him further away from the bench. One never knew when defeat might turn to sour vengeance. He took her retreat for weakness and lunged. Her blade found its home.

As he fell, she looked around once more. No third man. The first was carried downriver, perhaps drowned. In the distance, other promenaders had seen the struggle and were fleeing or approaching as their natures took them. Barbara knelt and pulled the cloth from the man's face.

"Damn him," she said under her breath. Then more loudly, "Damn him!" It was Perzin from the count's ball. The one who had been so full of himself at being hired as armin to a baron. If she'd needed any proof of who was behind this, he was it. But it would never stand as evidence before a magistrate, not against a titled man. She cleaned her blade on his coat.

Margerit was still huddled behind the bench, despite her aunt's urging, but at a reassuring word she rose, her hems muddy to the knees and her bonnet askew. Barbara hurried toward her to hide her view of the corpse.

"Is he...?"

"He's Estefen's man," Barbara said, ignoring the more obvious answer. "You're safe enough now." She looked around and spotted a handful of young boys among the gathering onlookers. Pulling a small coin from her pocket, she showed it to them and said, "There's five *teneirs* to share between you if you run and tell the magistrate's men." She shrugged apologetically to Margerit. "Better to send word ourselves than for someone else to report it. But we need to get you home and out of the matter."

At the edge of the crowd she saw a friend of the Fulpis riding in a light chaise and signaled to them, urging Margerit over toward the carriage. "Your aunt can see you safely home. The magistrate will want to speak to you, but better it's done in private."

Margerit was taking the matter more calmly than she'd feared. "But what about you?"

"I need to stay to answer for this. It makes explanations simpler if I don't leave the…the place where it happened."

"I'm staying with you," Margerit said firmly.

Maisetra Sovitre's urgings had no more effect than her own did, so it was three of them who met the black-coated official and waited while his men examined the body and shooed off the bystanders. He blinked bewilderedly as Barbara recited the standard legal formulas she had last used—was it only four months ago? It seemed a lifetime.

"You are…?"

"Armin to Maisetra Sovitre," she answered and clarified, "Maisetra Margerit Sovitre."

His eyes widened slightly and he bowed to the other two women. "My apologies, I didn't recognize…but you shouldn't be standing here." He took in Margerit's muddied state. "Like this."

Margerit took a step closer to her and said, "I understand there are certain questions you need to ask."

Barbara was amused to note that Margerit had the air of one granting, not seeking, protection. With a few brief sentences she laid out the bare facts of the attack, with Margerit adding confirmation. And then more quietly, for the magistrate's ears only, the other details: what she knew, what she guessed. It made no difference, she knew that. One couldn't go around accusing a baron of attempts at abduction and rape for no better reason than a jilted proposal.

The magistrate asked only, "What is your proof?" Barbara raised her hands helplessly and he sighed, more in relief than resignation she thought. "Well, there's no harm done," he said with an air of dismissal.

It was the best she could hope for: that he would rule the death as falling within the legitimate scope of her employment. There was little doubt of that. There had been no doubt of it the time in Rotenek either. The trouble there had been political, not legal.

He offered his own carriage to carry the ladies home, to her relief. The onlookers had long since drifted off; no doubt some had carried the word ahead to Chaturik Square. Maistir Fulpi had not been home but he had been sent for and arrived hard on their heels. He took only a moment to satisfy himself that Margerit was unharmed, then Barbara found herself the target of his glare and he said shortly, "In my office."

This was no time to play games of waiting to be questioned. She reported to him as she would have to the baron, sparing no details and omitting no conjectures.

"There is no doubt," she concluded. "Mesner Chazillen—Baron Saveze, that is—was behind this. If he had succeeded—"

"If he had succeeded then you would have failed at your duty."

"I didn't fail," Barbara said evenly. Years of practice kept her temper on short rein, but he seemed to delight in goading her. "I doubt there will be another attempt of the same nature. He won't have the resources." It was tempting to ask him whether he still doubted the need for an armin. She counted that battle as won.

"Was the killing necessary?"

She found the question odd. Did he think it amused her to murder untried boys? "Yes."

He tried and failed to stare her down but hid the failure in a distant look as if he were thinking of something else entirely. She waited.

"Do you think it is wise," he asked at last, "to take her to Rotenek? When he will be there?"

Barbara's mind raced. Nothing must divert that plan. "Rotenek is no more dangerous than any other place. There are more eyes, fewer lonely places. And more people to disapprove should he go too far."

"Well, perhaps so. And perhaps there are additional measures that can be taken."

But if he had thoughts on the matter, he chose not to share them.

CHAPTER TWENTY-ONE

Margerit

The shock of the attack faded but in the days that followed Margerit felt a wall rising between her and her guardians. Uncle Fulpi watched her with a speculative and measuring eye when he thought she didn't notice. Did he regret refusing Estefen's offer now that he'd shown his teeth? Was he considering the possibility of hurriedly offering her up to some other noble suitor, less dangerous but just as hungry? He spoke of a season in Rotenek now more in the way of a treat for good behavior and not for the marriage market. Aunt Honurat sorted through her invitations ruthlessly for those she might and might not accept. The favored ones included far fewer of the suitable young men than before. There were no more balls at the great houses. Had her aunt dared to decline them or was she no longer enough of a novelty to be amusing? She didn't care about the dinners or parties themselves but she was nagged by hints of unknown plans and by the constant scrutiny. Axian Park was banned to her entirely. She protested at last to her uncle, "Am I being punished? Do you think it was my fault?"

"We only want to keep you safe," he answered in a tone that allowed no contradiction.

If the strictures had kept her from going to Fonten Street she would have rebelled. LeFevre's lessons and the treasures of her library remained as consolation. But even those visits were more closely watched. There were no more walks across town accompanied only by Barbara. Now she was required to send for her carriage and there was always another in attendance, even to the transparent stratagem of sending Sofi and her governess along to try her hand on the clavichord in the yellow parlor.

Once, she might have turned to Aunt Bertrut, who seemed unchanged through all the shifting tensions. She went on as she always had: playing *vizeino* when it pleased her, retreating to the company of her own friends when she quarreled with Uncle Fulpi. But Bertrut would never support her at the cost of her own comfort. And, as LeFevre repeatedly cautioned her, her uncle had both the right and duty to do as he thought best for her. So she walked meekly and patiently on the paths they allowed and kept her eyes on the distant goal of Rotenek.

On the first day of summer, the tension eased abruptly with the unexpected arrival of Cousin Nikule. To be sure, the university term was over. Last year he'd returned early and there were shouted arguments behind closed doors. But she knew he'd had other plans this year: friends to visit, a more meandering path back from the freedoms of the city to the smaller world of Chalanz. She felt suddenly shy in his presence. Three years past, when he'd first been sent off at considerable expense and trouble to collect a gentleman's education, she'd pounced eagerly at every return visit for stories of Rotenek and the university. And when he'd deigned to humor her with droll stories of his fellows and their adventures, it was with the air of indulging a baby sister. He found her zeal for scholarship amusing. His own studies were clearly fit in between less mentionable masculine pursuits to the barest extent necessary to satisfy his father's ambitions.

Now so much had changed between them. Even simply being out in society might have been enough to shift the balance and there was so much more. Nikule clearly looked at her in a new light, bowing formally and kissing her hand, in contrast to the light-hearted teasing he'd shown previously. She saw him in a new light as well. When he was her only window on those distant lecture halls, his scraps of stories had fed her fantasies. Now she was impatient with his indifference. She would have made any sacrifice to be in his place and he'd always treated his studies as a tedious chore. If he looked at her as a grown woman now, she saw him as a careless boy, breaking his toys in the certainty that he'd be given new ones.

The attention that would have been flattering the year before left her skeptical and curious. He was attentive over dinner. Instead of disappearing afterward to spend time with old friends, he was content to enjoy a quiet family evening, listening to Sofi play and sing and even indulging Iulien by joining in childish card games. And in the morning, when he saw her and Aunt Bertrut putting on their bonnets to go out to the waiting carriage, he offered to escort her instead.

"After all," he said, "you need to have more care taken of you now."

Margerit laughed and gestured at Barbara who had come up the back stairs to join them. "You're quite unnecessary on that account! Didn't Uncle tell you? My fortune came with its very own bodyguard."

She saw his eyes narrow in annoyance as he looked around. Barbara, in turn, bristled at the scrutiny. "Indeed?" he said. "Well, today you can dispense with all that." He took her gloved hand in his own and tucked it under his elbow. "It can be just us two, like old times."

It was tempting to ask him which old times he was thinking of, but she only slipped her hand free and said, "If I go out, Barbara goes with me. Your father is quite firm on that point. But I'd be happy to have you accompany me as well. I have some books to deliver back to Fonten Street, which you may carry for me. And Aunt Sovitre finds LeFevre's account books hopelessly boring so I'm certain she'll be delighted to let you take her place." She took mischievous delight in handing him the two substantial tomes waiting for her on the sideboard and watching him juggle them along with his brass-knobbed walking stick as they climbed into the carriage. Clearly the illusion of assistance would have been undermined by simply handing them off to the footman.

He bore patiently with her errands or at least he pretended to. It was tempting to see if he would suffer having a visit to the milliners inflicted on him after the long hour with LeFevre, but since she found the choosing of bonnets equally tedious, it hardly seemed worth the entertainment.

That entertainment wore thin over the next week. He must have been called home to help watch over her, for now Aunt Honurat presented her with a new and more extensive list of social engagements to attend and it seemed that Nikule would be available to escort her to most of them. It wasn't entirely a burden; he was a competent dancer and a witty enough dinner partner. But if she'd been eager to secure a fiancé, the hovering presence of someone who was practically an older brother wouldn't have been welcome.

CHAPTER TWENTY-TWO

Barbara

Barbara didn't care much for Nikule Fulpi. Perhaps it shouldn't be counted against him that his looks echoed his father's so strongly: the same long face and arrogant mouth. He had picked up a dandy's habits in Rotenek and his light brown hair was more daringly styled, but there could be no doubt whose son he was. No, it was the clumsy attempt that was being made to throw him in Margerit's path. Margerit had laughed when she pointed that out. "Don't be silly; he's my cousin!"

"Dispensations can be had for a price," she'd countered.

What confirmed her opinion was the principle that the servant reflected the master, and the fellow Maureld that Nikule kept as his valet was a poor reflection. He was boastful, his hands made too free with the younger kitchen maids and he was working to discover exactly how far he could needle her without giving her an excuse to respond. He was, for all of that, harmless in the ways that mattered to her. And so she ignored him.

She didn't care to ignore Nikule but he was outside the scope of her duties. With Estefen's stillborn proposal, her concern had been for the threat of force. That was easy to face. Harder was the thought that one of these silly young men would succeed in winning Margerit's heart. Not Nikule, perhaps, but there would be others—more deft, more subtle. It was no part of her job to come between them, though he raised her hackles.

That was what she was pondering one afternoon over a late lunch in the kitchen when the house had fallen still. She had left Margerit reading in the parlor, Maisetra Fulpi had taken to her bed with a sick headache and the elder Maisetra Sovitre had taken the younger children out for a walk to preserve the quiet. The men were about somewhere, doing whatever it was that men of leisure did in the middle of the day. And Barbara was so lost in thought that it took a moment for the conversation to rise to her notice. Maureld came down the stairs with his usual swagger and blocked the path of the maid who was about to go up with a tea tray. "Now where would you be going with that?"

In a voice sharp with scorn she replied, "It's for Maisetra Margerit and it's none of your business!"

"If you'll take a hint from me," he returned slyly, "I'd keep clear of the parlor for a bit yet."

It wasn't his words that set off the alarm bells, it was the shade his face turned when he realized she'd heard them. She upended two chairs in her plunge for the door to the stairs. The corridor was a blur. She thrust the parlor door open on the heels of a thud and crash to see Margerit struggling in Nikule's embrace. In two steps, she grabbed his shoulder and wrenched him aside, throwing him to the ground to the sound of tearing cloth as she planted herself between them. Behind her, she heard Margerit breathing heavily.

Nikule picked himself up from the hearth, looking more bewildered and chagrined than angry. Her memory flashed back to her own misstep at the reading of the will. But his transgression had been deliberate. When he saw who faced him, he cursed at her and—looking around—snatched up the poker from the stand by the hearth.

Barbara went into a crouch, reaching reflexively for her sword—the one left upstairs in her chest. After all, what need would she have to carry a weapon in Maistir Fulpi's own home? On the street it would have been a fatal mistake but instead the forced hesitation let good sense creep back in.

"Ho! Help! Murder!" she shouted, caring nothing for the inaccuracy of her words.

That gave him pause. He looked down at the poker as if unsure how it had come to his hand and began, "Margerit, I…" He seemed to realize there were no words that could mend the moment.

The tableau was broken by a clatter of approaching footsteps and voices. Nikule froze, visibly unsure of his next step. Fulpi's voice cut through the babble. "Go about your business!" The small cluster of servants scattered. Barbara watched him take in the scene, glaring from Nikule as he dropped the poker with an expression half sheepish, half defiant, to Margerit, holding the torn edge of her bodice closely over her bosom where she stood by the sofa, and back to his son.

A brittle silence stretched out. In the distance came the sound of a door opening and a burst of cheerful laughter, as incongruous as a canary at a funeral. The laughter was silenced and a patter of quick steps heralded Maisetra Sovitre bursting in exclaiming, "What in heaven?"

Nikule found his tongue at last. "You were the one who told me I should make sure of her."

"I meant," his father said icily, "that you should engage her affections. Not that you should compromise her virtue." He slapped him lightly across the face. "Get out!"

The young man reddened and left the room without a word. Barbara stepped back from the center of Fulpi's attention, watching to see what might be needed. Margerit's mouth was set in grim determination. Her aunt had taken up a shawl from the back of the sofa and draped it around her shoulders, looking from one figure to another in confusion. Margerit's fingers twined in the fringe, hardening into fists.

With Nikule's departure, her uncle turned to her and said in a conciliatory tone, "We won't speak of this. No harm was done. It was a misunderstanding."

Maisetra Sovitre began a sharp reply but Margerit uncharacteristically gestured her into silence, announcing, "I will not continue to live under this roof."

"Don't be a silly child," her uncle began. "You can't—"

"In the future, I will be living at Fonten Street. Aunt Sovitre will live with me as companion and guardian."

Her aunt was startled but Barbara could see her mind working in calculation. She quickly lent her support to the plan: "Mauriz, you can see how impossible this has become. The two of them...you could hardly put your own son out on the street. It will be simpler this way."

He tried a voice of authority once more. "It's impossible. A girl like you, living alone, without the protection of a man..."

"Clearly a man's protection is not sufficient," Margerit answered steadily. "I will live there under my own roof, with my own household, with my own protection. Or I will find myself explaining to all of Chalanz why I find it necessary to keep an armin at my side at every moment, even in my guardian's parlor."

Barbara was tempted to step a pace closer to her and scowl at him, playing the part, but that would be beyond the line. She remained still.

Maistir Fulpi was clearly shaken. He ventured, "Margerit, think of your reputation. What will people think—what will they say?"

"Perhaps you should think of an explanation," Margerit said coldly. "Otherwise the truth might occur to them."

Barbara knew it for a gamble. Margerit had far more to lose by the truth than Nikule or her uncle did. But he nodded slowly at last and said, "I'll send word that they should prepare to expect you tomorrow. Your things can—"

"Today," Margerit insisted. "Aunt Sovitre can arrange for my belongings tomorrow. Send a message that I will be there by supper tonight and have them send my carriage."

He looked one more time between his niece and sister-in-law as if he saw all his hopes for the future crashing to the ground. Then he stepped back as Margerit swept past him and out the door. Barbara kept close on her heels up the stairs, hearing the beginnings of a heated discussion behind them. When the door to Margerit's room closed behind them, Barbara recalled her first day in the house and braced herself for hysterics. But when Margerit turned toward her, her eyes were shining not with tears but with triumph.

"He lost. He gambled and lost and he gave me the key to the door."

She wasn't certain whether that meant her cousin or her uncle. The triumph was almost as unsettling as the tears she had dreaded. "Maisetra, your uncle is right in one thing: people will think it very odd for you to leave his roof. They'll need to be told something."

Margerit frowned. "Tell them…I don't know, tell them I didn't see the point in leaving the staff idle."

Barbara began to shake her head, but then a thought came to her. "Tell them you plan to hold a ball of your own, in your own house. It will only make sense for you to spend most of your time there for the preparations. Some might not believe it, but it's a plausible excuse." She could see the idea take hold. "There would only be one real problem," she added.

Margerit's face had started to brighten but the frown returned. "What?"

"You'd need to actually hold a ball."

CHAPTER TWENTY-THREE

Margerit

When Margerit woke the next morning, it was the first moment when she truly realized and utterly believed in the legacy she had received. As Maitelen drew the curtains open, the morning sun streamed through a series of windows reaching above her head. She stretched out across a bed that could have held five people comfortably and yet failed to dominate the room. A tray at her bedside held a pot of chocolate prepared the moment she'd been seen to stir sleepily. There was an almost palpable sense throughout the house of expectancy, of people waiting only to know what she wanted for it to be done. Luxury tempted her to enjoy the moment to the fullest, but long ago she'd taken to heart that you must begin as you meant to go on. And to go on she needed to convince everyone that this had been a sensible decision, that coming here wasn't just the whim of a willful child.

If Aunt Bertrut had surprised her with the strength of her support, LeFevre had done the same with the depth of his disapproval. Thinking on it, Bertrut's enthusiasm made sense. She'd always chafed at her neither-this-nor-that place in Uncle Fulpi's household. Overseeing this household was the closest she could expect to being mistress of her own. Her usual air of detachment had evaporated the moment they walked through the doors and she'd spent the remainder of the evening establishing a working relationship with the upper staff.

But LeFevre, having obeyed her announcement to the letter in preparing the house for her, had whisked her immediately to his office for a raking down that rivaled the worst Uncle Fulpi had ever delivered. She had withstood it in silence, sure of her decision but unsure how to defend it. It was Barbara, standing behind her, seething at the tirade, who told him in one pithy sentence what Nikule had tried. At that, LeFevre fell silent for a long moment then sighed, "I see." And though he never questioned the move again, Margerit was determined to convince him that a separate household made its own sense.

It was at his urging, before a week went by, that she had reached a truce—if not a reconciliation—with her uncle. The Fulpis were her first guests in her own home. Though the air was strained, they too kept the pretense that all was well between them. Aunt Bertrut had the management of her invitations now but Aunt Honurat was asked to escort her regularly. Nikule was not included in the truce. Word was that he was off visiting friends in the north. Gossip, it seemed, had been averted.

* * *

In that first week, Margerit nearly forgot the public excuse given out for the move until Aunt Bertrut raised it over breakfast. "You need to set a date. I was thinking perhaps in mid-September. That would give us plenty of time and the calendar isn't as crowded."

"No, that's much too late," Margerit replied.

"Too late for what?"

It wasn't time yet to mention the university. Not until her place there was secure. But the term would be starting by the date she'd named. Another excuse was needed. "Barbara says everyone important returns to Rotenek in time for the Feast of Saint Mauriz." He was the city's patron. It was more than enough reason to travel earlier. "I'll need time to get settled before that—to find my feet. I'd rather have the ball in early August and have plenty of time."

"Completely impossible," Bertrut answered with no room for argument. "You can't plan a ball in only two weeks. That would be barely time to send out invitations."

"What about three? I don't want to spend all summer working at it. You know I don't care much for balls."

Her aunt considered the matter. "Three is possible, with help. But remember, this is supposed to be why you left your uncle's roof. Show a proper enthusiasm to the world."

Margerit had thought the days would drag but she hadn't accounted for everything she had to learn. Aunt Bertrut was willing to let her forgo all but the most important parties in favor of the preparations but she wasn't willing to let her slip out of her new household responsibilities. There were meals to approve, refurbishment to oversee, minor invitations to issue, correspondence to take up. LeFevre began to introduce her in earnest to the complexities of managing her holdings. "I need to go to Rotenek to prepare a few matters," he pointed out. "Draw up your own responses to everything that comes in while I'm gone. I'll still need to approve your replies, so you needn't be concerned about making too great a mistake." She knew enough to be flattered by the offer.

And then there were the more practical preparations for her move. A stiff and sharp-tongued woman from the city was hired to instruct her in how not to appear a hopeless provincial. It wasn't entirely outside of possibility that she might be invited to be presented at court. In any event one must be familiar with the complicated web of forces at play that could entangle the naïve or unwary. A dancing master was brought in, despite her protests that she knew all the popular dances well enough for the purpose.

"You know the dances popular in Chalanz," he said dismissively. "Half of them haven't been danced in Rotenek for years."

And because dancing could not be taught to a single pupil, she invited Sofi and other friends to join her, and even Barbara was regularly drafted to make up the sets.

It was Barbara who filled out the remainder of her time by piling the library table with books that she said every university student would know.

"Your Latin is excellent but your Greek…has not seen the same attention."

Her Greek was barely passable, Barbara's diplomacy notwithstanding. And though Aristotle was no longer considered the bedrock of philosophy, any lack there would be felt when she tackled more modern works. Sister Petrunel had been systematic with the classics and the humanists, but she had touched only lightly on the esoterics, and for philosophers of the last century she had cared not at all. Those could wait, but Barbara ruthlessly set her passages of Fortunatus to work out on her own.

"Do you know he was the foundation of the university in Rotenek?" she mentioned, by way of inducement. "The tutors he gathered around him began lecturing in the Plaiz Vezek to gain more students and those students attracted more teachers and it grew from there."

That would have been an exciting time to live, Margerit thought. When seeds were being planted and new ways of thinking were being explored, both inspiring and dangerous. She added history to the list of subjects she might pursue, given time.

Before she knew it, Aunt Bertrut handed her a stack of invitations to sign and send and the final fittings for her new gown were scheduled.

CHAPTER TWENTY-FOUR

Barbara

Moving back to Fonten House was like emerging from a cave into a riotous garden. Maistir Fulpi's house had been cramped and narrow in many ways more than the physical. There, she had been an irritating anomaly among the staff; here, she was a familiar one. Here no one questioned her right to come or go, to act as she thought best to fulfill her duties, to enter any part of the house or to have access to her charge. And Margerit—she was the rose blooming in the center of the garden. It was a joy to watch her unfolding and reaching out to seize her destiny. Not the inheritance itself—that was the least of the matter—but what it made possible.

The moments she treasured most came on those evenings when Margerit stayed in and Maisetra Sovitre had gone off to sleep. The two of them would meet in the library to argue philosophy, digging through thick volumes for quotations and exegesis, debating competing translations. It was the one time Barbara allowed herself to forget the gulf that lay between them. Margerit's mind jumped easily from thought to thought, making connections and finding parallels that would then take an hour to pin down and trace through in detail. Barbara worked more meticulously, pulling from her memory elaborate structures of logic and evidence.

"You should study law," Margerit laughed accusingly after losing one particularly convoluted debate.

"I have. A little," Barbara answered. It was a field where women students were less tolerated than philosophy but also one easier to study outside the lecture halls. "LeFevre suggested it at first. He said you never know when the deadliest attack may come from a lawyer."

Indeed, LeFevre illustrated that point when he returned with the latest news from Rotenek. "Estefen's latest challenge has failed."

"I thought you said the court refused to hear him," Margerit said.

"That was the challenge to the will itself. The greatest danger was that it would be heard and take years to settle. But it doesn't require a charge or a judgment for him to demand an accounting. The baron's strategy relied on the fiction that Estefen had, in effect, already been treating the title-estate as his own." Among the three of them, "the baron" always and only meant the old man. "But that strategy left him open to a charge of mismanagement of the Saveze lands or even outright theft, strange as it might seem. The clerks went over every slip that Estefen signed over to the baron and matched them against the revenues of the property. His accusation that the estate was deliberately gutted found no footing."

"Will he try *res patrum* do you think?" Barbara wondered.

"On what grounds?" LeFevre countered. "The title-lands were the only thing Marziel inherited from his brother. When he began investing, he was careful never to purchase any property that had been in the family within two generations back. I know, because there was a very pretty little orchard he had his eye on, but when we traced the title there had been a connection in his father's day and he let it go."

She could see Margerit struggling to follow the thread of the argument. "Why was it so important to him? He must have been making these plans since long before Estefen was grown. It couldn't only have been to spite him."

LeFevre shook his head. "That's the baron's business and on that my mouth is closed. But you needn't worry about the law. There's nothing left he can do except make noise."

* * *

The weeks passed more swiftly than she would have predicted. As the day neared, preparations for the ball swallowed increasingly more of their lives. Barbara let most of it pass by. The aunts and LeFevre took command of it like a military campaign. Even many of the ordinary security preparations would be handled by the staff, just as they had been in the baron's day. Margerit's safety was her main concern—but in the end that encompassed all else.

For all that the ball had been her idea at first, Barbara grew steadily more uneasy about the project. She preferred the Margerit who found morning visits tedious and dinner parties merely amusing, not the one who reviewed her guest list with rising excitement. How many of the young men who attended would see this as their last chance to catch her interest? Who was to say there wouldn't be someone acceptable who caught her eye? It wouldn't be the first time a woman with scholarly aspirations had decided to turn aside at the last for the conventional prize. If she could see Margerit safely to Rotenek the university would cast its own lures, but until then all was at risk. And it would be such a waste. That was what she dreaded: the waste. And the complications a husband would bring for the remaining time they were bound together. That was all, she told herself. Truly.

In the end, the preparations rushed down on them like the river in spring flood. And underneath it all, the packing and closing down of rooms in preparation for the move. The first baggage carts would leave the next morning. The day itself was a blur with only the image of Margerit always in her sight among the crushing crowds. Watching everyone, everything. Alert to any possible threat. But no threat came, not even so much as a clumsy dance partner stepping on her toes.

It was nearly three in the morning when Ponivin came to tell her that the last of the guests were gone, including the Fulpis. As the butler left, the tension began draining out of her, leaving her exhausted. The staff would be cleaning and setting things to rights until dawn after the temporary help had left, but Margerit could go to bed at last. Her Aunt Sovitre had been chiding her to go for the last hour, pointing out that her guardians were the nominal hosts of the affair and could handle the official farewells. Barbara could tell that it was less a sense of duty than the excitement of playing hostess that kept Margerit circulating among the stragglers.

She found her in the ballroom, surveying the scene of her triumph. "That's the last of them, Maisetra," she announced.

Margerit pirouetted in the middle of the room, spreading her arms wide. "Wasn't it glorious?"

Barbara grinned in spite of herself. "It was a bit too glorious for someone who claims she doesn't care for balls."

The strains of a fiddle came floating down from the gallery where one of the musicians, in the midst of packing up, had paused to demonstrate a new waltz to his fellows. Margerit came over, stepping in time to the music, saying, "I like dancing, I just don't like being on display as merchandise." She playfully held out her hands, saying, "Dance with me!"

Barbara's heart started beating like a hammer. "I...I can't," she stammered.

"Don't be silly," Margerit said. "You've had the same lessons I've had. And you haven't had a chance to use them all evening. Dance with me."

Lessons under the eye of a dancemaster were different. Barbara had schooled herself to view them as training, as a supplement to sessions with Signore Donati. She had carefully avoided thinking of them as anything more. Now Barbara's shoulder burned where Margerit laid her hand across it and her own hand burned across the curve of Margerit's waist. But reflexes ruled her life and she guided the two of them in graceful arcs across the empty floor. Their heads lay closely enough that Margerit's chestnut curls brushed against her cheek and she could easily trace the profile of her upturned nose and the curve of her lips, parted with the exertion. Their bodies moved as one while the music lasted. The fiddler stopped, abruptly, in the middle of a line and they were left suspended, standing closely face to face. Barbara felt the world pause and knew that in another moment she would drown in those shining eyes, those sweet lips. Maisetra Sovitre coughed loudly from the doorway. Barbara stepped away stiffly, aware of how guilty she was acting. But Margerit was the one who was blushing hotly and rushing to say, "We were only having some fun, Aunt Bertrut. Did you need something?"

Barbara watched as she crossed to the door and took her aunt by the arm, heading for the family rooms and rest at last. *It was only a bit of fun,* she thought. *It didn't mean anything. How could it?* When they disappeared, she spun abruptly toward the stairs to the gallery and went to hurry the musicians along. They couldn't lock the doors until the last of the strangers had gone and she couldn't take her own rest until the doors were locked. And she needed her rest, for tomorrow the work would begin in earnest.

CHAPTER TWENTY-FIVE

Margerit

Their cavalcade had lessened by one carriage shortly after entering the old East Gate as Uncle Mauriz and Nikule turned off toward the university district. There had been no arguing with LeFevre that the presence of both her guardians was essential to establishing her respectability. And even to her it would have felt petty to demand that Nikule travel separately. But she was relieved that there was no question of her cousin entering her new home.

Margerit's first thought when she saw the baron's—her—house in Rotenek was how small it was. When Barbara had spoken of Tiporsel House she'd envisioned something as grand and spacious as the house on Fonten Street. From the East Gate the broad avenue had arced gently until it reached the southern side of the *plaiz* that lay between Saint Mauriz's Cathedral and the palace. But then as the main road swept widely south around the elbow of the river, the coachman turned more sharply left to double back on the Vezenaf, an old cobbled road lined on the right by a row of narrow compounds that lay cheek-by-cheek along the river's edge. On the left, the mews and coach houses that served those households were tucked under a steep rocky rise, topped by the spill of gardens behind the houses edging the *plaiz*.

The stone arch through which they turned on the riverward side of the street seemed to fill a third of the width of the property. And when they emerged from the arched tunnel, the courtyard that filled the entire span seemed barely wide enough to turn the coach even with dexterous maneuvering. The house rose up before them barely more than two stories, but on entering through the iron-bound doors, Margerit found that it ran deeply back from the yard, inviting in the golden September sunlight with a series of stepped levels, broken by broad balconies. The steep slope seen at the upper side of the street continued down to the river's edge. The two stories of the house visible from the courtyard were augmented by three or four more descending to the terraced gardens by the river wall where, as she'd been told, there was a private dock.

It was the docks that had given the street its name, back in the early days of the city when all trade ran through the hands of the oldest families. The cramped elbows were—she soon came to understand— the very mark of the old city center, where wealth had been measured in river access before the building of the new docks and warehouses farther downriver outside the old walls. The newly rich might have their broad boulevards and sprawling estates on the northern edge of the city, but old money—or enough money—bought you a slice of the heart.

As the house filled with the bustle of luggage being sorted out and the newly arrived servants chatting with the resident staff and those who had gone ahead, Margerit walked out onto the terrace that opened off the hall to look down over the spill of railings and roof tiles, past the lush green and pink of the gardens, and to the glinting water beyond. She heard her aunt come up behind her repeating in an awestruck whisper, "Oh my! Oh my, will you look at that!" And then the moment was no longer her own and she turned back into the house.

* * *

The truce that had held between her two guardians during the journey lasted until supper that evening. Aunt Bertrut opened with, "I've sent cards to Maisetra Faikrimek's cousin and my old friend Lufise to let them know we've arrived. We'll go out visiting tomorrow and that will be an opportunity to make more introductions. Before you know it, you'll be invited to all the balls you could wish for."

Uncle Mauriz countered her drily, "I hardly think your 'old friend' will be able to introduce Margerit into the sort of society she came to

Rotenek to join. She would do better not to encumber herself with social connections that will do her no real credit."

But in the end it was LeFevre who arranged for her first contact with Rotenek society. Not directly, of course—he didn't move in those circles himself. But in the course of arranging a settlement of one of the late baron's charitable bequests, as he explained to her later, he'd happened to mention to Mesnera Arulik that the young Maisetra Sovitre might be inclined to continue the charity. That led promptly to the leaving of a card and an invitation to a musical evening. Not an event of the season proper, but a place to start. So not three days after arriving, Margerit found herself preparing to make her entrance.

She had, in fact, begun to chafe under her confinement to the house. She'd left it only to attend Mass up at the cathedral. Though an evening of strangers was not the first or second or even third choice on her list to see, it would do for the sake of getting out. The moment they'd arrived in Rotenek, Barbara had extracted a promise from her not to set foot outside unescorted.

"Not even into the gardens, never alone. At least have one of the servants in sight when you're on the grounds. The neighbors are safe enough—I know them. But the river can be used for coming as well as going. And not out into the street without me or another guard. This isn't Chalanz."

But Barbara had been hardly to be seen in those first few days. There were arrangements to be made, she'd said. One of them came clear when she turned up the afternoon of Mesnera Arulik's salon in company with a stranger: a man of early middle age who was introduced as Marken. It was clear from his manner and the sword he wore that he followed Barbara's profession—an ordinary armin, not a duelist. He was far more what Margerit had imagined for the type: broad-shouldered and stolid, his sandy hair cropped close as if always in expectation that his next employer would be old-fashioned enough to require the wearing of a periwig. Margerit could see her uncle bristle at this unconsulted addition, but he said nothing as Barbara explained, "You'll need more eyes than mine if you want to go about freely. If you go out in your carriage, take one of us. If you plan to walk about in the streets or markets, take one of us. If you have visitors, make sure one of us is here and knows—it doesn't need to be in the room, but within earshot. I've worked with Marken before. He's sound. He knows the rules and the game. Mostly you won't notice he's there, but if he ever tells you to do something, do it. No questions."

Later, well after that first social call had been survived, Barbara explained her other reasons for the new addition to the staff. "I'll speak plainly," she said, "because I know you prefer it. I can't spend all my time only watching over you. I have my fencing training at Perret's academy and there are arrangements to be made for when you go to anything more public than a dinner party. You'd hardly want to be sitting home half the day while I have business to take care of. It was different in Chalanz—" She smiled apologetically. "It always comes back to that, doesn't it? Everything was different in Chalanz. And when the university term begins—" Barbara glanced away as she did when she felt she was treading uncertain ground. "You said…that is, you wanted me to continue my studies…"

"Of course!" Margerit broke in. "But—oh! Of course, you would have your own lectures to attend at times. You said you were following law."

Barbara shrugged. "It's useful. I follow philosophy too, of course, but law—that's more practical."

Margerit jumped to her first concern. "When does the term start? Who do I need to ask…?"

"Lectures begin after the feast of Saint Mauriz." Barbara pulled a small folded paper from her pocket and continued, "That will give you time to plan." She unfolded the paper and Margerit saw that it contained a list of women's names. "Remember what LeFevre told you: well-bred young ladies play at being students, they don't come to Rotenek for the purpose of becoming philosophers. These are some of the more serious students you're likely to meet socially. They all attended at least some lectures during last year's terms. There'll be others who are less serious but they wouldn't provide you with cover. I've marked the names of the ones you were introduced to at the Aruliks'. Befriend one or two of them, be curious about their studies. Then ask if you could join them for the lectures. There's no point in asking the professors for permission; you'll have no official standing in any event and LeFevre will take care of the fees. But show up in company with this set and no one will question you."

Margerit took the paper and worked to fit faces to the ones she must have met. Cheristien Riumai. She recalled a tall willowy girl with mousy brown hair, fiddling relentlessly with her fan throughout the performances, despite reproofs from the older woman at her side. Verunik Felix—no, she couldn't bring any face to mind. Amiz Waldimen was the only one she recalled speaking with. Her eyes had sparkled constantly with humor above a pursed bow of a mouth and a daintily pointed chin. Perhaps two years younger than the others. She wasn't properly out yet in society—the concert had been a special treat—but Margerit guessed she would cut quite a swath when that day came. "I can't do this. I can't go and befriend someone just to use her as…as a stalking horse."

"Why ever not?" Barbara seemed honestly confused. "It's done all the time. One befriends the sister to make eyes at the brother. One laughs at the old man's jokes to be invited to his niece's ball. One pretends to love carriage rides in order to be seen parading back and forth. It's the way of the world; there's no point in having scruples."

"But I've never been any good at it. That was what I dreaded most about my season: having to pretend to enjoy it."

"Then you'd better learn," Barbara said shortly. "I warned you before that there would be more gates to pass than your uncle's displeasure. Do you want this enough to work for it?"

Margerit held back a heated answer. She needed this. She needed honest words from someone who wished her only good and who knew the rules. And she knew how easy it was to send Barbara retreating back into stiff formality. "Of course I'm willing to work for it, I'd just prefer honesty." She placed her finger on Amiz Waldimen's name on the paper. "Her, I think, to begin with. I liked her. That makes it easier."

Margerit soon found that the combination of Mesnera Arulik's seal of approval and pure curiosity brought a welcome to nearly any drawing room suitable for her station. And once she set her mind to it, she found that laying siege to the scholars' set was not as daunting as she'd feared. She had only to suggest to Aunt Bertrut that an afternoon visit to the Waldimens might be a suitable first step in society. She was less certain of seeing Amiz in more formal contexts; the concert had been a rare public outing for her. Then, with a mention to Amiz of the university in an offhand way, the next thing she knew she was being regaled with tales of what this professor had done, or how the alchemy scholars were hopeless bores but the theology students were the most fun to tease.

"Cheris is such a bluestocking," Amiz said carelessly. "I think she actually does the readings. And Antuniet is determined to make a name for herself either in thaumaturgy or alchemy. But I just go to get out of the house and away from my sisters. You have no idea what it's like with two older sisters still on the market. Well, no, you wouldn't know. My mother swears I won't have a dancing season until one of them is betrothed, but she doesn't mind if I go to the lectures and amuse myself as long as I don't commit the sin of falling in love with a scholar. Well, no chance of that—I'm not such a fool. But the boys don't know that."

Barbara's strategy bore fruit when an invitation came later that week to join Amiz and some of her friends in the university district to take note of the schedule of lectures and debate the merits of the professors. Margerit was reminded that Amiz's loose talk of "amusing herself" was limited to what might be done in the watchful presence of a sharp-eyed governess. Cheristien Riumai's family felt the need to augment the watch over her morals with the protection of an armin in addition to the obligatory *vizeino*. The subtleties of hazard and protection in Rotenek society were only beginning to make themselves clear. Amiz's family might be every bit as wealthy as Cheristien's, but the money was new and there were older sisters competing for it. So she was protected against her own folly but was considered no temptation for the greed of others. Verunik's family was old but their fortunes had dwindled. Her parents were likely to favor any suitor for her hand so there would be little advantage to seeking to compromise her. And there was little enough to tempt a wayward suitor. Nature had blessed her with mousy hair that stubbornly refused to curl and was drawn back in a severe style that brought unfortunate attention to her prominent ears.

In contrast to those two, Antuniet—not part of Amiz's circle but thrown together with them by common interest—was shadowed by a dour swordsman. Evidently family pride demanded it, regardless of practical need, though she broke with tradition in disdaining female companionship for informal public gatherings such as these. Antuniet was older than the others. Past the age when the girl scholars were expected to put by their books and look for an offer of marriage. Margerit wondered if she 'hadn't taken' as the saying went. It would be easy to see why. A straight blade of a nose lent a haughty expression and her black hair made no nod to fashionable curls, being pinned into a severe and practical bun. Her piercing eyes reminded Margerit oddly of Barbara, though there was no other resemblance. There was a depth of hardness in them as if no obstacle could daunt her. And perhaps she needed that hardness to pursue…what was it Amiz had said? Alchemy? Not a topic that could be passed off as a girl's foolish fancy.

The temptations of dowries and inheritances bound by family honor were only part of the matter. That was brought forcefully to mind by the absence of the last member of Amiz's circle from the university expedition. Margerit was confused at first by the whispers with wary glances at the coterie of escorts. Mari's name had been on Barbara's list, she recalled, but like several others she hadn't yet crossed her path. Now she learned why.

"Her mother's cousin! Who would have thought it?" Amiz exclaimed in response to Verunik's whispered question.

Cheristien shrugged. "It's the cousin more often than you might think. Usually they hush it up and pretend to a long-standing arrangement and all you ever know is that a wedding date is set."

That could have been my story, Margerit thought.

Cheristien continued, "The only reason it's a scandal is because he'd been refused so publicly. His only family legacy is his army commission. They thought she could do better."

"But she'd fallen in love?" Verunik asked eagerly. Verunik hungered for others to have the romantic adventures she was ill-suited for.

Margerit had wondered the same thing, but Cheristien made a scornful noise. "Hardly! I don't think she'd given him a thought. But she was stupid and now she's stuck with him."

Margerit ventured to ask, "How was she stupid?" The others turned to her as if deciding whether to consider her inside or outside the circle.

Amiz was the one who answered. "It was his sister. Anywhere else, Mari wouldn't have gone out unprotected. They were in negotiations with Mesner Pelnik and everyone was being very careful of her good name. But Lenze invited her over to meet a new dressmaker—sent her own carriage and everything. It was pure carelessness that she went out with just her maid. And then, when she got there, Lenze wasn't there but Simun was. No need even for an abduction—Mari'd been there alone with him for six hours by the time they went searching for her."

"Alone?" Margerit asked. "But there was her maid and the servants…"

Cheristien laughed scornfully. "Surely you don't think they count!"

"But an armin would have counted?"

Antuniet commented for the first time after standing aloof from the gossip. "An armin would have gotten her out of there the moment Lenze failed to greet her."

"Never trust a man's sister," Amiz said with a laugh.

Margerit saw a strange look pass between Barbara and Antuniet. Not only did Barbara know everyone in Rotenek, she had all manner of unknown history with each of them.

Amiz lowered her voice and said, "They say Pelnik's sent his duelist to make the challenge."

"To Simun?" Margerit asked, trying to sort out all the names.

"No, silly! To Mari's father! For making him look a fool. It'll only be to the touch, for the sake of his good name."

Margerit gave up on making sense of it all. Perhaps she'd ask Barbara about it later, but for now there were decisions to make. Whether to follow Alessandro for a grounding in the humanists or to plunge directly into Mihailin's lectures covering the modern philosophers. And further, whether to follow the standard course of study at all or to take full advantage of being officially invisible and follow her own whims. The university was a banquet in the grandest style and at the moment she had barely tasted the soup. There would be more than enough time to sort out her dining partners when that first hunger had been appeased.

CHAPTER TWENTY-SIX

Barbara

When they entered the East Gate, Barbara felt a deep tension drain from her body. Which was strange, she thought, for Rotenek presented more hazards and more difficulties than Chalanz ever could. But here she knew who she was, where she stood and what needed to be done.

The first week was over-full of renewing contacts and negotiating new relationships. Matters that had been long established and assumed under the late baron were changed now. There was assistance to be hired. She needed to review all the servants carefully. The temptations and penalties for betrayal were different now. It was even possible that some might consider that their deepest loyalties passed with the title and not with the household. Even familiar surroundings were changed: she had silently abandoned her old room for a smaller one up under the eaves. There was no lack of space on the main floor but she no longer felt comfortable occupying one of the family rooms. It had never truly been hers, only lent for her use. But Rotenek itself— that *was* hers and it was home.

In planning Margerit's protection, Barbara had foreseen the conventional rituals of society and the more practical hazards of the university district. But her own venture into the scholar's life had been a solitary matter and she found she hadn't considered that for

Margerit the two worlds would collide. Antuniet Chazillen's presence among the coterie of girl scholars had been unsettling.

There was no question that Antuniet knew who Margerit was. She gave at least the pretense of polite indifference for now. Whatever her brother might have told her, she was not choosing to be Margerit's open enemy. But Barbara was not yet ready to embrace the truce. She raised the issue as the carriage returned them to Tiporsel. "Maisetra, the name Chazillen should mean something to you."

Margerit looked at her curiously. "There have been so many introductions! I'll learn all the names in time."

Barbara nodded to acknowledge the truth of it. "It's the surname of the new Baron Saveze—Mesnera Antuniet is his sister." She watched the implications sink in.

Margerit frowned a little. "She was perfectly nice. I rather liked her. Do you really think she'll cause trouble?"

"Just remember what Maisetra Waldimen said: never trust a sister. Family will always come before friendship." She was disturbed by the faintly mulish look that came over Margerit's face. It wasn't time to push the matter. She would put a word in Marken's ear.

* * *

LeFevre suggested the next stop on Margerit's grand tour of Rotenek society. "You must go to the opera," he said at the end of one morning's review of accounts. "Everyone goes to the opera. You have a box, you know."

Maisetra Bertrut was clearly far more excited by the prospect than Margerit. While her aunt went into raptures over the prospect of seeing all of society and the music and the fine gowns and perhaps even a glimpse of the princess, Margerit suppressed a look of boredom. Barbara sighed inwardly. Margerit was impatient to move forward with her studies, but this wouldn't do. The mask of a debutante was still important. Maistir Fulpi planned to stay into the new year and would be working tirelessly to promote a good match. If he thought it necessary, he'd drag her back to Chalanz. She must at least pretend to play the game.

The role of advisor was new and uncomfortable. The reflexes ingrained under the baron were to watch, to hold her tongue, to step in to smooth the way without ever criticizing the path. And so she waited for the right moment. In Rotenek they'd lost the habit of their bedtime conference to discuss the next day's plans and needs. There had seemed to be more breathing space—less need to set a united front to the world. But now Barbara again tapped lightly on Margerit's door in the last hours of the evening and slipped through without waiting for an answer.

Margerit's eyes lit up as she entered. "I'm so glad you've come. I've missed this. Maitelen, you can go—I can finish myself." The maid nodded and slipped out.

Barbara gestured vaguely to the house around them. "Is it everything you expected?"

Margerit picked up the brush that Maitelen had been wielding and resumed tending to her hair. "I don't know—I hardly knew what to expect. I suppose I thought…well, this is more comfortable than what I thought. We rattled around so on Fonten Street. But Barbara—" She left the brush hanging for a moment and her eyes were shining again. "To be here at last! Just walking through the square it was like I could hear the echoes of Romazzo and Rodulfus lecturing from the steps before the Chasintalle was built. And all the students bustling around in their robes like…like bees in a hive! There's so much to learn—so much to know." She gave a little laugh.

Barbara bent to a sudden impulse and took the brush from her hand to draw it slowly through Margerit's chestnut curls. She wished she could prolong the moment but there was business to be done. "When you've chosen the lectures you plan to attend we should look through the library and see whether the baron had all the books you'll want. I know something of what's there of the older texts, but he didn't collect the modern philosophers. You can fill in the gaps easily enough. There's an entire street of bookshops off the Plaiz Vezek by the university."

Margerit laughed again. "I asked Verunik what she planned for her reading and she just stared at me. I don't think it ever occurred to her that she might actually learn something. I'll need to be more careful to keep my disguise!"

Barbara saw her opportunity and put the brush down. "Yes, you will."

The serious tone made Margerit turn to look at her.

"Maisetra, may I suggest that you pretend more interest in," she thought how to phrase it, "in the more conventional attractions of a Rotenek season. Go to the opera and enjoy it. Go to the suppers and balls and concerts and talk of something other than philosophy. Let your uncle believe you're open to his 'good match' but you want to take your time. You have the excuse of it being your dancing season…

but only if you dance! You need his complaisance. It's still well over a year before you can think about defying him, if that's what you choose."

Margerit sighed. "You're right, of course. The opera it is. After we go hunting for books!"

* * *

Barbara would not for the world have given up the duty of escorting Margerit on her expedition to Booksellers Lane in the heart of the university district but she gladly left it to Marken to take the late night duties at the opera house. The place held ghosts for her and she wasn't yet ready to face them. And so it wasn't until their return, when he tapped on her door to report in, that she heard the details of what had passed there.

"It seems," he began, "the young Baron Saveze has been confused about whether the opera box went with the title or not."

Barbara's heart raced. *I should have been there!* But the time of their return argued against any serious encounter. "How much trouble did he cause?"

Marken waved his hand dismissively. "Wasn't even there. Only the mother and sister and a few hangers-on. The old lady cut up all stiff but the house manager was there. Knew there'd be a face-off but not worth his trouble to interfere until the maisetra came to town. He set things clear quick enough but the old lady was mortified."

Barbara could just imagine her expression. The late baron's sister was most punctiliously correct in everything she did. She must not have known. "And the maisetra—was she upset?"

"Well now, that was a bit curious. It seems she knows the Chazillen girl and invited them to stay as her guests. You can imagine how Mesnera Chazillen took that! You could have froze a pond with her refusal."

That was interesting, she thought, after dismissing him for the night. There was certainly no harm in Margerit being seen to be a peacemaker but it would complicate matters if she got too close to Estefen's family. Fortunately the Chazillen matriarch was unlikely to forgive her brother's unexpected heir. *Froze a pond.* Yes, she could well imagine the baron's sister pulling together every ounce of pride and delivering a withering refusal from her lofty height.

Elsewhere in the house she could hear the creak of boards and the indistinct murmur of voices as the opera-goers settled in for the night. From her old room she could have told within inches where each person was moving. There were times when the attic felt like exile. The windows were narrow and looked only on the walls of the neighboring house, not the courtyard view she'd had before. She preferred being able to see the comings and goings. At moments like this she thought she would give anything to turn the clock back a year. Anything except knowing Margerit.

CHAPTER TWENTY-SEVEN

Margerit

Margerit tried sincerely to throw herself into Rotenek society. There was no rushing the start of the term and she was only beginning to feel the gulf between the foundations that Sister Petrunel had been able to give her and the structures—the walls, rooms and hallways—that the professors would take for granted in their lectures. But teasing out the players on the social stage was just as deep a puzzle.

In Chalanz, society wasn't just the handful of noble families whose summer villas dotted the outskirts of town. Invitation to one of their balls might be an envied and sought-after prize, but the meat and bread of life was among the pillars of the town: old families, but untitled. The two worlds mingled rarely.

Rotenek was different. The nobly-born and the merely moneyed intertwined on the landscape like roads and rivers. In Chalanz, Margerit found it easy to speak only to those she'd been introduced to because everyone knew everyone. In Rotenek, she was in constant fear of stepping across those solid but invisible fences that wove through every gathering. It was no faux pas to dance with a man of titled family, but heaven help you if you unwittingly addressed him as *Maistir* and not *Mesner*!

Cheristien and Amiz eased her path to some degree: the first because she moved easily among all ranks, the second because she did not. Amiz knew far better the delicate balance required of someone welcome only for the size and cleanliness of her bank account. She might not be out yet herself, but she'd watched both her older sisters tread that path and vicariously charted her own future plans within her advice. Margerit drank up every word. Aunt Bertrut was learning quickly but for the moment she was of little practical use except as *vizeino*, providing the chaperonage expected for any unmarried woman. Her connections—and they were few to begin with—were older women with no marriageable daughters. They neither held nor received invitations to the most sought-after events. And by the complex rules of hospitality Margerit couldn't issue invitations in her own name to anyone she didn't yet officially know or to anyone of higher rank to whom she had no ties.

Barbara knew everyone and all the rules, of course. Margerit found herself on more than one occasion staring across a crowded floor from her aunt's side to the clusters of watchful armins, wishing that Barbara could be there instead: whispering names in her ear, explaining the braided threads of lineage, history and influence that would allow her to make sense of what passed before her eyes.

It was the feast of Saint Mauriz—coming hard on the heels of the start of the term—that gave her the opportunity. A house on the Vezenaf meant the cathedral also counted as her parish church and services there had become familiar. But Saint Mauriz was not only the patron of the cathedral and the district around it but, by extension, of all Rotenek. Like all else in the city, the celebration of mysteries was a complex intertwining of participants. Ordinarily the highest nobility—the prince and his family—attended private ceremonies, ruled by long established guilds and presided over by no priest less than a bishop. But the celebration for Mauriz overlaid the ordinary mystery of the Mass with the pomp of a Great Mystery, intertwined with the familiarity of a local festival, belonging to all whose residence fell within its ambit. And as that extended from the palace to the riverside townhouses, Prince Aukust would preside as the chief lay participant, the same as any mayor in his parish church.

So Margerit led Aunt Bertrut—for Uncle Fulpi declined to attend the mysteries, even for his own namesake, unless he saw some clear benefit—through the crowd of witnesses out in the *plaiz* to take the place guaranteed to them in the nave. Margerit had studied the general forms of the service in Bartholomeus, but his *Lives and Mysteries* dealt in generalities, and what was asked of the common worshippers was little more than the standard responses that she could have performed in her sleep. So she took the opportunity to quiz Barbara on the richly clothed nobles who took the lay parts of honor, welcoming the saint and listing through the *markein* that defined the ritual's scope.

Barbara bent to whisper their names and give their stories. "There is the prince—Aukust Atilliet—there in the seat to the left of the altar by the choir."

"In the blue?" Margerit asked, looking for the one who best fit her image of a prince.

"No, no, the older man. I don't think you will have seen him before. He never goes out in public these days. Not unless he must."

Margerit peered at him as he rose to intone the *invitatio*. His thin gray hair draped limply over his high stiff collar and his eyes were sunken and hollow. But now that she looked again, Margerit saw command and determination in the set of his mouth and the way those deep eyes swept across the crowd. Later in the ceremony, as she recalled from her reading, he would also act in his role as prince, but now he spoke on behalf of the people of the district. To the far side of him sat a tall sturdily-built woman in a gown of that just-out-of-date style that marked it as formal court wear. The traces of a grand beauty still lingered in her dark arching brows and the dainty curve of her mouth, but the eyes below those brows darted back and forth as if she were ever mindful of an audience. "Is that his daughter?" Margerit whispered.

Barbara gave her an odd look. "That's Her Grace the Princess Elisebet, his wife. Second wife. It's true she's younger than his daughter, Duchess Annek, but *she* isn't here of course. She married an Austrian duke back in the middle of the French Wars. The alliance proved useless for the purpose at the time, but at least it saved her from being married off to one of the Corsican's cousins."

"Oh, of course." Margerit thought back to her history books and did the calculations. "She would have been just a child."

A shrug acknowledged the truth of it. "A daughter of royalty grows up quickly. Her brothers fell in the battle of Tarnzais. Prince Aukust knew he was facing surrender. The Austrian alliance was a last chance and there wasn't time for a long courtship."

They rose then to give the responses as they moved into the body of the ceremony and Margerit felt her heart swell as the spirit moved through her and swirled around the columns like vine tendrils in the sun. She recalled what Barbara had said in Mintun in the spring. Did others see the mysteries in drifts of transparent color and soundless music? The vision rose up like bright smoke above the altar and dissipated in the darkness of the arches above. She sighed amid the rustle of the crowd as they sat once more and her mind came back to picking out the unfamiliar faces surrounding the prince.

"The young boy…"

"Yes, that's young Chustin—Aukustin—Princess Elisebet's son. Her only child and that's caused some talk. It's said the prince wouldn't have remarried at all except that a single remaining daughter was a thin thread for the succession, even with a scattering of eligible cousins. She was one of the French exiles—Isabelle de Villemont she was then—but her mother was Baron Perient's daughter so she wasn't too foreign."

Margerit looked back at the fidgeting boy on the ornately carved bench. "Then he will be prince hereafter?"

"Shh! Not here."

Their voices had been pitched low so as not to disturb those near, but Barbara looked around sharply as if to see if anyone had heard.

One of those hidden traps, Margerit thought as she moved on to the next rank of unfamiliar celebrants. As Barbara laid out the web of family connections their faces and names began to settle into patterns in her mind. There was where Estefen's family fit into the pattern. There, an odd gap where an entire lineage had been lost to war and the disease that had come in its wake. And there, the welling up of a new family to fill the gap. New blood could even become noble through the proper refinement, it seemed.

The archbishop turned from the altar to signal the closing exchanges of the mystery and Margerit once again became aware of the currents swirling around her. This time they seemed to circle in the space around the altar like a slow whirlpool. With the final blessing the clear light pooled into one of the faintly carved paving stones at the right-hand foot of the altar and faded away as if it had been a drain. Margerit wished she could go examine the stone to see if it held some clue but now was not the time, for the ceremony shifted to the regular rhythms of the Mass. The dramatic visions that accompanied the special ceremony settled into the almost invisible glow that Margerit associated with the sacraments.

* * *

After the dignified procession of the royal party down the aisle and out the massive doors, the remaining celebrants emerged into the *plaiz* with a burst of chatter and the excitement of a market holiday. Barbara hurried her through the jostling crowd and off to one side where the carriages would meet them. When they paused, Margerit realized Aunt Bertrut had been left behind somehow. No sooner was this discovered than she emerged slowly among the stragglers, leaning heavily on the arm of a strange man. Was he someone they had met at the Aruliks? She tried to match the reddish-blond hair and florid complexion against the names she'd been working to learn.

As they approached, Bertrut began a soft stream of apology, which the stranger ignored steadfastly until they had come up to where the others waited. Then he bowed slightly to Bertrut and murmured, "I think the foot is not too badly twisted, but you have a carriage?"

"Yes, yes," she said in some confusion.

He looked up and Margerit saw him glance at Barbara in recognition and then back to her. His expression worked its way through surprise, calculation and curiosity, but he said nothing further, only bowed again and left.

The carriage came up and as the footman busied himself with the door and steps, Bertrut said, "Barbara, you know him I think. Who was that?"

"One of your neighbors, Maisetra. One of the Pertineks, although not near to the title. Mesner Charul. He lives with his cousin's family in the house with the spiral columns at the gate." She fell silent to help the older woman up the steps.

Margerit followed her aunt in and as the door was shut behind her teased, "Do you have an admirer, then?"

"Don't be absurd," she said quickly. "He was only kind enough to help when I stumbled in the crowd and put a foot wrong."

CHAPTER TWENTY-EIGHT

Barbara

With the feast of Saint Mauriz past, the university term was upon them. Lectures filled half the mornings now and free afternoons were spent studying. Barbara found herself on the move from dawn until late into the night when there were evening invitations. The day visits that had been a staple of Chalanz society were less important here, but they fought for attention as well. The baron's schedule had been less hectic and the house had been quieter in his day. Margerit had declared the library her sanctuary against her guardians and for now they were willing to humor her. Barbara also treasured it as their place of absolute truce: no mistress and no servant, only two scholars in pursuit of truth. It was there that she found Margerit several days after the Mauriz mystery when the new schedule had settled enough to bring them together.

Margerit looked up from her books as she sat beside her and asked, "What couldn't you tell me about the prince's heir?"

Barbara looked over her shoulder by reflex to make sure the door was closed. "It isn't a safe thing to discuss where others can hear. To ask is to speculate. To speculate is to predict. To predict is to plan. To plan could be treason. Princess Elisebet naturally wants her son to succeed. But the law is complex and unclear. The bridal charter for the Princess Iohanna, Aukust's first wife, specified that her children would have first right to the crown." She went to a shelf and pulled down a volume covering the history of the Atilliets. "You see here, in this lineage, Aukust has two cousins and they both have children. The inheritance isn't fixed. The council of nobles elects the successor, though it's rare to go against the prince's will. If Aukust had died," she crossed herself reflexively, "when his children were young, the choice would normally have fallen elsewhere. But Iohanna's family had influence and he needed the alliance at the time. It's said he was also deeply in love. So he pledged that their descendents would have first place."

"But they were killed in the war."

"Only the two sons. Remember that daughter who married in Austria? There's no bar to the female line, if it's determined to hold the best choice. And she has two sons."

Margerit frowned. "Then one of them will inherit?"

Barbara closed the book and returned it to its place on the shelf. "Maybe. There are those who argue that marriage should cut the legal line between a father and daughter. There are some precedents for that position, but it isn't clear if they apply here. Some seem to be purely a matter of timing rather than an absolute barrier. There are others who argue that a contract overrules everything but that can't be true. The prince couldn't have contracted to pass the crown outside his lineage entirely. And even the contract only holds weight because it was approved by the succession council at the time. Most agree that even if Iohanna's children have no special right, Elisebet's don't either. You can tell which line a man favors by the language he uses. The *Charteires*—those who hold by Iohanna's marriage charter—will speak of Aukustin as 'the French woman's son.' Elisebet's supporters—and she's been working hard to gather them—speak of 'the Austrians' and call themselves *Chustines*, though the boy himself is little more than a symbol. In the end, it's for the council to elect the best choice when the time comes. And the prince is an old man." Barbara watched Margerit digest the complexities. "You can see why it's not a subject to debate on street corners. There are duels being fought over questions of allegiance."

Margerit nodded, looking thoughtful. "What did my godfather think about it?"

It was like an unexpected touch on a bruise. She worked so hard not to see the baron in every shadow and hear him behind every door in this house. Maisetra Bertrut had been starting to remake the place to her own taste and style, which helped. But now she could see him there, standing by the glass-paned panels of the door, looking out over the river terraces, speaking coldly to Estefen, *I will not change my pledged word for mere advantage. Even for me, some things are sacred.* And Estefen raging at him for a shortsighted fool.

A small noise brought her attention back to the present. "It wasn't my place to know the baron's political opinions." On second consideration she continued, "Estefen, that is, the new baron supports Princess Elisebet." She let that observation settle into Margerit's awareness, then continued briskly, "It's nothing to concern you and you're well out of these matters but it's good to know the players on the board. Have you read the passage from Erasmus on formalism yet? I remembered that there was a commentary on it in Desanger that specifically applies to that question you had on the Great Mysteries. It might give you some ideas."

The distraction was successful and she watched Margerit cross the room to hunt out the green-bound volume. Did she realize how much more difficult her studies would have been if the baron hadn't been something of a scholar and collector himself? She would have been spending all her time—and a great deal more money—trying to track down rare but essential works for her studies. Or struggling for a share of time in the cathedral library or any of the other paths an ordinary scholar used. But then, if he hadn't had inclinations in that direction, he likely never would have had the whim to send Margerit a private governess from the Sisters of Saint Orisul and she might never have stepped on this path at all. It meant Margerit could study in the security of her own home. She would even have an excuse to invite her new friends to come to her rather than always being out and about. At heart, she found it terrifying every time Margerit left the house in someone else's care. Not that she didn't trust Marken's competence. Not that she doubted Maisetra Bertrut's watchfulness. Not that she was even capable of being at Margerit's side at every moment.

She tried to return her attention to the passages from the Statuta Antiqua that Chunirez's lectures would dissect in the weeks to come. The only thing that kept her from gnawing guilt over the time spent on her own study of law was the belief that it too would some day serve as protection.

When had she started seeing herself watching over Margerit's safety long past the day when the baron's will set her free? Was it sensible to dream that far? She looked up from the page that had been struggling for her attention and gazed across the room. *What will we be to each other when I know my history and my true name? When I know whatever shameful secret the baron concealed all these years?*

The smile that crept over her face every time she looked secretly at Margerit faded. What if that truth drove them apart? She shook the question away. There was no answering it now.

CHAPTER TWENTY-NINE

Margerit

What she had seen—or perhaps experienced was a better word—during the Mystery of Saint Mauriz puzzled Margerit enough that she went back to Bartholomeus. There were so many types of mysteries: the Holy Mysteries of the sacraments, the everyday rituals of praise and worship for telling through in private when you wanted to go beyond the prayers for the day. There were the public mysteries, like that of Saint Mauriz, that invoked aid and protection and prosperity for the community. There were the private rituals of the mystery guilds that had purposes known only to their members. Uncle Fulpi had mentioned once in a sour moment that the Guild of Saint Mark in Chalanz seemed to concern itself more with the state of roads than the state of souls. She knew that professional guilds were often little more than social clubs. Then there were the sharp and desperate pleas—for healing, for mercy, for a son—more often learned by word of mouth than kept in books. Or performed for you by old men and women in the marketplace who claimed to have the ear of the saints. Most who made that claim looked rather in need of the saints' blessings themselves. With their signs and herbs and scribbled charms and rhyming chants the street-corner mysteries were scorned by many as mere superstition but where was the line drawn? Then there were the Great Mysteries, celebrated for the benefit of the nation and performed only by those of the highest rank.

Margerit scribbled notes on what she remembered as she worked out her questions. Saint Mauriz's work partook of the Great Mysteries, but in structure it was an ordinary public *tutela*—a celebration of a patron—merged with the *turris* format used for all manner of protective rituals. In its words and symbols it was meant to seek the saint's blessing on the parish, to ask protection against harm and disease. Back in Chalanz the mystery performed in high summer for Saint Andire had much the same form, using the symbols and images of the fisherman, rather than the warrior. She had expected this one to be similar, but that was the puzzle. She hadn't always noticed visions during Andire's mystery, but when she did, the light flowed up and out from the altar and seemed to pour through the stones and out into the town. But in the Rotenek cathedral that day everything had seemed to swirl around aimlessly and then sink into the floor. She'd read through the text in Bartholomeus again, but it had only the skeleton, not the details of the ritual. She'd never before thought to question the connection between those details and their effects.

When she asked Barbara, she only shrugged. "I've never seen anything like that—only when something actually happens, like the early blossoming at Saint Chertrut's Spring or when Saint Iohen healed the kitchen maid's burn overnight. But she might not have been burned as badly as she thought."

She asked Amiz as they waited for the start of Desalamanca's theology lecture, but she only laughed and asked why it would matter. "Say your prayers and burn a candle to the Virgin and trust the priests to know their own rituals. If you need a charm to get a good husband, I can tell you who has the best ones. But if there were something wrong with Mauriz's mystery someone more learned than you would have noticed."

Margerit knew better than to ask why Amiz was studying theology if not to better understand divine workings. And then the professor began speaking and there was no chance for further questions. But when the session had passed she signaled to Marken that she wanted to stay behind while the others left. There were always a few questioners detaining the professor at the end and she began down the theater steps to join them.

A hand on her shoulder drew her back and Antuniet said, "Don't bother."

As she turned, Margerit saw the two armins shift position with their eyes flicking back and forth from each other to their charges. *It's not just Barbara*, she thought fleetingly. *They all do that: those little movements and looks that say, "this one is watched and guarded."*

Antuniet either hadn't noticed the mutual bristling or considered it of no importance. "He won't answer your questions. What you need to do is make friends with one of the real scholars and ask him to propose them. Don't you know any of them?" She gestured generally at the regular seats.

Margerit shook her head. "Only my cousin Nikule and he...doesn't go to the same lectures." No need to explain why Nikule was the last person on earth she'd ask for favors.

"What were you going to ask?"

Margerit recalled that Antuniet had come in late, after the lecture had started. But she hesitated. If Antuniet had not been particularly warm, neither had she been unfriendly, for all that she had reason. Was it a sincere offer? Amiz had said Antuniet was interested in thaumaturgy so she might have answers.

"It was just something I noticed in Saint Mauriz's. At the feast day. I don't know what it means. In Chalanz, at the public mysteries, sometimes something...happened. But I'm not always sure what I'm seeing."

"You see things?" Antuniet asked sharply. "What?"

Margerit tried to find words to describe it. "Colors...that aren't really there. And music that moves—" She gestured in the air trying to give the shape. "Bartholomeus doesn't say anything about—"

Antuniet snorted. "No, he wouldn't. You're reading a dictionary when you want a history. Next you'll tell me you've tried Fortunatus. Everyone assumes that everything must be found in one or the other." Margerit began to explain but she waved her hand to cut it off. "Oh, they have their place for babies, but if you're seeing visions then what you need is Gaudericus." She stared long and hard until Margerit wondered what response was expected.

"Thank you," she began.

"Not everyone does, you know," Antuniet interrupted, then turned and left without another word.

* * *

The baron's library might have been extensive, but for once it failed her. Even Barbara was stumped. "Are you sure it was Gaudericus? I'm not very familiar with the practical mystics. I know there's a book by Chautirik—but no, that's an atlas of the old pilgrim's road through Nofpunt. Not likely to be what you want." She frowned in thought. "Who was it that suggested the work?"

Margerit felt oddly hesitant to mention Antuniet. She saw how Barbara still went all hackles-up around her. "One of the girls mentioned it—I don't remember who. Back to the booksellers then?" She laughed. "How dreadful!"

Barbara seemed on the verge of questioning her further when the door opened and Aunt Bertrut entered holding a folded paper and with a puzzled expression.

"Margerit, I know you don't like being disturbed when you're studying, but this invitation…"

"You know I trust you to sort them out." Even in a strange city, Bertrut had developed an instinct for what to accept and what to decline. "Is there a problem? What am I invited to now?"

"Only a barge party on the river—I turned it down because of the damp. No, it's not you; it's for me." Her aunt offered her the paper to view.

Margerit ran her eyes down the formal text. Although it would be unthinkable for her to attend dinners and balls alone, Bertrut's expected presence was normally indicated by the simple formula *cum vizeino*, "with escort." But here, in plain black ink on the pale cream-colored paper, was "…request the presence of Maisetra Bertrut Sovitre for dinner…" and tucked between the lines, the formula *"cum vizeino"* as was proper for an unmarried woman.

Margerit looked farther up the page for the identity of the host. Mesnera Pertinek, Lady Marzim. The surname sounded familiar—yes, the kind gentleman at the cathedral. His wife? No, Barbara had said he wasn't near to the title. But at his request perhaps? That would make sense. It wouldn't be proper for an invitation to come from him—not only as a man and a stranger, but as he wasn't master of the house he lived in. And there was the address, just a few doors down, as Barbara had said.

"You've accepted it, of course?" Margerit asked. From the corner of her eye she could see Barbara suppressing an amused grin where her aunt couldn't see.

"I don't know, dear. Why would he—would they be inviting me? I'm nobody."

The obvious answer was too fragile to mention aloud. Margerit suggested slowly, "Well, they're our neighbors…and I don't know if there's anyone in their household that I might meet socially. So if they wanted to become acquainted with their new neighbors, perhaps they thought it more proper to approach you?" It was an unlikely possibility. Nobody in Rotenek worried about becoming acquainted purely on the basis of living on the same street. Either your families had known each other already for generations or one of you was too new for notice.

Uncle Fulpi had the same thought when the matter came up over dinner, but he didn't try to disguise it. "What nonsense! They want something and you'd best take care until you know what it is. It's Margerit they want to get to, though heaven knows why as they haven't any marriageable sons. If you feel you must go, I'll accompany you of course, but it would be better to find some excuse for now."

It was the wrong tactic to take for the desired end. Margerit could tell the precise moment when her aunt's decision was made.

"Mauriz, you are neither my brother nor my father and I'll thank you not to behave as if you were! I'm not being invited off to some den of iniquity, I'm being invited to dinner by Mesner and Mesnera Pertinek, who happen to be well-respected people in Rotenek and happen to be our neighbors. I will be taking Margerit as my *vizeino* and I believe that should suffice to protect my reputation!"

It would more than suffice for propriety, Margerit thought, since it meant that either Barbara or Marken would accompany them— something her aunt couldn't justify on her own account.

Uncle Fulpi angrily waved away the footman who waited silently by the door to the passage. And then again more impatiently when the man hesitated and sought Margerit's assent before slipping through the door. Where, no doubt, he would hear everything that passed as clearly as if he had remained, Margerit thought. But the illusion of privacy must be maintained.

"It seems," her uncle said in an icy tone, "that my presence in this house is superfluous. I have left my affairs in Chalanz unattended for too long as it is. Since my niece seems to have no need of any assistance I can offer, and since some seem determined to plunge my name into scandalous and undignified goings-on, it would seem best for me to return home. Maisetra Sovitre," this was addressed to Bertrut, of course, for he'd never yet promoted Margerit to that dignity, "I will hold you responsible for informing me of any discussions or decisions to be held concerning our ward and I will expect regular reports from that French clerk regarding expenses and funds. Margerit, I leave you to your aunt's care and hope that she has a greater concern for your good name than she has for her own."

And that, it seemed, was his unmovable decision. The next day he ordered his trunks to be packed and arranged for the hire of a coach—declining the loan of her own.

"I will have no one suggest that I am a parasite on my ward's fortune," he said with a meaningful glance at Bertrut.

Margerit saw her aunt redden slightly and held back a hasty defense. It had taken a good deal of persuasion to convince her aunt to let her pay for the gowns and other everyday personal expenses that made the difference between respectability and appearing a dowdy country matron. But now was not the time for more arguments.

"Uncle, I hope…I would like for the whole family to come visit at Christmas. I think the girls would enjoy it." They had already planned the visit. It was the best olive branch she had to offer at the moment. He harrumphed and said he'd consider it and that was as good as a promise to her mind.

* * *

The search for a copy of Gaudericus did not begin well. As soon as she uttered the name of the book, Margerit could tell she'd stepped in deeper than she knew. The shop proprietor, who until that moment had been all obsequious solicitude, composed his face and said evenly, "I'm afraid I'm not familiar with that work."

She tried again, describing the contents that Antuniet had indicated it covered. No change. "I'm afraid I'm not familiar with that book."

So Margerit shrugged and moved on to the next bookseller. His answer was somewhat different, but the tone was similarly quelling. "I have no copies of Gaudericus for sale."

As they turned down a narrow alleyway to find the cramped open stall of her third choice, Margerit studiously avoided catching Barbara's eye. The third merchant said plainly what Margerit suspected the others had been thinking. "What would a young lady such as yourself be wanting with Gaudericus?"

She squirmed inside. "A…a friend recommended it."

"Well," he said, leaning closer over the counter and continuing in an overly familiar tone, "you might want to rethink your friends. But if it's Gaudericus you want, then I suggest you look down on Rens Street. The work's a bit too rich for my taste. The printers still won't touch it, so all there are is hand-copies. I don't have the kind of capital to stock that sort of thing. Try Eskamer, but don't say who sent you."

When they were out of hearing around the next corner, Margerit turned to Barbara at last and ventured, "So…Rens Street?"

"No. Absolutely not." It was clear she had crossed the line from attendant to armin.

Margerit's thoughts pressed forward. It would be Marken with her for tomorrow's lectures. Maybe he…

Her intentions must have shown on her face because Barbara's voice turned pleading. "If you must have the book, I'll find you a copy. But promise me—*promise* me—you won't go off to the wharf district. Not with Marken, not with anyone. Even the baron took armed men with him when he visited his warehouses there. I'm not talking about genteel kidnappings, I'm talking about men who would slit your throat to steal your shoes."

It was that frightened tone more than the words that convinced her. She nodded. Then when that didn't seem enough, she said, "I promise," and was grateful that the question of just who had recommended the book was left lying.

* * *

The dinner at the Pertineks was—after the initial row—remarkably ordinary and even bordering on tedious. Margerit knew that Barbara had paid a formal call on their staff, just as she did for all such events. But this wasn't a formal ball with a gallery of lowering armins, just a small family dinner of ten in the cramped space of a riverfront mansion. After witnessing the reception in the front hall, Barbara had disappeared silently into the understairs realm and Margerit was left to the old familiar tedium of listening to the empty pleasantries of the older generation.

It could almost have been a quiet dinner among the pillars of Chalanz society. Lord and Lady Marzim, it seemed, were the support of a host of unpropertied cousins and bachelor aunts and uncles. As she watched her aunt bask in the gallant charms of her rescuer, it occurred to her that—noble family or no—he might well see it as a step up in the world to trade being the hanger-on of a titled cousin for being the hanger-on of a wife's plebian niece. She suppressed an amused grin. How did one go about these things? Would he apply to her for permission to court her aunt? Well, no need to worry about it yet. Let Aunt Bertrut enjoy a season's flirtation of her own. She was strong-minded enough not to take things badly if it came to naught.

Once again Margerit wondered what Bertrut's own youth had been like. Had she had suitors? Why had she never married? She vaguely knew that the Sovitres had been comfortably enough off. The funds that had given Bertrut a measure of independence—if not comfort—over the years would surely have been sufficient dowry for a respectable marriage. And although being saddled with the guardianship of an orphan niece might have posed a bar, that hadn't happened until well after Bertrut would have been dismissed as on the shelf.

With such speculations distracting her, the dinner passed more quickly. As they strolled the few doors down to home afterward, Margerit tucked her aunt's hand under her arm as an excuse for leaning closely and teased, "What do you think? Will he do?"

Her aunt shushed her in embarrassment, but there was a contented glow about her.

CHAPTER THIRTY

Barbara

The expedition to Rens Street, Barbara determined, called for discretion beyond the ordinary. Disguise, to be precise. For all that the past few years had seen her wearing breeches far more often than skirts, it had never before occurred to her to try to pass entirely as a man. But in her own person, anything she did there would be tied to Margerit. And an ordinary woman would have too many distractions to deal with in that district. So she assembled her preparations down at the end of the gardens, making adjustments to an unfamiliar suit: plain cloth, but a more fashionable cut than what one wore in service, long pants and odd neckcloths and a hat that could be jammed down to overshadow the face. She set out from the small private quay where she'd tied a skiff of the sort used by ordinary working men to travel up and down river within the city. No witnesses would see her leaving by the main entry. When the errand was done, assuming no mishaps, she could return by the same route.

She had left the sword behind, of course, but a serviceable knife, short enough to conceal under the skirts of a coat, took its place. And the uncomfortably large fold of bank notes that Margerit had given her lay concealed in a hidden pocket of the waistcoat. There was no point in making the transaction in disguise only to have the bill sent to LeFevre for payment.

Rens Street was home to a number of small shops that catered to the pawning of a desperate man's last luxuries or to a less public market in small, portable items of high value. Books were not an ordinary item of trade on the street. The first establishment Barbara tried proved as fruitless as the more respectable shops but not, in this case, from any lack of enthusiasm of the proprietor. He could get it— he was certain he could. If the gentleman would come back in two days? Maybe three?

Barbara shook her head. "My client isn't that patient. If I can't find the thing immediately the deal's off." In truth, she was hesitant to risk the same disguise twice.

She had begun with an establishment of at least tolerable repute. But Eskamer had been mentioned by name and perhaps it was best to venture into the lion's den directly.

The place was entered through a door at the back of a wharfmen's tavern. It ran back through the building in a maze of linked rooms and passages. Barbara walked slowly through the dim entrance toward a light at the end of the first passage, trying to project an air of confidence and curiosity. The curiosity was easy.

The pawnshop's rooms were filled haphazardly with all the odd sorts of things one might expect, but one wall was covered with row on row of books. A surprisingly tidy little man with a sharp fox-like expression greeted her from behind a table cluttered at the edges with trinkets and ornaments of uncertain value. There seemed no particular order to the contents of the room, but Barbara suspected he was the sort who could lay hands on any item in his inventory without need to consult a ledger.

"I understand you might be able to supply me with a book," she opened.

His expression might have been amusement or indigestion. "Would that be for pleasure reading or perhaps you have a table that needs propping up?"

"Gaudericus," Barbara answered. "I believe the title is something to do with visions."

He stared at her silently for a minute, stretching into two. Barbara felt she was being evaluated, but for what? The sincerity of her intent? As a possible trap? How deeply did his scrutiny go?

At last he turned silently, signaling her to wait, and returned in several minutes with two slender leather-bound volumes and a third, much thicker, with broken binding and loose boards, held together by several wraps of cotton tape tied about it.

He laid the first two before her. "Fine, clean copies—said to be the work of Raifrit back in the sixties. The first has some unfortunate damage due to damp, but there are a few interesting annotations that appear to have been made by an owner with practical experience. The second is a lovely little piece—an ornament to any library."

Barbara picked each up in its turn and leafed through it with the pretended air of one who is only a courier, verifying the identity of the cargo. "And the third?" she asked.

"Well," the man said, "it depends on your...client. You strike me as an uncommon customer, so perhaps you would be interested in an uncommon item. Back during the wars there was a trunk left in the care of my predecessor with instructions that if it were not redeemed by the end of twenty-five years, its contents were mine to dispose of. As it happens, that term is recently up and you are the first client to inquire about this particular item since it became available. It's highly unusual—perhaps unique."

"Also nearly fallen to dust, I notice," Barbara interjected, recognizing a spiel intended to inflate the price to improbable heights. "My client wants a readable text, not a relic for a curio cabinet."

The man shrugged and made as if to return the tattered volume to its original resting place.

Barbara played along. "But since you've taken the trouble to bring it out, tell me what makes it so unusual."

He turned back and laid the book on the table and began carefully untrussing the ties. "I have my suspicions regarding the owner of that trunk, but never mind that. The text of Gaudericus has been bound together with Petrus Pontis and Chizelek, quite some years ago from the look of it. There's some additional material added to the unused pages at the end. Probably by the last owner, as the hand is quite similar to a number of the more recent glosses and notes elsewhere. The text of Gaudericus is the usual one. Petrus is lacking the end of the fourth chapter. It appears to have been missing when the parts were bound together, but the lack can be supplied easily enough. But Chizelek includes several extensive citations from Tanfrit that are not part of the standard text and, as you know, no originals of Tanfrit are known to survive."

Barbara hesitated before examining the features he had described. She could keep up the mask of a disinterested agent and take one of the finer volumes, which would adequately fulfill her promised errand.

Or she could confirm the man's suspicions that he was dealing with a serious scholar—agent or no—and guarantee a higher price. She carefully turned the pages to confirm the presence of the promised citations. Petrus was the only author she recognized from the list. Fortunatus was as far as she'd gone in the mystics, and that for his logical arguments and because he was, after all, a classic. But Fortunatus dealt in theory; these texts addressed practice.

"I think my client might be interested, but I also think your price will exceed what I'm authorized to pay."

"And what is your authorization?"

Barbara laughed out loud. It broke all the rules and customs of bargaining. On impulse, she named the precise sum she carried.

He gently closed the book and tied it securely again with the tapes. Barbara was just about to reopen negotiations for one of the slimmer, finer volumes when he pulled a sheet of heavy paper from a shelf under the table and began wrapping the book into a nondescript and sturdy package. After tying it up in an intricate net of string, he finally looked again at Barbara with an eyebrow quirked.

She nodded and turned away slightly to extract the sheaf of notes from its hiding place. The two exchanged hands simultaneously and the money disappeared with a practiced motion. "If your client has any other needs, it would be a pleasure to do business again," the man concluded. But he didn't offer a hand to shake.

Barbara simply nodded once more and left.

* * *

If she hadn't been taking such pains to move unrecognized, she might not have noticed that she was being followed. He was a very ordinary-looking man—the sort you might see on any street corner. But not on *every* street corner. And now that she'd taken note of him, she thought perhaps this wasn't the first time she'd seen him.

Trying not to give any hint of her notice, she changed her route with a thought to drawing him off to a more lonely place and ensuring that she had only one tail to deal with. There was an empty warehouse she knew of—not one of Margerit's, that would risk tying the matter back to her. Once, the building had stood along the branch of the river that ran behind Escarfild Island. But when the river shifted and that branch silted up it had been allowed to decay and now the flooring was too uncertain to store anything substantial. In another decade, it would collapse in on itself and no doubt fresh buildings would take the debris as a foundation. But for now, it was a place where one could have hopes of having a private conversation…or leaving a body where it might take some time to be found.

As she slipped through the broken door—taking care to leave clear footprints in the muddy road running by—it occurred to her that simply disposing of him would not only be simpler but would be safer as well. If she could manage even minimal surprise, she had no doubts of her ability to kill a man efficiently. But disabling and immobilizing him enough for questioning—that was another matter. The most important rule that her first instructor had impressed on her was that if she let it come to grappling, she had already lost the fight. That rule held whether he had only a knife or carried a pistol.

If it were still the baron she answered to, she would have felt on surer ground. That was a conversation they had had when she first learned to fight. But Margerit…she tried to imagine asking, *Maisetra, under what conditions may I kill on your behalf without asking permission first?* And then, the baron had had enough influence not to worry about repercussions. Margerit didn't have the same resources. So it was necessary to be more careful and thus to take more risks.

She eased her way around the edge of the room, avoiding the rotted spot in the center where the boards sagged and dodging around the empty crates still littered about. She laid the book in its wrappings on top of a crate by a window whose shutters hung crazily enough to let in a band of light. Just so—so that he'd see it and move *that* way. She stripped off the fashionable coat and hat and stuffed them out of sight behind the box. Her pinned-up hair would give her away if he saw it, but that was the least of her worries at the moment. Using the sturdiest of the crates she leapt up to grab a rafter and swung herself up into the shadows under the roof. *Blessed Saint Barbara watch over me!* she thought—not a proper prayer, but perhaps her namesake wouldn't mind.

When he came through the door she froze. He did as well— looking and listening until he was satisfied. No pistol in sight, so she didn't have that to worry about. He advanced cautiously across the floor until he felt the weak spot, then retraced and looked around again. As she'd planned, he spotted the package. She'd been carrying it openly enough; he would know it for hers.

He scanned the room again, saw her tracks in the dust and followed them along the safe footing. When he passed beneath her, she dropped.

There were three possibilities. She could hit him harder than she meant and have a corpse to dispose of after all. She could miss her mark entirely or fail to bring him down. Or…she swung against his back, knocking him forward, and grabbed his coat to ensure she followed him down to knock the wind out of him. She didn't pause to see if she'd knocked him senseless but pulled off her stupid fashionable neckcloth and used it to tie his hands behind him. He groaned and tried to kick as she used his own less savory cravat to do for his ankles. Then she stepped back out of the reach of any thrashing and retrieved her coat and hat. The truth was better kept under another layer and the hat once again hid her pinned-up braid. Secure in her masculine disguise, she drew out her knife and skirted carefully around her prisoner to where he could see her.

"Explain yourself," she said coldly.

There was a flash of panic in his eyes as he took in what had happened, but it was replaced immediately by bravado. No doubt, Barbara thought ruefully, he had correctly concluded that if he were still alive at this point he was likely to remain so. A pity, but there was no help for it.

She crouched closer—still out of reach of even the most extreme contortions—and twiddled the knife so that it caught his eye. "Explain yourself," she repeated.

"I don't suppose I could have been looking for a dry place to sleep," he offered without any attempt at sincerity.

Barbara shook her head.

"Did you think to slip around unseen? He knows who you are. He's always known."

"He?" Barbara prompted.

"My employer."

A long minute stretched out as she waited for him to continue, but no details were forthcoming. "And why should your employer be concerned with my comings and goings?"

"He wants what's his. He's been patient a long time but his patience is running thin."

Estefen, she thought immediately. That was no surprise. But what was his angle in this? "Tell the baron that he should trade patience for resignation. He's received everything that's his. The rest belongs to others. And you might want to consider that the last hireling of his I crossed paths with is dead."

Genuine confusion crossed the man's face mingled with the return of fear. "Baron? I know better than to get tangled up with titled folk. This is strictly business." He added with a touch of panic, "You get no special license for killing me over your own private affairs."

Barbara laughed outright at that. "I have no private affairs. If this is nothing to do with my…ah…employer, then you have the wrong mark entirely." She stood up and slipped the knife back in its sheath. She could safely leave him. Eventually his shouting would bring someone to cut him loose.

"Oh no, Barbara No-name. My employer knows exactly who his debtors are."

She froze. It wasn't the piercing of her male disguise—she'd known that would fool only casual observation—or the use of her name. It was the implication of some deeper truth. One that even she wasn't privy to. "If your employer knows that much, then he knows I haven't a penny of my own and he can whistle for whatever debts he claims."

"I'm sure there must be someone who considers your life of some value. Perhaps some legacy you could lay hands on? Your mistress has a few pretty pennies and might find it worth it to—"

The knife was back out in a flash and pressed closely into the line of his jaw. "Now you do make this about the maisetra and within my legal mandate. Would you care to reconsider?"

When she released the pressure sufficiently to allow him to speak he offered, "I'll take your answer back to my employer."

Seeing that he believed her intent, Barbara withdrew before his fear drove him to struggle further. Always best to keep the illusion of control. "I'll be watching for you." And as an afterthought, "All of you."

After she had retrieved the book and was heading for the door he made a small noise. Without looking back she said, "Shout if you like."

CHAPTER THIRTY-ONE

Margerit

Aunt Bertrut's strictures about an afternoon lay-down before a late evening were finally beginning to make sense. Feminine frailty had nothing to do with it; early mornings over readings and translations made for a long day. Margerit glanced at the angle of the pale wintry sun and it told her Maitelen would soon come scratching on her door to lay out the evening's clothing. But this time she began with, "Maisetra, that armin wants to speak with you."

Margerit wrapped a dressing gown around herself, not wanting to go to the trouble of dressing twice, and said, "I wonder what it is that Barbara can't take care of."

"Barbara isn't back yet," the maid offered.

She felt a twinge of guilt and concern. Had book shopping indeed turned into a hazardous venture? If there were anything sure in the world, it was Barbara's reliability. She hurried downstairs and down into the servants' level where she found Marken waiting.

"I'm supposed to be off tonight," he began with his usual lack of ceremony, "but she's not back yet and I know you're planning to go out and she'd have my hide if I left you on your own." Margerit had noticed that for Marken there was always only one "she." He seemed to regard Barbara with an odd combination of the affection due a younger sister and the deference due a commanding officer. "So I was wondering," he continued, "if she'd mentioned anything about it to you?"

Margerit shook her head, but before she could feel serious concern, there was a bustle in the corridor leading off to the back gardens and Barbara herself entered, carrying two bundles. The roll of clothing tucked under one arm was of no interest, but the other was a large, rectangular, paper-wrapped package.

Barbara took in the scene and gestured briefly to Marken, in a single movement acknowledging and releasing him. Then she held out the package to Margerit saying, "I suggest you wait to examine it until you have plenty of time."

She sighed. "I suppose it wouldn't do to send my excuses to Maisetra Enien because I'd rather stay home and read!"

* * *

Throughout the evening she almost managed to leave off thinking of the package—now lying on the library table—long enough to make pleasant conversation over dinner. And she kept herself from mentioning the acquisition when she briefly saw Antuniet at the concert afterward, in part lest Barbara should overhear and make guesses and in part because she wanted to wait until she had something of substance to discuss.

But when midnight had passed and she was back home and had changed her gown for nightclothes, she sent Maitelen to bed and took up a candle to slip back downstairs to the library. She had expected the room to be dark and cold. Instead a cheery fire was glowing in the grate and all the lamps were lit. And in her usual chair, next to the table where the unopened package lay, Barbara waited with an amused smile playing on her lips.

A laugh burst out. "You know me better than I do myself! I swear I planned to wait for morning."

As she picked the knots out of the string and gently unwrapped the volume, Barbara stood beside her and told a tale like something out of a gothic novel: cramped rooms filled with sinister objects and a mysterious proprietor; secret treasures and the fortunes of war; and speculations that might be made of the book's history. Margerit guessed that the tale was both embroidered for effect and edited for—well, there seemed to be odd gaps, but no doubt Barbara had her reasons.

When she opened the cover, trying not to damage the binding more than time and ill-handling already had, the significance of what had come into her hands struck her. On impulse she turned and threw her arms around Barbara exclaiming, "I knew you'd find it! I knew it! This is—"

She turned back to the table. Barbara's arm had begun a movement but it shifted to resting across her shoulder as they both bent over the book and began to take stock of its contents in greater detail.

By the time the lamps began to gutter and require trimming a third time, there was a sheaf of papers with closely-spaced notes and lists scattered across the table. As Barbara made the rounds to adjust the lamps, she coughed deliberately and Margerit looked up to see the palest glow of dawn peeking through the curtains. And now that she listened, in the depths of the house she could hear the sounds of the kitchen staff beginning their day.

"Aunt Bertrut will kill me," she muttered without conviction.

"More likely she'll kill me," Barbara offered, and grinned. "But that's my job, after all—to throw myself in the path of danger for your sake!"

Margerit found herself yawning uncontrollably as if the mere realization of the hour had brought on exhaustion. "I suppose it's too late to sneak into bed unnoticed and too early to claim I've already slept. There's no help for it. At least I have no classes this morning."

"Whereas I," Barbara countered, pulling back the curtain to gauge the hour more closely, "have a lesson with Perret in less than two hours."

"Oh! I'd forgotten," Margerit said contritely.

Barbara turned back from the window. "Nonsense. Do you think I expect you to keep track of my duties? And did you think I'd miss out on this?" She swept her arm out to take in the product of their night's work. "I'll do well enough. Perret will say it's good practice to work tired."

Margerit tidied their working notes and weighted them against errant drafts. The servants knew better than to move or disturb anything in this room. She began snuffing the wicks on the lamps—there would be enough stray tendrils of dawn to find her way up to bed—when a stillness made her look up. Barbara was tracing a finger over the decorations on the book's cover and considering it with a fixed gaze.

"What is it?" Margerit asked.

"Who was it who told you to read Gaudericus?"

Last time, she had evaded the question. It occurred to her briefly to lie. But then a guilty anger bubbled up insider her. "Antuniet," she said, trying to keep her voice neutral rather than defiant.

If Barbara had questioned her—had warned her or given so much response as a weary sigh—she would have been ready with her defense. But she said nothing; did nothing except turn back to close the curtains against the now-rosy light.

Against all logic, Margerit felt angry. The camaraderie of the night had faded away. She pulled her robe more closely about her and left without another word.

CHAPTER THIRTY-TWO

Barbara

Although LeFevre came by the house two or three times a week for ordinary business, Barbara had questions for him that were not ones she cared to have overheard. So at her next free afternoon she made her way to the Lamsiter district that he called home in Rotenek. He'd always declined the baron's offer to take residence at Tiporsel, preferring a small measure of privacy and independence. His apartment itself was fairly small—just a few simply furnished rooms above his business offices which he shared with his secretary Iannipirt. Barbara knew the appearance was deceiving: he owned the entire block in which those rooms were located. Another man might have picked up a taste for luxury from associating with the baron but LeFevre's bond with him had been forged in the early days when ruthless penny-pinching and shrewd dealings had built the fortune that made the later luxuries possible.

The office door was locked, as might be expected at a time when businessmen took dinner. No late hours in this part of town. She pulled at the bell that would ring upstairs and in a few minutes Iannipirt was there, greeting her as an old friend. He motioned her up the stairs ahead of him, not so much for courtesy as from the stiffness of an old wound. That wound and his raffish moustache were the only souvenirs he'd kept from a brief stint conscripted into the hussars during the French Wars.

LeFevre rose from the table in some concern on seeing her. "There's nothing wrong?"

"No—that is, Maisetra Sovitre is well. I—" She looked over at Iannipirt as he bustled to clear a pair of plates from the table. "I want to ask about…a personal matter."

He looked at her oddly for a moment then laid a hand on the other man's arm and said, "Ianni, leave that for now. Could you set us up with some tea then make yourself scarce?"

When they were alone, Barbara found it easiest just to pour out the tale of her shadow and the confrontation. She would have preferred to leave out the matter of the book, but then how to explain her disguise? And it would be against a lifetime of habit to lie to him. There was no one alive who knew more of her secrets, not even her confessor. He listened carefully and nodded occasionally and when she had finished asked, "And so?"

Here Barbara faltered. "I know there are things you can't…you may not tell me. But what if the secrets of my past make me a danger? Who is this man? And what does he think I can pay him?"

LeFevre sat silently, staring into the bright coals that did double-duty in warming the room and heating the kettle. It was the same look he had when calculating long sums so Barbara waited patiently for the equation to resolve.

"The baron had his reasons," he began at last. "Even if he'd had none except his whim, my tongue would still be tied. But there are reasons still current why you must remain in the dark. I *can* tell you that those reasons will end when the terms of the baron's will are fulfilled, and you may know however much you choose on that day. But there are plans still in train that would be marred or broken beyond repair if the wrong people knew all the baron's secrets. Even I don't know all his secrets," he added.

Barbara stood and began to pace impatiently. "But the danger is *now*. I'm being followed and watched. And if I'm being watched then Marg—Maisetra Sovitre is being watched."

"And is she doing anything that won't bear watching?"

She turned on him and said, "No!" a bit too hastily. "But I don't like it. And he threatened to make the Maisetra pay whatever this debt is I'm supposed to owe."

"No," LeFevre said confidently. "He tried to make you *believe* that he could make her pay—which nearly got him killed, I understand.

But he has no power to touch her by law. And if he tries other means, that's what your protection is for. And—believe me when I tell you this—he currently has no power to touch *you* by law."

She frowned at him uncertainly. "How do you know?"

"Let me—hmm." He tapped a finger against his lip as if working through a problem. "I believe I can thread my way between the baron's commands to give you something of an understanding. Let me think on it."

He escorted her down through the office to the street but at the moment before taking leave another thought came to her.

"What do you know of Charul Pertinek?"

LeFevre shrugged. "A nice enough fellow from all I've heard. A neighbor of yours, isn't he? The family are sound but they've tended to breed beyond their income. I think there was some illness in his youth that kept him from trying military life. No politics that I'm aware of. He—" An incredulous expression came over his face suddenly. "He's never made a play for Maisetra Sovitre!"

Barbara grinned. "Well, yes, perhaps. But not the one you're thinking of."

"The aunt?"

Barbara nodded and he shook his head wonderingly.

"There's nothing been said in so many words yet, but—" She shrugged. "I find it hard to believe he's fallen madly in love, as they say. But neither does he seem to have illusions of fortune-hunting. Still and all—"

"—perhaps I might make discreet inquiries?" LeFevre finished for her.

"Only because it touches on the maisetra's security," she added hastily.

"Of course." Unexpectedly he burst out laughing. "Oh Marziel! You had no idea how far the ripples would spread!" And to her, "Go, go. I'll see what can be done."

She was left wondering which of her errands he covered with that assurance.

CHAPTER THIRTY-THREE

Margerit

It was nearly a week before she'd worked her way sufficiently through Gaudericus's circuitous prose to begin answering the question that had sparked her interest. There had been promise enough at the beginning. That was clear from the allegory with which he began.

A blind man may shoot an arrow, but how can he know whether the target is struck? A one-armed man may tell him where the arrow strikes, but if he has never pulled a bow, how can he tell him how to improve his aim? A charlatan will shoot ten arrows then name the targets after they are home. In battle, forty archers loose a flight of shafts and one strikes the enemy, but each man takes the credit. So it is with the working of mysteries.

Barbara had said something much the same on that day they first debated Fortunatus together. The Mechanistic Heresy she had called it: the idea that the mysteries could be teased out into equations and formulas if only one knew how to measure them. Fortunatus may have flirted with the heresy but Gaudericus was a serious mechanic.

It was another thing entirely to move from that promise of understanding to its fulfillment. Gaudericus seemed to have created his own language to describe his philosophies: a bastard mixture of the Latin of formal theology with bits of Greek that he used to distinguish his own theories and occasionally a wordless glyph when all available language failed.

At first, Barbara dove as deeply into the text as she did, sorting out the places where he left familiar paths to strike out into the wilderness. Barbara's Greek was far better than her own and better suited to the obscure language of Gaudericus's code. But when it came to matching the text's descriptions with her own experiences and memories she could sense Barbara's growing frustration.

"You talk about *charis* and *periroe* as if you could see it right in front of you!" she burst out one evening after another puzzled description of the oddities at the cathedral.

Antuniet's words came back to her. *Not everyone does, you know.* Did Antuniet see things? She wasn't ready to ask. There was something in the other woman's cool aloofness that made her want to be sure of her own ground first before exposing herself. Now that she was analyzing them, she saw her memories in a new light. Her childhood visions were coming back in more clarity through the habits of dismissal and denial that had been imposed on her. It was time to unlearn those habits—to stop simply accepting the movement of trees and clouds and re-learn to see the wind.

Margerit put her pen carefully back in the stand and rubbed her eyes. When she started thinking in Gaudericus's flowery metaphors it was time to stop for the day—the night, really. Once again she'd outlasted any trace of movement downstairs. She felt a twinge of guilt. Barbara had long since gone to bed but Maitelen would be waiting up for her, or more likely napping in the chair by her fire. Margerit had once suggested that she didn't need to wait up when she was only studying and didn't have the complexities and ornaments of an evening gown to undo, but Maitelen had responded tartly that she hoped she knew her job better than that.

Once she was changed into nightclothes and alone again, Margerit slipped out of bed for one further question. It seemed strange that she couldn't recall ever noticing the *fluctus*—the swirling flow of colors that tracked the forces at work—during her private prayers and celebrations of minor mysteries. It only appeared during the formal public rites. She pulled out the small medallion of her name-saint that she always carried and called to mind the oldest of the daily mysteries she'd learned. One she knew best by heart. The familiar Latin formulas rolled off her tongue almost without thought.

She strained her perception, trying to see actively what had always been a passive thing before. Nothing. Was it a matter of setting? Did it need more people? Was it the nature of the petition? Was it that she, herself, was only a Seer and not a Doer? But no, there had been Chertrut's blossoms. For all that Gaudericus took a practical approach, her questions still seemed more specific than his answers. Perhaps the best plan was to begin where she had last seen the greater effects. Not at Sunday's Mass; the Holy Mysteries just…were. If anything, the contemplation of Christ emptied her mind rather than filling it with visions. No, she'd try afterward, when people stayed behind in the cathedral for more personal and pointed conversations with the saints. That would be the time to watch and see what was to be seen.

* * *

Aunt Bertrut was not so much surprised as amused at her apparent sudden devotion. "Is there something in particular you need to pray for?" she teased.

"I'm…studying," Margerit offered as explanation. "There's no need for you to stay. Barbara will be with me, of course."

And Mesner Pertinek, who had happened by no chance to be standing near, offered quietly to see her aunt home. Margerit saw him exchange the briefest of glances with Barbara and found herself wondering what might have passed between them in those hidden negotiations of the world of armins. At what point did Bertrut's personal life become Barbara's professional concern?

"Take the carriage," she offered. "I don't know how long I'll be and it wouldn't do to leave the horses standing. We can walk home." Indeed, it was only the rules of fashion that made a carriage necessary for the short trip to the cathedral at all.

When the others had been swept away in the crowd of departing worshippers, Barbara asked, "What do you have in mind?" Her tone implied some doubt of the stated purpose. Margerit realized that she hadn't had an opportunity earlier to share her plans.

"Watching some small mysteries. I didn't ask—that is, I know I don't usually need you after Mass on Sundays."

Barbara shrugged, but it was the shrug that said whatever plans she may have had were set aside.

Those coming to the church to work personal mysteries, Margerit reasoned, would choose the side chapels: the spaces and altars dedicated to the favored saints of the city. She chose the Lady Chapel as her starting place, mostly for the greater traffic it saw. On the opposite side of the aisle from the chapel proper, set against a screen that stood between two pillars, there was a plain wooden bench. Margerit settled herself where she could easily see all those who knelt at the altar, bringing candles, relics, prayers and the other essentials of their petitions. She schooled her mind to a waiting—if not entirely patient—stillness.

Although the Virgin's petitioners were many—there were rarely fewer than six or eight figures present—it seemed nearly an hour before the first hint of *visio* brushed against her senses. It came when an elderly woman, a widow by her clothing, drew out a slip of folded paper. She spread it out and tilted it to catch the flickering candlelight. As she stumbled indistinctly through the words written on it, the paper seemed to take on a soft glow. Margerit caught her breath and leaned forward. From the corner of her eye she saw Barbara stiffen and shift her stance to look around, then relax once more. Now the widow folded the paper once more and lit a candle from one of those already burning around the base of the altar. She held the twist of paper into the flame. The light flared, blooming into a quickly-fading haze that enveloped the woman's hands until the heat of the flame forced her to flick the last scrap into the pooled wax beside the wick. The widow seemed to notice nothing. She whispered her way automatically through an *Ave* then crossed herself and struggled to her feet and moved slowly out of sight through the next archway.

If she had looked away for two minutes she would have missed it. From another angle, the *concrescatio*—the flare when the petition was concluded—might have been lost against the light of the earthly candles. And from the look of patient resignation on the widow's face at her departure, she had no knowledge that her supplication had been heard so clearly. What had she asked for? The shape of her petition was a common one, differing only in the nature of the verses, the symbols on the paper and the saint to whom they were addressed. Gaudericus had indicated that the form of the *visio* would often echo the nature of the mystery, but as always he had been maddeningly unclear. Perhaps something to do with her hands? But that could mean anything from relief for rheumatism to a plea for skill in some work.

While she was still contemplating those questions, a second flicker of *fluctus* caught her eye but this time it was brief and off to one side. By the time she had turned her head to follow it, it was gone.

When another hour had passed, Margerit had learned one important lesson: she had been looking too large. The splendid swirls and swellings of color of the formal public mysteries were as the noonday sun to starlight. And like starlight, the flickers and glows of these small personal mysteries were often best seen obliquely. On two occasions, when she stared directly, only mundane objects remained, but when her eyes slid past, the other light returned.

She was beginning to suspect one other thing that Fortunatus had hinted at. The notice of the saints—if that was indeed what she perceived—was not granted for need or for devotion or for depth of learning or even to those most in want of grace. The young mother, come to plead for the life of a child wracked with fever, was lit only by the golden candlelight. An older man who had not brought any petition at all but was making a circuit of the side chapels was followed by the faintest of afterglows as he moved, as if his whole self were a mystery waiting to be invoked. The young man in scholar's robes who laid out the paraphernalia of an elaborate invocation stirred a bright, complex vision that dissipated abruptly, leaving him untouched by the Virgin's blessing. For some who were touched, the *fluctus* sometimes seemed to come from within; for others it centered on the objects and actions of their celebration. Once, when a cloaked figure passed by without pausing, the altar itself shimmered briefly, like the ripples on a lake caused by a passing breeze.

Margerit finally stood, stiff from the chill, knowing that if she were seeing more now than when she sat down, it was because she was learning how to look. And to listen, though she was far less confident that she could distinguish the ordinary noises of the echoing space from any whispers of the saints. But now she knew that if she could learn to look properly, there was much to observe.

She could tell that Barbara was all curiosity but she wouldn't ask here in public. Margerit leaned close so her whispers wouldn't intrude on others. "I want to go look at the floor by the main altar. The strangeness during Mauriz's ritual seemed to happen there."

In appearance, it was much like the space near every cathedral altar—at least, those that had stood for more than a handful of centuries. Tiles that once had formed careful and artistic patterns were patched with repairs and renovations and intruded on by flat stones whose inscriptions were lost to long years of footsteps. Most of those would mark the graves of men prominent enough in life to earn a more holy resting place after death. Somewhere below, if tradition were believed, was the chamber housing the relics of Mauriz, dating back to the founding of the first church on this site. Once there might have been a stone marking that location, but more likely it had been assumed that the knowledge would endure down the years. And stones might be moved, new foundations laid. The cathedrals of capital cities outgrew their origins and were rebuilt time and again, erasing the traces of the original plans.

Margerit closed her eyes and tried to remember just where it was that the swirling lights had seemed to settle. A meaningful cough from Barbara's direction brought her attention back. A man in priestly vestments was approaching with an expression poised to choose between helpfulness and officiousness. Margerit didn't recognize him from the earlier service but there were any number of junior priests at an institution of this size.

"Is there anything you need?" he asked.

She considered an evasive reply. There was no predicting what his opinion might be of women scholars and she wasn't even certain how to phrase her request. But it was no small thing to speak anything but truth to a priest.

"I'm a—I'm studying at the university and I was…curious about something that happened during the *tutela* Mass for Saint Mauriz."

"Perhaps I could explain if you wish."

Margerit shook her head without thinking how it would look. "It wasn't that. It was something I saw—something…"

She must have given a certain emphasis to the word "saw" because a look of unexpected understanding came over him. "Are you blessed with *phasmata* then?"

She nodded with relief at not having to explain.

"I am not so fortunate," he continued, "but our late archbishop—it was said he sometimes heard the singing of angels during the mysteries. Was that your question? Is this the first time you've seen them?"

"No, not the first," Margerit explained. "It was…there was something different about the service than what I've seen back in Chalanz."

"Chalanz?" he echoed. Another layer of understanding dawned. "You're the Sovitre girl, aren't you?"

Margerit could hear what he didn't say: *the heiress*. But it showed in the more conciliatory tone to his voice.

"Naturally you must understand that the forms of the mysteries will be different here than in the country." He sounded as if he envisioned Chalanz as a market crossroads, peopled with farmers and superstitious charm-wives.

She tried not to be offended. "I was trying to remember the forms of the ceremony—what the priest was doing when I had the visions. Bartholomeus only has the general order but none of the liturgy itself. Is it written anywhere?"

"Of course. We keep an *expositulum* for every mystery performed here. Let me—you say you are a scholar at the university?" From his tone she knew he'd placed her with the mere dabblers. "Then you know how to handle books, I assume. I think I might get you permission. I'll give your name to our librarian. Come back on an ordinary day and ask for the clerk Iohannes. He'll help you find what you want."

* * *

It had gone far better than she feared, despite the priest's maddening condescension. So the previous archbishop had been an *auditor*? That made her doubt her concerns. Surely he would have noticed if Saint Mauriz's rites were flawed in some way. What had led her to think she had made some momentous discovery? But she would see it through and if nothing else today's exercise had brought her a step closer to understanding Gaudericus.

CHAPTER THIRTY-FOUR

Barbara

As Barbara watched over Margerit's vigil in the Lady Chapel, what struck her was how difficult it might be to distinguish divine visions from madness. It was one thing to read a philosopher's discussion of *charis* or *fluctus*, but it was deeply unsettling to see Margerit start at nothing and watch her eyes dart here and there following...what? Small wonder that few people discussed such things openly. How many *vidators* had chosen to doubt their own senses and keep a fearful silence? How many had been thought possessed? Not all visions had divine origins; who was to tell the difference? She had learned enough of Margerit's childhood to see how she might have balanced between those paths. So much of what she loved had been dismissed as irrelevant by her guardians. This would have been only one more thing that was never discussed between them. But the rest of the world might not be inclined to that benign neglect. A word, at the right time, might save future grief.

The unexpected watch in the cathedral meant that it wasn't until Tuesday afternoon that she was able to learn the results of LeFevre's interview with Mesner Pertinek. Perhaps that was for the best. It would have been a conversation most comfortably held between men alone. She was trailed again on her way to LeFevre's office. Now that she was watching for them, there had been more than one occasion when she was certain she'd spotted her unknown creditor's men. Never following as closely as the last time—and not the same man— but neither trying for concealment. She met their eyes, glared daggers and ignored them. So long as they never tried to follow north of the river they were no more than an annoyance.

But still she mentioned the matter to LeFevre. "Have you decided what you can tell me? It would help to have some idea of who they answer to."

He took out one of his calling cards and wrote a few lines on the back then set it aside for her to take when the ink was dry. "Read this commentary on the *Statuta Antiqua Alpenniae*. It's a start, at least, and not one that breaks my word. It won't explain anything important," he cautioned, "but it should give you reason to trust that you're in no legal danger. For what they may do outside the law?" He shrugged. "There's never any defense against that except to be careful."

They went from the front office into the smaller room in back where there would be no interruptions from casual business matters.

"He does intend marriage," LeFevre began with no other introduction. "He understands now that Maisetra Bertrut has no significant income of her own. Even so, he himself suggested that it be tied up beyond his reach."

"But…why?" Barbara wondered, waving a hand to encompass the situation as a whole.

LeFevre fixed her with a thoughtful gaze. "He's a lonely man. Oh, to be sure, the house is crowded enough—too crowded I think for anyone's comfort. But he's been trapped by his birth as surely as any debutante. Too well-born to take on a profession that could support a wife. Not well-born enough to attract an heiress. Too poor to support a household on his own. If I may be indelicate, I doubt he's lacked entirely for female company, but he could hardly afford the class of mistress who could be a true companion for a man of his taste and education. Maisetra Sovitre came to his attention and he learned enough about her to think he might have something of value to offer in exchange for her hand and what comes with it."

It sounded remarkably cold-blooded when put that way but no more so than most matches. "What is it he has to offer? I assume he expects to take up residence at Tiporsel. Whatever allowance he receives from his family must be barely enough for him to make a respectable presence in society."

LeFevre held up a finger to stop her there. "That is exactly what he offers: a respectable presence in society. I confess that I've been uneasy since Maistir Fulpi returned to Chalanz. However useless he may have been as a social escort, the presence of a man in the household makes a difference. And there will certainly be doors that will be opened for Maisetra Margerit by a Pertinek that couldn't be opened by money alone. The advantages are hardly one-sided."

Barbara made a wry face as a thought came to her. "And will she then become Mesnera Bertrut? That would take some getting used to."

He waved dismissively. "I doubt it. There would be no real advantage to it and I doubt she'd care to be burdened by the requirements of the rank. She doesn't strike me as the sort to be dazzled by the illusion of nobility and we can hardly expect that there will be children to think of. No, I think they'll choose the simple contract and she will be plain Maisetra Pertinek."

"If she accepts."

LeFevre chuckled. "Yes, if she accepts! I don't know her well enough to guess at that, do you? But I think he won't delay long in making the offer." He laughed again. "Mesner Pertinek mentioned that he had been expecting something like our little chat but hadn't the vaguest idea who to approach. I assured him that there were no brothers or cousins lurking in the wings—that she was *femina sola*—but that if she asked I would be happy to draw up the contracts and settlements for her approval. He seemed much relieved. I don't think it would have suited his dignity to beg permission from some *burfroi* to pay her suit."

It wasn't until she had returned home that Barbara remembered the scribbled card still sitting on LeFevre's desk. It hardly mattered—he'd admitted he could tell her nothing important. It was hardly likely there was anything in the ancient legal tract that could help her deal with her shadows. Only time could unravel that puzzle.

* * *

Barbara put less stock than Margerit had in the promise of access to the cathedral library. But whether it was an unexpected respect for the sincerity of her scholarship or a less surprising respect for the likely size of her donations, the name Sovitre had indeed been passed on to the clerk who oversaw the books and archives and they were allowed to enter and grudgingly told to request what they would.

"I was told you had a written text for the ordering of the public mysteries performed in the cathedral," Margerit explained.

He only grunted and disappeared for some time among the shelves, returning with an old-fashioned tome whose binding might have been almost any color before centuries of handling turned it black. He set it out on the central table, shared only with two young boys who seemed to consider their time there more punishment than treat. The librarian's laconic demeanor dropped briefly as he recited a long list of instructions. "The book stays on the table; when you're done, you call me. Corners only, no smudges. If you can't read without dragging your finger across the page you don't belong here. No pricking, no underlining. No notes."

It would have been the height of condescension if it weren't so clearly a rote speech. Barbara had heard it many times before, back when it had been the baron's name opening the door for her.

As Margerit sat and began to turn the first few pages to get her bearings, habit stepped in and Barbara glanced around the room to note all the entrances, the hidden spaces, the lines of sight that would allow the least conspicuous watch. She saw the librarian taking note of her precautions with a sniff and a shake of his head. Well, he guarded his own and so did she. Both rituals might be equally unnecessary in this case, but neither would be omitted.

Margerit's identification of the desired text was marked by a quickening of breath and a twitch as she remembered in time to keep her finger from the page. Barbara found it hard not to smile as she noted both the librarian's dagger-gaze and Margerit's careful tracing in the air, half an inch above the parchment.

"Barbara, look here," she whispered, beckoning.

She stepped closer and bent over the table. It was a long text, of course, with the parts for the main celebrants picked out in rubrics and centuries of notes on the staging directions cluttering up the margins.

"Here. This is when the *visio* went strange." Margerit pointed above the page to a benediction marked for the principal priestly celebrant. "But," she delicately turned over to the next page, "I don't remember this. It was shorter, I think, and then there was a bit from the choir that I don't see anywhere in here."

She looked up and caught the eye of the librarian who still glared, ready to pounce at the slightest infraction. He came over and asked, "Are you finished?"

Margerit shook her head. "Maistir Iohannes—"

"Brother will do," he interrupted.

"Brother Iohannes, I was wondering…the *expositulum* for Saint Mauriz's mystery—the formal one for his feast day—it looks different from what I remember from last month."

"Well of course it does," he said sourly, "since our Mauriz wasn't good enough for the new archbishop. Too antique he called it. Too countrified. Well it's been good enough for Rotenek since the days of Bishop Dombert but now we must follow the habits of Lyon. Of Lyon! If it's the new ceremony you want, I'll find a copy." He once more disappeared back among the shelves.

"That must be it," Margerit said excitedly. "If the new archbishop made a change, that explains why—" She didn't complete the thought for Brother Iohannes was returning with a folder of loose pages.

"It hasn't been copied out fancy yet. His Excellency wants it bound in place of the old one, but that would mean taking the binding apart and the prince won't have it. Not his choice, of course, but no one wants the fuss now when—" He shut his mouth abruptly. Even his newfound garrulousness evidently stopped short of reference to Aukust's mortality. "Well, here it is. Don't worry about keeping the sheets in order, the catchword will keep them straight. The round hand there, that's what's left from the old text. Hard to change the common responses, of course—no one would follow them. And the parts there marked for the prince, don't mind them. He said he'd been speaking the same part for near sixty years and he was too old to change now. So what's written there isn't what he used. But these here—the priest's lines and the hymn that you mentioned—those are from the Lyon model. Had to change them round, of course, since Rotenek's not Lyon and Mauriz isn't Blandina. It's a patchwork mess if you ask me, but nobody asked me." He retired to his writing desk still muttering.

Margerit's eyes flicked back and forth between the two texts. "It's not as changed as he makes out," she said quietly. Barbara wasn't sure whether it was to avoid reaching the librarian's ears or because she spoke only to herself. "This phrase, here…and those two lines. And here the original has all these repetitions. That's what made it seem much longer."

Barbara leaned in to compare the sections she indicated. "That's the style of the Penekizes—the old Benedictine house at Eskor. You see it all the time in the chronicles the monks kept there. It only seems repetitive to us but in Dombert's time each piece had a slightly different meaning."

Margerit looked surprised. "Really? It doesn't look anything like the old Latin that I studied. What's this word here?"

Barbara felt off balance. She didn't like shifting between the roles of armin and fellow scholar in public. She compulsively took another look around the room. There was nothing any more menacing than the glowers of the two schoolboys who perhaps felt that Margerit was setting a bad example by waxing enthusiastic over her studies.

The two texts were set out in strikingly different manners. The older one was the more familiar style. The new text was written out in a flowing copperplate that marked the change in speakers only by a brief initial at the head of each line. It took some time to match the two to compare the passage Margerit had questioned.

"*Stet dedicatum tuum in aeternum. Dedicatum*—is that the word you meant? I've seen it before in the chronicles. It's something between 'shrine' and 'chapel' but it can also mean 'home.' Or even 'palace' if the text was speaking of kings. It's—I guess something like a special dedicated building. It could mean 'home' in a poetic sense but you'd never see it for an ordinary house. It's not proper Latin at all. The older texts have a lot of that." She traced the same passage on the new page. "See, here, this is where it should be in the prince's lines and here the bishop's line echoes it using *aedificium*." She frowned.

"What is it?" Margerit asked eagerly, leaning in to follow the lines.

"Just a matter of style, I suppose. The old text in this part is a fragment of Mauriz's *lorica*—a protective prayer using military images because he was a soldier. But when they borrowed the pattern from the Lyon mystery there wasn't anything parallel—their patron Blandina was a fairly ordinary martyr. So instead they used bits of the Martin *tutela*, which makes sense I suppose since he was a soldier too. Armand's Martin mystery is considered the ideal model for new liturgy, but his Latin is very much in the French style and the flavor is different. Look here." She pointed. "If I saw that phrase in the Penekizes chronicles, I'd read it as 'the building and its walls.' Sides, more literally. But here it's clearly meant to be understood as 'the parish and its surroundings.'"

"Does the meaning really change that much?"

Barbara shrugged. "Words change, sometimes. If you walked up to a man in Paris or Barcelona or Vienna and said, "A blessing on your head!" in the vulgar tongue, everyone would understand what you meant. But if you took those same words and put them into Latin, you might end up blessing his cookpots or cabbages."

Margerit stifled a giggle and glanced quickly in the direction of the librarian for fear of another disapproving glare. But he still sat unmoving at his desk, no longer muttering imprecations against newcomers who mucked about with the old rituals. She slid the next leaf of the rewritten text to the front of the stack. "So here the prince said his line the same, but the bishop's part—"

"—takes out all of the repetitions. The older law texts always said things five times in five slightly different ways to make sure everything was wrapped up tightly. I think this was doing the same. See here in the prince's old lines: strength…protection…wardship…shielding… and then the new text has only protection. Shrine…memorial… dedicatory stone…altar…church—but the new text uses *sepulcrum* in this part which wouldn't have made sense in Dombert's day because it would have meant only the actual grave where the saint's body lay. And then here grounds…district…this is an archaic word meaning the people served by the specific church. It's the same problem. They boiled it down to one word and it doesn't capture all the meanings."

Margerit broke in, "And then the prince has the line about Saint Mauriz protecting us with his shield and defending us with his spear. I remember those because it matches the image in the window so well. And here it finishes—"

Barbara took over once more. "—with a repetition of the previous bit, but now it's the archbishop speaking it so we actually got the simple version this time. Before it would have meant something like 'Grant your protection to this place dedicated as a memorial to you and to its people and the lands surrounding it,' but he's gone straight to Armand for the model and if you read it in the Lanpert dialect back in Dombert's day there's no way to understand it except 'to your grave and the body in it and its walls.' And that doesn't make any sense because Saint Mauriz isn't even buried here. I think we have a finger bone and that's it."

"But that's it!"

It took a moment to realize that Margerit wasn't simply echoing her own words. "What?"

"The vision. The *charis* was supposed to rise up through the church and spread out over the whole district—the way it always did at Chalanz. But it got confused. At the end, instead of being told 'protect and bless the church and its surroundings' it was told 'protect and bless the saint's grave.' The closest thing it could find was the relics buried in the foundations. They must be down there under the corner of the altar where the *fluctus* sank away."

As the meaning of her description sank in, Barbara's gut clenched. "Margerit, hush!" she ordered, looking over to the desk. Had Brother Iohannes heard? Had the schoolboys understood enough to repeat it?

Margerit followed her glance, first in fear, then confusion. "What—?"

The librarian glared at them but only with the expression of one distracted by noise. Barbara lowered her voice. "Maisetra, it might be best to save your thoughts for a more private time."

After another moment of confusion the message went home. Margerit dropped her eyes to the bundle of papers and shuffled through them once more as if nothing unusual had transpired.

But in the close privacy of Margerit's own library that evening it was a different matter. "I can't believe it's that dangerous to discuss the details of a mystery out loud." There was frustration but no hint of reproof.

"Perhaps, perhaps not. If I err it must be on the side of your safety. When you talk about the *fluctus* and *charis* doing this and that—as if they were angels or demons carrying out our commands—it goes beyond what most would consider orthodoxy. In a philosophy class it could be safe enough, but within the grounds of the cathedral I'd rather not take the risk."

"But—" Margerit was pacing back and forth before the fire like some wild thing in a cage. "How can the text of the ceremony get fixed if no one dares to talk about it? Does no one care that the mystery failed?"

Barbara was stunned into a brief bewildered silence. "What did you think you were going to fix?" she asked at last.

"But it's all…wrong. However you want to describe it, the city isn't being protected by Saint Mauriz the way they all think it is."

"And how do you know? How would you *prove* it?"

Margerit had no answer.

"Didn't you hear what Brother Iohannes said? If centuries of tradition made no difference, if the disagreement of the cathedral canons made no difference, if even the opposition of Prince Aukust made no difference, why do you think the archbishop would listen to you? This isn't about the mystery, it's about power and influence. And that's an even better reason to watch what you say and who hears you say it."

"But…gah!" she exclaimed in disgust.

In her heart Barbara agreed—assuming that what Margerit had seen was true and not a trick of her own senses. But the world had its ways and it wasn't easy getting around them.

CHAPTER THIRTY-FIVE

Margerit

Mesner Pertinek had proposed. Margerit wasn't exactly surprised but she was a little shocked at the rapidity with which it happened. To go from a first introduction to asking to name a date in the space of a month might not be unheard of for a girl in her first true season, but somehow it seemed precipitous for older people.

"And what was your answer?" she asked, not even trying to keep the excitement out of her voice.

Bertrut was sitting in the soft chair at her bedside. It wasn't her aunt's habit to claim late evening tête-à-têtes but it was one of the few opportunities for a truly private conversation. She was staring down at her hands twisting nervously in her lap. "I told him I would need to discuss it with you."

Margerit laughed. "Isn't that a bit backward?"

"Margerit, be serious. Don't think I'm asking your permission because I'm not. But you're my first responsibility and I'd never give marriage a second thought if it interfered with that. I don't have any illusions—his proposal was more in the line of a business proposition. He says he finds me charming and pleasant to talk to and I find him the same. But his intent would be to live here, with us. It would be out of the question if he wanted to set up his own household—well, but if he could do that he wouldn't be talking to me. It's not very romantic to be told you're someone's last hope at leaving the house he was raised in. Although when you think of it," she added wistfully, "I suppose there have been spinsters enough who have accepted an offer for no better reason than that."

"Do you love him?"

Her aunt pursed her lips with a faraway look and shook her head. "I enjoy his company. And I believe, in time, we have a chance to become quite fond of each other. There isn't much point in talking about love. If I'd married at your age, it wouldn't have been for love. I'd like to tell him yes. He seems like a good man and he's been very honest about his life and prospects. Do you know, he even went to LeFevre to reassure him that he had no designs on your inheritance!"

Margerit's mind went back to the look he had exchanged with Barbara that day in the cathedral. Had she too been asked to approve the proposal?

Bertrut continued, "The advantage wouldn't only be on his side. He pointed out that his presence would add to the respectability of your house without imposing any hardships on you. He neither wants nor expects any authority over your life, but if you wanted, there are doors he could open for you. You still only see a small part of Rotenek society, you know."

"And will you be Mesnera Pertinek?"

"No, no." She shook her head, smiling. "I don't want the burdens of that! And for that he'd need permission from his cousin and a *carta equinoma* from the prince. And…it would complicate matters."

Margerit privately completed the unspoken. Those in the nobility who had welcomed them for the sake of her inheritance might change their mind if she aspired too high.

"He said if I liked he'd present me at court—and you too, of course—and that would be the end of it, but I told him there was no need for that. What do you think?" For all her attempted diffidence she seemed anxious about the answer.

Margerit wanted to exclaim, *Of course!* and begin the congratulations, but too many people were schooling her to caution these days. Did LeFevre truly believe he lacked ambitions for her wealth? What did Barbara know? Would this cause difficulties for her? She replied more carefully than she wished. "Just as you wanted to consult with me, I need to discuss it with—well, with others." No need to rub it in that Bertrut's future might depend on the critical opinion of a mere armin.

"Yes, yes of course," her aunt replied, returning to a businesslike manner. "But not your uncle," she said firmly. "I won't have him thinking he has the right to say yes or no on what I do. If we wed, we can do it before everyone comes for Christmas and that's how I'd want it."

"I'll have an answer for you tomorrow," she promised. It would make for an interesting family holiday. And with that thought she remembered that it was past time to steel herself to talk to Nikule. He was unlikely to come if he thought the invitation came from his father and not from her.

* * *

The answer was yes, with all her advisers concurring that Charul Pertinek was most likely exactly what he seemed. And if he weren't... there were safeguards in place.

It seemed it was the time for betrothals. Cheristien Riumai had left the coterie of girl scholars to prepare for a more conventional pursuit. Verunik Felix, though with no similar excuse, had become bored with the exercise and came less and less often. Amiz still gamely showed and there were others Margerit didn't know as well due to differences in their schedules. And Antuniet, of course. In her, Margerit recognized a fellow enthusiast, if not a comfortable companion.

Working over the changes in Mauriz's mystery had given her confidence in her grasp of the basic principles but also a gnawing hunger to share her questions with someone else. Barbara—well, the problem was that Barbara was blind to the visions. She would listen raptly to Margerit's descriptions of a particular effect, but once they worked past the physical forms of a ritual she could only shrug. Antuniet had hinted at more.

It was easy enough to broach the subject as they waited for the men to exit after Desalamanca's lecture. "I haven't thanked you yet for that book you recommended. He's opened my eyes in so many ways."

"Was that meant to be a joke?" Antuniet asked drily, looking down at her with a hint of laughter in her dark eyes. Margerit felt herself blush. The other woman had a way of making her feel like a foolish schoolgirl without saying anything the slightest bit offensive. Antuniet continued as if nothing had happened. "Did you have much trouble finding a copy?"

"No—not much anyway." Barbara had never told her whether it had been easy or hard. And why not let Antuniet think she'd found it herself?

"How far have you gotten?"

They had descended the steps to the street, followed of course by the armins. On Wednesdays it was usually Marken. Barbara stuck close to her on philosophy days but for theology she was happy to trade off. And though Margerit wouldn't have suggested it, she was just as glad to have time with Antuniet that didn't involve Barbara scowling in the background. It seemed she couldn't forgive her for being Estefen's sister.

"I've read through the whole, but I'm still trying to work out his language. It's nice to have names for things, I just wish they made more sense. But even having names…now I can explain, *the charis underwent concrescatio at the missus*, rather than waving my hands around and saying, *and then the colors all swirled together when he said 'amen.'*"

Antuniet looked at her sharply. "Indeed. And is that what you see?"

"It depends. That's the whole part I don't understand. Why is it so often different? Why is one person's celebration so brilliant and another's invisible? Why is it sometimes the same, even when different mysteries are being followed? What do *you* see?" She had been hesitant to ask so blunt a question but it came tumbling out.

"I see…bits, wisps, enough to know there's something I'm not seeing. It's only really clear at the grand mysteries." Antuniet stared at her thoughtfully for a minute. "Do you have time to come with me to the university chapel? I want to try something."

Margerit turned to Marken. She knew the rules. Any unplanned venture was for him to say. He shrugged to indicate he knew of no objection. "I have time. What—"

"Not yet," she said.

They crossed the square toward the small church that formed part of the heart of the university buildings. Halfway across a familiar long face caught her eye and she called out before her courage could falter. "Nikule! Cousin Nikule!" She might not see him in passing again for a week or more. Always before she had avoided any sign of recognition.

He stopped, both puzzled and suspicious as she closed the distance, trailed curiously by the others. The need for introductions gave her a chance to find her voice. "Nikule, may I present Mesnera Antuniet Chazillen. Antuniet, my cousin Nikule Fulpi."

He bowed over her hand, making his best attempt to be charming as she echoed, "Fulpi? Do you perhaps know my friend Mihail Salun?" He nodded. "I've heard him mention the name but I never realized there was a connection."

"Nikule," Margerit ventured, "I've asked your father and mother—and your sisters, of course—to spend Christmas with me here in the city. I was hoping you could join us."

If he was surprised, he covered it well. "But of course, cousin. I'd be delighted. Mesnera!" With a second bow to Antuniet he slipped on past.

There. It was done. One mistake needn't tear the family peace apart. "I didn't realize you knew my cousin," she said.

"Hardly," came the reply. "But eventually one always knows someone who knows everyone. It's all just a matter of keeping your ears open and your wits about you. Shall we?" She nodded toward the church.

She pushed past the idlers in the porch and proceeded directly to the small side altar dedicated to the apostles. "I'm going to do four things. I want you to watch carefully then tell me what you saw."

Margerit nodded somewhat bemusedly and stood just to one side where she could take in both Antuniet's kneeling figure and the altar itself. Antuniet reminded her of one of the carved mourning figures on the old tombs in the cathedral, with her back stiff and straight, her chin raised, and her hands held clasped before her in a prayerful attitude. What was it Verunik had called her once? *Proud Antuniet!* But was it pride or only the confidence of a master craftsman? With little preamble, Antuniet launched into a careful but rapid recitation of a prayer for good fortune and especially fortune with money. Margerit guessed it was one that a gambler might be apt to mutter over his cards. Did Antuniet gamble? Probably—it was a common enough vice among the nobility and had ruined more than one fortune. Or perhaps it was simpler than that. The baron's will had destroyed any hopes Antuniet might have had for a generous dowry. She'd never seen any hint that Antuniet was short of money but—

Her attention snapped back to the present as a brief *visio* arose: a net-like flare stretching from candle to candle along the rim of the marble platform. And then it flickered out. Margerit was about to describe it when she remembered that Antuniet had said there would be four things to watch.

The first time she had spoken the words with her hands kept still at her sides. This time she moved them: now in a sign of prayer, now raised in supplication, then closing with a brief cross. The effect was much the same as before. In the third repetition the prayer was changed slightly—just a word here and there—but in response the net of holy light glowed and held fast, lingering in the darkness after the words died away.

With the last repetition, she drew out of her purse a new wax candle and lit it to stand with the others as she wove the altered prayer. The response flared brilliantly enough that Margerit gasped in surprise. As Antuniet signed herself and rose she said, "The fourth one then," with a tone of satisfaction.

"Can't you see it?" Margerit asked, amazed that all eyes in the church hadn't turned toward them.

Antuniet's eyes narrowed. "No. At least, not enough to tell the difference between them." She reached out and snuffed the candle wick between her fingers, tipping out the small pool of melted wax and returning it to her purse.

"It's gone," Margerit said quickly as the net too snuffed out.

"Interesting. Well, that would explain certain things. We're done here."

Those ten minutes had left her mind reeling. Could you experiment like that? As if you were testing a recipe? As they emerged into the daylight again she started and abandoned several questions until Antuniet stopped and demanded, "Well?"

The questions she wanted to ask all seemed too dangerous. At least Barbara was teaching her some caution. She fell back on the merely rude. "Why don't you hate me for taking your brother's inheritance?"

Antuniet blinked at her in confusion then broke a rare smile. "Is that what you expect? My brother is a fool. Marziel loved nothing more than intrigues and games. Estefen thought he could win against him in the end. He was a fool and he took the rest of us with him. But I don't recall it being said that you threatened my uncle into changing his will. Or that you seduced him on his deathbed."

Margerit felt her face burning in mortification.

"So I fail to see on what basis I should blame you for my lack of prospects."

In a debate on logic it would have been a presentation of the simple truth. But it never seemed possible to discern Antuniet's real thoughts behind her wit. And she sometimes seemed to speak truth to hide truth.

"Then we are friends?" Margerit ventured.

"No," she replied with a firm shake of her head. "But I think we have certain interests that lie together. You have questions. I know where some of the answers can be found. And you have skills that I find useful. In comparison with that, friendship is an uncertain thing."

* * *

The betrothal of Charul Pertinek and Bertrut Sovitre was announced formally at a small family dinner held by Lord and Lady Marzim. As everyone who attended the dinner was already well aware of the situation, the announcement was repeated for more public consumption at Mesnera Arulik's salon the next evening. Aunt Bertrut blushed and glowed as if she were a girl again and if Mesner Pertinek were anything less than proud and happy, no one could have proven it. Listening to gossip afterward, Margerit found people divided equally as to who had the advantage in the match. One opinion seemed universal, although she overheard it only by chance while talking with Verunik in a secluded window seat.

"It makes no difference to the prospects of the little Sovitre, of course." The voice came around the corner, not meant for her hearing. "No one who found her fortune sufficient would be put off by a lack of titled connections."

Verunik reached for her hand and squeezed it gently. "Don't you mind them," she said kindly.

But Margerit hardly gave a thought to what others thought of her marriage prospects. She was rather relieved that the trickle of proposals her uncle had fielded had fallen off with his departure. Aunt Bertrut might have a guardian's authority, but evidently fortune-seeking young gentlemen were less inclined to lay their case before her. She giggled at a sudden thought.

"What?" Verunik asked.

"I will wager you—that is, I won't really wager because Aunt Sovitre wouldn't like it—but watch and see. Before the night is out, someone will petition my soon-to-be Uncle Pertinek for his influence in winning my hand. He may yet be sorry for making his offer!"

CHAPTER THIRTY-SIX

Barbara

Her shadows had broken the rules. They had never agreed to any rules, of course, but she'd told herself, *As long as they never show when I'm with Margerit, it doesn't put her at risk,* and *As long as they never follow me north of the river, it doesn't touch on my job.* There was one who always seemed to be loitering at the end of the Pont Ruip when she crossed the river heading for Perret's academy in the morning. He was never there afterward—not that she ever saw. There was one who had followed her past the Tupendór Gate when she rode out on an errand for LeFevre.

There had been more books to hunt down at Eskamer's shop; more recommendations from Antuniet. At least this time there'd been no dissembling about where the idea came from. That had bothered her more than the source. This time they were titles she recognized. Not dangerous, as such, but could any book be considered truly safe when the reason it was so hard to find was that no printer cared to take a chance on it? To keep matters simple with Eskamer she had used the same disguise as before. Perhaps he'd seen through it as the shadow had, but he'd understand the purpose. And though her shadow was a different man this time, she knew the masque was pointless on that end already.

But the next day they broke the rules. After lectures were done, as she and Margerit sheltered from the rain in the arcade around the Plaiz Vezek while a boy was sent for the carriage, the man from Pont Ruip stumbled by in the guise of a lame beggar, making his pitch to Margerit from a safe distance. When she began to reach for her purse, Barbara stepped in between them, touching her sword hilt and warning him off. He made a good enough show of cringing as he scuttled away that Margerit chided, "Was that necessary?"

"He isn't what he seems," she answered.

"Few of them are, after all."

Barbara left the matter. While there was any way to avoid it, Margerit had no need to know. She itched to challenge them, but over what? The nobility might start duels over a look or a gesture, but she would need something more solid.

Several days later, the same man—all clean and tidy and in the clothing of a hired hackman—was mingling with the carriage drivers waiting outside the cathedral after Mass. He had been talking with Margerit's coachman, looking at one of the horses. Barbara checked her impulse to dart forward and looked around instead. Was he only a feint? When he saw her in the approaching party he touched his hat and grinned at her and slipped behind the carriage to disappear.

They'd broken the rules. And even if it were just to torment her, she couldn't let it stand. A word to the coachman—she had no serious doubts about him—and the grim look on her face let the others know something was amiss. She explained in as simple terms as she could when the front door of Tiporsel House was shut behind them. Bertrut accepted her reassurances but Margerit demanded more details later when they were alone.

Barbara searched for the line between truth and discretion. "I really know nothing more than I told you before," she offered. "I don't know who he is or what he hopes to gain by having me followed—only that he claims I owe him some unspecified sum. LeFevre says I have nothing to fear under the law regarding the debt but if I strike at these men without cause then I cross the line and I won't bring that trouble on your head."

Margerit was outraged. "But you're protecting yourself!"

She shook her head. "No I'm not, not yet. They haven't attacked me, only followed me. If I thought they threatened you, it would be different. The law is quite generous on the question of an armin's license. What he did today was close to the edge but I think they're trying to goad me into going too far. What I don't know is why—what it would gain him. Whoever he is."

"What sort of debt could he possibly think you owe him? How could you not know what it is?"

"I think—" She hesitated. Margerit knew her history, enough of it at least. But the last time the topic had come up it had caused a quarrel between them. "I can only assume it has to do with my father."

A frown crossed Margerit's brow. "But that would mean he knows who your father was."

It should have occurred to her before. She turned the thought over in her mind to examine from different angles. "I suppose he must. But what does it matter? After all, LeFevre must know as well, but that's never been any use to me. Even now he just gives me riddles about legal precedents and a promise that everything will work out. And Mesnera Chazillen—the baron's sister—I assume she might know whose orphan her brother had taken into his household. So my unknown creditor knows as well; what am I supposed to do? Go begging for the answer?" She recalled that first encounter in the empty warehouse. *Barbara No-name.* He knew—and knew she didn't. He'd been taunting her with that. No, she wouldn't beg. Not from him and certainly not from the Chazillens. "The only thing I need to know is how to get rid of these shadows without causing trouble for you."

"LeFevre gave you what?"

It took a moment to return to what she had said. "Some citation from the *Statuta*. I think I left it in his office. But that was only to show that I was immune from the debt somehow. It doesn't solve my problem."

* * *

She thought that had been an end of it. The household staff had been warned. There was nothing beyond the usual precautions for them to do and this wasn't their affair in any event but with the preparations for Bertrut's marriage it was no time to be lax.

The wedding, like the betrothal dinner, would be small and private. Nothing like what Margerit's might someday be. Margerit's wedding. The thought was a cold stone in her gut and she turned her mind away from it. Even the disruption to the household from Mesner Pertinek's arrival would be minimal. He would bring a valet, of course. She doubted he would feel his station required the addition

of a personal armin. His cousin had one, of course, because one did.
But on the rare occasion that pride and ceremony might require, she
supposed he might borrow Marken and no strangers need be reviewed
and approved. It was possible that there would be more entertaining in
the future and thus more staff to hire but that wasn't her responsibility.
The house was currently empty and echoing compared to what it was
capable of holding. Bertrut already occupied the second-best rooms
upstairs. No, there would be little enough change in the household
arrangements. The guests at Christmas would cause far more chaos.

She had already spoken with Mesner Pertinek in her office. They
understood each other well enough with regard to Margerit. He
might serve as a social escort but not as a substitute for professional
protection. She wondered if he would resist the temptation to profit
from the illusion of influence over Margerit's fate. Well, that was his
choice and nothing to do with her as long as he knew it for an illusion.

* * *

She had forgotten once more about LeFevre's hints until Margerit
presented her with a thick book one afternoon in the library.

"Another obscure philosopher?" she asked in an amused tone.
Dozzur Mihailin had lately been challenging his students to read
beyond the standard texts and Margerit had been combing the less-
frequented shelves to see what minor works the baron had laid in store.

"The commentary on debt from the *Statuta*. I've marked the
section that LeFevre recommended."

Her mood darkened. "You shouldn't have bothered. He's playing
games with me—he has no intention of telling me anything useful."
An irrational resentment rose in her. This was her history, her family,
not something for Margerit and LeFevre to discuss behind her back.
Nothing was left to her of privacy.

"Be fair," Margerit said. "He can't be direct. I think he would if he
could."

Barbara pressed her lips together tightly. *Easy for you to say.* She laid
the book on the table and opened the section LeFevre had marked.
Concerning the laws of debt and the inheritance of debt.

"What use is that? I already know—"

"Just read it. Knowledge is power, as they say."

"Is that an order?" It came out more stiffly than she'd intended.
She sighed. "As you wish."

Margerit shot her a stricken glance and closed the book. "Don't. Don't do that 'as you wish' thing. Not when it's just us."

"As you wish," Barbara said, quirking up a corner of her mouth in a smile. She set the book aside by her usual chair. "I'll look through it tomorrow when you have visitors. There are, after all, obscure philosophers to hunt down."

* * *

The text would have been fascinating if she were studying it for its own sake. It was in the archaic language of the code set down by Domric—or at least that was known under his name. There were several layers of commentary and summary interleaved with the original tract, with the occasional peculiar precedent to liven up the mix.

A man's debt cannot be denied by any person, whether man, woman or child, who has claim as of right to his property as income, for those who have right to the benefit cannot be free of the responsibility. However no claim of liability for debt can be brought to court in the abstract. Repayment is due only when the sum or property has been identified, specified and sued for, and judgment has been awarded in court. If a person falls from the status of being due the benefit, he cannot be sued for the debt.

For a legal tract, it seemed a remarkably coherent summary and Barbara was unsurprised to see a note in the margin identifying it as the work of Rodulfus. What followed was considerably more dense.

A wife is liable for her husband's debts in all times and places, for those debts contracted after the betrothal, or after the marriage if no betrothal announcement is made. If a woman is betrothed to a man who then contracts a debt but the wedding does not take place, she is not liable for the debt, except for debt concerning his wedding clothes if it was she who broke the engagement. If a man dies with debts, his widow may be sued for payment until the day she remarries, but on that day she is free of his debts forever if no suit has yet been raised and laid at that time.

A man's son or daughter may be sued for his debts whether they were contracted before the birth or after, until that child stands separate from his purse. This is a child who stands separate from his purse: any child who has attained the age of majority, for no man is obliged to maintain an adult child by law; any daughter who is wed, save that her dowry may be sued for until she attains majority; any son when he takes holy orders or a daughter when she takes the veil.

She returned to the earlier passage: *Repayment is due only when the specific sum or property has been identified, specified and sued for.* That answered the immediate concern—she was safe from the debt because she had no property they could specify. A case could not even be raised against her in court so long as she owned nothing. But was this what LeFevre wanted her to understand? Was that why the baron had done what he did? To protect her from her father's creditors?

It made a strange kind of sense if the debt were all that mattered. If she had no possessions under law—being a possession herself—there would be nothing to sue for. But with both her parents dead, she had no claim under law to any man's purse. Would it truly have been worth anyone's time to sue her for whatever gifts and trinkets the baron might have given her? To be sure, it could have been vastly annoying to spend twenty years answering in court for claims on every dress or necklace. And perhaps it really was as simple as that. The baron had disliked petty annoyances and interference. If it had made his life simpler and smoother to keep her in the status in which she came to him, perhaps that was all the reason he had needed. And as for the concealment of her name—that too could have been simply to avoid the attention of the buzzards. Or even perhaps some sense of shame to tie an ancient and honorable name—for he'd said as much that it was—to what he'd made of her.

If the hints had been meant to satisfy her, they had utterly failed. Barbara sighed and scanned down the remainder of the clauses. They began with the obvious and trailed off into the bizarre.

A minor child is not entitled to contract debts without permission and therefore his debts are his father's debts. A minor child who is an orphan is not entitled to contract debts for he has no father to stand surety for him and he has no claim by right on the purse of his guardians. He is entitled to promise what he holds in inheritance but if his guardians forbid the contract it may not be collected until he comes of age. If a minor daughter marries, her debts are her husband's from then on, as for any married woman, unless her husband has yet to come of age and then it is determined by the marriage contract. Any child born to a man's wife may be sued for his debts, just as any child born to his wife has a claim on his purse unless it be that another man acknowledges the child and the debtor denies the child. And if it happens that another man acknowledges the child and the mother's husband does not deny him, that is a child of two debts, for just as two purses have been opened to him, so he may be sued for either man's debts. If a woman lives from her own purse and has a child without having a husband, then her child may be sued for her debts. But if such a woman still lives from her father's purse, though she be of age, then her child is a child of her father's purse, both for right and for liability, unless he disown both her and the child before it is baptized.

Barbara read through to the bitter end without receiving any further enlightenment. She was still lingering over the precise forms of suit and countersuit in court when Margerit came in after the last guest had left and the last tea tray had been carted away.

"Was it worth the time?"

"I'm not sure I learned anything I care to know," she answered. She read aloud, for Margerit, the passages that showed her free from suit, but her thoughts about the baron's motives she kept to herself.

* * *

Her shadows had broken the rules, but she had been careless. She knew to watch for the man at the Pont Ruip in the mornings but she hadn't looked for him coming back at dusk from one of LeFevre's errands in the driving wind and rain of an incoming storm. And with her mind set on dry clothes and the warmth of a fire she'd been slow to take note when he fell in twenty paces or so behind as she climbed the gentle arch of the span. It was a carelessness she wouldn't have allowed herself if she'd been on duty.

At a sense of wrongness she paused and glanced back. He halted, echoing her own movement and barely visible in the flickering light from the lampposts. Her fingers played at the hilt of her sword, not in threat but in contemplation of the choices. The man's presence annoyed her, but a fight and the consequences it would bring would be vastly more annoying. He had made no overt threat and she hadn't the excuse of Margerit's presence to justify more precipitous action. And the warmth of Tiporsel House beckoned. She sent one last dagger-look and continued toward the northern abutment. The next two men were standing idly but purposefully in the middle of the pavement before her. Her heart dropped and she glanced back the way she had come, drawing her blade at the ready. From the corner of her eye she could see several passersby scatter. The first man was advancing slowly. There were only seconds to escape the trap. This was no time to play one of Perret's waiting games. She took their measure in an instant as if she were in the practice *salle*. She could fight her way past on the northern end—not one of them carried more than a knife, that she'd seen—but it would mean bloodshed and at least one death. Better to dodge back the way she'd come, where there was only one attacker to avoid, and lose them in the twisting alleys of the southern bank. She moved, not wide around to the far side of the road as he expected, but leaping up onto the parapet and running that precarious path, with a feint to throw him off balance as she passed and then a leap down to the cobbles again.

She didn't see the fourth man until his club caught her in the side with an explosion of pain. Her blade went skittering into the darkness and she rolled aside just in time to miss the second blow. Without counting the cost to her ribs she grabbed the weapon and sent her attacker sprawling over her and past with a sickening thud. She scrambled to a crouch. Two to her left and home beyond them; one looming to her right with a glinting blade in his hand and the uncertain darkness of the south bank alleys behind him. She chose the better odds, despite the knife, and with all the strength she could summon, drove her shoulder into his belly. Pain licked across the side of her head but she was past and he was down.

Her body protested the thought of a long chase but there were other escapes. She dodged down the water-steps at the southern end of the parapet to the landing below where the rivermen docked. On a night like this there was sure to be someone waiting for a fare for a quick trip downstream. She tumbled into the first boat she saw untied and barked an order. "Tiporsel House, as quick as you can!" Upstream would be slower, but once they were in the middle of the current she'd be safe.

He worked his oars with a will and as they passed under the arch of the bridge, she could see her attackers peering over the side and heard curses. Let them curse. The boatman was staring at her strangely. The rain felt warm across her cheek and when she touched it she could see a dark stain even by the wan light of the boat's lantern. "Footpads," she said by way of explanation but her head suddenly felt light. "You know the Tiporsel landing? The marble steps just after the bend?" She pointed ahead where her goal was a pale smudge against the river's darkness and gasped at the movement's consequences. He rowed and the steps loomed closer as she gritted her teeth to avoid crying out. "That's the one." She contemplated the current impossibility of fetching the coins for the fare out of her breeches pocket. "Come by in the morning, you'll be well paid."

But he hung off from the small stone wharf, working the oars to keep even with it a few feet away. "And what business do you have at Tiporsel House?" he asked gruffly. "It's worth my license to dock there without leave."

Barbara had no will to argue the point. She knew she must look rather a ruffian herself at the moment. She judged the distance and the current and suddenly dove over the side into the dark waters. Swimming would have been out of the question but her hand reached out to grasp one of the heavy iron rings, heedless of the cost to her ribs, and she felt her way around to the slick stone steps as the boatman let his craft slip downstream once more.

CHAPTER THIRTY-SEVEN

Margerit

What she enjoyed most, so far, from Aunt Bertrut's betrothal was a new opportunity for socializing that fell between the routine of a dinner at home with only her aunt for company and the rigors of an evening out in society. Margerit had found herself missing the Fulpi family dinners in Chalanz, formal though they may have been. She didn't mind not having the position to host elaborate events but she did wish on occasion that the rules of society made allowance for a quiet evening with a few friends—something more than the rituals of afternoon visiting.

She wished even more that Barbara's strict propriety would allow her to join them at the long empty table. Hadn't she said that she'd shared the baron's table on occasion when they were informal at home? But the farthest she would unbend was on those rare occasions when Aunt Bertrut went out alone and Barbara would consent to share a supper sent in to the library while they studied.

But Uncle-to-be Pertinek had fallen into the habit of dining at Tiporsel House on any evening when they stayed in, always accompanied by one of his cousins for form's sake. It brought a sense of family back into her life. He was witty and well-read and seemed genuinely interested in her studies. It was easy to see why Aunt Bertrut thought they would suit.

* * *

It was one of those cozy dinners, on a rainy night that made her glad to have skipped the opera. An unusually long delay before the serving of the fish course was explained by the butler's harried, "Maisetra, your presence is requested downstairs. Barbara…there's been an accident."

Her heart skipped a beat at the possible events that word might cover. Even as Aunt Bertrut was asking "What—?" she was up and making her excuses to the guests.

As she followed Ponivin quickly down the back stairs toward a noise not quite rising to uproar he reassured her, "She's in no serious danger but I've sent for a surgeon."

In the next few seconds a cascade of images passed through her mind. Thrown by a horse—no, there was no place she would have been going today that would be far enough to ride. The night was dark with the storm and windy—a carriage accident? Timbers blown down from a building?

Barbara was seated close by the hearth in the servants' common room, soaking wet and hunched over to clutch her ribs while a splash of blood trickled out from under the cloth pressed to the side of her head by one of the grooms. As Margerit entered she struggled to rise but was held none too gently down in the chair.

Margerit flew to her side. "What happened? Where—?" She turned back to Ponivin. "You sent for a surgeon—who? Delecroix?"

"Not him," Barbara said thickly. "Muller. He does for Perret when there are accidents at the academy. Army surgeon. Knows what to do with a scratch."

"Scratch!" She knew Barbara was making light of it for her sake, but there was so much blood. "How bad is it?" She directed the question at the groom, figuring that would get her more truth.

"Hard to say, Maisetra. Scalp wounds always bleed like a stuck pig. But I didn't see any bone, so—"

"Hold your tongue, man!" Ponivin ordered and he fell silent.

Margerit knelt where she could see Barbara's face more clearly. "What happened? Who was it? That same man?"

She began to nod, then evidently thought better of moving her head. "Him and three or four of his friends." She told the story in short, clipped fragments. "I had to jump and wade the last bit—that's where all the water comes from." Her jaw was clattering by the end of the speech.

And no one had thought to get her out of the wet clothes. Margerit began barking orders. Hot blankets. Build the fire. When she began unfastening Barbara's coat the groom hastily handed over his position to the least squeamish of the kitchen maids as Ponivin shooed the male servants out of the room.

The sodden clothing had been replaced by blankets by the time the surgeon pushed his way through the crowd outside the door. He took in the scene at a glance and set to work. His first words to her were, "If you mean to swoon, get out now. If not, make yourself useful and bring me as much light as you can manage."

He grilled Barbara on her injuries then pulled back the blankets to poke and prod the places she had been holding close. Margerit felt a flash of outraged modesty but Barbara seemed not to care. She looked so thin and fragile like this: near-naked and bereft of her usual driving energy.

"Not broken, but cracked perhaps," Muller said. "Some sort of club? Well, cracked is likely. Now let's see about sewing this up."

Enough hands were required for the process that Margerit found herself holding the lamp, though she had to look away once he had begun. By the end, she suspected she was nearly as pale and shaking as Barbara was, though with less cause.

The surgeon took her aside as he washed his hands and tools afterward. "She guards for you?" he asked.

"Yes."

"Not for the next couple of weeks, she doesn't. The ribs should heal well enough if she stays quiet but watch out that cut doesn't fester. Heads are a bad business. Have someone sit up with her this first night. If she starts breathing oddly, try to wake her. Give her as much broth as she'll take down—nothing solid until I've seen her again tomorrow. And give her a drop or two of this in each cup." He handed her a small vial from his bag. "I'd say only if she needs it for the pain but her sort never admit to that, so just give it to her anyway. I'll be back tomorrow sometime."

"Wait," Margerit asked as he gathered up his things. "What about… are there any charms, any mysteries that would help the healing?"

His face was tired when he answered her. "You'd probably know better than I would. They say a prayer to Benedict helps against the fever and I suppose it can't hurt. I'll put her in my prayers but I don't deal in charms. I'll stick to the work of my hands and leave that sort of thing to you."

* * *

Barbara was too exhausted to protest when she was carried as a limp burden up to her room. While she was being made comfortable, Margerit sought out her aunt. The dinner guests were long since gone.

"I'm sorry for leaving you alone. Did Ponivin explain? It all got so busy I forgot to send word."

"He told us something," she answered. "But…Margerit, your dress!"

She looked down. No point in asking the housemaids to try to get those stains out. "Never mind, it's only a dress. Aunt, I'm going to sit up over Barbara tonight—the surgeon suggested it. So don't expect to see me in the morning."

"Surely someone else could—"

"No," she interrupted, "they can't. This is my responsibility."

Not alone, of course. Some unlucky girl would draw the lot of popping in every few hours to bring a fresh tray and make sure the fire was kept going. But Margerit claimed the right to sit at Barbara's bedside and hold the cup for her to sip and talk softly while she tossed and moaned trying to find a less painful position to sleep.

Muller's drug seemed to do its work eventually and she fell quiet for several long hours. Margerit prayed—to God, to Saint Benedict, to everyone—and for the first time wished she knew all the little charms and rhymes that every dairymaid and scullery girl seemed to learn. Against burns, against the scab, against bleeding, against the wet cough, against the cramp. She'd always considered them little better than fortunetelling, but what good were grand cathedral mysteries when what you needed was to close the cut of a knife? Barbara looked so pale. Another hour passed, then there was wakefulness and pain once more. More broth, more drug.

Sleep failed to come this time and to distract them both, Margerit began asking questions—meaningless everyday things at first. Why was the house named Tiporsel? For the crest of the first owner carved over the gate. You could still trace the outlines of the bears in the worn stone. Who had it belonged to before the baron purchased it? She didn't know. The drug slowed her answers but not her wits. What would the garden look like in the spring? Rows of tulips and daffodils lining the paths. It was left rather wild down by the landing because of the floods. In summer the lavender filled the air, but the household was rarely there in summer. And then the question that had been teasing at Margerit ever since the evening they first met. "How did it happen that you became my godfather's duelist?"

Barbara closed her eyes and for a while Margerit thought she might have fallen asleep again. The story, when it came, chilled her. "I was…oh, eleven? Twelve? Barely of an age when the first signs of womanhood might appear. Estefen had newly decided he was a man. And he had decided that his uncle's possessions were his to play with. I was lucky—someone happened by before it went too far and the baron took matters in hand. He gave me a choice. He would order that I was never to be alone with Estefen and he would make sure that I was always protected. Or he would have me taught to fight and I would have his authority to do whatever I needed to protect myself. I chose the second.

"My teacher—this was my first teacher, not Perret—my first teacher was a thug who specialized in dark alleys and tavern brawls. The next time Estefen laid a hand on me I nearly killed him. He's never forgiven me for that. I couldn't have done it a second time at that age; surprise is a powerful weapon. But once was enough. When the baron saw that, he put me in training for an armin.

"I was just a girl. I worked hard—I always worked hard for him. But what he saw at first wasn't strength or even skill but the sheer bloody-mindedness necessary to kill a man if that was what the moment called for." She opened her eyes but stared off at the ceiling rather than meeting her gaze.

"People don't understand. It isn't about being strong. I'm not—not compared to most men. Nine times out of ten, being an armin is just a matter of being there. And in that tenth time, nine times of ten it's your wits that win the day. I've only ever killed two men: one for him and one for you. And the one for him was more a matter of honor than protection. But when I had to, that's what I did. That's what keeps you safe. This—" She reached up to touch the bandage on her head and winced. "This wasn't about you. This was someone telling me 'I want something from you and I can hurt you if I don't get it.' I made a mistake. I thought they only meant to scare me. Now I know better." She was quiet again for a while and this time her breathing slipped into the slower cadence of sleep.

Margerit rubbed a hand across her cheek to smooth away the moisture there. She had always thought there was something silly about the obsession Barbara put into her training. The near-daily lessons. The repetitive drills, alone in her room, when she could be studying or resting. She'd never wondered what it might take to keep yourself at that edge of readiness every moment of every day. And all to keep someone else safe with no shield left for yourself. No shield... but there were other kinds of shields.

She picked up the notebook she had been studying before to pass the time and turned to the section where she had been analyzing Saint Mauriz's ritual. There was one section that she had traced back to an ancient *lorica* quoted in Pontis. Only the words were there, but *loricas* had a typical shape and form and Antuniet had shown her the way. She might not have the original mystery, but she could build a new one. She glanced over at the medallion of Saint Margerit that she'd been fingering during her prayers. Mauriz had been a soldier and the symbols of armor came naturally for him. Margerit had survived attacks as well—though it wasn't part of her usual patronage. She knew all the standard mysteries for her namesake. There were parts that could be interwoven into the *lorica* easily. The first step was a fair copy of the text with room to note her experiments. There was a pen and ink on the table and a third of the night yet to fill.

In the hour just before dawn, at the twentieth variant, the *charis* rose up under her hands as she invoked the saints' names. She watched in awe as it spread in a golden shell to cover Barbara's sleeping form. And then, with the final words of the prayer, it coalesced around her, sinking in past the bedclothes to form a second skin just under the fleshly one—a breastplate and shield to keep her safe from harm.

Margerit stared at her hands as if they belonged to someone else. A wave of exhaustion passed over her—and no wonder; she'd been awake the night through. But this—this was what Fortunatus hinted at. This was what Gaudericus struggled to describe. This was what had built Tanfrit's reputation. She had created a new mystery and called on Saint Mauriz and Saint Margerit and they had answered her and lent their grace to her will. And now that she'd done it once, she could do it again. From now on, whether she knew it or not, Barbara would no longer be standing alone against her enemies.

CHAPTER THIRTY-EIGHT

Barbara

The surgeon had ordered she was to do nothing until he had come again, so Barbara decided to be up and about as usual by that time. But even leaving the bed for necessary things left her with a pounding headache and every movement clutched her ribs like an iron band where the bruise was taking on the color of raw liver. She had woken at dawn, groggy and suspicious of the surgeon's remedies, to find Margerit curled asleep in a chair at her side. Some of the night came back clearly; other parts were blurred.

The day dragged out in fretful inactivity and she tormented the housemaid who came to see to her needs until Margerit returned, still yawning and pale, to scold her and require obedience.

"You aren't going downstairs today, so there's no point in demanding help to do so. If there's anything I need, Marken is here full time for the moment."

That was hardly what she wanted to hear. She slapped at the bedclothes in frustration and winced at the effort. "There's no need for that. I'll be up and about by tomorrow for certain."

Margerit stood over her, making her feel like a petulant child. "You won't be on watch until you're properly healed."

"But you don't understand," Barbara burst out. "This had nothing to do with you. I won't let it interfere with my duty."

Margerit stared at her in bewilderment. "Nothing to do with me? Anything that happens to you has to do with me."

"No." Barbara fumbled to explain. "I mean, I had no right to be injured on my own business and deprive you—"

"Don't be an idiot," Margerit interrupted. She sat down on the edge of the bed. Barbara looked away, uncomfortable at the scrutiny. "Something you said before, about not crossing the line. Is that...did he know he could push you into that trap last night? Because you were afraid—not afraid, but reluctant to defend yourself from the start? Because it wasn't in my defense?"

It was a surprising insight. Barbara thought back on every move she had made since that day in the warehouse. "I don't have a legal standing," she explained once more, "to attack in my own defense."

"But you do in my defense," Margerit countered. "And if I lose your protection, that's an attack on me. It doesn't matter what they intended."

Barbara considered the argument. It might hold before a judge if it came to that, but she wasn't sure she cared to test the case.

"From now on, you do whatever you need to in order to be safe. If it ever comes to a matter of law, I'll swear it was by my orders—and it'll be true. Whatever comes after can fall on me."

She shook her head. "You don't understand what that could mean."

Margerit's response was sharp. "I understand what it would mean if I lost you! Promise me. Promise you won't let yourself get cornered again out of some mistaken fear of bringing trouble on my head. You told me last night that when the baron trained you to fight he gave you permission to do anything necessary to protect yourself. Why won't you take that same permission from me?"

Because you aren't the Baron Saveze. You have no power, no influence to let me get away with murder. But did it matter? Money could buy a great deal of forgiveness. And these thugs weren't courtiers with friends in high places like Estefen's friend Iohenrik had been. "I promise," she said at last.

* * *

The first week, it was easier than she would have thought to do nothing. The stiffness made it a challenge simply to dress and manage the stairs. The dull throb in her head made books no comfortable refuge. And the constant sullen drizzle of the rain ruled out the gardens as a safe place for slow limping walks. She had quarreled with Margerit once more on the question of leaving the house but the risk of encountering her creditor's men while still lame won that argument. It was still maddening to stand idly by and watch another take her place, however temporary it might be. The only thing that sealed her obedience was the promise that—barring reinjury—she would be back at her duties by the time the Christmas guests descended on the household.

By the second week she had returned to her own studies and noticed how empty the house seemed when Margerit was out and about. It was Marken who saw her to all her lectures and kicked his heels at the afternoon teas and mingled with the other armins at the evening affairs. She would have felt a twinge of jealousy except that he was as eager as she was to get back to sharing the rigorous schedule of looking after a scholar-debutante.

In odd moments that week her mind went back to the problem of how to settle those shadows from her past. She looked again for the copy of the debt tract that Margerit had brought but it was gone. Only borrowed, no doubt, and returned. So she found herself setting out the key points anew on paper.

Item: Her father had died encumbered of a large debt. Large enough to swallow not only his own wealth and his wife's dowry but enough of his family's resources that their name itself was abandoned as poisonous. Large, but not unusual. The last generation had seen many upheavals and turnarounds and not all the fault of their victims. Most such debts were pursued for a time then abandoned as the potential targets fell away or disappeared. If it were only the sum involved, it might make her worth the trouble of pursuing, but there had to be some hope of payoff. Chances were the debt itself had changed hands more than once. These things were bought and sold in hidden markets and not always only with gold in mind.

Item: She had been protected from the liability for that debt by virtue of having no resources to pursue. It had been a brutally crude method, but not originally by the baron's choice. Indeed, it had only been made possible by her father's last act of greed. By selling his child—however base his own motivations—he had set a wall about her. For nearly twenty years that protection had held with no assault. Or had there been? She couldn't know what sorties might have been deflected over the years. No, there would have been some sign. The sort of man she was dealing with now would have had no compunction about exposing a child to his maneuverings. No, there had been some other bar. And why now? When the same legal shield still stood? The answer was no doubt the same. Whoever it was—perhaps several whoevers—had feared the baron. Margerit was not the least frightening. Whether they thought to work on her by threats to Margerit, or work on Margerit by threats to her, they believed there was some hope of gain.

Question: Would there be any use in identifying her father by name? Her father...well, she hardly had any fond thoughts for that unremembered individual, but she cherished the promise of a return of her name as she hoped for salvation. And the baron had promised she would know. But he'd made other promises that lay broken. Was there a point to waiting patiently for another year—just a year and a bit? Would anything change? Why wait? That name was her only inheritance. Why not claim it for herself?

Item: She had been born at the end of the year in the twenty-eighth year of the reign of the current prince. There would be a record of baptism some time in the month following. At some church. Somewhere in Alpennia. Listing as father some now-forgotten nobleman—and many had been forgotten in the time since then. She knew nothing of her mother's family except that they had abandoned her in her time of need, but the clues were there. It wouldn't be the first time a family of wealth and ambition had married off a daughter in the hope of buying nobility for their grandchildren.

So all that was needed was to search in one month's records in the entire country for an entry recording the baptism of one Barbara, daughter of a now-extinct line, who could not be otherwise accounted for among the Barbaras now living. It was a name neither common nor unusual. And many families had vanished during the war or the chaos that came after. Prince Aukust had found those gaps very useful for renewing the ranks of the nobility from the ablest of the middle rank.

Barbara sighed. Well, perhaps it was simpler than that. Most likely, she had been born here in Rotenek. And if her father's family had been prominent, there were only certain churches that would have been sufficiently dignified for his child's baptism. It wasn't such an impossible task.

She was still poring over her notes when Margerit came in, excited to share the latest arguments from Dozzur Mihailin's lecture on the new philosophers. And how he had led one pompous student into such a tangle of argument that he ended up denouncing Aquinas by accident. Barbara unobtrusively slipped her notes under a ledger to take away later. This was her puzzle, for her to solve.

CHAPTER THIRTY-NINE

Margerit

Margerit wondered if Aunt Bertrut had been overly cautious in timing the wedding itself. She'd declined to send announcements of the betrothal to Chalanz on the technical grounds that such notices were really invitations to the wedding and no general invitations would be issued. The wedding itself was held a bare week before the Fulpis were due to arrive, guaranteeing that the personal announcements would cross on the road, giving Uncle Mauriz no opportunity either to cancel the visit or to complain of not being told. In the hubbub of arrival and introductions Uncle Mauriz kept his response to a startled silence. Afterward, his ability to rage about it was damped by Mesner Pertinek's calm insistence on staying at Bertrut's side and doggedly repeating, with no wavering of the cheerful expression on his pleasant round face, "The matter is really none of your affair, Fulpi." Short of destroying Aunt Honurat's and the girls' enjoyment of the visit, that left nothing but acceptance.

With the family crisis past, Margerit was free to enjoy playing hostess and showing off what the capital had to offer. Sofi and Iulien were too young for there to be any question of begging invitations to formal dances at the grand *salle* but there was the opera and the lesser theaters. There was shopping and the exotic sights at the Strangers'

Market in the wharf district. There was the simple opportunity to walk out and see people and things that were only fairy tales back in Chalanz. Even the excitement of coming across a formal duel one afternoon in the Plaizekil, though Aunt Honurat hurried the girls away in an excess of caution. And above all there was the unmatched pageantry of the seasonal celebrations at the cathedral.

With her newly sharpened perceptions, Margerit found the holiday services fertile ground for new questions. Was there truly a distinction between mysteries of worship and petition? The joyful Mass of Christmas Day produced the same dizzying effects of *sonitus* and *visio* that the more purposeful ceremony on Mauriz's feast had. Yet in several sessions of close observation on ordinary days, it was only—or mostly—the petitions whose answers could be perceived. Perhaps it was an effect of numbers. A packed crowd of worshippers each contributing his mite, blazing like the Milky Way to a single star. Perhaps that was the reason for the guilds—beyond the simple human desire to gather in groups. Even those blind to the immediate response of the saints might have found that the petitions of groups were more often answered than solo ones. Yet the visions seemed tied to purpose. Where was the purpose in celebrating the Nativity? So many puzzles still to solve! In the ordinary way of things, she would have closeted herself in the library afterward with only Barbara and her books for company, hunting down what this author or that might have opined. But there were few quiet moments with the house full and entertainments to organize. And there were entire days when she didn't see Barbara even in passing.

Margerit stretched the rules sufficiently to invite Amiz and her parents to a small dinner party. There was no bar of rank between the Waldimens and Fulpis and one could make allowances for the charm of country manners on occasion. Even Nikule brought little awkwardness and both of them were able to pretend that day in the parlor on Chaturik Square had never happened. On the last day before the visit was to end, when Nikule was making noises about returning to his lodgings for the evening—for even student rooms were more spacious than what he would have gotten at Tiporsel with all the visitors—he took her aside and asked to speak with her privately.

"I have a…a proposition to pass on to you," he began and then hastily protested, "no, no, nothing like that!" at the wary look in her eyes.

So she went aside with him to a corner of the drawing room to listen.

His explanation was hesitant, as if he were afraid to provoke her into a swift refusal. "There are some fellows I know, they've been talking about starting a new mystery guild at the university. Not one of those stuffy old men's clubs like Papa always complains about and not...well, I know that student guilds have a reputation for being drinking clubs and...and worse. They want to begin something that's actually focused on celebrating mysteries. Maybe researching and reviving some of the older ones. Maybe trying to create new ones."

Her interest was caught. She nodded, trying not to show too much excitement in case it were only teasing as he used to do. But Nikule seemed in earnest.

"One of the fellows—he thinks it's important to have a mixed guild: men and women both. He thinks it—well, I forget how he described it. All abracadabra stuff. But they want to invite some of the girl scholars. The serious ones. And they asked me to invite you. Truth to tell, I think I only got included so they'd have the chance to ask you. You have a bit of a reputation, you know."

That was a surprise. It had never occurred to her that any of the regular scholars had even noticed her as an individual, rather than as part of the annoying gaggle in the top rows of the lecture theater. But she could see many problems. "I don't know. It doesn't sound entirely... proper. I'm trying to imagine any of my friends being allowed to join something like that."

"It's all very respectable," he insisted. "Your friend Mesnera Chazillen has already joined. And Mesnera Nantoz as well."

The latter Margerit knew only by reputation, but that reputation was impeccable.

"Don't imagine these are wild student parties, wandering through the catacombs by candlelight. At the moment we're meeting at Dom Amituz—the count's son is a member—although I think they're looking for someplace more formal for the mysteries themselves. What can I tell them?"

Margerit could hear the story he wasn't telling. He'd come to the notice of well-born men. Men whose families had influence. And they wanted something they thought he could provide: her. And if he failed, likely that would be the end of their notice. But a guild interested in treating the mysteries as more than simple ritual—as something to be explored and tested? And who wanted her specifically? She wondered if Antuniet had suggested her. But then why hadn't the invitation come from her?

"I would need to ask Aunt Bertrut's permission—to see if she thinks it's proper."

He seemed relieved and even teased, "But not Papa?"

She shook her head. "He doesn't understand how things work here. He'd either be against it for the wrong reasons or approve for different wrong reasons. Aunt Bertrut doesn't know all the rules but she knows whom to ask. She's never set me on the wrong path yet."

Nikule nodded though he looked as if he'd hoped for a more certain answer. And then he ventured, "Margerit...," in an even more hesitant tone than before.

She waited.

"Margerit...I'm sorry. That matter. Back in Chalanz. I didn't—"

"It's forgotten," she said firmly. And somewhat to her own surprise, she meant it. He'd been a pawn in Uncle Fulpi's plans as much as she had. And it had been those plans that set her free. Nikule was no more a villain than he was the icon of her childish fancies. And if the guild's invitation were a peace offering, they could both consider the matter closed.

When Bertrut was petitioned, she took several anxious days to consult with a few well-chosen acquaintances. And in the end, the answer was yes. The judgment had been made that this new guild was a harmless enough diversion. The principals were from some of the oldest families and the ordinary members at least had no bad reputation. And if it brought the young lady scholars together with men who would never be admitted to their parents' drawing rooms, as long as the proprieties were observed it was no worse than attending lectures in the first place.

With that answer in hand, Margerit turned to what she thought might be the harder problem: presenting the matter to Barbara.

CHAPTER FORTY

Barbara

Barbara held the lamp closer to the mirror and craned her head to one side. The scar might fade in time. A fashionable style with her hair frizzed over the temples would hide it but that was hardly practical. She sighed and set the lamp down to braid and tie her hair into a loose club like the styles of the last generation. Pinning it up still pulled painfully at the new skin. Had she become vain?

On impulse, she opened her wardrobe and drew out a gown of pale blue silk to hold against her before the glass. The baron had given it to her on her last birthday. Given—well, presented it to her to wear, in any event. Only a year ago. She had worn it that once. Or was it twice? Would it still fit? There had been no occasion to wear women's clothing since the baron's death. Her world had been wider then. Now there were so many things—like the gown—shut away to wait until there was a place for them again.

At the moment nothing much seemed to fit. December had passed in contrasts as sharp as moving from a fireside out into the east wind. The house was more full than it had been at any time she could remember. It wasn't a small house—none of the north bank properties could be considered small. But the baron had purchased it with no vision of a sprawling clan of cousins and grandchildren. Between

Margerit and the Pertineks and the Fulpis, all the family rooms were inhabited for once. Even the bare minimum of Fulpi servants had strained Mefro Charsintek's ingenuity to find room, though in the end the housekeeper found beds for everyone. And yet Barbara found herself alone in the bustle nearly as often as in the weeks before, when her wound and her promise had bound her to the house.

Her recovery still seemed maddeningly slow. Perret knew how to bring you back from injury—when to push and when to call a halt. But for all that, she still found herself dancing around the fear of pain. At the moment it gave her little concern for Margerit's safety. Playing the hostess, she went nowhere questionable and was surrounded at all times by so much of her family that an armin felt superfluous.

Then in a rush of bells and crowds and lights the season was past and the entire city of Rotenek seemed to sigh and sit back for a moment's rest to gather strength for the next round. It felt like the slow promenade before the start of the waltz. Looking forward, January would pass in a long frozen slog. February would pick up the pace. The university's short Lenten term would begin even as the social world paused in contemplation. Even farther ahead, with Holy Week past, there would be the double burden of the long Easter term and the rush to finish the season before the unpredictable spring floods. But for now Barbara watched the departing carriages of the Fulpis and hoped life would return to normal.

* * *

Though it would be weeks before lectures started again, Margerit suggested they venture out to the university quarter to see the postings and catch the gossip on what would be offered. Many of the *dozzures* preferred the traditional approach of lecturing on whatever topic pleased them that term, certain that their particular students would follow. Even so, someone would know what was planned and would be passing it on in coffee shops and huddled discussions as friends passed in the street. It wouldn't do for Margerit to be seen loitering in a student café but enough could be gleaned by listening. Some of the lecture subjects would be posted as handbills by those professors who didn't trust to reputation alone to draw an audience.

Even in those familiar streets, Barbara found herself on edge and constantly twitching at movements caught from the corner of her eye. This was their first excursion alone since the attack. She'd seen no sign of her shadows since she'd returned to going out—not even the loiterer at the bridge—and that was suspicious enough on its own. But it was different when she had a charge to keep. She couldn't trust to whatever strange luck had protected her so far. Given her own mood, she failed to notice that Margerit was also distracted until she announced abruptly, "I've been invited to join a guild."

Barbara nodded vaguely. Good. That was a sign of true acceptance. Invitations to balls were one thing, but it could take generations in Rotenek to be invited into the old private guilds. The Waldimens most likely, she thought. They were— She noticed that Margerit was staring at her expectantly. "I'm sorry, was there more?"

"It's a student guild."

Barbara didn't try to keep the wary look from her face.

"A mixed one—it's perfectly respectable. Aunt Bertrut asked around." The whole story of Nikule's offer tumbled forth.

Barbara considered the matter carefully as she listened. Well, why not? It was a safer place to explore her questions about the mysteries than the cathedral library. Students were expected to debate and flirt with all the more questionable philosophies.

Margerit's explanation trailed off with, "…but I wasn't sure you would approve."

With that word, the world shifted again between them and Barbara replied stiffly, "It isn't my business to approve or disapprove if Maisetra Sov—Maisetra Pertinek has no objections. I'll need to know where you'll be meeting, of course, and who will be present, if you know." It was, after all, just another social function. And she would be there to assess the gameboard and the players and to see that her token made it across the squares unscathed.

* * *

But when it came to the first gathering of the newly formed Guild of Saint Atelpirt, it seemed one of the principals had other ideas. Mesner Choriaz looked over the motley cluster of chaperones and armins and exclaimed, "No, I'm sorry, this is impossible. Is this a guild or a carnival? Rather than naming ourselves after the great theologian we should have called ourselves harlequins and had done with it." He waved dismissively at the group of attendants. "They'll have to wait elsewhere when we get to serious work."

Barbara looked around at the invitees. In addition to Choriaz and their host, Filip Amituz, she recognized three scions of the nobility. Of the noblemen present, Choriaz most looked the scholar, his severe plain coat and spectacles contrasting with Iohennis Lutoz's boyish looks and garish waistcoat. She wasn't much familiar with the Salun brothers except by name. On the distaff side, in addition to Antuniet there were two slightly older girls she knew mostly by reputation: Ainis Nantoz and Iosifin Rezik. Back when she had first started attending the baron as his duelist, they'd been moving from their dancing seasons into the serious pursuit of suitors. But whether from personal inclination or a lack of offers they'd returned to a preference for books over balls.

The numbers on the male side of the guild were filled out with studious looking men that she didn't know. Ordinary scholars had never intersected her duties under the baron. She noted their names carefully for further interest. And Nikule, of course. He seemed oddly out of line with the ordinary run of invitees. She didn't recall him being described as more than dutiful in his studies. The remaining women were taken from the ranks of the poor-scholars. Barbara recognized one of them. Akezze Mainus was known for her work on formal logic. If she had been well-born she might also have been known as a beauty, with her pale skin and masses of red-gold hair, but even years spent over books hadn't erased the drift of freckles that an outdoor childhood had left across her nose. The other poor-scholars, she presumed, had been chosen for similar talents. There were no other women of Margerit's class. She wished that Amiz Waldimen had been invited, but it would be impossible for a girl not yet out.

The poor-scholars were accompanied by two older women to watch over them. It was a requirement of their studies that there be no blemish on their morals and clearly they were taking no chances on that end. Another companion covered the two older girls. She had more the look of a lady's maid. Antuniet had her armin, of course, and two of the men had also seen fit to be so accompanied. All together it made for quite a crowd. It was easy to see why Mesner Choriaz objected.

It was Antuniet who put a stop to the rising grumbling. "You want three things, Iakup: a mixed guild, the participation of respectable women and no chaperones. You can have two of them." And with that, the matter was settled, if not entirely to everyone's satisfaction.

* * *

Through the crawling progress of those first few meetings of the guild, Barbara could see Margerit's frustration. But what had she expected? To her, the purpose of the group might be obvious, but each member had come with different expectations. And while university debate might pay lip service to equality, in the end it came hard up against the wall of noble privilege. The ensuing struggle was an ideal chance to size up the players on the board.

She had thought at first that Amituz had been the seed for the guild's formation. By courtesy of his father, the count, he was their host for these initial gatherings and his was certainly the most prominent name. But for all that he was known as an avid student of history, he seemed indifferent to the details of more spiritual topics. Iakup Choriaz had shown his hand from the first: impatient, hot-tempered and yet genuinely dedicated to unraveling the same sorts of puzzles that fascinated Margerit. Frizo and Mihail Salun were ciphers as yet. They stood back from the arguments over structure and purpose, though Mihail was clearly fixed as one of the principals from the start. It was Hennis Lutoz that Barbara finally pegged as the unlikely leader. His face hadn't lost the softness of youth and he gave the impression of caring more for the cut of his coat and the arranging of his cravat than the content of his studies. He spoke little in the discussions, but when he did, she noted that the decision always went his way. He was the one who brought them back to firm principles: that the purpose of the guild was to understand and practice effective mysteries, not simply to perform the traditions of ages past by rote. He was the one who gave respect to the proven talents of Maistirs Albin and Perfrit, to Antuniet's systematic experiments, to Mainus's rigorous logic and— much to her delight—to Margerit's reputation as a keen *vidator*. And how had he known that? Barbara wondered. Antuniet, no doubt. What else was being said of her behind closed doors?

The interplay of personalities was amusing to watch, but when it came to her duty Barbara narrowed her focus to two questions. Would there be a physical danger? Not likely for the meetings at Dom Amituz, and not likely in the presence of the whole company, but they hadn't yet chosen a site for the rituals. The one time she ventured to interrupt the deliberations was when Lutoz suggested the abandoned chapel of Saint Chermen just outside the city walls. No, she objected. Lonely travel to a deserted location was not acceptable. The second question, of course, was the danger to Margerit's reputation. Maisetra Pertinek might have approved the guild in concept, but it was still a perilous mix. Throw together young men and women, working closely with only a token nod to chaperonage, side by side with others who were not at all suitable as social partners. One never knew who might think to take advantage or who might simply be careless of the proprieties.

And yet, watching Margerit's enthusiasm when they settled finally to work made all the effort worthwhile. Balls and concerts felt like a tedious chore, knowing that Margerit was indifferent to their attractions and attended mostly for show. But this work was what she had envisioned for Margerit that day back in Mintun when the cherry blossoms fell. She would take every care necessary to see that nothing interfered.

CHAPTER FORTY-ONE

Margerit

The guild wasn't quite what Margerit had envisioned, once they worked past the initial arguments over organization. Her debates with Barbara had been ones of exploration. The two of them had picked to pieces the writings of those who had gone before and mapped out what they could understand of her own observations. But now when the question came to composing a new mystery, there were many branching choices. Iakup wanted to resurrect an old *instantaria* of Saint Aukustin that he'd unearthed in a collection of charters—a meditative ritual to promote diligence in an undertaking. Giseltrut urged a brick by brick approach to identify the common elements across the familiar mysteries—both great and small—that seemed most essential to success. Morpirt objected that they had no way to define success, and wasn't that the eternal problem with a mechanistic approach?

Hennis, as usual, waited until the others had had their say and then pointed out that every serious writer on thaumaturgy agreed that the combined efforts of a practiced guild were essential. Clearly, their first task was to work together on some simple ceremony to learn each others' strengths and skills. And having chosen Atelpirt for their namesake—as a patron of philosophers and scholars—it made sense to choose the *memoriosa* ritual he was best known for as their starting point. There was the added benefit that the success of that aid to memory would strengthen their later efforts.

Finding a venue for the guild's mysteries remained the largest hurdle. Even Morpirt, whose doubts of the divine nature of the mysteries bordered on heresy, was not ready to claim that a sanctified space was unnecessary. But such spaces—consecrated and yet available for use—were hard to come by within the city walls. The old traditional guilds each had a long association with a sponsoring church. But that would mean closer oversight than any of the principals cared to submit themselves to.

The search dragged out into the start of the Lenten term. For a time, it looked as if the guild might founder before it began. Lectures and readings began to fill up the days. Efriza, one of the poor-scholars, stopped coming, noting scornfully that she had no time for children's games and to ask her again if they ever settled to real work.

At last, a place was found: a travelers' hostel built by the Iulin Brothers just inside the southeast gate which had fallen into disuse when the new port shifted traffic to the west. The hospitallers had sold it to a speculator who had not yet turned it to a new purpose and the chapel had been kept open for the use of the neighborhood. A search was made for the new owner to inquire about an arrangement and to everyone's surprise—including her own—Margerit found that she held the deed.

* * *

She hadn't been among the small group that examined the hostel for suitability. Her first glimpse was after she'd asked LeFevre to make arrangements to see that it was cleaned up and provided with various necessities. But from the reactions of Hennis and Iakup he'd worked a minor miracle in the few days since she'd spoken to him. The chapel alone was little altered, as the neighborhood folk had been expected to keep it up as the price for access. Behind it, the old refectory had been provided with tables more suitable for study and writing. The understory had been returned to its original purpose as a stable. And one of the former guest rooms had been refurbished and an old veteran installed as caretaker and porter.

As the members wandered through the rooms inspecting their new guildhall, Giseltrut commented, "It must be nice to be so rich that you could simply forget you owned a place like this."

Margerit's first thought was to protest that she hadn't forgotten, she simply hadn't known. But that wouldn't answer the woman's jab. Even more than she needed to help bind the guild's diverse personalities, Margerit wanted the friendship of this loose community of woman scholars. "A year ago," she began, "I would have been desperately jealous of you."

Giseltrut blinked at her in puzzlement.

"A year ago, I wasn't poor enough to be a student. When I was a girl, I dreamed about running away from home and disguising myself as a boy to attend lectures. There wasn't any other way it would have been possible. They would have tracked me down and locked me up, of course. My guardian had my reputation to maintain. I didn't even know about the poor-scholars then, but if I had I would have been willing to throw away everything I had for the chance to be one of you."

"Then you would have been a fool," the woman said scornfully. "I enjoy the study of course—I'm good enough at it and it's better than taking in laundry or mending. But I'd trade it in a heartbeat to marry a merchant's son and have a household of my own. It's well enough now at the scholars' hall but I'll be lucky to find work better than clerking or as a copyist. I have no talent at teaching, so there's no governess post waiting for me."

They had wandered around again to the refectory where the others had gathered. Margerit tried once more. "Of course I was a fool. I won't pretend I don't prefer being rich enough to study over being poor enough. But I would have taken either gladly."

Giseltrut shrugged and moved away. Margerit could think of no further answer to her. It was a waste, an injustice. There should be other callings for a learned woman than scribbling or trying to drill some lawyer's daughters in French and Latin. Perhaps she could…what? Hire a handful of them to manage her library and do translations? That wasn't an answer. They needed real work—something that wasn't dependent on a single patron. And she had no idea what that might be.

* * *

It wasn't until the fourth visit to the hostel that the guild managed anything resembling serious work. At that first convocation of the whole guild, there had been a fumbling attempt to read through the Atelpirt ritual. But no one had thought to review the requirements in advance. When they had finished sorting out the stations and roles, it was found that they had only plain altar candles and not the thin tapers called for or any of the other minor *apparatus*. At Hennis's insistence they went ahead, but though Margerit watched carefully throughout the ritual, she neither saw nor felt any of the signs she had come to associate with the notice of the saints.

Perhaps that was to be expected, she thought. How much practice did it take to bring the parts together? What proportion of the participants needed to bring some level of skill? The same questions were on others' minds. Frizo turned to Hennis and shrugged. "Nothing. I hope we aren't wasting our time."

"It will come," the other said.

Iakup broke in impatiently. "How many times do we need to go over cradle prayers before we move on to important matters?"

"Enough times to succeed in touching the divine—or whatever you choose to call it." It was Antuniet who answered him, as usual. If Iakup were impatient with the slow methodical development of the guild, she was impatient with his impatience. "If our *vidators* say nothing happened, then nothing happened and we need to try again. Otherwise how will we know why our 'important matters' fail—as they will at first."

"So we keep repeating ourselves until Frizo says we're done? What makes him the expert?"

Giseltrut interjected quietly, "Not only Mesner Salun. I felt no response. It's not a certain sign—I miss a lot of the smaller workings. But something this focused? And with no distractions? I should have felt something."

"How many of us are there who can recognize a *visitatio*?" Petro asked. "I know I wasn't invited for my sensitivity to visions. I assume there are others who bring a different set of skills as I do. But how many of us will know when we've achieved something?"

They had discussed the importance of signs and portents in the theoretical, but Margerit had picked up only fragments of information about people's specific knowledge and talents. Everyone looked around at each other, unwilling to be the first to speak. Was it reflexive caution for skills as often condemned as honored? Or in this particular crowd was it a reluctance to admit their lack?

Hennis made no move to press the question but at last Frizo offered, "No secret here. During some mysteries I hear…feel…no, hear a sort of buzzing—like a gnat. From what others tell me, it happens only when the saints are answering. I can't tell much more than that." He chuckled. "I got kicked by a horse once and my ears were ringing for a month. Christ himself could have been talking to me then and I wouldn't have noticed, but it came back with time."

When he'd finished, Morpirt offered that the saints had never spoken to him and he had some doubts they spoke to anyone. "But once I was there for a physical manifestation, so I know that mysteries can work true miracles. And if mystic visions make it easier to craft true mysteries, that's good enough for me."

Margerit waited until nearly all had spoken, expecting someone to offer an experience similar to her own as each laid claim or disclaim to *visitatio*. There were only a handful of *vidators*. For others, the response came as a ringing in the ears; a touch of warmth like sunlight; a glow; Antuniet's unreliable flickering lights. At her turn, Margerit hesitantly described her experience at the mystery for Saint Mauriz. "It isn't always like that," she added. "It seems to depend on the celebrants and the nature of the mystery. Only the old public ones have such grand effects."

Several of the guild members made noises of disbelief. Filip voiced his aloud. "You don't need to invent details to impress us. You got that out of one of the old saints' *vitae*."

Margerit looked over to Antuniet, expecting some confirmation. She'd believed in her visions enough to test them. But Antuniet ignored her plea, staring off past her at some suddenly fascinating corner of the chapel.

* * *

Nikule was the only person who seemed genuinely impressed. He hadn't spoken up at all in the sharing of skills. It seemed common knowledge that the talents he brought to the guild were minimal. But as the others drifted out to the streets or stable to leave, he came to her—she almost would have said shyly—and asked, "Has it been like that for you all your life?"

She nodded.

"I remember—" he began. "I remember when you were small, you could never be still in church. Always talking and pointing and trying to run off into the aisles. Was it because…?"

Again she nodded.

He breathed a mild oath and shook his head. For a moment it looked like he would say more but thought better of it and turned to leave with the others.

* * *

In the confusion of the start of the new university term and the beginnings of the guild, Margerit had begged off on most of the engagements that Aunt Bertrut offered up. The restrictions of Lent gave her some relief but even in that season there were too many invitations and visits to be juggled easily.

Bertrut finally put her foot down one wet afternoon, finding her staring out at the rain and fretting that the weather would keep half the guild at home as it had kept half the students from lectures. "This won't do, dear. People are asking after you. I can't tell them you've become an anchorite. Now Charul has brought us a very kind invitation to the Ovinzes' to hear that new poet and I want you to accept."

Margerit knew not to push too far. Barbara had been harping on the same note lately.

The events that Mesner Pertinek brought access to were not different in the kind of people attending, only in the balance. There were fewer representing the new money—mostly those with a personal connection to the hosts. There were more from the fringes of the noble families, the people who had known each other for generations, even if their stars might be in eclipse today. These were not the hot-blooded marriage mart events where guest lists were ruthlessly pruned to eliminate the unsuitable. Discussions in the card room were more likely to cover politics than the cut of a new coat and the dancing ran to old-fashioned long sets.

After introductions to the hosts, Margerit was shown to her seat by a distant cousin of some sort of Uncle Pertinek—it was still odd to call him that—who thus fell in the category of safe but entertaining. He filled the space around the recitations with engaging but totally meaningless conversation. When the audience rose at last to take refreshments, Margerit looked in vain for her aunt and ended up instead being delivered to the orbit of her uncle where he stood in conversation with a uniformed man of similar age.

"But Charul," the other was saying, "do you think they'll actually carry through with the succession council this time? We've heard it all before."

Mesner Pertinek turned slightly to acknowledge Margerit's presence and said, "I believe your aunt was abducted to make up a hand of quadrille. Chalfin, have you met my wife's niece? Margerit, this is Mesner Tombirt Chalfin, Major Chalfin I should say. Chalfin, Maisetra Margerit Sovitre."

He took her proffered hand. "Yes, I'd heard you'd fallen into the noose at last. Sovitre? Why is the name familiar?" He fixed her with a piercing glance and frowned as she dipped a curtsey. "Sovitre…yes, old Marziel's mystery heiress. That tweaked the nose of the *Efrankes* party right enough. Young Estefen was counting on that fortune."

And at that his interest in her was at an end for he picked up the previous thread. "Now Charul, will he go through with it at last? I swear he was trying to wait out the old guard past the grave."

"As the prince wills, but there will be a council before or after. I think he knows as well as any that it would be better now."

Chalfin scowled. "It's the French woman making him wait. Every year her boy gains a step closer. And as they say, an unclaimed horse goes to the man in whose pasture it's found. But I'll be damned if I let some foreigner take up the crown."

Uncle Pertinek answered mildly, "There are plenty who say the same but mean the Austrians."

"Do you?"

"My friend," he said, throwing up his hands in a grand shrug. "I will not be sitting on that council no more than will you. What I might say means nothing. But I will tell you, if my cousin asked for advice, I would tell him to choose the heir most likely to keep us strong and at peace." He hailed another passing cousin. "Simun, would you be so kind as to take my niece in to dinner? She's bored to tears listening to old men talking politics."

As she was led off, the debate continued. "Charul, I swear you are either the most spineless man I know or the most honorable. Damned if I can choose."

Her new companion rolled his eyes conspiratorially and muttered, "Save us from old men and politics! Are you enjoying the evening?"

She hardly knew what she answered. The close of the party could not come too soon. There was nothing here to interest her as much as the contents of a single page of her waiting books.

CHAPTER FORTY-TWO

Barbara

For the first few meetings of the guild, Barbara had claimed watch over Margerit. But when they settled into serious work she grew restless. These matters had always been theirs to share—Margerit's and hers. It was difficult to be there and yet not there, playing the invisible servant with the other armins. The last straw came as the guild debated what text to use to develop their new mystery.

"There's no point in creating out of nothing," Iakup Choriaz argued. "Everyone agrees that the Lyon rite provides the simplest and most elegant models. The university at Rome uses nothing else these days for new compositions."

Some agreed, but the objections were many. "Better to adapt the existing mysteries for the saints we're invoking," Mesnera Rezik insisted.

Amituz objected, "That guarantees an ugly patchwork. Some sort of uniformity of style would be good, but I don't care to go to the French for it."

They ran through all the arguments that she and Margerit had explored while working their way through Fortunatus. As if no one had ever thought them through before.

Margerit had been finding her feet in the debates and entered into the fray with confidence. "You can't treat the saints as if they were interchangeable pieces, like a set of plates you could serve any dish on. Why else would we invoke Mauriz to protect Rotenek but back in Chalanz it was Saint Andire? It isn't just the chance of who the church is dedicated to. If Saint Peter protects Rome, why can't he protect every city? Why do we invoke Chertrut in our tongue but celebrate Aukustin in Latin? There's more going on than just elegance of language."

"You're making this too complicated," Amituz countered. "The meaning of the words is the important thing."

"But meaning isn't that simple," Margerit protested. "When we were working out what went wrong with the new Mauriz *tutela*, Barbara pointed out that they'd changed all the old Helvizen dialect for the simple Latin of the Lyon rite and even though the words were supposed to be the same it entirely changed the meaning."

Barbara tensed at the mention of her name. *This won't go well.* She pretended not to notice the stillness that fell and the sharp glances in her direction. Choriaz broke the silence, drawing off his spectacles to glare angrily. "It's bad enough we put up with the hired swords hanging around, but I don't care to have one school me in languages. Perhaps we could confine ourselves to the opinions of guild members?"

After that, Barbara let Marken be the one to stand idle in the hostel common room while the guild argued and experimented. When they came up with anything interesting, Margerit would let her know.

And she had a new occupation for her spare hours. Each church kept a register of the baptisms and marriages and deaths it presided over. The date of her birth was one thing she knew for certain. And though her baptism might have fallen even months later, that gave a starting point for the search. Her given name, the baron as godfather—it should be enough to find the record. And that record would contain two more names at least: those of her parents.

The registers were open for anyone to view who came at reasonable hours. Deciphering them was another matter as each clerk had his own hand and often his own shorthand, though the structure of the entries was fixed. Only the names needed to be puzzled out. She began at Saint Mauriz's. It was the obvious choice for a noble family. To balance that, the volume of material to work through was vast. The sessions became part of her routine, alongside practice with Perret and reviewing Margerit's engagements with Maisetra Pertinek and reading enough of the *Statuta Nova* to keep up with Chunirez's lectures.

In her movements, she tried to avoid routine. That mistake had contributed to the disaster in December. Now she kept to no standard routes when she moved around the city. There was no way to avoid a predictable schedule—the university lectures were fixed. But she became far more familiar with all the back doors, hidden hallways and unexpected alleys. Margerit hadn't questioned the need, once she had explained. Near the Port Ausiz, she happened by pure chance on one of the men she had wounded in the attack. From his shock and the speed with which he dodged around the corner she didn't think he'd been following her. Perhaps her defense had put caution into them, for when she encountered him again in company, the two of them melted away as if Saint Mihail himself stood at her back with a sword.

She spotted another of them at a distance late one afternoon—the same man who had followed her to the warehouse the day she bought the Gaudericus. *And why not turn the tables?* she thought. She had no training in trailing a man unseen, but it was as if she carried some ophthalmic stone as a talisman shielding her from his notice. Barbara read his intent as she followed his movements along the road heading west toward the river. He was purposeful but not furtive, brisk but not rushed. He was clearly going somewhere to meet someone, but that gave no guarantee of useful information. He might have any number of employers or business of his own. But there had been something in the way he'd spoken of her creditor that sounded like more than casual employment. It was a chance.

At the river he crossed over rather than turning off to the old warehouse district where they'd clashed before. Bridges made for poor cover but the street was crowded and Barbara paused only slightly to give him space. After that she nearly lost the trail, for she'd assumed he would continue on toward the West Gate. Glancing up the cross streets by reflex, she saw him pushing his way through the crowd along the Nikuletrez, following the road by the river north toward the better part of town. Now that was odd. Perhaps he was taking a message to some unfortunate whose income no longer entirely supported the lifestyle of that district. That would make this entire exercise a waste.

The farther they continued in that direction the more he stood out among the passersby and the more she blended in. There was the Waldimen's house on Plaiz Nof—she recognized it despite approaching from the opposite direction than usual. Off another street lived the Chazillens. It was a more than respectable district yet it must gall when they'd hoped to be living on the Vezenaf by now. She hadn't seen or heard any sign of Estefen since…since they'd arrived in Rotenek, she realized. That too was odd. Had he retreated to his title-estate? He didn't seem the sort to be content rusticating.

Her tail—now tailed—left the main street for one of the narrow alleys that gave access to the yards and kitchens of the fashionable houses. The foot traffic was thinner here but dusk was closing in and she decided it was worth the risk to keep close. He was making no attempt to conceal his movements and seemingly had no concern for being followed. But then, why should he? No doubt most of the unfortunates he was sent to dun were perfectly aware of the identity of their creditor. No doubt she herself could have known for the asking if she'd been willing to admit ignorance.

He turned at last into a wicket gate leading to the back entrance of an older brick structure. In quick succession she heard the clacking of a knocker and saw a brief glow of light as the door was opened and closed. And he had entered, so that meant he was recognized and welcomed rather than being left to kick his heels on the step waiting for a response. So. That was as good a sign as she was likely to be given today. She took careful note of the house position and shape and counted down from the end of the block. It would be easy enough to discover who lived there. Easier still if she could simply ask LeFevre, but he'd disapprove of her interest.

* * *

It was a week before she had time to track down the name and it surprised her: Langal. To be sure, he was well known for buying up the debts of the high and falling—or the newly rising—and brokered them as much for influence as for profit. But he was also the princess's man and his lackey in the warehouse had sworn there was nothing of politics involved. Or…wait…he'd said that *he* knew better than to get mixed up with the nobility. That could mean only that he was used for ordinary debts, whatever else his master dabbled in. Langal was long established, but not long enough to have held her father's debts from the beginning. So why would he have bought them up when there was no sensible hope of recovery? He was sure to have gotten them cheaply, but cheap with no return was still expensive. No, there must be some larger plan.

He was known to be one of the *Hertes* party—the ones who held Aukustin to be the only direct heir. Was there some benefit there?

Unlikely. With rumors of a succession council at last, what they wanted were votes or influence on votes. She had no influence over anyone. Unless...

Barbara's imagination spun out of control. Votes. And only the titled and their heirs-default held votes in council. What if...? What if her father had not merely been well-born but titled? That would explain why his family had destroyed itself to support him. And the title wouldn't necessarily be extinguished with his death. She had a vague recollection that in default of direct known heirs there was some provision for a delay against potential claimants. What if she had a right of claim? How long would that right last? Langal would lose the ability to sue her for her father's debts unless he acted before she came of age. Was there a similar limit on what she could claim? No, that wouldn't make sense. An adult cousin or brother—any near relative—could raise a claim to the title of a childless man. The only thing she would lose at her next birthday—in addition to the burden of his debt—was any claim on her father's nonexistent purse.

No, not his purse. His nonexistent estate. Except there *was* an estate—the title lands without which the title couldn't be held. That had been the baron's joke on Estefen: he couldn't have the title without accepting the title-lands and their mortgages. And that was what Langal held over her—if she were right. If he had bought up all her father's debts, it would include the mortgages that surely must burden any title-lands. And if her father's last heir failed to claim them before losing the right to do so, the lands would default to Langal. If the title weren't extinguished already, that would do so for any useful purpose. If there were a title.

Was that what he hoped to gain from her? A bargain to trade a meaningless title and a gutted estate for her vote in favor of Chustin?

The house of cards came tumbling down with one further thought. If that were the goal, then why not approach her directly, as a business proposition? Why make her his enemy with shadows and threats and attacks in the dark? It made no sense. But that returned her to the problem that it made no sense for him to pursue her at all.

She needed to bring another mind to bear on the matter—someone she could debate and test and argue with. LeFevre was out of the question. His oath to the baron would forbid him from helping her to any useful conclusion. But perhaps it was time to open her secrets to Margerit. If anyone could help untangle the puzzle she could. Still the voice whispered at the back of her mind, *This is yours alone. It's private. She owns every other part of your life, why this?*

Having made her mind up to break her silence, Barbara waited impatiently in the library after supper for Margerit to join her. That was still their time together—in the absence of outings—to read and debate and learn.

Margerit came at last, bubbling over with the news of the day. "We did it! The Atelpirt ceremony was brilliant today and even the doubters are convinced that between us the *vidators* will be able to guide the development of a true mystery. And we have a goal finally. Hennis said I was the one who gave them the idea, because of the changes in the Mauriz *tutela*. We're going to work on a shield for the entire realm—not just Rotenek. The *turris* from the old Mauriz mystery will be the basis for it but we'll weave in all the other major patrons to create a *castellum* complex. And they asked me to draft up an outline for the structure."

Her eyes were shining and her cheeks flushed. Barbara had the same thought that had come to her back in Mintun. This was what she had been born for. This was her calling. And she'd had the luck to tumble into a guild that recognized her value. Barbara pushed her own questions and puzzles back into their box. They would keep. The moment had passed. She spread some blank sheets of paper out across the table and they plunged into the work of outlining what they remembered of the old Mauriz rite. Tomorrow there would be another trip to the cathedral library to begin copying it out in full.

CHAPTER FORTY-THREE

Margerit

When Margerit asked Brother Iohannes about arrangements to copy out the older Mauriz *expositulum*, the cathedral librarian gave a flat refusal. "Pens and ink in my bookroom? Are you mad?" She negotiated finally for the loan of a set wax tablets still used for drafting correspondence. It was twice the work; twice the chance for error. And then there was the need to carry the awkward tablets back and forth from home. After the first session, she was ready to find another way.

"I should hire Giseltrut or one of the other poor-scholars to do the copying."

"Would that be kind?" Barbara asked, pausing a moment in the tidying up of writing supplies. Margerit had no concerns about mixing ink and books in her own library but the limited working space still called for care.

"More than kind, I should think. I've been thinking about it—what could be done to help women find more work as scholars. Scribbling isn't the answer, but if I need the work done…"

"No," Barbara interrupted softly. "I mean, is it kind to turn a guild-sister into a mere hireling? I won't pretend your guild treats all the members as equal, but they all swore to give their time and skills for the love of learning. What would it say if you paid one of them for the time she pledged to give freely? It lessens her."

Margerit didn't see it. Why should it make a difference? If she paid Giseltrut to do copywork, it wasn't taking away the time she gave to the guild, only the time she might spend on other odd clerking jobs. But she would drop the matter if Barbara were so very certain it would be taken amiss.

If it hadn't been for the slowing effect of Lent on the social calendar, the copywork would have been difficult to fit in. The short term was winding to a close and the guild research had doubled her list of readings to complete. A second copying session at the cathedral was managed two days after the first and went more smoothly. Brother Iohannes had recovered from his terror of spilt ink enough to inquire curiously about their project, noting, "Some of the monasteries have compiled collections of the older mysteries. Not only the ones they use themselves, but any they had access to. Copies sometimes find their way into the market when new ones are made."

That plucked at something in her memory. "Barbara, didn't you—?"

"Yes, Maisetra," she answered. "That…ah…bookseller you frequent thought he might have a collection of that sort from Saint Penekiz's. If you like, I could—"

"Yes, please," Margerit responded eagerly. The book hadn't sounded as interesting when she was immersed in theory, but now it might be quite useful.

The librarian turned to Barbara. Ordinarily, Margerit noticed, he treated her with the invisibility she pretended to. "I found that second register from the beginning of the February you were interested in. The one I thought had been misplaced. It was only a few quires that really should have been bound in the next volume but were kept separate for some reason. Did you want to see it now?"

Barbara shook her head. Knowing her reticence, Margerit waited until they were out in the *plaiz* to ask her about it.

"It's nothing," she responded. "Some research I was doing." Her face closed down in the way it did when questions of her family history came up. Margerit had learned not to push.

* * *

The Easter term at the university was looking to be lonely if not for the guild. Of the seven women in the loose group of girl scholars she had joined back in September, she would be the sole survivor at the lectures she attended. Antuniet still studied, of course, but she'd moved beyond the topics favored in Mihailin's philosophy lectures and was casting about for a private tutor who would match both her standards and her purse. And she had little use for history and theology but recommended, "You should spend more time on arithmetic and geometry," when they were comparing their planned courses.

"I can do my own accounts well enough," Margerit protested. "And Sister Petrunel gave me as good a grounding in the basic quadrivium as anyone has here. If they'd let me read for a degree it would be a different matter. As they won't, I don't see wasting my time on subjects that don't interest me. You never do."

Antuniet had given her a scornful look. "I'm not talking about reckoning and plotting angles. If you want to build mysteries, look to the structure of proofs. They'll take you further than formal logic alone." Margerit tucked that thought away for future reference.

Amiz bade goodbye to the group when the Lenten term ended. "My oldest sister settled her choice at last. They announced the betrothal last night. Mother's unbending enough to let me join the round of evening parties even though my dancing season won't begin until autumn."

Margerit found it hard to understand. Amiz had been a good student. The work came easily to her and if she'd put in the effort she could have been brilliant. But she'd never viewed the university as more than a pleasant distraction while waiting for her true calling.

Barbara still accompanied her, of course. She watched over all her classes now. Margerit never inquired into the details of how Barbara and Marken divided their watch, but it was clear that Marken now had responsibility for the guild time and Barbara had shifted to cover all the lectures. The evenings and other outings they split in some unknown fashion.

"Are you still studying law?" she asked Barbara one day when she realized the subject no longer featured when schedules were negotiated.

She expected Barbara to give the shrug that meant she had once again silently rearranged her life for another's convenience. Instead she frowned and shook her head. "There isn't much more I can get from lectures alone. They're all moving on to disputing cases and—" She gestured to indicate the invisible wall that faced her. "I'm still reading, when I have the time. And LeFevre has been giving me advice. He may not be a doctor of law, but he's spent most of his life untangling the baron's affairs."

* * *

The rituals surrounding Holy Week, both great and small, once again offered a riot of sensation for her newly opened eyes. She felt guilty, almost, to be watching and analyzing and planning when by rights her heart should have been filled only with piety. She sometimes found herself thinking of Sister Petrunel. Her governess had spoken of mysteries only as a means to experience God. What would she think of her former pupil? Did she ever think of her at all or did her duties for the *Orisules* take all her attention? The guild provided Margerit with plenty of opportunity to explore the mechanistic side of mysteries but few of them were interested in the simple experience of the numinous. In the long hours spent at services, bits of memory kept floating back. Things that Sister Petrunel had said. Margerit realized now how thoroughly and subtly she had discouraged her from questioning her *visitationis*. Why, if she had no doubts about their divine source?

It was easy enough to be swept away by the play of light and sound. Easy enough for ecstasy to take concrete form. But it was just as easy to start picking apart the patterns of cause and effect; the correlations between the priest and choir and the congregation's responses and the way the *fluctus* answered them; the difference between the calm peace of some services and the driving energy of others. And then, in the event that there were other *vidators* in the crowd, those effects were cover for her own workings.

It had proven surprisingly difficult to find opportunities to renew the *lorica* over Barbara that had been her first success. Most of the difficulty stemmed from a shyness in telling Barbara about it. There was no good reason not to, but having kept it to herself at first, it became harder and harder to raise the subject. She had a nagging suspicion that Barbara would find it embarrassing to be protected by the one she was sworn to protect. And Margerit was certain that the *lorica was* protecting her. There had been no further attacks, no sudden street corner encounters, no lurking shadows pointed out warily. To maintain that, she seized every chance to renew the protection when the necessary words could be said in Barbara's presence with no notice taken.

CHAPTER FORTY-FOUR

Barbara

Barbara's search through the baptisms at Saint Mauriz had failed to turn up any likely candidates. With the birth in December, the baptism surely would have happened by Easter. It must have been performed elsewhere. A lesser church in Rotenek was less likely than the parish church on the family lands—wherever that might be. That road went nowhere. A marriage, on the other hand, would only have been made in Rotenek. Especially since—she counted nine months back. If they had gotten to the begetting of heirs promptly, the marriage would have fallen solidly within the social season. She tried to envision her mother: a young girl, newly out. Flattered by the notice of a nobleman. A wedding. A child. The slowly dawning realization of the trap she had fallen into. Barbara turned the pages of the register to March and started working backward.

That search was no more successful than the first. No solemn marriage of Mesner This to Maisetra That, as she guessed her mother must have been. After a month of stolen sessions at the archives she let it go and cast about for some other clue to follow.

* * *

With Easter past, Rotenek was trying to squeeze all possible activity in before flood season. In the grand *salle* the floor was so crowded that the dancers were doing half-steps to avoid one set running into the next. It was odd, among all that, how one footfall could stand out in a crowded ballroom. Barbara couldn't have said how she managed to hear the sound: a step behind her, registering first for its intent and then for its familiarity. In the first moment, she stiffened; in the second, she relaxed. A low laugh sounded and the matching voice said, "I know better than to take you by surprise, *chérie*."

The woman stepped up beside her at an intimate distance and pressed two fingers to her carmined lips. Barbara tried not to respond when the fingers were brushed against her own mouth. That was all past.

"Mesnera," she acknowledged with a token bow.

"What's this? Once you called me Jeanne."

"Not when I'm on duty," Barbara said, moving half a step apart. "And not in public."

It had been inevitable that she would see more of the Vicomtesse de Cherdillac now that Mesner Pertinek's intervention had brought their orbits together once more. This was the first time Jeanne had sought her out. They had parted on perfectly amicable terms but Barbara had no interest in beginning again. From the corner of her eye she could see Jeanne's black curls spilling out from the bindings of a ribbon fillet to frame that familiar face. Her cheeks were still as delicately blushed, her lips still as rosy as she remembered, though both owed something to the cosmetic box. And the glint in her dark eyes as she leaned closely…Barbara kept her gaze deliberately out toward the dancers.

The vicomtesse glanced in the same direction. "I've been watching you watching her," she said with an edge of mischief in her voice.

"It's my duty to watch her." She tried to keep her tone entirely neutral but Jeanne was not put off the scent.

"What's this? No poetry?"

That drew a startled glance. "I beg your pardon?"

"There was a time when you'd start spouting poetry every time you were flustered. But perhaps you've lost your taste for verse."

"Perhaps you've lost your ability to fluster me," Barbara countered with a faint smile.

Jeanne pouted and turned her gaze back across the room. "And how does she like your poetry?" When she declined to take the bait

Jeanne shrugged. "I haven't yet had a chance to meet Marziel's little protégée. I think I shall procure an introduction."

Propriety forbade her from seizing the vicomtesse's arm to restrain her. Common sense kept her from begging her to leave well enough alone. Jeanne would do as she pleased. Barbara watched her make her way to Maisetra Pertinek's side and lean close to say a few words. At the next interval, introductions were performed. They were too far away to catch what was said. It went on for more than polite greetings and compliments. How indiscreet would she be? Jeanne had a spirit of mischief that forgot that other people's lives were more complicated than her own.

The question was answered somewhat in the carriage returning home when Margerit asked Mesner Pertinek, "The Vicomtesse de Cherdillac—" she stumbled uncertainly over the name. "Is she actually French? Her accent sounded more like Helviz."

He laughed lightly. "The title is genuine enough. She's the widow of an émigré. It was quite the scandal at the time for she was barely out and he was nearly seventy. It amused her to become even more French than he was. I think she aspires to be scandalous but has only achieved eccentricity."

And if she hasn't succeeded in being scandalous, Barbara thought, it's because she's more discreet than she pretends.

Mesner Pertinek continued, "It's for your aunt to say, of course, but I'd be careful about being drawn into de Cherdillac's circle. I wouldn't go so far as to say she isn't quite the thing, but her friends have established reputations that can survive a little wildness. A girl in your position must be more careful."

Maisetra Pertinek asked, "Did she invite you to anything, dear?"

"No," Margerit said. "She asked me what poets I liked. And then she said I should be sure not to miss Vittoriani's new opera. She said she saw it in Florence and thought I would enjoy it. But I don't know why she thought I would like it; we didn't talk about music at all."

"I think that's a marvelous idea," her aunt responded. "Your box has sat empty since December. And I've been saying for weeks that you need to make the most of the end of the season."

"But Aunt," Margerit protested, "I'll be staying in Rotenek through the end of the university term, so I have two more months at least."

"No one else who matters will be staying much past the floods. It isn't students you need to be meeting. When autumn comes, we need to start thinking seriously about your marriage."

Even in the dark, Barbara could see a mulish look settle over Margerit's face. She hoped Maisetra Pertinek was less perceptive. There was more of the game to play out before Margerit could afford to defy expectations openly.

* * *

The last time Barbara had ventured in disguise to Eskamer's pawnshop he had suggested that he might be able to lay hands on a copy—a transcript only, and somewhat corrupted—of the Mysterium of Saint Penekiz. And now that Margerit had expressed an interest in it, Barbara once again put on the guise of a fashionable young man and set out by circuitous ways to Rens Street.

She paused just inside the door of the tavern to let her eyes adjust. When her gaze fell on the pair of men at a table just by the passage to Eskamer's entrance it took all her nerve to walk casually past, confident in her disguise—her disguise and whatever mysterious luck had been concealing her from her enemies' eyes. Estefen. And Lutoz with him. Not so strange, she reassured herself. They ran in the same circles and were of an age. It was only expected that they would know each other. But why here?

It seemed Lutoz had the same question, for as she paused just out of their sight around the corner he was saying, "But why this godforsaken hole of all places?"

And then Estefen's answer, "I don't care to have anyone know I'm in town. And especially not my mother." His voice dropped to inaudibility and Barbara moved on. This was a place where eavesdroppers would likely be noticed and challenged.

So he was staying away from Rotenek. That would account for the lack of any unfortunate encounters in the salons and ballrooms. No doubt he too had creditors to avoid. And a mother to avoid, evidently. Barbara recalled the times she'd crossed paths with the late baron's sister. A formidable woman. Perhaps one who had not yet forgiven her son for how badly he'd handled his family relationships.

The Penekiz book was not available. Alas, the owner had decided not to sell after all. Barbara wondered idly if the owner had ever been aware he was considering selling. More speculations about the availability of other books were offered but she declined. It was too risky to keep coming down here without a specific need or a solid certainty.

The two men were no longer in place when she emerged. Too brief to have accomplished much of business. Perhaps this had only been a meeting point? It made her uneasy that someone so prominent in the guild was close to Estefen, however unsurprising it might be. And yet, with Estefen's sister Antuniet a member, why not friends of his as well? Lutoz had never treated Margerit with anything less than civility and respect for her talents. She was being overcautious. And it would take more than caution to be worth trying to pry Margerit loose from the guild now.

* * *

No one went to the opera planning to listen to the music. No one who inhabited the ranks of boxes along the mid-levels, that is. When Barbara realized which performance the vicomtesse had recommended her heart sank. Had Jeanne meant the allusion for her? Or had she guessed there was something more between her and Margerit to be teased out? *Ifis e Ianthe* was not the most subtle of stories. But who paid attention to the stage when there were people to be watched and gossip to exchange?

Margerit paid some attention at first, no doubt wondering why the recommendation had been made. By the end of the first act her attention had wandered and Barbara relaxed enough to appreciate the performance herself, save for that part of her that always stood guard. The story of Ifis had echoes for her: a father's malice, a daughter concealed and disguised, raised more in the ways of men than women and excelling at it. And then, in the second act, Ianthe offered as the reward for a hero. Betrothed and—in the ways of the stage—willingly so and in love.

The lights came up for the interval and Margerit insisted on the long walk around to the Aruliks' box where she had seen the Waldimens were guests. Barbara had been keeping a wary eye out for the vicomtesse and she appeared at last as they returned to Margerit's box.

"And how are you enjoying the performance?"

Margerit curtsied and invited her to join them but the offer was waved off. "The music is very pleasant," she answered politely. "I confess my Italian is better for books than for singing."

Jeanne leaned toward her with a conspiratorial air. "You should ask Barbara to translate for you. Her Italian is excellent and she loves opera."

Margerit smiled faintly and thanked her as the sounds of the orchestra called them to their seats.

Barbara took her accustomed place by the door but as the singing began Margerit beckoned her over to her side. "I haven't been following it much except that it's all ancient Greeks and battles and such. What's happening now?"

Barbara knelt beside her and leaned close to whisper so as not to disturb the rest of the party. A brief synopsis of what had gone before took up the time while the chorus escorted the principals to the center of the stage. "I haven't seen this performance before," Barbara added, "but I imagine this will be the grand love duet." As the soprano began she concentrated on the stage to follow the opening phrases. The chorus had abandoned the field to the principals who faced each other against a backdrop of fluted columns.

"O! What strange fate is mine!" Barbara paused as the signature line was repeated several times. "I loved you in the guise of Mars, but now I am betrayed by Venus. The iron in your glance turns soft beneath my touch. I am undone. O Venus, you are cruel to mock me so." It continued on in the same vein until it was the mezzo's turn. Her lyrics ran much in parallel with the soprano's. With less concentration required, Barbara ventured a glance to see Margerit's reaction. Margerit turned at the same moment and their eyes met as Barbara whispered Ifis's lines.

"O! What strange fate is mine! In the guise of Mars I loved you, but now as Venus I'm betrayed. The iron in my soul turns soft beneath your touch." Unconsciously, Margerit placed a hand on hers where it lay on the arm of her chair. "Fire runs through my veins—I am undone." Fire indeed ran through her veins. Her hand burned sweetly where Margerit touched it and she dared not take it back. Her voice grew husky. "Why do the gods mock me with desire I cannot sate?" Their eyes were still locked and Margerit's lips had parted in a little "o" of wonder. "O Venus, have mercy on one new come to your shrine."

When the soprano joined again for the duet, Margerit breathed along with her, "O! What strange fate is mine!"

With an effort, Barbara wrenched her gaze away. "And now they'll repeat the whole thing over again for another quarter hour." They both turned to watch the stage again as the singers joined hands and sang an intricate counterpoint of their two themes. When the next scene began, Barbara confined herself to merely glossing the lyrics in short descriptions.

The finale was grand and triumphant and hollowly disappointing. Barbara could see it left Margerit troubled and she dodged the opportunity for awkward questions by sitting up with the coachman for the return home.

It was less possible to escape when the Pertineks had headed upstairs and the servants had dispersed into the back hallways. Margerit stayed her with a hand on her arm when she would have slipped away as well. "It didn't seem fair or…or just."

Barbara waited. She didn't want to second-guess what Margerit meant.

"It was as a woman that she loved her. There was no need for the gods to change her to a man."

Barbara shrugged. "That's the way these stories always end. If there isn't a miracle then there's a convenient twin brother waiting in the wings."

"And what if there are no brothers or miracles available?"

They were standing on the edge of a precipice. Barbara wanted to do something irrevocable—to take that plunge against all duty. Instead she kept herself to a wry smile. "In that case, I guess they'll have to muddle through as best they can. Good night," she added firmly and turned to mount the stairs without looking back.

CHAPTER FORTY-FIVE

Margerit

Margerit had envisioned the spring floods as coming with a torrential downpour, the skies dark and roiling with clouds, the gutters swelling with runoff until you couldn't tell the difference between streets and streams. But they started on a bright sunny day. A light sprinkle had passed through just around dawn and there were still a few wisps of clouds overhead. The mountains to the east were cloud-capped, as always. It started with a change in color. The center of the great Rotein where the current ran quickest grew pale and muddy. The color spread and the surface grew troubled, hinting at activity below. Along the banks, the water began to rise. You would look away for a moment and then back to see another bit of pathway swallowed up.

The gardens had long since been cleared of any movables—the heavy marble benches were not counted as such. The early flowers had bloomed and gone but later there would be work for an army of gardeners setting things to rights and setting out the summer plantings. The lowest levels of the house were cleared. It wasn't common for the water to come so high, they said—only once in ten years or so—but prudence was best. Everything crowded upward, like petticoats lifted to avoid a puddle. Boxes stood in every hallway.

But however much inconvenience it caused, tradition ruled that flood season didn't begin until water covered the feet of the statue of Saint Nikule where he stood watching over merchants and boatmen at the wharfside. Late one afternoon Margerit heard the bell at the saint's chapel ring twice to mark the event. Then, like an echo, every other church took up the simple two-tone signal and the city was released from the bondage of custom. A few carriages passed through the gates before dusk—those that had only a short distance to go, or those whose road required them to cross the bridges before leaving and who didn't care to gamble on what the footings might look like in the morning. But for the most part the departures began in the morning with the stately dignity of a ceremonial procession, not the air of hurried flight.

It seemed, like all else in the city, that the exodus at flood-tide had its layers. Those at the top dispersed to their country estates. For them, the floods weren't the end of the social season but only marked its transition to a less formal venue, like the annual arrivals in Chalanz. Next were those who flowed out in their wake, taking advantage of whatever ties and obligations could be claimed to enjoy a week's holiday. They would return to their homes in Rotenek neighborhoods not quite fashionable enough to have been in danger from the waters. Lower down were those for whom flood-tide meant only a temporary bar to movement and a pause in all but the most desperate river traffic. If their homes were threatened by the rising waters, they had nowhere but the streets to flee to.

The university held to a stricter calendar than society. While the students might have their flood-tide holiday with the rest, the lectures stretched out until the term was complete, whatever the river might do. And as Chalanz was too far for a week's holiday, at first Margerit thought to join the Waldimens and another family in nearby Iuten for the festival there. But once again she bent to Aunt Bertrut's ambitions—no, ambition was the wrong word. The invitation from the Pertineks was only to be expected and it would be rude to refuse regardless of what advantages it might confer. Particularly as her aunt would be constrained to accompany her whichever invitation she accepted.

The Pertineks' country home reminded her in many ways of Aunt Fulpi's family home at Mintun. It had the feel of a working estate— the sort that supported a family's wealth rather than draining it. The multitudinous Pertinek clan that rubbed elbows so closely on the Vezenaf spread out and blossomed here. Cousins who had been silent faces at a dinner grew garrulous and good-humored. Names that had previously eluded memory acquired personalities. And, of course, there were any number of people—some merely acquaintances of the family—that she hadn't met before.

They all knew her, it seemed. New additions to the gathering were not so common that she and Aunt Bertrut hadn't been discussed and speculated over long before they stepped down from their coach. In the strict and formal confines of Rotenek, such obvious scrutiny would have been intimidating. Under the relaxed atmosphere of flood-tide it had more the air of marketplace gossip. The consideration was not all one-sided. In ten days of picnic luncheons and garden walks, Margerit learned more about the prominent figures of Rotenek society than she had gleaned in the previous half year.

The old Pergint place on the Vezenaf had finally been sold after years tracking down the last heir and of all people Estapez had purchased it. "And you know he got his hand in before anyone else because he has the right friends in the palace. Chozzik thought it would be his. He even tried to challenge Estapez over it but his duelist wouldn't fight. Said there was no insult to being the princess's friend so there was nothing to defend."

"Friends won't be there forever. Chozzik's ship was left high and dry when old Lumbeirt died. No one cares for his opinions now but the wheel will turn for Estapez some day."

Even the royal family and the question of succession evaded their usual constraints. "Elisebet must have smelled the wind changing. I hear she's talking to the old men these days and not just their sons."

And among those of an age to remember, Alpennia's small part in the French Wars was refought at tedious length. "Tarnzais should never have happened. They should have known long before the battle that it was no mere border skirmish where a handful of bright uniforms and a cavalry charge could serve the needs of honor."

"I don't think they could have known. The world was turning differently. Our alliances had always held the balance—" the speaker crossed himself reflexively "—and the protection of Saint Mauriz, of course. How could we see this was a new age with new ideas and new rules?"

"All I know is we lost the flower of our youth that day and for what? For a shameful treaty and years of tribute."

"The Atilliet did the best he could, and that considering what he himself had lost."

There were nods all around at that and a few murmured blessings for the souls of the lost princes.

"Not everyone lost that day," came a querulous voice. "She's proof of that."

Margerit realized this was being said with a nod in her direction.

"Yes, Marziel Lumbeirt turned out to have quite a knack for turning manure into roses."

There was a pause, as if waiting for her to make some objection. She ventured, "I really know very little about my godfather's history."

As if to oblige, the topic turned in that direction with a confused jumble of voices. "I'm not sure you could count it part of Lumbeirt's luck that his brother died at Tarnzais. Remember that the title wasn't worth much then. It was afterward he turned things around."

"Turned around—that's one way of putting it. There's a name for a man who turns a profit in wartime when all around him are wearing last year's clothes. And that's aside from the matter of soiling his title with trade."

"Well, when the profit was made at the expense of foreigners, I'm willing to make that name 'patriot.'"

"But what did it get him in the end? Never married. He certainly wasn't doing it for his sister's boy—those two were always at cats and dogs. I know he was a strange and acid fellow, but you'd think that some woman would have dared the chance."

"I always rather fancied that his heart was broken by an unrequited love."

"The way I heard it, it was requited well enough. Problem is, it was another man's wife. And that would explain rather a lot, I th—"

The speaker broke off, calling more attention to the thought than completing it would have. Margerit once again saw eyes turn toward her. She rose, feeling her face flush brightly, and fumbled for a response in the sudden hush. "I don't...you..."

From behind her, Barbara's voice cut through in a carefully even tone. "You have come perilously close to slandering Maisetra Sovitre's mother."

There was a nervous titter from the direction of the speaker. Someone else said, "Come now, it was only ancient gossip, nothing more. No names were named."

And then Uncle Charul was taking Barbara aside and speaking rapidly and intensely to her, too low to hear. Margerit stood frozen, not knowing what to do, knowing only that she couldn't face these strangers at the moment. She turned and strode out of the garden, heading blindly out along paths that led back toward the manor.

The tiny room she shared with two other guests was an uncertain refuge. By luck it was empty and she locked the door behind her. There hadn't been tears before but they came now. *Is that what they all thought?* It was ugly.

There came a tap at the door and Barbara's voice. "Maisetra? Margerit?" Of course. There was no question that she could be left alone.

"Go away," she called out, knowing that Barbara would do no such thing.

There was a brief respite and then a hand tried the door and Aunt Bertrut's voice came through. "Margerit, let me in. Don't be such a child."

The idea of throwing herself on the bed sobbing had already lost its appeal. Her aunt, of all people, could answer her questions. She turned the key in the door.

"It's not true, is it? What she said?"

Aunt Bertrut entered with a brisk no-nonsense response. "Do you even have to ask?"

Bertrut took her face in her hands and gazed at her with sympathy. "These people may know old gossip about the late baron, but I knew your mother. She and my brother came to love each other very deeply. I saw how happy they were together. The only mystery around your birth was the one your mother went to Saint Orisul's to ask for." Her voice became softer, remembering, as they sat together on one of the beds. "They had been trying for so long. You had a brother, you know, who only lived for one day. The others—not even that. Your father wanted to…to let things be. Each time it was harder and she wasn't strong to begin with. She thought the only hope left was a miracle— and here you are. Does that sound like a woman who had need for a passionate affair with a stranger?"

Margerit shook her head. She had never really doubted, but it helped to hear the matter laid out so plainly. "How did the baron come to be my godfather?"

"That I don't know," she answered briskly again. "He's some sort of very distant cousin but that wouldn't have mattered. I think the connection was through an old school friend. Your parents were living in Rotenek then."

Margerit was startled. "I never knew that!"

"Your father wanted a physician in attendance; there was a man there who was highly recommended. That was a quarrel between them but he insisted. When they brought you home to Chalanz, I don't think the matter of godparents was ever discussed. Not until those last days when the fever came through and—well, until those last days. Your mother was so insistent that we contact the baron and remind him of his obligations. For the rest, you know as much as I. Now wash your face and let's go back. They'll be talking about something else entirely by now and it will all have been forgotten."

Perhaps no one had believed it. Perhaps no one thought it mattered. But for Margerit the light holiday mood of flood-tide had faded and she found herself looking forward to the return to Rotenek as eagerly as most had anticipated the exodus.

* * *

Rotenek after flood-tide felt not so much empty as thin. In spite of all, the streets still bustled. The university district was near unchanged and the river traffic was busier than ever and more noticed as the activities of the household spilled out into the gardens. There had been a hasty clean up of what the floods had deposited and the new plantings were not intended to be seen to full advantage until late summer. Margerit thought longingly of the baron's gardens—her gardens—in Chalanz. She would miss their best flowering.

Without the overlay of salons and balls and visiting, it felt easier to breathe. True summer, she knew, would be far less pleasant in the city but by then the term would be finished and the household would make its delayed departure. Aunt Bertrut looked forward to that, she knew. The Pertineks rattled around now with nothing much to do. There was a limit to how many carriage rides into the countryside one could enjoy, how many lazy boating excursions one could take up the now-placid waters and how often one could make excuses to visit the few families still in residence. Margerit felt a twinge or two of guilt for holding everyone hostage to the university's calendar. But none of them would be there at all except for her. It was the bargain they had taken up.

The guild had entered into a half-life. The noble members had mostly scattered to the countryside but Hennis, uncharacteristically impatient with the turn of the season, had parceled out tasks before his own departure. Margerit took the largest part: to create the scaffold of their *castellum* and somehow test its structure even as others crafted the individual stones that would fit together to build it.

It wasn't until the presence of the guild faded somewhat that Margerit realized how much she'd missed the close partnership she and Barbara had forged over their books and debates. She hadn't seen how far Barbara had stepped back until her days were emptier. Now that partnership returned, filling the library once again with the joy of search and discovery. And then, at last, lectures were at an end, the household was packed up and sent ahead, the last agonizing over which books to take and which to leave was past and Rotenek was left behind.

CHAPTER FORTY-SIX

Barbara

Barbara remembered the sense of relief she had felt on returning to Rotenek the previous autumn. The familiarity of old haunts and old habits had given a false promise of simplicity, even in the midst of the tangled rhythms of the city. But Margerit's household was not the baron's and there would never again be a return to knowing her place in the world that precisely. Now the sight of Chalanz brought a more reasoned relief, the more appreciated for knowing it would end.

The household that returned to Chalanz was not the one that had left it either. More than half a year of being mistress in her own house—and despite her nominal position, Maisetra Pertinek had been too clever to dispute that—had changed Margerit enormously from the girl she'd known in those chaotic weeks around the baron's death. Maisetra Pertinek returned changed as well, Barbara reflected, leaving as an old maid, barely better than a paid companion, and returning with a well-born husband in tow. There was little time to speculate what Margerit's uncle would make of the changes. No sooner had the weary travelers been welcomed at the doors on Fonten Street than Margerit was presented with a small envelope whose contents caused her to venture a very mild oath as she crumpled the sheet in her hand.

"He expects! Expects—not requests or invites—my presence at dinner this evening. I'll barely have time to wash the dust off. What's so important it can't wait a day or two?"

Maisetra Pertinek seemed to be swallowing a similar reaction as she ventured, "He hasn't seen you in months, after all. I'm sure he wants to hear all the news."

Margerit eyed her skeptically. "He wants me to remember that I'm under his orders." Barbara hoped it was only the wear of the journey that provoked her rebellious impulse.

Mesner Pertinek, perhaps hoping the same, offered an uncharacteristic, if mild, rebuke. "As you are. It might be well to remember it. But if you want a brief respite," he continued, "I think we might stand by a point of etiquette."

And so it was that Barbara found herself employed as messenger, carrying a formal invitation card to Chaturik Square, along with the words of an intricate and apologetic explanation.

Maistir Fulpi was put in no good mood by the identity of the messenger and her decision to follow city customs and direct her errand to the front entrance. He held the small card up before her, as if it were something unsavory, asking, "What is this? 'Mesner and Maisetra Pertinek request the company of Maistir and Maisetra Fulpi at dinner on the morrow by the gracious hospitality of Maisetra Sovitre.' What is she playing at?"

Barbara repeated her carefully rehearsed lines. "Maisetra Pertinek was certain it was a mere oversight—the matter being so complicated. But she knew you could not have meant to entertain Maisetra Sovitre without her presence. And of course she could not be expected to come without the company of Mesner Pertinek," she placed just the slightest of emphasis on his title, "but of course it is for him to offer the first invitation. And not keeping lodgings of his own, he has accepted Maisetra Sovitre's generous offer to use her house to entertain you." It was convoluted, absurd and totally unassailable. For all that they had rubbed elbows for weeks as fellow guests in Rotenek, any visits between the two men must be initiated on the side of higher rank. And Margerit could pretend to complete innocence in the skirmish.

When presented with the matter in that light, Maistir Fulpi scribbled his response on the card and handed it back with ill grace. Barbara felt no pity for him. If he followed the rules, he could play his new brother-in-law into no small profit of prestige among his circle here. No matter that a minor Pertinek cousin meant nothing much in

Rotenek. The boundaries were harder to cross here in the provinces and the tie was worth a minor retreat.

Though born out of pique, that first family dinner seemed to have set a tone for the summer, and an agreement that all could be content with. Barbara was amused to learn the details of the negotiations as they came back to the kitchen with the empty dishes. Maistir Fulpi would not argue over Margerit's maintenance of her separate household—well, that was hardly a concession. To arrange otherwise would be impossible at this point. He had approved of her lack of haste regarding offers of marriage. When the time came to move these things further along, he would be to hand to see them done properly. That, again, was hardly a concession on Margerit's part. But she was expected to take on the full round of dinners and parties and visiting that Chalanz society offered for the summer. Barbara knew she had hoped to enjoy more of a holiday. After all, Maisetra Pertinek had her own circle here, not needing the excuse of escorting Margerit in order to find her own welcome. But Maistir Fulpi was adamant. Margerit was not to give the impression that one season in Rotenek had made her too proud to mix with her old friends back home. Well, a few dinners and such were more than manageable. After all, Barbara added to herself, there were no lectures to accommodate. And it would be good if Margerit herself planned an entertainment. Yes, that was agreed. Perhaps at the end of summer as she had last year. And with the Pertineks in residence there was more scope for smaller invitations. That, she would leave to the aunt. LeFevre was to give Maistir Fulpi a full accounting. Naturally—he would be traveling through in a month or so. It was his habit to visit all the properties over the summer. Not the foreign ones, of course, although those had mostly been sold off by now.

There were a few more minor matters and Barbara suspected that some of the details had been left behind as uninteresting. All in all, Fulpi's requirements were harmless—and likely would have been so even without having been thrown off balance from the start. But he was still the most likely hazard to Margerit's ambitions and Barbara made a note to compare the kitchen version of his visit with Margerit's own.

* * *

With barely a day or two to get settled, they plunged into the designing of mysteries. Margerit laid claim to LeFevre's office, leaving the library free for sprawling piles of books, each fluttering with ribbons marking passages to be reviewed and referred to. LeFevre's desk was pushed aside and a long table was brought in from the ballroom. Page by page, the skeleton of the *castellum* took shape down its center, weighted in place by decorative oddments borrowed from here and there around the house. Piles of scribbled notes and comments branched out at intervals as key points were examined and planned.

"I just don't see how you can do it," Barbara marveled, looking over the shaping chaos. "You don't have the prayers, you don't know the apparatus. You don't even know which saint is going to be petitioned here." She pointed to a section of the plan that was bare of details.

"But I know the…the shape of what it needs to look like. I know what needs to happen during that piece. We'll try a few alternatives until we find someone who fits that shape. It's—" She gestured widely, taking in the entire length of the table. "It's like planning a garden. You lay out the walkways and the beds. You know that *here* is where your stream is flowing, so you can direct it *there* or *there*. And you have a copse over *here* so you could work around it or remove it but you couldn't move it *here*. And maybe you don't know exactly which flowers you're going to plant yet, but you know what color they should be and how tall and that *these* ones should bloom before *those*."

Margerit stood in trance, staring out as if she could see that garden blooming. Barbara felt a shiver of excitement. She might not be able to see that vision in detail, but she could see it reflected in Margerit's face. She loved helping create it for her. Margerit shook her head, as if to disperse the imagined structures. "Or if not a garden, it's like I'm a painter and I *know* what the image will look like but I have to figure out which brush and paint to use."

Barbara laughed. "I like the garden better. It allows for the part of divine interference in the plan. But speaking of gardens, you promised your aunt you'd walk out in the park with her this afternoon." She started moving along the table, replacing the weights that kept the notes in order. "You really should take advantage of the beautiful weather more. Fresh air is good for you and you spend so much time in here."

"Oh Barbara, not you too!"

Barbara turned at the waspish tone in her voice.

"Everyone in the world is always telling me what I should do. I'll keep my promise to Aunt Bertrut, but please don't badger me about it."

Barbara stiffened and inclined in a slight bow. "Forgive me Maisetra."

"And please don't spoil our time with that 'yes, Maisetra' nonsense. But leave the nagging to my aunt."

* * *

For Barbara, Axian Park would always be associated with that unlucky boy's death, but there had been pleasant times as well: long restless walks in the days before Margerit had left her uncle's house, when it was a welcome chance for her to be alone. Now the opposite was true. At home, Margerit could shut the world away, but here in public anyone with the proper introduction could approach her. And in a close community like Chalanz, that meant almost everyone.

True to form, they hadn't been walking more than a hundred yards before chance-that-was-no-chance brought another party's steps alongside hers. There was a show of making up to the aunt, of course—greetings and a mention of the doings of mutual friends. But then matters turned in the usual direction.

"Maisetra Sovitre, I swear the roses have left their stems to bloom in your cheeks. Are you enjoying the gardens?"

"I was enjoying the walk," Margerit answered. "I have roses enough at home."

She never quite warned them off—that would earn a scolding later from Maisetra Pertinek. But her answers were always calculated to throw her petitioners off balance. The young men of Chalanz were brasher than those of the city, no doubt sensing that they would have little time to make their case. It amused Barbara to watch them assail the fortress and find no chink. She'd lost the fear that some provincial gallant would turn Margerit's head from the delights of Rotenek.

He made another essay. "I'll be riding tomorrow if the day is fine. Perhaps you might ride with me?"

"I don't ride," came the reply.

"Ah." He stumbled a bit, trying to keep up with Margerit's brisk pace while still facing her. "Perhaps a carriage ride?"

She seemed to be considering the matter. "Perhaps I might take a carriage ride tomorrow. What a pity that you can't join me."

"But why not?" He was clearly taken aback.

"Because you'll be riding tomorrow—you just told me so. And I know you're a man of your word."

He gave up at that. Even Maisetra Pertinek couldn't help laughing once he was out of earshot. "Oh Margerit, you shouldn't tease him so!" But then she took herself in hand once more and added, "Perhaps you should think of learning to ride. It's a useful accomplishment."

Margerit shook her head. "If I decide to learn, it won't be with some would-be suitor at my side, laughing at all my tumbles."

* * *

The summer continued in that vein, with the time marked first by the slow accumulation of papers on the office table and then by the ebbing of the paper tide as decisions were made, references were completed, details were specified and all was copied out in a fair hand. Barbara thumbed through the sheets when they had completed the best version that was possible without the contributions of the other guild members. It was nothing like the Mauriz text they had pored over so many months ago. Rather than the cramped layers of hands and emendations, adorned with the rubrics and flourishes of an older age, it was a crisp, even copperplate, interspersed with boxes and diagrams that gave it more the air of an astrological chart than a ceremony. Seen as a whole, it was hard to believe that something so... so *created* could have the same force of ritual as those handed down across the centuries.

She didn't voice that thought. If Margerit were free of such self-doubts, it wasn't for her to raise them. But another matter did tease at her mind. "I know the intent was to create a *castellum*—a protection for the land—but there are parts here that feel less like a set of walls and towers and more like an army sallying through the gates." She pointed out one of the passages in question.

"It's all just symbols. The protection is meant to be many-layered, after all. Against plague, against drought, against curses, against misfortune. We thought about putting in layers against foreign invasions—the old wars are always on everyone's mind. But mysteries are little match for a strong army. We learned that well enough. The intent here is to guard against more subtle things."

Margerit took the papers from her and rolled them up to fit into a stout leather case. No risk of all that work being damaged before it got back to Rotenek.

"Too late for LeFevre to have his office back!" Barbara pointed out. He'd arrived two weeks before and made do with the corner into which his desk had been crammed. But now, having reviewed all accounts for the Chalanz house and having satisfied Maistir Fulpi of his stewardship, he was gone ahead of them back to the city.

"And now," said Margerit as she set the case aside, "all that's left of the summer is to hold a ball."

* * *

Last year there had been the heady excitement for Margerit of taking up the reins of her own life and first stepping into society as a hostess rather than a pawn on the board. This year it felt more routine. A great deal of the planning was handed over to Maisetra Fulpi as a sweetener for having left her out of most of the summer's entertainments. Details that had been skirmishes in the battle for independence last year could now be placed on the table as peace offerings. And for Barbara, the nerves that last year had been tensed to near breaking by the weight of her responsibilities were calmer with the ease of habit and—she dared to admit—the long months with no sign of any overt threat to her charge. In truth, Estefen seemed to have abandoned the gameboard.

CHAPTER FORTY-SEVEN

Margerit

The Estrausiz Road that stretched east from Rotenek had a reputation in story for being haunted by bandits. Margerit had thought it just a staple of romantic novels. What she'd seen of it before had been a well-kept carriage road, dotted at intervals with villages sporting quaint, friendly innkeepers. It was frequented by enough traffic to make care necessary on blind turns but not enough to slow the journey significantly. Barbara's caution in hiring extra outriders for the trip, equipped with pistols, had seemed overdone until she leaned in toward the open carriage window from her saddle to warn, "Be ready! We're followed." When Margerit craned her head out to see the clot of riders pacing them a quarter mile back, Barbara shouted at her to sit back and hold on.

She felt a change in the pace of the horses as the coachman gathered them in readiness for a sprint. Long moments passed. Shouting could be heard clearly over the sound of the hooves and she braced her ears for the sound of a shot. But in the end nothing came of it. When they stopped to rest the horses and take refreshment at the next inn, Barbara said only, "They decided we were more of a bite than they cared to chew." And then, quietly, almost as an afterthought, "I see no reason to think Estefen could have been behind it."

That hadn't occurred to her. She'd stopped worrying long since whether the new Baron Saveze was still planning revenge—or something more practical.

They reached the city with no other excitement. Overlaid on her view of the familiar streets was the memory of her last arrival: the cathedral that had towered so imposingly, the glimpse of the gilded ornaments of the opera house, the imposing bulk of the palace, the row of deceptively simple facades along the Vezenaf. It had all been a wonder out of legend and now it was just home. Margerit smiled to herself at that thought. One year had made Rotenek home. Chalanz was where her childhood lived—that shy, dreaming, fettered girl. Transplanted to Rotenek she had finally found the chance to bloom. In another echo of her previous arrival, she'd come out onto the narrow balcony behind the library to look out over the tumbled riot of gardens falling down to the river's edge. Behind her on the round table lay the roll of papers representing her summer's work, carried carefully in hand throughout the return journey. Last year she had been surrounded by newly opened doors, wondering what lay behind them. This time was better because she knew exactly what they offered.

* * *

The mystery guild re-formed slowly as the traveling members returned from their summer haunts. If there had been any acceptable way to do so, Margerit would have gone calling on Hennis Lutoz to present the results of her work. But outside the license of the guildhall itself she had no social entrance to his life—no sister of his she might visit as an excuse. She could have used Nikule as go-between but he was one of the last to straggle in. There had been arguments between him and Uncle Fulpi, she knew. She hadn't been privy to all the details but the field of their battle had been whether he would take another year at the university or stay in Chalanz and start in his father's business. Nikule had never been serious as a scholar and he had fulfilled the requirements of a gentleman's education. But the guild had changed him. He knew—they all knew—he'd only been included to give cover to her own invitation. But just maybe he'd decided to prove he brought some value of his own, for he'd insisted on another year in the city. And in the end he'd won on the argument to his father that the connections he made there would pay off in the end.

It wasn't until lectures were already begun that Hennis sent word round to gather at the guildhall and renew their work. Margerit laid out the pages of her framework along one of the long refectory tables, echoing the office in Chalanz.

"It opens here," she explained, "with the standard prayers. Then we define the limits of Alpennia with a *markein* invoking the local patrons in turn, beginning at Helviz and working around to Feniz, then it ends in Rotenek with Mauriz, finishing with our own patron Atelpirt to set the seal. Each point has its own small structure based on the traditional forms for that saint. That's where the mistake is often made, I think. People want to bring the parts together under a single rite, whether it's the Lyonnais today or the Roman in our grandparents' time or whatever the fashion is. But these are local saints and I think they should be spoken to with their local tongues and habits."

Hennis interrupted, "Which is why the rest of you have been working separately to fill in those spaces."

As Margerit moved down the table to gesture at the next section, the others followed her in a cloud. She thought momentarily of how students would cluster around the *dozzures* as they moved between lectures. Did it feel like this? "So that part is raising the walls. Then we move on to touch on the different protections we request. For each one we raise a tower. Each saint is called on to lay a course of stones and here there's a unifying structure to the repetitions but each petition still keeps elements native to the patron. And then here," she moved down to the last section, "the threads are woven together to tie it up as a whole. That's not quite the right image. Perhaps more like setting up a network of signals and messengers between the towers so that any harm is answered by the whole. I know what the *fluctus* will look like here, but it doesn't fit so well with the image of walls and towers."

She looked up to see whether the others had followed her explanation. Iakup was peering at her over the edge of his spectacles and the Saluns were staring in something bordering on astonishment. The rest were bent over the papers to study them in more detail. "Do…do you think it will work for our purpose?" she asked in sudden uncertainty.

Akezze barked out a laugh. "Will it work? Even if it doesn't you've created a wonder here. Is this really the first mystery you've crafted?"

"Not exactly. The first was—" No, the *lorica* was a private matter. If she hadn't told Barbara about it, it wasn't right to tell them. "The first was much smaller." And it pained her not to give Barbara the credit she deserved for her own contributions. Small wonder she'd once again assigned Marken to oversee guild days. Margerit knew she wouldn't have been able to stand by silently if she were in Barbara's place.

* * *

The return of the Rotenek season hit like a river flood. Last year there had been the long slow accumulation of contacts and introductions. Now suddenly she found herself committed in a single week to two musical salons, one formal ball and playing nominal hostess to an opera party of Aunt Bertrut's friends, as well as the usual rounds of visiting that her aunt insisted on. At that she put her foot down.

"Aunt Bertrut, this is too much. I need at least three days in a row with no going out. I have work to do."

Her aunt indulged a rare moment of impatience. "And 'no going out' doesn't include running off to your lectures or chanting mysteries with your bookish friends. No, Margerit, I'm not blind and I know you don't care much about making a good match. But I had to give a promise to your Uncle Fulpi that I would try to turn your mind more to serious matters."

There had been arguments between them, she knew. Bertrut was keeping a fine balance between her roles of guardian and dependent and she had grown sharp and nervous over it. Margerit knew her face showed her own growing annoyance because Bertrut continued quickly, "And if he isn't happy with my reports, he's said he'll fetch you back to Chalanz. It wouldn't be pleasant for any of us, but he has that legal right."

"Only until February," Margerit interrupted.

Bertrut fell silent for a moment. Margerit realized she'd never quite so plainly indicated her intention to go her own way the first moment she could.

"Margerit, if you want to spend the next six months locked in a bedroom in Chalanz, all for the pleasure of telling the entire world to go to the devil a bit sooner, then I don't know you at all." She had clearly been building up to this talk for some time. "It's not for me to judge why your godfather thought it wise to put that power in your hands so young, but how long do you think you'll be happy to sit here alone with your books and writings when the world takes you at your word and goes to the devil? When no one of any sense or standing will greet you in the street because you've trampled every convention they hold dear? When even your family refuses to receive you because you destroyed the hopes they have for you?"

Margerit blurted out, "You mean the hopes you have for yourself that depend on me! Where would you and Mesner Pertinek be if I were locked up in Uncle Fulpi's attic and didn't need you to keep house for me?"

That went too far. Much too far. Bertrut began crying. Margerit felt her anger melt away.

"Aunt! Aunt, I didn't mean it! I'm so sorry." She took her aunt's hands as she crumpled into the nearest chair, then knelt at her feet. "It's just all too much. I'm tired. But the studying and the guild…that's what I live for. It's *important*. Not just to me. What we're doing, it will be important for everyone, you'll see. But I can't do that and be out dancing every night as well! Aunt, have you ever wanted something so badly that it *would* have been worth telling everyone to go to the devil to get it?"

She reached up to touch her aunt's face, to wipe away the tears, to erase all the poisonous words.

Bertrut turned to her with a faraway look and just the hint of a smile in the corner of her mouth. "Yes, dear, I have. But it wouldn't have been worth it." She pulled out a handkerchief and dabbed at her eyes. "I know you're tired. But you can't shut yourself away from society. And if I left the choice to you, that's what you'd do and not count the cost until too late. I'll tell Mesnera Arulik you aren't feeling well and we'll stay home tonight. But you need to meet me halfway." She stood up and smoothed her skirts out then added in a brisker tone, "And if it helps, think about how your guild would manage without you if you were locked in that attic for the next six months."

CHAPTER FORTY-EIGHT

Barbara

To those who listened, there was a frantic edge to the voice of the city. Prince Aukust was ill. No, he wasn't ill; he had left the city for a religious retreat. No, he was in the city but would see no one. His visitors were being refused by Princess Elisebet and he didn't know it. No, he had been seen at the opera the night before, laughing and in good health.

Barbara declined to believe or disbelieve any of the rumors. The one story she did believe was that he had sent ambassadors to Austria over the summer to request the presence of his daughter and his grandsons at a council on the succession of Alpennia. It would take months to arrange their travel—if it could be done at all before winter closed the most convenient passes. That left a long time for rumors to sprout and bloom and die.

The unrest touched Margerit not at all. For that, Barbara was grateful. The levels at which the merits of the prospective heirs were debated lay far above her head and no one expected her to have a favorite, much less to support a faction. And there were factions in plenty: the *Chustines*, Aukustin's party—or rather, Elisebet's; the *Charteires* who held by the prince's contract to his first wife; two or three Atilliet cousins who ventured to offer themselves as alternatives. And for each supporter who took a principled stand, there were two who looked to their own profit, whether in influence or gold. Only the strict rules of polite behavior kept parlors and ballrooms from fracturing into open hostility. The streets were another matter. Every week saw swords drawn in the *plaiz* at least once over some point of honor spilling over from the debates. With luck, the opening of the council and its truce would come before there was a death.

And the season must go on, whatever the undercurrents. Barbara moved farther along the upper balcony of the *salle* to keep an eye on Margerit as she found a seat for the concert. The floor was too crowded to allow for armins as well as guests. It made the watch more nerve-wracking, though in truth it would take a bare half-second more to fly down the stairs in case of need than it would to push through a crowded dance floor. A few of the guests found the vantage of the upper level preferable as well so she took note of the approaching woman only when a familiar voice greeted her.

"I haven't seen you for entirely too long. One might think you were avoiding me, *ma chere Barbre*."

"Vicomtesse," she responded, nodding without taking her eyes off Margerit. The last thing she wanted at the moment was the distraction of Jeanne de Cherdillac's attentions.

"And how are things progressing with your little *bourgeoise*?" Jeanne raised a hand to stroke her cheek. Barbara fought the reflex to lean into it.

"Mesnera, with all respect, that is none of your affair."

Jeanne leaned closer. "Once, it would have been my affair. Ah, forgive me, you're serious."

Barbara risked a glance at her. "Your pardon, Vicomtesse, but with things as they are," she gestured to take in the entire city and its restless mood, "I'd prefer not to be distracted from my duty."

"Ah yes, the succession is poisoning everything at the moment. I even had young Lutoz pestering me to support Elisebet's boy. As if the fact that she was born Isabelle de Villemont and so part French should be enough for me. He forgets who *I* was born."

"Do you have a vote on the council, then? I thought—"

"Oh *la* no! I've been invited to witness the debates but de Cherdillac had no Alpennian lands to give me a vote."

The other matter was even more surprising. "Is Lutoz for the *Chustines* party? I had thought he would follow his father's lead."

The vicomtesse shrugged. "She's been courting the young men for years now. I don't know if she expected to have more time—few enough of them have inherited to the titles yet."

Now that was unexpected, Barbara thought as the vicomtesse drifted away once more. She reviewed the list of guild members in her mind. The Saluns she knew leaned toward Elisebet's party. And Filip Amituz followed his father in the same direction. And Iosifin Rezik as well. Antuniet—she was hard to read. Her brother was solidly at the princess's side but how close were they? And their mother was outspoken in support of whoever Aukust's choice would be. Antuniet might go either way or have her own opinions.

The ordinary scholars, male and female, were harder to assess, but her curiosity was up. They would have no direct interest in the deliberations but there were endless webs of ties and obligations. Where did their families live? In whose district? Were they supported in their schooling by a patron's bequests? What were their prospects for advancement? Who stood at the gates to their chosen careers? Again, what of their families? Was a father or cousin in the employ of a partisan to one side or the other? How could that not be the case?

The place to start was the university registers. With the same zeal she had brought to searching for her own origins, Barbara followed each thread in the web. The hunt was more difficult than it might have been in the palace district. She had few existing contacts and the excuse of scouting out Margerit's safety held little weight with the university clerks. But slowly a pattern emerged. A few of the ordinary scholars had no known ties to any faction. They were, on the whole, among the more skilled. The women from the poor-scholars fell entirely in this group. That made sense in the emerging picture. They had no immediate obligations beyond the Scholars House itself; by definition they were residents of Rotenek. And it had been clear from the beginning that they had been invited to the guild for the reputation of their work as much as to keep the balance of men and women.

But the bulk of the guild membership—both high and low— were either partisans of Elisebet or in their patronage. Could it still be chance? Or, more likely, a simple consequence of that web of connections? But then, why Margerit? Yes, she was invaluable to their work but they couldn't have known that at the time. If she were looking for a conspiracy, it was as if they had designed the guild as a lure to draw Margerit in: a mixed guild to satisfy proprieties, a few personal connections to disarm suspicion, the promise of serious study of the mysteries as bait. Once the idea had seized her, it was hard to shake loose.

She ventured the topic with Margerit one evening over books. "At the guild meetings, is there much talk of politics?"

Margerit thought a moment. "Not much—not like at parties, where the old folks go on and on. We talked about the succession at the beginning, of course, when we were choosing a mystery to work on. It was one of the thoughts, that the land would be unsettled and vulnerable and that our *castellum* could help keep it safe for whomever was chosen."

"Did you know," Barbara ventured, "that most—almost all—of the guild members lean to Princess Elisebet's side?"

Margerit shrugged. "What of it?"

The ground was growing tricky. "I've been wondering whether the guild's work might be meant to her benefit in some way."

"It's meant for the benefit of all the land; why shouldn't it benefit her as well?" Margerit seemed genuinely confused.

"It seems odd that people so strongly partisan would put this effort, at this time, into what did not raise the chances of their favorite over others."

"You've seen the mystery," Margerit protested. "You helped write it! Is there anything of favoritism in it?" An edge of annoyance was emerging in her voice.

"I don't know. I haven't seen the full ceremony—not with the saints all filled in." Her further suspicions weren't strong enough to stand on their own.

"But I have. Barbara, I wish we could be working on it together, like we did this summer. Then you'd see."

Does she think I'm jealous? Barbara wondered. And of course she was. But that had nothing to do with it. "Just be careful. There's something at work here. If it turns out to be dangerous…" If it were dangerous it would fall within her hands and then Margerit would have to listen. But it was too soon to point that out.

* * *

The pattern of the loyalties had emerged as she traced connections back and forth from the south bank to the north bank of the Rotein. Another thing emerged during that search. Her old shadows were back. The same men—some of them—who had dogged her errands the previous year were appearing in view with disturbing frequency.

Others were strangers but met too often for chance, even given paths of habit. She'd grown sloppy in those paths of habit. That would change again.

What had brought them back? The last time the question had teased at her, she'd spun an elaborate fantasy around her father's supposed title and estates and the trading of debts for influence. That explanation had been abandoned as implausible. But now the shadows were back and tangled up in questions of the succession debate. And this time those questions crossed Margerit's path. If she were right...

It wasn't a question she could share with Margerit. And Marken—well, he'd been told what to watch for, but he had no curiosity about the larger doings of his employers. She thought briefly of taking Mesner Pertinek into her confidence but he was still too newly come to the household for her to trust entirely. She would drop him a word or two. In the end, the habit of a lifetime took her to LeFevre's door.

"And you think these are the same men as last winter?" he asked when the bare facts had been laid before him.

"Some of them are the very same men, the others have the same feel. I never told you—I learned they were in Langal's employ."

"Ah."

From his expression she knew the comment was on her discovery and not on the man's identity. He would give her no confirmation of her other guesses. She didn't bother to rehearse them.

"But now," she continued, "I don't know whether I'm the target or Maisetra Sovitre is. There's something odd happening around the guild. I don't know how to protect her if I don't know what it is."

He watched her closely, as if waiting to be certain she'd finished. "And what would you like me to do?"

What *had* she wanted? What had she expected? "I don't know. I...I needed to tell someone."

"You could protect her by removing her from the guild," he said mildly.

Barbara threw up her hands. "And how am I supposed to do that? This work means everything to her. I don't think even Maisetra Pertinek would be able to forbid her and have her obey."

"Maistir Fulpi could. He would be quite capable of dragging her back to Chalanz willy-nilly if he were given good reason."

Barbara envisioned the scene. "She'd never forgive me," she said, shaking her head slowly.

"Then you may need to decide which is more important to you: her forgiveness or her safety." He waved a hand as if dismissing the question. "I don't say I think it would come to that. But Barbara—" His voice became quietly intense and she marked his words carefully. "If you ever find yourself in desperate straits—you or Margerit or the both of you—take sanctuary at Saint Orisul's."

"That's five days journey away!"

"And well away from Rotenek if it comes to that. If you're at Saint Orisul's, I'll know where to find you."

CHAPTER FORTY-NINE

Margerit

It had been raining steadily for a week. Not enough to leave small lakes in the low spots of the *plaiz* but a steady drizzle that quenched spirits as if they were candles. Margerit had been damp more often than dry for days. Every time she returned to the house, Aunt Bertrut fussed and warned against taking cold. There was no help for it. They were spending long hours in the chapel working through the task of stitching the local patrons into the *castellum* and she couldn't be spared. The other *vidators* could tell whether a particular draft had succeeded or failed but only she could see the shape of *how* it failed or how it had almost succeeded. As yet, the guild work had not displaced the time she spent on lectures, but she could see a time when it might.

"Go upstairs and get those things off immediately," Aunt Bertrut ordered, heading her off when she would have taken her satchel to the library. "Leave that here, someone will see to it. I told Maitelen to keep the fire up in your room. I knew you'd be coming in all wet again. You look like you drove across town with the carriage open."

"No, Aunt," she sighed. "It's only that there's no way to get from the guildhall to the carriages except across the yard and of course it poured for the two minutes that took."

"And you couldn't take a parasol?"

Margerit didn't try to answer. She hated the bother of carrying too many things. The satchel kept the books and papers dry—that was the important thing. "Where shall it be this evening?" Aunt Bertrut had insisted she be back in plenty of time, but Margerit hadn't bothered to take note of the details. She stripped off her soaked gloves and tossed them on the side table with the book satchel.

"It's just a small musical supper at Mesnera Arulik's. Let me see your hands."

Margerit held them out, knowing what was coming. Gloves might hide the ink stains but one couldn't wear gloves every moment of the day and even lemon juice failed to fade the marks entirely.

But Bertrut only sighed and continued where she'd left off. "You wanted a quiet week. I think there's some new Italian soprano she's showing off. There's no dancing so wear something warm."

The instructions were hardly necessary. Her maid would have chosen the dress already with far more care than she would have taken herself. Maitelen might have started out as a country girl, but from the start she'd determined to live up to the expectations of the lady's maid to an heiress. She'd made friends and gathered advice in all the neighboring households with the determination of an invading general. After only a few false starts, Margerit had stopped worrying over whether she'd be turned out properly. Tonight it was a pale fawn merino with black piping and her heaviest shawl.

The care came to nothing. Margerit was waiting with Aunt Bertrut in the front parlor when Uncle Pertinek entered, dressed not for the evening's excursion but as if he had just returned home. Barbara followed him in from the entry hall and Margerit saw them exchange an odd look.

"My dear," he said to Bertrut. "I think it would be best to stay in tonight."

"What is it? What's wrong?"

"Nothing dreadful, I promise you. More a case of bad taste. It's—" He looked more embarrassed than concerned. "I've learned some unfortunate things about this evening's planned entertainment." He looked over at Barbara again and Margerit was certain she was the source—or at least the inspiration—for that knowledge. "It seems the songs to be performed this evening are…somewhat pointed in commenting on the suitability of various persons for positions of responsibility. To attend might be taken for support for those opinions.

I don't believe Mesnera Arulik intended to put Margerit in an awkward position. The choice of music was changed quite suddenly."

Margerit was vexed. For all that she would have preferred to stay home, it seemed a silly reason to withdraw at the last minute. "No one cares what I think about politics. Won't it look just as odd to stay as to go?"

Aunt Bertrut looked back and forth between the two of them. "Your uncle knows best in these matters. We can always say you've caught a small chill—that's easy to believe. We're only thinking of your good name." More cheerfully, she added, "I'm disappointed too, but we can have a cozy dinner at home instead."

It wasn't disappointment but the sense of being driven in harness. Now go; now stop. She frowned. "I'll take supper in the library, if you don't mind."

She expected Barbara to join her there after they'd both changed to more domestic clothing. The supper tray came with soup and cold meat and whatever else the cook could manage on short notice, but without Barbara. It was taken away an hour later and still no Barbara. *How dare she use Uncle Pertinek to control which parties I might and might not attend?* She found herself reading the same passage for the third time and shut the book. Where was she? Barbara couldn't have had other plans for the evening—not when she'd been expecting to escort them to the concert. One of the lamps guttered and she got up to trim the wick. She put a hand on the bell pull then turned away again. That wasn't how she wanted it to be. A cold finger ran down her spine. When Aunt Bertrut had painted her picture of sitting alone with her books and writings, it hadn't touched her because in her mind Barbara was there at her side.

She snuffed the lamps, taking a candle to light her way to bed.

* * *

The morning dawned clear and dry. Her mood felt washed clean with the streets. There were no lectures today and she'd told Hennis she could work until midday.

With Giseltrut's help, they finished polishing the *turris* against plague. Hennis sent the other off to the guildhall to copy out the changes but asked her to stay a moment.

"I've been thinking. When we discussed the design of the towers, we decided not to include protection against invasion and foreign armies. We had good reasons at the time, but I'm not so sure now. I was thinking…could you sketch out—not to include necessarily, but just to consider—a tower against foreign invasion?"

Margerit considered the problem. "It shouldn't be too difficult, but I'll need to think about the symbols and the best patrons."

He pulled out a small sheaf of papers. "Here are some ideas. I don't have the same talent you do, but I think you might find them a useful starting point."

Margerit took the pages and looked through them with a pleased grin. "This will certainly help. I think—" She shuffled back to the beginning of his notes. "Yes, Ainell for protection against invaders. But why Saint Viz?"

"It's part of the echoing layer," Hennis explained, "representing foreign armies as wild beasts attacking."

Margerit nodded absently, continuing on. "Then the patrons of the major passes and Nikule…to cover the river as entrance? An odd choice."

"The idea is more for his protection against robbers—to turn away pillaging and those who come seeking what isn't theirs."

"Yes, this should work," Margerit concluded. "I can have a draft for us to try in a couple of days. Do you think the rest of the guild will want to add it?"

He shrugged. "We can only suggest it. But it will help if we have the text prepared."

* * *

They were so close to being ready. Another week, perhaps. A couple more days if they added the new material. Only a few of the members had been following the whole text; most knew only the parts they'd helped to polish. That would take more time. The fluency of the celebrants made a significant difference in the shape of the *fluctus*. Though as Ainis noted there was nothing to say that the saints might not respond to a sincere though awkward petition.

She was still counting through the calendar in her mind when the footman who relieved her of her coat mentioned that Barbara would like to speak to her in the library, if that were convenient. She glanced questioningly at Marken, but he only shrugged as he left for whatever occupied his off-duty hours.

Barbara had a restless look as if she'd been waiting impatiently for some time. "Maisetra, I need to talk to—" She stopped and said bluntly. "You need to stay away from the guildhall and the guild for a while."

The words didn't even make sense. And why the formality here? Where they always left such things behind? "What do you mean?"

"I've learned—" Again the hesitation. "I've been following Lutoz and Perfrit and some of the others. They've been meeting with Estefen. Regularly. And when they meet, they talk about two things: the guild and the succession."

Margerit still didn't follow her. "Everyone's talking about the succession."

"I wish I could trust it was only that but I fear something deeper is at work. And I don't know if the trap is aimed at you or if you're only meant to be spattered with someone else's mud. But you need to stay well away from the guild until matters are more settled."

Margerit's mind went back to the heady successes of the morning's work. Barbara wanted to take that away? When they were so close to finishing? And for fears that she couldn't even put a name to? A hot anger rose in her.

Barbara continued, "Margerit, this isn't forever. But for now you must—"

"No! Don't say 'must' to me!" In her own ears her voice rang icy and brittle. "You are neither my guardian nor my governess. You forget your place!"

As soon as the words left her, she wished them unsaid. But the strength of Barbara's reaction shocked her. Her face went as white as bone. Then, after long seconds of deep silence, she sank smoothly to one knee and bowed her head. Margerit's first impulse was to laugh at the absurd melodrama of the scene; the second was to beg her pardon. But then the anger returned and she turned away without speaking and left the room, pushing past Aunt Bertrut who had come to investigate the shouting.

CHAPTER FIFTY

Barbara

The tapping sound of Margerit's shoes echoing down the hall filled her ears, drowning out the sound of Maisetra Bertrut approaching, saying, "What under heaven?"

Barbara rose and walked past her, stumbling half-blindly down the back stairs and out into the gardens. Her only recognizable thought was to find a place to be alone. She came at last to the marble bench tucked away down near the river's edge. It had been her refuge many times before. She sat down crosswise, tucking her knees up to her chest and hugging them tightly to keep the pain from bursting out. Periodically her mind darted forth to examine the nature of that pain and then retreated into numbness again.

Several hours must have passed because, when the sound of voices intruded, she roused enough to notice that the sun was low and she should be feeling chilled. She looked up at the two approaching servants. They must have been sent to find her but she wasn't ready yet for human contact. She snarled an oath in their direction and they retreated.

Time passed and another figure neared. Without looking up, Barbara recognized the footsteps as LeFevre and so she ignored him, hoping he too would go away again. Instead he sat down next to her, allowing long minutes of silence to stretch between them. When at last he spoke, he said, "Only love can hurt so badly."

Barbara raised her head with a wild and wary look.

"Did you think I hadn't noticed?" he asked.

"Does she—?" Barbara looked back over her shoulder toward the house.

He shook his head. "The two of you stand too closely to be able to see each other's hearts." LeFevre sighed heavily. "It wouldn't do any good to tell you that this storm will pass. In time things will be better."

"Better?" Barbara said bitterly. It was tempting to say that death would be better than this but even in the depths of her black mood she didn't believe it. And armins who started talking that way about death tended to come to bad ends. Her eyes bored into LeFevre's face, trying to see the things he would not—could not—tell her. He'd been keeping the baron's secrets since before she was born. He would say so much and no more.

A more immediate thought came to her. "What are you doing here?" She nodded indicating the garden rather than the house itself.

He shrugged and made a dismissive gesture. "I came by with some papers. They sent me out to find you because...well, because Margerit refused to speak about what passed between you two and no one knew what to do and because they thought you would be unlikely to kill me."

That, at least, cracked a smile out of her as it had been meant to.

"All will be well in time," he repeated. "In less than half a year the terms of the baron's will will be complete. Many things will be easier then. For now, just do your best to keep her safe."

"And if she won't let me?" Barbara uncoiled herself abruptly from the bench and stood.

"Oho! So that was the quarrel?"

"No!" And then, "Yes, that was the quarrel, but not—"

"Not the reason you've been hiding out here for hours."

Barbara bristled at the word "hiding" but didn't contradict him. She took a deep breath and tried to find that place inside where she was a professional and nothing more. The air was full of damp rising from the river and she could taste the coming change in the seasons. "I do my best, but she doesn't make it easy."

LeFevre quirked an eyebrow. "And the baron did?"

"The baron could take care of himself. Mar—Maisetra Sovitre doesn't know what the dangers are."

"And doesn't care to be reminded of that by you, of all people." He rose as well and they began walking back toward the terrace. Before they reached the steps he asked softly, "Whatever she said to you…is it forgivable?"

Barbara struggled to keep her composure from crumbling again. Her heart cried no! But her mouth said, "It must be, I suppose. But I don't know if I can—"

"Then forgive her if you can," he interrupted. "And protect her because you must. And remember, if there seems no other hope in sight, take her to Saint Orisul's. What seems impossible today may become clear tomorrow if you can keep yourselves safe until that day. And if you take refuge with the *Orisules* I'll know where to find you."

Again that odd urgency. "Do you know anything that might send us fleeing into sanctuary?"

He shook his head. She couldn't tell whether his oath bound him or whether he was as much in the dark as she was.

She slipped up the back stairs to wash her face and make herself presentable once more. And then there was one excuse and another to avoid descending until the odd stillness from the rooms below brought her back to the moment. *The Pelnik's ball—was it that time already?* She rushed down to the empty hall and accosted a footman. No, the Maisetras had left already, nearly an hour before. She calculated quickly: foot would be faster than any other method, a change of coat only and she could pass in that venue. What was Margerit thinking to go out unprotected at times like these?

A quarter hour later she presented herself at the back entrance to the *salle* and slipped along the edges of the rooms looking for a familiar face. She spotted Marken first and felt the tension drain away. So, at least she'd had that much sense. She followed his gaze out through the crowd and spotted Margerit where she was dancing with some forgettable young man. In less haste, Barbara worked her way around to the colonnade where the armins were loitering. She disliked the layout of this room. The back of the colonnade gave way to a row of curtained alcoves overlooking the gardens. A favorite for assignations but the hidden spaces always left her neck prickling.

Marken acknowledged her arrival with a sideways look and a grunt. "They said you weren't feeling well."

Barbara shook her head, "I'm well enough."

"Can't be," he replied. "If you were feeling well you wouldn't have abandoned your charge."

"I didn't—" Barbara began hotly, but it was true in its essence. "I'm here now."

He shrugged. "As you please, but I'm on duty for the evening."

It would be too much if he turned against her as well. She settled herself in by the next pillar and turned her gaze to the dancers. Watching Margerit as she moved down the line, the ache in her gut was still there but duller, more faded. How had she allowed things to go this far? That a simple rebuke could tear her world apart? When the couples moved through a turn she thought Margerit's eyes met hers—thought she saw a blush on her cheek—but no doubt it was only the exertion of the dance. The hour stretched on eternally.

A rustle of silk behind her barely impinged on her consciousness but the spicy scent of a familiar perfume brought her back to herself. The one person she least wanted to speak to in her current mood. "Vicomtesse," she said without turning.

"Barbara." It wasn't her usual teasing tone. "A word, if you please."

"I'm on duty." She heard a rude noise from Marken's direction and sighed. Well, since he was there…She gave him the hand signal for a transfer of responsibility—he had the grace not to comment—and followed Jeanne back into one of the half-curtained alcoves. The glow of the candles in the hall reflected in the dark glass of the window like stars lending barely enough light to see each other.

"What's wrong, *chérie*? I see it in your face…and hers. What has she done to you?"

"Does everyone in this damned city know my business?" Barbara asked sharply.

"Only the ones who care for you. Barbara, it will end badly, this passion. I fear for you. If you want…if ever you need a friend—a place to go—think of me." In the flickering light Barbara saw her pull something from her gloved finger. Jeanne pressed a small hard object into her hand and curled her fingers around it. "If you need me, send that and I will stand more than your friend." And then she leaned forward and kissed her. For a moment Barbara relaxed into the sweet, familiar sensation but they were the wrong lips, the wrong hands.

At the sound of an indrawn gasp they drew apart. Barbara barely had time to see Margerit's silhouette against the backlit archway before she turned and darted away. *How long was she standing there?* She made no apology to Jeanne as she followed to the edge of the dance floor, tucking the ring away into a pocket. Margerit had ducked between the lines of dancers, heading for the far rooms where the refreshments were laid out. There was no point to compounding the scene by chasing after her. And what could she say? What was there to explain?

She started to follow at a more circumspect pace but Marken stopped her with a hand on her arm. "Barbara, go home." She glared at him. "Barbara, I don't know and I don't care, but you aren't in any fit state to stand watch tonight. Go home. I'll see her safe."

* * *

She was still awake when she heard the carriage return and heard the opening and shutting of doors that signaled the family's return. She strained her ears for footsteps and muffled voices. Later, when quiet reigned, she thought the night air carried the sound of sobbing but it might have been a nightingale in the garden.

* * *

It wouldn't do, she told herself on rising. There was too much at stake to let herself be crippled now. She was an armin. She had a charge to guard and far more peril than over zealous suitors or even highwaymen. Whatever else she had dared to imagine…that was past. As she dressed, she saw Jeanne's ring lying on the table where she had left it the night before. Perhaps someday her heart might be ready again, however impossible that seemed at the moment. She rummaged in a box to find a small silver chain and threaded it through the ring to place around her neck.

Three hours later she was still waiting in the library, her heart pounding every time there was a footstep outside the door. Once past the first words it would be easier, she knew. But when the door finally opened, it wasn't Margerit but Maitelen, her maid. She closed the door carefully behind her and looked to be steeling herself for a fight.

"She cried herself into a sick headache last night," Maitelen said sharply. "I thought you ought to know."

And what business is it of yours? She fought the words back. *Stick to your ribbons and mirrors.* And most bitterly, *You forget your place.* But she had need of allies and here was one with more eyes and ears than most. "I need your help," was what she said at last. The disagreement about the guild—that much she could share. And the hints of plots and deeper currents. She could tell it appealed to the maid's romantic nature. "You go out and about and hear gossip from every household on the north bank. If you hear anything—*anything*—about your mistress, about the mystery guilds, about the university, you come tell me. It could mean her life. And if she's unhappy for a day or two, let that be the least of her troubles."

It was a lie, the part of it about the argument. But Maitelen took it in with widened eyes and hastened to assure her that she'd be watching and listening. And that was all that could be done for the moment: watch and listen and wait.

CHAPTER FIFTY-ONE

Margerit

It was the work that kept her from going mad. The rest of the world was off-balance. Barbara wouldn't speak to her—not beyond what was necessary—and yet she went everywhere with her, a silent shadow two steps behind. Aunt Bertrut had threatened to write to Chalanz. She had stopped going out at all except to the guildhall. But then the mystery was finished, the last sections polished and tested. Even the new tower was completed, though Hennis had decided not to try to add it to the whole for the nonce. They had been working so long piecemeal that it took a week to find a date when the entire guild could meet to read it through for the first time. This wouldn't be a true celebration, only a sort of actors' rehearsal. They would sort out roles and movements. Each member would take note of their parts on their own copy of the whole.

The guildhall was oddly silent when Margerit entered with Barbara trailing behind. Only the caretaker who had let them in and Nikule, sitting awkwardly at one of the tables, a look of relief washing over him when he saw her.

"Did I have the time wrong?" Margerit asked him. "Are they all in the chapel already?"

"If you have it wrong, you're early, not late," he answered, rising to meet her. "No one else is here, only him," nodding his head toward the old man.

"How strange." Margerit spotted a sheaf of papers on the next table and wandered over to examine it, thinking a note might have been left. It was labeled with her name, but she had her own personal copy of the *expositulum* in her hand. Then whose was this? She put down the roll she'd been carrying and leafed through the pages of the other. Not only the common text but the tower against invasion as well. Had Hennis changed his mind once again?

She turned at the sound of steps and the door opening. Iakup Choriaz came in looking startled to see the place inhabited.

"What are you doing here?" he asked. And when they stared at him blankly, "Didn't Lutoz send you word? A problem came up and we've changed to Wednesday instead." He went to the cabinet where the copies of the *expositulum* were stored. "I only came to get my text since I'll have some time to study it after all. A good thing too or you might have been waiting here all day."

The old caretaker said sourly, "And he might have sent *me* word as well, for all that. Maisetra, I'll go tell your man to put the horse back to. With luck he won't have started yet."

"That's odd," Margerit wondered as Iakup left. "I wonder how the message went astray. But I could get some work done by myself, since the chapel's been opened up already."

"No," Barbara said suddenly. "This goes beyond odd. The both of you not notified? We're leaving now."

Margerit bristled. The silent, compliant Barbara of the last week had disappeared. But before she could respond, there was a sound of flying footsteps in the passage outside and a slight figure burst in. To Margerit's astonishment, it was Maitelen. She was gasping with the effort of the run and only Barbara seemed to understand when she managed to say, "Palace guard…coming…"

Barbara grabbed her arm. "Where? How long?"

"Just…crossed the bridge…when I did. I ran."

Barbara spun around, saying, "You've been betrayed. I don't know what's been said or what they think to find, but we need to leave *now*!" She turned on Nikule. "If you had anything to do with this, you're a dead man." But the shocked and bewildered look on his face must have convinced her of his innocence. Margerit still stood frozen. Barbara took her by the shoulders and shook her. "This is no game, this is your life!" She pushed her toward the door to the courtyard.

Margerit stumbled down the steps, rolling up her *expositulum* and thrusting it into a pocket of her cloak for safekeeping. She was followed by the still panting maid and by Nikule. As she and Maitelen were pushed into the carriage, the driver asked, "Where away? Back to home?"

"No," Barbara answered. "Get down. I'll be driving. Maistir Nikule, get yourself away from here as quickly as possible and lie low until you know what's happened."

But Nikule ducked into the carriage after them, saying, "If you think I'm going to abandon you when you're in danger, Margerit, I don't know what you think of me."

Barbara looked as if she wanted to throw him out bodily but she only swung up into the seat the coachman had vacated and took up the reins, telling him, "Go to LeFevre in Lamsiter Street. Tell him—it doesn't matter what you tell him. He'll know what it means. Go, man!"

She urged the horse forward almost without waiting for him to step away. It was when they turned the corner onto the street running toward the city gate that Margerit saw the distant uniformed figures advancing down the road, light glinting from the rifles on their shoulders. It was real. Not something Barbara had conjured out of fears and shadows. She sat back against the cushions and barely breathed as they negotiated the crowded traffic through the Tupendor.

* * *

They were half an hour out on the highway before she learned anything further. Once past the outskirts built up against the city wall, there was space to put the horse into a trot and they made more distance. At last the carriage slowed to a stop and Barbara climbed down. "The horse needs to breathe a bit—the poor thing never bargained for going this far solo—and I need some answers."

Margerit wanted answers too but hardly knew what questions to ask. Barbara saved her the effort by addressing Maitelen. "How did you know? What did you hear?"

"I was keeping my ears sharp," she began, "like you asked."

Margerit wondered briefly just how many of those around her had been asked to keep their ears and eyes sharp on her behalf.

"I was out with Anniz, the Riumai's lady's maid. I needed a bit of ribbon to match and we stopped for a cup just off the *plaiz* when there was this big to-do—people running and calling out. I went out to see and it was a troop of the guards marching out. And someone said they were going after a ring of traitors and someone else said no, it was a guild that was doing witchcraft and that was when I took off running."

"You ran all the way from the palace to the guildhall?" Margerit asked in amazement.

"Not all—I had to ask directions a couple times. I knew it was hard by the gate and that Market Street ran that way but I've never been in that part of town before. When I was a girl I used to run all over. I tell you I thought my heart would burst."

Nikule burst out, "Treason! What can they be thinking of?"

"It must be a mistake," Margerit agreed. "Did we do the right thing to flee?"

Barbara was adamant. "Do you understand? If the accusation is treason, that means death. This was no mistake. Someone's been planning it—I think from the start. I don't know how but we can all guess who. I would lay a wager that hidden somewhere in your guild's work they will indeed find treason. And everyone will tell them that you were the one who created that mystery."

A suspicion began forming in her mind and she clutched close the text she still carried. "Where do we go now?"

"That," Barbara said slowly, "is a problem. My plans didn't include four of us."

"You knew this was going to happen?" Nikule interrupted. "You had *plans* for it and you didn't tell anyone?"

It was a poor time, Margerit thought, for her cousin to take up his father's habits of command. Barbara had tried to warn her and she—she'd done worse than refuse to listen. She shied away from that memory for now.

Barbara hadn't deigned to answer him. "Maisetra, you and I need to disappear until we can discover what it is we need to disprove on your behalf. LeFevre told me—" She glanced at the others. "No, better you shouldn't know, in case you're questioned."

Maitelen said, "Questioned?" with a little yelp.

Barbara was staring at Nikule with a speculative eye. "Maistir Fulpi, you said you wouldn't abandon your cousin when she was in trouble, but would you be willing to abandon her to help her? I have a mind to lay a false scent." Nikule looked skeptical but motioned her to continue. "The guard isn't likely to be after us yet—they'll be searching the guildhall until they find what they were meant to find. They may not even know we've fled the city. But I expect that as soon as he knows we've slipped the net, Estefen will be sending men on our trail. Being helpful. Showing his loyalty. They'll be looking for a well-dressed young woman accompanied by a armin wearing men's clothing."

Margerit could see understanding dawning in the others' faces even as she grasped the plan. "So Maitelen and I exchange clothes, and you and Nikule—"

"That would hardly work!" her cousin interrupted.

Barbara agreed. "You'll have to make do with what you're wearing. Your coat's all wrong and you don't at all look the part, but if you keep quiet and stand right people will see what they expect. I'll lend you my sword to help you pass as an armin. Take the carriage to Chalanz. Charge your expenses on the way in Maisetra Sovitre's name and you won't even have to lie to leave a trail. There's a posting inn a few more miles on. You can hire fresh horses and a postilion—you'll need a pair hitched to make any time at all. Maisetra, tell the innkeeper's wife that your maid has torn her gown and the luggage has all gone on ahead. Ask to buy an old dress—that will also give us cover to borrow a room for the change."

"But what do we need with another dress?"

Barbara grinned humorlessly. "They'll be looking for me in men's clothing. What better disguise than to return to skirts? It would be easier to travel if we put you in trousers instead, but I don't think you could carry it off. And it would complicate matters later."

* * *

The innkeeper's wife did, indeed, have an old gown she could part with for a few coins. And while the hired horses were being fetched and the harness reorganized for a pair, they played a conjurer's hide-and-seek game to bring three women into the borrowed parlor to change while leaving the impression there were only two. Margerit stood quietly while Maitelen worked to fit up the inn-wife's dress to her smaller frame. Barbara was stripping off her coat and waistcoat to don the supposedly town gown that Maitelen had discarded. When she pulled off her shirt a small chain swung free, dangling a heavy gold ring with a crest between her breasts.

The sight of it stabbed Margerit in the heart. She'd almost managed to convince herself that she'd imagined things, that evening in the shadowed alcove. The kiss, the token slipped into Barbara's hand. She bit her lip to keep from crying out. She had lost…lost she knew not what. Only that there was a hollow in her life that couldn't be filled. She tore her gaze away. There was no mending things now and no time for weeping.

More sleight of hand tucked all four into the carriage hidden from view, with the spare horse saddled and following behind. Just far enough along the road to be out of sight of the inn they halted again and sorted themselves out to part ways. It was only when the carriage had disappeared down the road that Margerit thought to exclaim in dismay, "But I don't ride!"

CHAPTER FIFTY-TWO

Barbara

The first day's travel was light. The horse wasn't fresh and Margerit was unsteady, even held tightly in front of her on the saddle. That was near to torture: the feel of Margerit's body pressed against her, the scent of her hair filling her nostrils. And through it all Margerit stiff and silent and distant. They went far enough to leave behind the carriage roads and took to narrow country tracks where two farmwomen riding tandem home from the market would cause no comment. Or riding on pilgrimage to Saint Orisul's—that was true enough. At least they needn't fear sleeping too rough. There had been enough coins pooled among the travelers—most of it from Nikule, truth to tell—to cover food and a place to sleep from countryfolk. The first evening found them in a small snug barn with borrowed blankets.

Barbara surprised herself by sleeping soundly.

With the dawning light she came awake quickly but lay still, enjoying the first morning in entirely too long when she wasn't waiting for the trap to spring. Strange: to find that the fear had been a heavier burden than the disaster itself. The next danger wouldn't come until they had to follow the main road for a space hard by Saint Orisul's. It also passed through the Saveze title-lands. That would strain the nerves whether Estefen was in residence or not.

She could hear the restless movements of the livestock and the sound of Margerit stirring a short distance away. She opened her eyes lazily. Margerit was standing by the sheepfold, staring past her toward the door with an expression of such bleak despair that Barbara rolled instantly to her feet, swearing at the tangling skirts and reaching for her absent sword, certain that there must be an armed troop waiting there. Nothing. She asked, "Maisetra, what's wrong?"

Margerit had turned away. "Nothing…nothing."

But there were so many things: concern for her family and those left behind, fear of what lay ahead. Even the possibility that she *had* unwittingly worked treason in some way. Barbara was trying to frame some sort of reassurance when Margerit turned back, wiping tears from her cheeks.

"I've lost you."

"Maisetra?"

"In a few months you'll be free of me. Then you'll go back to her. And it's my fault. I said…even if I could take it back—what I said—it wouldn't matter. You're wearing her ring. I saw it."

Barbara's hand went to her breast where the chain hung beneath her gown. Was that what this was about? Was that why the distant silence? What was it LeFevre had said—that they stood too closely to see each others' hearts. Was it possible…?

She began hesitantly, "Maisetra…Margerit, I…" She swallowed and took the plunge. "Jeanne de Cherdillac and I were lovers—it's true. But that was some time ago. It's over now. The ring…She thought I might need…that you might…The ring was her pledge that her door would be open to me if I had nowhere else to go."

Margerit looked confused, but by which part? "Lovers," she repeated slowly, as if tasting the word. "And you said that you and I couldn't even be friends."

Barbara struggled to find the right question to answer. "Margerit, she was neither my employer nor my charge to protect. And I wasn't in love with her—that made things simpler."

"And me?" Margerit breathed.

"It isn't simple at all," Barbara answered, shaking her head slowly. Or perhaps it really was that simple. The frightened sorrow in Margerit's dark eyes could not be left unanswered.

She took half a step forward. Another. Her hand reached out to trace the line of Margerit's cheek and twist an errant curl around her finger. She leaned forward, watching for hesitation, for retreat. Their lips brushed softly, then more surely. She had been wanting to do that for entirely too long. She felt Margerit's arms go around her and moved to kiss the tears that traced down her cheeks. The salt turned to sweetness on her tongue.

* * *

The day might have been lost to long-delayed delight but for the farmwife coming bustling in to milk the cow and turn her out. They recollected themselves and packed up for the road. Except for the looming threat of arrest and execution, the journey would have been idyllic. Autumn had turned warm and golden in that way it often did just before cold set in. Sometimes they rode two on the horse, sometimes Barbara walked beside. In either case their speed couldn't rise above an amble. At least the direction was clear: they need only keep an eye on the peak of Mont Neplek and they would come to Saint Orisul's nestled at its feet.

If not for the need to spare the horse, Barbara would have mounted behind her the whole time. Where the touch of their bodies had been stiff and awkward the day before, now Margerit melted against her and Barbara's arm circled her in an embrace, and not just to keep her from falling. There were endless opportunities to leave kisses and whisper endearments as their heads leaned together.

They paused at midday for grazing and rest. To stave off the risk of other distractions Barbara asked, "Can you think of anything in your *castellum* that could be seen as working against the prince? I know the structure is sound, at least what I've seen of it. But could there be something in the paraphernalia or the movements that might cast a more sinister impression?"

Margerit looked sheepish of a sudden and fumbled beneath her skirt in the pocket that hung there, drawing out a thick folded packet of papers. Barbara had seen her hide them away when they all changed clothing but there were always papers around and it had meant nothing.

"A few weeks ago Hennis thought we might work up an additional *turris*: the one against invasion that we discarded at the beginning. And after we'd done all that work, he decided not to present it to the guild. But then yesterday it was there, sitting out on the table, included in this copy. In the confusion, I left my own *expositulum* and took this one." She unfolded the packet and thumbed through to pull out two close-covered sheets. "It's much in the style of the other towers. A bit more poetic than I prefer, but Hennis did half the work—putting together the saints and symbols—so it would have been ungrateful to start fresh."

Barbara skimmed down the pages, then caught her breath and read through in more detail. "Mother of God!" she exclaimed, looking up at Margerit. "You didn't know? No, you wouldn't have." It had been a safe wager that a girl of her class would be ignorant of the crests and arms of distant nobility. She spread her coat out on the grass to keep off the damp and laid the pages down in order. "See here: the references to hunting down the leopard and here to plucking out the thorns from the garden." Her finger traced the passages.

"But what does it mean?" Margerit asked anxiously.

"The leopard is the crest of the Dukes of Maunberg and the thorn is their badge. One symbol alone might be coincidence but both together? This isn't a mystery to repel invaders; it's a curse aimed at Prince Aukust's grandsons."

There was a long silence, then Margerit abruptly stood. "We have to go back. We have to warn him."

"Are you mad? You wouldn't even make it through the gates. And once you've been taken and charged no one will listen to you. You aren't even allowed to stand your own defense until you're of age and I have no standing at all in law until then. I doubt Estefen would let them stay the execution that long. That's why LeFevre warned me to take you to find sanctuary. We can't return until we can prove our innocence—or rather, our ignorance, since it seems we *are* guilty."

"Not us, just me. You had no hand in this…this abomination."

Barbara waved off the objection. "It comes to the same thing. Lutoz may have acted purely out of loyalty to Elisebet but it's Estefen who will have cast this net and he means both of us to be caught in it."

Margerit frowned. "You're very sure of that. That Estefen is behind this."

"The two of them are thick as thieves. At first I thought it was no more than friendship, but when I started asking questions…there was more. Much more. I suspect Estefen even suggested forming the guild in the first place. Lutoz may not even know all his plans. What would it benefit Lutoz to have you accused? If his game is to cut off the Austrian line, then dragging the mystery into court as evidence would only hinder that. But Estefen—" She laid out the matter as plainly as she knew how. "If you were to die in the ordinary way of things, your property goes to your heirs. If you died before you come of age, it might count as breaking the baron's will, but that would only mean that it goes to Saint Orisul's. But if you are executed for treason the crown seizes it all. And tradition holds that the one who brings and proves the charge is granted half. It's Estefen's last chance to take what he considers his inheritance and be revenged on you at the same time."

Margerit's attention seemed to have wandered. "If the mystery is brought as evidence…but they won't find it! Not at the guildhall. Not the damning part. Only Hennis and I had copies. Mine is at home—I didn't expect to need it for the celebration. And this one—" She picked up the papers again and examined them closely. "This is Hennis's copy. Those are his notes in the margin. Someone's added my name on the front, that's all. There's nothing for them to find at the guildhall except copies of the regular *expositulum* and there's no treason in that."

"Your working notes and drafts?"

"At home. Oh!" she exclaimed with returned agitation. "What if they search the house?"

Barbara could see the scene unfolding in her mind: Maisetra Pertinek in hysterics, not even knowing Margerit was safe; the library plundered in a search for who-knows-what. "There's nothing we can do right now," she said grimly. "But there's at least a hope that they may not have any certain proof. Estefen will have to work harder to bring the charge. And if Lutoz has no copy then the Austrians are safe."

Margerit shook her head. "He could reconstruct it, I think. We worked closely on it. I know I could write it out again from memory if need be."

The thought clearly worried at her for the rest of the day. Barbara forbore from breaking in on her concentration, many though the temptations were. There would be time. For now it was enough to have swept away the walls and misunderstandings that had stood between them. Whatever came, their hearts now beat as one.

They stopped finally for the night at a small cluster of houses at a crossroads. Not enough to be deemed a village—no church and no tavern. But one of the local women brewed and her neighbors gathered in her house most evenings for good company. So there was more welcome for travelers than there might otherwise have been. Barbara shared the story she had devised of a pilgrimage, a desperate petition. Something ordinary folk would accept as reason to be taking the road so late in the season. It was entertainment enough to earn them a bed by the fire when the others drifted away at the end of the evening. And it was natural enough to roll their blankets together for warmth without inviting questions. There were quiet caresses and sweet kisses before exhaustion took them.

Riding out in the morning, Margerit announced, "I think I can amend what I've done."

"Hmm?" Barbara inquired softly in her ear.

"The curse—we have a little time. I've been turning it over in my mind and it isn't set to act unless the border is crossed. So even if Hennis were to work the *turris* immediately there would be no harm done until they arrive at the border."

"But that could be in only a few weeks. They can't leave it later unless they plan to wait for spring."

"Or take a longer road. They could always go down along the coast and up from Marseille. And the tower can't be celebrated alone—it was designed to be part of the *castellum* as a whole. He still needs a guild for that. Not necessarily the whole group but at least half a dozen."

"I'd count easily that many *Chustines* among the guild. Whether any of them might balk at murder if they realized the intent…But how do you think you can prevent them from carrying it through?"

"I don't. I think—" She twisted slightly before the saddle to look back at Barbara. Two days on horseback had given her some confidence along with the sore muscles. "I think I can devise a new mystery that blocks it. Not the whole *castellum*. That would be difficult because it—" She shrugged. "It *wants* to be done. But just the invasion tower. It's weak because it *is* an attack. That's one of the reasons we left it out at first. Once you start asking the saints to smite your enemies, things tend to go wrong. Chizelek has an entire chapter on that. I thought I'd avoided the problem because the *turris* worked in abstracts, but if it's used against specific people, there are cracks that can be opened."

As usual, it all made perfect sense when Margerit explained the problem but Barbara couldn't see how to move past understanding to action. "How will you put together a whole new guild to counter it?"

"I don't need to," she answered confidently. "It's a much simpler matter. You address the patrons of the border points and petition them to treat all within their sphere with love and protection. It's what they *want* to do, so it doesn't need to be elaborate to hold their attention. You and I could celebrate it at any church we pass. Perhaps…do you think we could ask the sisters at Saint Orisul's to perform it? That would be even better."

Barbara grinned to herself at the thought of Margerit proposing new mysteries to that august and learned body. "Best not to count on it."

"True," Margerit agreed, not seeing the grin. "And I'd rather not wait that long. I've had another thought: a petition that they stop their ears against those who wish harm on others. If Hennis hasn't acted yet, that might make the counter even stronger."

"And thwart every local busybody who's praying for his neighbor's milk to sour!" she laughed. "I think you reach too far with that one."

* * *

It took half a day casting about and asking directions to come upon a village church not too far off their path that would serve Margerit's purposes. An offering that halved their remaining funds convinced the priest that Margerit had a great deal of prayer to do that required a day of quiet and solitude. For it wasn't enough to perform the mystery she had worked out in her head. Margerit insisted on a full study: testing and adjusting and observing, until she felt the work was perfected. Barbara could only watch as Margerit gazed around, tracking and commenting on the visions only she could see, and then chime in with her own parts and choruses as directed.

But when they came at last to the true celebration, even she could feel a change in the air of the chapel: a movement, a soundless hush as if the stones themselves had paused to take note of their words. A prickle ran down her spine. It wasn't that she had ever doubted, but this…this she could truly believe.

For the rest of the journey they stopped at any church they passed and repeated the rite. It was a little thing, really. No more than a quarter of an hour from start to finish. The sense of hearkening that Barbara had felt was never repeated but it didn't matter. The saints had heard them, she was certain of it.

* * *

They both walked, the last day. The horse had cast a shoe and with no money left to pay a smith and no desire to lame the beast, they left him with a farmer with the agreement that the horse was his if they never returned to redeem its keep. He'd offered a wagon ride a few miles down the road into the bargain and Barbara was grateful for the chance to blend in. These were Saveze lands and she had been through them often enough on the baron's business—though never on foot in the now bedraggled gown of a lady's maid. There was hardly any need for further disguise. Soon enough they were climbing the stony path up to the convent gate.

The heavy iron knocker might as well have been just for show. Visitors could be seen well before they approached the entrance and the door opened just as Barbara reached for the ring. An elderly woman in the gray and black of the order looked from one to the other of them and asked, "Now which one of you would be Margerit Sovitre?"

CHAPTER FIFTY-THREE

Margerit

Margerit's first thought was to panic but even if word of the charges had gone ahead of them it should make no difference to their reception here. The portress smiled at her startled reaction but misread the reason. "No, I've had no vision of your arrival. There's a letter come for you. The Mother Abbess has asked me to bring you to her immediately on arrival."

They were allowed to wash and tidy themselves first, but beyond such niceties evidently the orders were firm. They were taken to an austere but cozy sitting room and, having made their courtesies, the letter was put into her hands.

She recognized the direction immediately as LeFevre's hand although the heavy wax seal was not one she had ever seen him use. When she broke it there was a brief flash of *visitatio*. To protect the seal? She had read of such things being used by royal scribes but it seemed excessive for a simple letter. She beckoned Barbara to join her and spread out the page on the table between them.

Maisetra, it began with no other salutation. *If Barbara has remembered my advice and if all the heavens are watching over you, this should find you safely. If not, then I pray God keep you wherever you may be. Do not reply to this letter. I will know if it comes into your hands and that will suffice.*

So that had been the mystery woven into the seal. Had it recognized her hands specifically? She tucked away the curiosity for later.

I send it now when there is news to tell but they have not yet thought to put a close watch on me. I think I will not dare to write again until this matter is settled.

And what did he know of the matter? She scanned ahead impatiently and then returned to continue reading.

All your people are well and safe for the moment although your aunt is greatly distressed as you may imagine. I do not know what came to pass at your guildhall, but the charge that has been raised is treason. And as the charge was raised by Estefen Chazillen—

She noticed that he, like Barbara, still balked at giving him the title of the man they had served so long.

—I suspect it was a trap laid for you in some fashion. Barbara can tell you of the reasons for thinking this. But his plan misfired when you escaped. No clear proof has yet been offered and treason cannot be judged in absence. If you return, it must not be until you are ready and able to defend yourself and demonstrate his guilt. Chazillen has already overplayed his hand. He tried to seize Tiporsel House but Mesner Pertinek laid claim of hearth-right—

She looked at Barbara questioningly who responded, "It's complicated. A nobleman can extend certain immunities to the place he resides."

—and called the prince as witness to uphold it. Chazillen has the backing of Princess Elisebet as you may have guessed and there are men in her livery who were seen leaving the city on your trail. I pray you will be safe. Do not leave Saint Orisul's unless you can answer the charges. And do not return, under any circumstances, until you have come of age and you both are free to act on your own behalf, no matter what news you may hear. I have no confidence in your guardians when the game is played at this level. Trust Barbara; she knows the law. And tell Barbara to remember the spotted pony. Your servant, René LeFevre.

Margerit sat still, letting the content of LeFevre's message settle into her understanding. Some parts were a complete mystery, others told little new but confirmed much they had suspected. So Aunt Bertrut was safe for now. Her library, her papers were safe. And if the breaking of the seal had sent a message, then LeFevre could pass that message along to the others.

The abbess waited patiently until Margerit met her gaze once more and said, "We ask for sanctuary. Is there something…a proper form we must follow in asking? Do we—?"

"No, child," she answered. "It's enough to say it to me. I won't ask how long you wish to stay—" she began.

301 of Mystery 301

Margerit interrupted. "We don't know." She turned to Barbara who shrugged. "We need to…to solve some problems and—"

The woman held up a hand to stop her. "I don't need to know what brings you here. But if you plan to stay for some time, then you need to know what we expect of you. You will lodge in the strangers' dormitory. There are only a few guests at this time."

Margerit felt a sharp disappointment, but what had she expected: a private apartment? The list of rules was short and not onerous. They were not to leave the grounds. They were expected to attend ordinary daily services but need not rise for the nighttime ones. They were expected to share in the daily work of the convent. And beyond that they were free of the place, including the gardens and the library. That was welcome news to hear. But of course there would be a library; the school at Saint Orisul's was famous.

They were shown to the dormitory and given clean, plain clothes of the sort the secular students at the convent school wore. The guesthouse was built to house considerably more visitors than it held at the moment. There was a woman come to deliver her daughter to the school—she would be leaving soon. Two had come for some unrevealed spiritual purpose. There was an elderly pensioner who clearly had settled in to spend the remainder of her life. Margerit looked around at the available beds and went to place her small bundle of possessions on one at the end of the room.

"Maisetra," Barbara said in her even professional voice. "Might I suggest one of the beds closer to the fire? I expect mornings will be cold."

Margerit barely heard the question. "Barbara, have I done something wrong again? Why the 'Maisetra'?"

Barbara looked around, then pitched her voice low for only the two of them. "Margerit, we aren't private anymore. Not here. I need to give you the…the respect of your position. For them. For the others who will hear it. And I need to do it all the time or I'll forget." She leaned closely and Margerit felt her warm breath in her ear as she whispered, "When I say 'Maisetra' to you, it means 'beloved.' Always remember that."

* * *

They met the community as a whole for the first time at the evening meal. In addition to the sisters and the few guests there were two groups of girls distinguished mostly by dress: the secular students, brought to take advantage of the convent's reputation for scholarship, as well as for the practical benefit of being removed from worldly temptations and hazards; and the postulants, learning alongside them but destined to take the veil. Margerit noticed something odd and in the brief period between the prayers and the reading, when ordinary conversation was allowed, she asked her neighbor, "Most of the sisters seem to be, well, older. But I see postulants and novices in plenty—what happens to them?"

The woman smiled. "We're a teaching order. After training for a while here they go out to our daughter houses to teach in the schools for a time."

"I know about the teaching," Margerit said. "My governess, Sister Petrunel, was of your order."

"Petrunel? She's in charge of the school at Eskor now, you know. Yes, some go out as tutors or governesses—it provides a great deal of our income. But that's for an age of steadiness and maturity. It wouldn't do at all for the younger women to be living in the world like that. Ah, the reading starts, we must be silent."

When the meal was at an end, the two new arrivals were called up to the abbess's table to be made known to the community at large, but as they approached, there was a sudden cry from the end of the table. An old woman—Margerit judged from her wrinkles and frailty she might be past eighty—fixed the two with a look of childlike delight and exclaimed, "Lissa and Bezza! You've come back! How kind of you to visit your old teacher."

Their escort whispered, "She means nothing by it. Sister Anna's mind has been wandering of late."

But after the introduction had been made, Margerit ventured, "My mother…she was a student here once. And I think she was sometimes called Bezza—Elisebet Fulpi she was then. They say I am very much like her in appearance. Do you think…?"

The abbess nodded thoughtfully. "Sister Anna would likely have been here in the house at that time. Perhaps she does see your mother in your face. She comes and goes through time, these days. Sometimes she's a girl again, sometimes she becomes lost at the door to eternity. We pray that she will find her path easily."

Barbara stepped forward, staring at Sister Anna in fierce concentration. "You put a name to me too," she said, almost to herself. And then she dropped to kneel before the old woman and grasped her hands. "Lissa—who is Lissa? Who did you see in my face?"

The nun looked around and moved restlessly. "Lissa? I don't know any Lissa."

But Barbara wouldn't be put off. "Was Lissa *my* mother?"

"Mother," she repeated vaguely. Then, "Mother—why did you leave me here, Mother? Why don't you visit me anymore?" It was the voice of a lost child.

Margerit took Barbara by the shoulder and pulled her away. "Let her be. Who knows whether she meant anything by it."

But Barbara turned to her with the same fierce look. "'Lissa and Bezza' she said. And your mother was Bezza. She said them as if the names went together."

But there was no more sense to be had from Sister Anna that evening and they were left to spin what-if tales between them as they lay closely together that night. That, at least, was allowed to them by the customs of the guesthouse. And if they were quiet and discreet, then after the lamps were out they might exchange caresses that made up for the distance maintained in daylight.

* * *

Margerit had heard the requirement that they share in the daily work of the convent with some trepidation. Her life had fitted her for very little of a practical nature. She knew how to dance and do fine embroidery but not how to mend torn clothing. She could plan and preside over a dinner party but not cook one. And she'd never come closer to housecleaning than knowing which of the servants owned each task to be done. She was willing, though she suspected they would find her of very little use. But when she laid out the matter to the sister who took them in charge the next morning, she was met by amusement.

"I don't think it will be necessary for you to scrub floors. I see by your fingers that you do a bit of writing."

Margerit reflexively hid her right hand under the other as if it had been Aunt Bertrut scolding her once again. Realizing what she'd done, she held up her fingers where even two weeks on the road had failed to erase the ink stains entirely. "More than a bit. I was studying at the university."

"We can always find a use for someone with a neat hand. And as you're a scholar, perhaps you might assist the teachers as well, if you have the skill."

Margerit hastened to add, "Barbara is a scholar too, for all that she's my armin." It had occurred to her that they might not see past Barbara's station when assigning work.

Barbara herself ventured, "Might there be something to be done with your archives and records?" She explained, "I want to search... to see what I can learn about the Lissa that Sister Anna mentioned. What better way to find my way around them than to help with the clerking?"

"There may not be a Lissa," the sister cautioned. "Last month she was telling us stories about the time she spent at court—all imagined. Or rather, you will likely find dozens of Lissas—it often seems like half our girls are named Elisebet."

* * *

It was easy to fall into the pattern of the days: morning services, a bit of bread and watered wine to sustain one, then laboring among the inkpots until the dinner hour. More services, a bit of time for themselves, more work, another common meal, then services and bed. Margerit was almost grateful that there was little time to think and fret. Barbara, as usual, could not be still. Usually she would be up before the morning bells to find an empty place to run her sword drills with skirts hiked up and a wooden rod for a blade. And in the free afternoons she buried herself among old registers and correspondence in search of the mysterious Lissa.

"Maisetra, what years was your mother here?" she asked at the start of her quest.

"I'm not sure exactly. I was born in ninety-eight so perhaps several years before that." She searched her memory for mentions of her mother's girlhood. "Oh, but Aunt Bertrut said—" She had listened only halfway to her aunt's story that day during flood-tide. "She said my mother had a difficult time, that she miscarried several times before me. So it would be some years before that, but I don't know..."

"Then perhaps I should start in ninety-five and work backward," Barbara mused. "Well, it wouldn't be the first time for that!"

When Margerit asked her meaning, she heard for the first time of the hunt through the baptisms at the cathedral. "But why didn't you ask my help?" she protested.

Barbara looked uncomfortable. "It was a...a personal matter. I wanted—oh, it doesn't matter now. It just seemed necessary to do it myself."

"Would you still prefer that?" Margerit asked hesitantly. She could understand, just a little, what Barbara was trying to say.

"Do you mind?" Barbara countered.

"Barbara, you *can* ask me for help, if you want it. You don't need to be strong all the time."

"But I do," she answered with a sad smile.

There was such loneliness in those three words. Margerit seized her hand and held it to her heart. "No! Barbara, promise me something: no more secrets, no more silences. Promise me!" And before Barbara had a chance to answer she added, "And don't you dare say, 'Yes, Maisetra' to me this time."

Barbara hesitated long enough that Margerit knew the answer would be the truth. "I promise to try."

* * *

The regular daily services might have been a chore to some guests but Margerit found them inspiring. Someone with true vision had developed their rites, both the ordinary daily worship and the special mysteries. To a *vidator*, the chapel became a symphony of *visitationis*, now quiet and peaceful, now like a blare of trumpets, now a swelling river of strings. Even the pure worship of God resonated in her senses. What made the difference? From Sister Petrunel's indifference to the idea of petitionary mysteries, Margerit had thought the whole order leaned only to devotion, but she was realizing that had been a personal stance. Indeed, the steady flow of pilgrims to the convent came not so much for simple prayer and a touch of the relics as for the benefit of the library of mysteries developed and gathered over the years, selected and adapted for their particular needs. Every few days another party of travelers appeared in the guesthouse to spend their days praying and, if they were so favored, to be taken in hand by the sisters who sorted through their needs and desires for the appropriate ceremony. Margerit longed to watch them with a student's eye, but the rule was for privacy.

She felt oddly shy about repeating her own mystery in such a place where she knew it would be noted and remarked on, though once or twice on those rare occasions she found the chapel empty, she had ventured it. And as October passed away she began to think that the ceremony must either have done its work or its time had passed. The first dustings of snow were lightening the lower slopes of the mountains and soon the passes would be closed. And how would she know if it worked? She thought of the charm that had been infused into the seal on LeFevre's letter. Was it possible to design a mystery that would communicate its eventual success or failure to the celebrants?

* * *

The Feast of All Saints, Margerit thought wistfully, would have been the ideal setting to celebrate their *castellum*. Best to petition a saint when there was a door opened in some way: a feast day, a dedicated chapel, a relic. But for a fabric woven of so many different strands, All Saints was surely the perfect time.

The services provided her the usual luminous glow of sensation—not the riot of colors of a true mystery, but more like the sun fighting its way through a mist. She thought at first she had nodded in sleep when a shadow crossed her attention. She jerked upright, aware of a sound: a rumbling like cartwheels on cobblestones or the buzzing of a swarm of bees. Another shadow slipped past the corner of her eyes—a sleek shape that seemed to move on four legs. It frightened her. Her visions had always seemed external. She could have traced the exact places and shapes in the air where they flowed past. But these...these *phasmas* seemed to move inside her own head. The air crackled like the snapping of dry twigs.

And then the chapel faded away and the shapes rose before her. A wall of stone, a spotted pelt, shining figures standing like the glass windows in the cathedral.

The turris, she thought wildly. *He's building the tower and they are come.* Had her workings prepared the saints against his petitions? She couldn't think of the right words over the roaring in her ears, but could only whisper over and over, "Hear not the words of he who wishes ill! Blessed Virgin, hear not the words of he who wishes ill! Sweet Jesus hear him not! Saint Mauriz, hear him not! Saint Challun, hear him not!" and on through the litany of all the saints invoked in the *castellum*. And she saw the Virgin cast her blue mantle over the thorn bush and the leopard was embraced by the Lamb and all went silent and dark.

CHAPTER FIFTY-FOUR

Barbara

Barbara had watched the reflections of visions in Margerit's face often enough to know instantly that this time was different. And when the urgent muttered litany ended with a small cry, she caught Margerit's limp form before it could crumple to the floor. With no interruption in the service, one of the sisters stepped in to help carry her through the cloister to a quiet room where they laid her on a low cot.

"She's only swooned, I think," the nun said and left to summon other help.

Barbara bent over her, chafing her hands and stroking her face and calling her name. She heard someone enter the chamber but didn't turn. Margerit's eyes were fluttering a little, though when she opened them she stared as if the visions still danced before her.

"Margerit, what happened?"

She was answered uncertainly. "He did it...the tower...the leopard...and Mauriz with his sword. But then he sheathed it...and the Virgin covered them but I don't know what it means. They've come...but are they safe?" Barbara felt her hands grasped tightly. "Did it work? Are they safe?" Margerit's eyes saw the world again and were fixed on her beseechingly.

"I don't know. We won't know until there's news."

There was a small cough behind her and Barbara rose to see the abbess waiting as one of the other sisters placed a small stool for her at Margerit's bedside.

"She isn't raving," Barbara hastened to assure her. "There's more sense in her words than you may think."

The woman nodded and took Margerit's hand in turn. "My child, do you often see visions like this?"

"Not…not like this," Margerit said hesitantly as she struggled to sit. "Just the…the ordinary ones. In the mysteries, when the saints are hearkening."

Barbara saw the abbess conceal a small bemused smile as she repeated, "Just the ordinary ones." After a moment's pause she said, "You should have told me."

Margerit seemed to take the admonition to heart and the story came tumbling out. Not quite everything, but her ambitions, the baron's legacy, the university, the guild, the mystery and finally the flight from Rotenek. The abbess heard it all to the end with no comment but when Margerit had finally come to the morning's events and their possible meaning she said, "Pride is not only a sin, it's a hindrance to wisdom."

Margerit flushed deeply. "I…I hadn't thought of it as pride."

"You have a gift. And you have a desire to use it for the good of others; that weighs in the balance. But your pride in that gift led you to think that only you knew what that good was. If I were giving penances, I would suggest that you pray in the ordinary way for humility." And then she laughed a little. "But I'm afraid I'm going to undo all the good that would do. When I suggested you should have told me you were a *vidator* it was for selfish reasons. We have a great many visitors who come to us seeking the benefit of mysteries and only a few sisters who have the gift of crafting new ones. If you like, I think we can find more interesting work for you to do here than as a copyist."

* * *

As Margerit was still shaken, she was sent off to bed for the rest of the day. Barbara claimed the right to watch over her. Her more immediate purpose, though, was to parse the strange visions and try to divine their meaning.

"I think we may have hope," Barbara said after Margerit told over what she remembered for the third time. The details were beginning to fade, like a dream after waking. "If they arrived safely, we should hear of it from travelers by the end of the year. If not…" If not, there might be no certain news ever. She continued, "We should lay plans for our return that cover both possibilities."

And that was the sticking point when they looked to the future: they could see no clear and certain path. Barbara laid out the matter in law. "Although the charge is treason, it will be brought against you in the ordinary courts. The royal court wouldn't come into matters until a judgment is made. It would be different if you were of noble birth— then you'd have the right to appeal directly to the prince's justice."

It shouldn't matter, of course. The law was the law and truth was truth, but yet it could make a great difference.

"The most important thing is that we manage to make the charges against Estefen and Lutoz before their charges are laid against us."

"But hasn't that already been done?" Margerit asked.

"No, the charges are raised but not laid. Treason can't be laid in absentia, otherwise we might stand convicted already. Between two parties, the first charge laid, not the first raised, takes precedence. Just as charges in the royal court take precedence over the common court. So if we can accuse Estefen and Lutoz in Prince Aukust's presence before anyone knows we've entered the city, then that charge must be settled first. If we can't, then we need to prove innocence, and that might be difficult. We don't know how much they know about that invasion text and we don't know whether it caused any harm. We need a plan for each of those."

Margerit looked properly dismayed at the task before them. "And if we bring the charges first, then what? How do we prove it?"

Barbara sighed. "I don't have an answer for that yet either. Did you have nothing written in Lutoz's hand?"

"No. There were some notes he gave me at the first but I remember he took them back. The rest was only talking."

"If all else fails…" Barbara had thought to keep the idea to herself, but there had been too much of that. "If all else fails and if it is confirmed—" She felt shy to say it, of a sudden. "If it is confirmed that my father *was* a nobleman, then I could challenge Estefen. Judicial duels aren't at all the thing these days, but they're still allowed by law." When Margerit brightened at that, she cut her short. "I might not win, you know. Estefen isn't entirely unfamiliar with a sword. There are ifs upon ifs." Barbara hesitated. "Or we could stay here. It would be the safer choice."

"Stay?"

"Take vows. Spend the rest of our lives within these walls." It was selfish that she hoped Margerit wouldn't consider it. It wasn't the life either of them were meant for, but it would be life, not the risk of death.

"And we could be together?" Margerit asked.

But Barbara could see she already knew the answer to that. Not together in the way they hoped for.

Margerit shook her head. "We'll find a way."

* * *

Barbara tried not to count the days as they passed. So many of their plans required waiting. On that point she agreed absolutely with LeFevre's instructions. The uncertainty of her status was not the only reason to postpone their return to Rotenek until Margerit came of age. If Margerit were charged while still under the care of guardians, it would be those guardians who would answer for her. That could be disaster. And there was no telling what charges she herself might encounter while she was still unfree. LeFevre had foreseen those difficulties. He hadn't needed to know exactly what they might face to know that it was better faced when they were both free to act on their own. No, they had time yet to plan and wait before anything could be done.

The convent's records had yielded up as much information concerning the elusive Lissa as ink could tell. Elisebet Fulpi had finished her studies in the year of Our Lord 1786. There had been at least three other girls named Elisebet who had finished that year, and four more in the years before and after. One surname, Barbara recognized and could eliminate. One had no surname at all—she was recorded only as "Elisebet, daughter of the miller at Vezemul." She too could be discounted. But of the five that remained, there was nothing to choose between and no clue which might have been the bosom-friend of the Fulpi. It would have been a name—only a name. But even that small treasure was still denied her.

And if the convent's school records were little help in tracking the identity of one former pupil, the comings and goings of the sisters themselves were even less. Teaching at Saint Orisul's was the provenance of the older nuns come home from more strenuous labors and seasoned at their work. Those who had taught twenty years before were nearly all gone. The postulants and novices kept apart from the secular students and then were sent out to teach at the daughter

311 Daughter of Mystery

houses. In between, the nuns might come and go, but took little note of individual schoolgirls. Sister Anna had served up no more memories despite gentle coaxing. And yet Barbara couldn't let it be. The search had become a secret point of honor for her: to return to Rotenek sure in her own identity.

* * *

Her birthday came and went. She marked it only because Margerit did, asking whether it changed their bond.

"The terms of the will hold until we're both of age," Barbara answered. "Nothing changes until February is spent. If you were the elder...but you have no legal power to free me yet. I could have seen fifty years and it wouldn't matter."

But one thing did matter, she thought. Whatever debt she might have owed in her father's name was now canceled. And whatever inheritance she might have had claims on was lost forever.

* * *

The gardens mostly lay under a thin blanket of snow now, but the stone pathways between the sleeping beds were a precious private space during the afternoon's break. Barbara had come to suspect that one of the local women who came to deliver eggs and gossip was in Estefen's pay. Certainly they had made no secret of their identities, and with the Saveze estate a mere hour's ride from the gate it was impossible that he wouldn't know they were there. So they saved the discussions of their plans for days when the weather was fine enough to walk out and they could see who might be eavesdropping.

On a day just after the turning of the year, when taking advantage of that private walk, they were approached on the pathways by one of the sisters that Barbara didn't recognize. Even in the dead of winter there were always comings and goings, so that was no great surprise. The nun looked from her face to Margerit's and settled on the latter, greeting her warmly. "Yes, it must be you—you do have the look of your mother! I wondered, when they told me the name of my new assistant. I'm Sister Marzina and I'll be overseeing the visitors' mysteries for the coming year. Mother Teres told me I would have some unusual help."

"You knew my mother?" Margerit asked, passing over the remainder of the introduction.

"Not when she was a student—I was too young for us to have noticed each other and we had very different studies in any case. It was when she came back later. I was in special training, because of my visions. No school teaching for me! She was my first real challenge in writing new mysteries. So you might say I was one of your midwives!"

Barbara's heart had leapt at the thought of finally finding someone with clear memories of those days but it sank again. A dozen years after leaving school, when Elisebet Fulpi had returned as Maisetra Sovitre, desperate for a child, her own mother would have long since been wed to her debt-ridden nobleman. There was no use in asking.

But Sister Marzina's gaze had been drawn to her curiously, as if there were a memory there to tease out. "And you...?" she began.

Barbara shook her head. "I believe my mother may have been a student here as well, but that would have been earlier, when Maisetra Fulpi was in school. She might have been called Lissa by some."

A look of surprised delight came over the nun's face. "But of course—the friend! How could I not remember, when she gave me the pattern I needed to build the mystery!" The story tumbled out even more jumbled than her introduction. "I was casting about for a model—it was a hard problem and the first tries brought no response. And then your mother came with Maisetra Sovitre one day. She wasn't staying at the convent—I think she had friends in the neighborhood. And I could see that she was newly with child. It was part of my *visio*, you see, to know that. I don't think even she knew yet. And it came to me at once—the pattern that is—with two close friends, one bearing and one hoping to bear. Sister Chazerin who was in charge of the mysteries then, she thought it might be presumptuous to build the work around the Virgin and Saint Elizabeth, but what could be more natural? Especially with the chance to celebrate it on the Feast of the Annunciation? The Reverend Mother approved and when we celebrated it I knew it had been the right choice. And...well, here you are! I knew the two of you would be bound together in some way—how could you not be?"

Barbara could see that Margerit was reeling as badly as she herself was. *Were we truly destined for each other from birth?* One question remained unanswered. "Please," she asked, with heart pounding. "What was my mother's name?"

* * *

Elisebet Arpik, Countess Turinz, once Lissa Anzeld. Barbara rolled the names over her tongue again. It had taken some explaining for Sister Marzina to understand why the question needed to be asked. Elisebet Anzeld, wed to Efrans Arpik for the sake of that title. Eventually Sister Marzina had bustled Margerit off to discuss thaumaturgy and practice and she had stayed behind in the garden, though the light was growing thin and cold. She needed to ponder this alone. Oh, she would share her thoughts with Margerit later—no more secrets, she promised.

The count and countess of Turinz. No, that meant nothing. The title was truly extinguished now. Elisebet and Efrans Arpik. Mother and father. She felt nothing at the thought. All these years—all the searching and wondering—and now she felt nothing. Barbara Arpik—it was a stranger's name. Not hers. She wanted to weep with frustration. It was supposed to have mattered. She was supposed to feel that she had come home at last. This was supposed to be her triumphant return: a free woman with a name of her own. And…nothing.

At the close of the day, Margerit was still lifted on the tide of Sister Marzina's enthusiasm. Barbara recalled that dismayed question after the mysteries in Mintun when she'd asked if her visions marked her for a religious life. Perhaps now it didn't seem so limiting. Here was scope for her talents and teachers who would know how to channel them. If things went badly in Rotenek, might it still be an option? She had suggested it once before but she was too selfish to urge Margerit to consider it again while there was still hope.

As they slipped under the bedclothes that night, enjoying what privacy half the length of the room might provide, Margerit joked, "And how was your day, Mesnera Arpik?"

Barbara winced. Once, she would have simply endured but now her promise bound her: no more silence, no more secrets. "Margerit," she said softly, trying to keep the stiff and brittle edge from her voice. "Please don't tease me about it. It's still a tender wound." And she poured out her thoughts haltingly: the paths her mind had taken since that revelation. It was like learning a new footwork pattern, this matter of sharing her heart. For now it was labored and deliberate, but she could see a time when it could become comfortable and familiar. "It makes no sense," she concluded. "I always thought…there must have been some *reason* why I wasn't to know. But at least my worst fears were pointless."

"What did you fear?" Margerit asked.

"That there was something worse than the debt staining my name. That my father had done something that left such a taint—what else could have required erasure of his name?—such a taint that it would come between us."

The response was immediate. "Nothing can come between us!"

"Margerit, have you thought—have you considered what we will be to each other when this matter of treason is settled? When I no longer have the excuse of serving as your armin to be at your side?" They'd never touched on that question out loud. She hadn't dared to, while so much was still unknown. And Margerit? Margerit didn't seem to realize there was a question to be asked.

"I thought…" The shift from confidence to doubt was visible in her face. "No, I hadn't thought. But you could continue—"

"—as your employee?" Barbara finished.

"Oh." There was a long silence. And then, hesitantly, "What do *you* want?"

What did she want? She'd only ever defined her hopes in the space marked out by her fears. "I want to be a part of your life—the most important part of your life. I don't want anyone to have the right to come between us."

"Who would—?"

"The man you marry." There. She'd said it.

"Silly. I have no intention of marrying anyone. I never wanted to and now I won't need to."

"I don't want you to sacrifice—"

"No." Margerit laid a finger across her lips to stop the thought. "Let me decide what I want to sacrifice."

"Your reputation? Your good name? Your status in society? There's no place for what we are, not one the world will recognize."

"What about your friend the vicomtesse?" Margerit asked.

Barbara sighed. "Jeanne is different. She married, after all, so she has the license the world grants to a widow and the status of her title, however little it means in the ordinary way of things. And me? When I was with Jeanne, I was nobody—less even than the opera singers and artists she dallies with. Nobody cared what I did. I'm still nobody, for anything that matters. But you have a great deal to lose. A fortune can't buy everything. As I told you before, it isn't simple at all. But we can find a way, if that's what you want."

Margerit snuggled more closely into her arms. "Do you need to ask? Promise me you'll always be at my side. Promise me we'll always share one heart and one life and we'll find a way."

Barbara bent and kissed her. "I promise."

* * *

With the certainty of her birth, Barbara could trace the branching pathways of their return to the city more clearly. "The most important part is to get to Rotenek before Estefen can get word that we've left the convent. And then we need to go secretly to LeFevre—he'll be able to tell us all that's happened in our absence and what evidence we need to be able to counter. Our best hope would be if no copy of the invasion tower came into the court's hands. Then we only have words to answer to."

"Why LeFevre?" Margerit asked. "Why not simply go home?"

"A whole household can't keep a secret, no matter how loyal they may be. And once you're in residence again, the protection of Mesner Pertinek's hearth-right is ended."

"And then we wait for a chance to find Estefen and Hennis Lutoz in audience with the prince," Margerit finished. "How likely is that to happen without some contrivance?"

"It needn't be the prince himself. That would be best, but Princess Elisebet would do as well—as long as there are witnesses enough to uphold the law. Or if the council has officially named and installed an heir, he would do as well."

The plans were as well-made as they could be in ignorance. Sister Marzina had brought one other piece of good news beyond her memories of the past: the Austrian party had arrived safely in Rotenek in the middle of the Advent season. She knew and cared no more than that, but the pomp at their arrival had been impossible to miss.

* * *

With no more questions for the convent's archives to answer and her zeal having left the records in better order than the nuns had seen in many a year, Barbara cast about for another way to fulfill her obligations. Later in the year she might have worn away her restless impatience with outdoor work. Instead she drifted from task to task, lost in her own thoughts half the time. She found herself among those sharing watch at Sister Anna's bedside. The old woman slept most of the time now but when she roused there were sometimes lucid moments. Barbara vacillated between considering it her penance for pestering her for memories and hoping that there might be one more crumb dropped for her before the end.

So it was, on the eve of Ash Wednesday, that she found herself alone in the infirmary to free the watching sisters for their devotions. As the night wore on, Sister Anna's breathing had become more ragged, signaling wakefulness. Barbara moved to prop her up more firmly against the pillows and trickled a few drops of wine in the corner of her mouth to see if she would swallow. She thought briefly of sending to the chapel, but what was the need? The woman had received last rites. There was nothing more to be done on this side of the grave except to make her as comfortable as possible. There was little chance that she would return enough to answer questions now. Tonight there was only the penance.

But unexpectedly the nun's eyes opened and fixed on her face with a glitter of awareness. Her voice croaked drily in an attempt to speak and Barbara propped her up further and fed her small sips from a cup, wary lest it lead to choking.

She pushed the cup away at last and asked huskily, "Is this how you try to win forgiveness?"

Barbara was startled to have her own thoughts echoed that closely. She nodded agreement.

"You won't have it from me, Lissa," she continued more strongly. "Oh, you were always so proud and haughty, but you're no better than you should be. You weren't as a girl and you aren't now."

She was being taken for her mother again, no surprise. But the venom in the old woman's accusation was startling. She reached for a response that might draw her out. "I've always tried to behave as I should."

"Tried! You think you've fooled them." A fit of dry coughing interrupted and Barbara held the cup for her to sip again. "They may be blind, but I know. I know."

"What do you know?" Barbara asked, leaning closer to catch anything she might say.

"I know you don't spend your nights inside these walls. And I know the look of a woman who's been with her lover. Repent that, if you can, else there's no forgiveness." She coughed again, repeating, "No forgiveness." And then she slept.

When the midnight prayers were done and others came to take the watch, Barbara tried to slip quietly into bed beside Margerit without waking her. But her mind spun endlessly turning over what Sister Anna had said. *I know the look of a woman who's been with her lover.* Was she still speaking of Lissa or were she and Margerit being accused? They'd tried to be discreet. Was it that obvious even to an addled old woman?

No, *proud and haughty* she'd said and Barbara was sure no one could accuse her of that. Had that been meant for her mother? Sister Anna had been wandering in her mind for some time. Yes, that was it. The accusations, the venom, it was only a phantasm of her failing memory. Because it didn't make sense. It didn't... The last pieces fell into place like stones dropping down a long empty well with only the faintest sound to mark their final goal. She gasped aloud at the realization.

Beside her, Margerit stirred sleepily, asking, "What's wrong?"

Barbara hesitated. She couldn't bear to be right, but even more she couldn't bear to be wrong. She had to be sure. *No secrets; no silences.* But there *were* no secrets—there was nothing to tell. Not for certain. Not yet. Into that hanging silence came the soft toll of an unscheduled bell, counting out years of service come to their final end. "It's Sister Anna," she whispered. "She's left us."

"Oh," said Margerit, more awake now. "Should we—?"

"No, there's nothing for us to do now. We can pray for her in the morning." The moment had passed. Her promise stood broken for good or ill.

CHAPTER FIFTY-FIVE

Margerit

When the day arrived at last, Margerit thought it should have been heralded by the ringing of all the bells in the tower. Even the ordinary bells for a Sunday hadn't chimed yet when she slipped out of bed, shivering in the dark. Barbara stirred beside her but was hushed with enough reassurance to return to sleep. There was no place in the dormitory to store personal possessions beyond a change of clothing, so she had whole distance of the building to traverse and down to Sister Marzina's office to retrieve the papers she had prepared. Signing and witnessing must wait until later in the day but this part needn't wait further. She brought them back, along with a small lamp, and sat carefully on the edge of the bed.

"Come back where it's warm," Barbara said sleepily.

"I have a birthday gift for you," Margerit whispered, trying not to wake the other guests.

"Aren't you supposed to receive gifts on your birthday, not give them?" Barbara teased. But she sat and swung her legs over the edge of the bed in order to draw the blankets around both their shoulders.

She knew, of course, what the document was. Margerit handed over and held the lamp, watching Barbara's eyes trace over the words.

Ego, Margareta Sovitre, manumisi Barbara Arpik…"No," she said firmly. Before Margerit could exclaim in confusion she explained, "Not by that name. I served you simply as Barbara. Release me by the same name." And then Margerit could hear a grin in her voice, though it was lost in the lamp's shadows. "Or if you will, say, 'The woman Barbara, who has served me well and faithfully as my armin.' It closes the circle neatly."

"If that's what you want," Margerit said doubtfully. "But will it serve in law?"

"There's no one else it could describe. It will serve well enough. Now put out the lamp and come back to bed. There's still an hour before rising and I think today will be a busy day."

* * *

They had the abbess and Sister Marzina to witness—the two who had been brought most closely into their secrets.

"And what will you do now?" Mother Teres asked.

"Leave you," Barbara answered. "But it may be best if we don't say when or to where."

The abbess had already explained carefully the limits of her assistance, whatever her sympathies might be. But when they'd left her, Barbara asked Sister Marzina to stay a moment. "There's a favor I'd like to ask. Could you arrange to send a message this afternoon to Mefroi Cherend? He keeps the hiring stable in the village. Ask him if the spotted pony is for sale—say there's a girl who needs a ride."

Margerit understood the message no more than Sister Marzina did but the latter repeated, "'Is the spotted pony for sale, a girl needs a ride.' It does occur to me," she added, "that if one of you were feeling poorly and needed the quiet of one of the infirmary cells, and the other were to stay to watch over her, it might take some time for most people to notice whether you were there or gone."

"Thank you," Margerit said warmly.

"For what?" And then she embraced her and asked, "Are you certain this is the right choice? You have a true gift from God. I'd hate to see that lost if things go badly for you. You could have everything you need right here."

It wasn't the first time Margerit had heard her urgings in the weeks they had worked together. She smiled, but she stepped away and took Barbara's hand, lacing their fingers together. "Not everything," she responded.

Sister Marzina looked from one to the other of them. Margerit could tell the moment when realization dawned. "I will deliver your message," Marzina said with sudden coldness and she turned away.

"That wasn't wise," Barbara whispered. "Have a care who you expect to share our joy."

* * *

Margerit took Marzina's suggestion and found she had developed a deep hacking cough that was sure to disturb the others staying in the guesthouse. She had to endure dosing with an unpleasant-smelling draught but it won them a small room to themselves, apart from the general traffic of the convent. It would have been an enjoyable luxury if they meant to use it. Sister Marzina duly returned with the response that the spotted pony was best seen to advantage by moonlight, if a buyer cared to view it.

"And what is that all about?" Margerit asked when they were alone at last.

"Do you remember in LeFevre's letter? He said that if we needed help to remember the spotted pony? It was something that happened when I was a small girl—only he and I and Cherend would remember it. Cherend—he was always Marziel Lumbeirt's man, not Baron Saveze's. Even if LeFevre hadn't made the suggestion I might have gone to him for help. At the very least, I know he won't betray me." She bit her lip, thinking. "The moon is up now, but we don't dare leave by daylight. He must mean us to come after dark. You might want to see what rest you can manage. We'll get little enough tonight."

* * *

There were other exits from Saint Orisul's beyond the front gates with their exposed pathway up from the village. There was the cellar cut deep into the rock that had its own entrance on the side where the wagon road came up. There was the sheep gate that opened onto a maze of narrow tracks climbing the mountainside. And there was the nearly forgotten door that had once been the shortest route to the old wellhouse outside the walls, before the new pipes had been installed to bring the water in. That was how they left, after the evening meal had been delivered and most of the community was at services. There was barely enough moon to see their way down the steep slope but that meant there was little to betray them to any watching eyes or even simply curious ones.

The season not being one for much travel, they were unsurprised to see only a single carriage standing ready in the yard. The owner would be spending the night elsewhere—Cherend kept a stable, not an inn, having little use for people and a great deal for horses. Still, there was no telling who else might be about. Barbara led them around the back—skirting the courtyard where dogs would bark—and into the shadow along the fence. The moon was nearly down when Barbara shied a few pebbles at an upper window then pulled back into the darkness to wait. A door opened with a silhouetted figure. Barbara must have recognized the outline for she started forward. Margerit trailed after.

The door shut behind them in a cozy kitchen with the stove built up to a level that said they were expected. "I've been awaiting you any time these four months," was all the greeting they received. "Ever since that *efrankis* sent word, for all he said you wouldn't move until now. That friend of yours has been eating me out of house and home and I couldn't even put him to work in case he was recognized."

"My friend?" Barbara asked suspiciously.

He'd crossed to the interior door and called out, "Hey! It's them."

Margerit had only a moment to wonder if they'd been betrayed after all when a second man came through the door. "Marken!" she exclaimed in relief, seeing his broad familiar face.

He nodded at them as if the day were nothing out of the ordinary. "Maisetra. Barbara."

Margerit couldn't resist making the correction. "It's Mesnera Barbara now."

He eyed Barbara narrowly but with no visible reaction. "Is it? That will take some getting used to."

* * *

They left as soon as light permitted in the dawn. A carriage on a frozen road with horses changed at regular intervals made for a far shorter trip than two riding in tandem through muddy farm paths. It was still a long time to keep one's face hidden away. The cold at least excused concealing mufflers and cloaks when stopping for the night, and the eccentricities of well-born travelers might account for meals served upstairs—not even in the comfort of a private parlor. But even before they came in sight of the sprawl outside Rotenek's walls, Margerit was exhausted and frayed to threadbare nerves.

The gates were the point of greatest risk. Perhaps no one was watching for them. It had been four months, after all. But there were only five gates to watch and it was within the gate warden's duties to examine every vehicle if he chose. Better to enter on foot, leaving Marken to deal with the carriage, as if they were only passing in and out on everyday business. LeFevre had sent an assortment of clothing and Barbara suggested the loose scholars robes of the sort worn every day for classes. It would conceal the ill fit of the men's clothing worn under them and one student was much the same as another to most observers.

"I thought you said I couldn't pass as a man," Margerit joked.

Barbara grimaced, sorting through the selection for the least offensive to her taste. "No, I said I could pass for a woman better than you could for a man. In any event, it's only for a short walk across town."

Short was an exaggeration. It was nearly the entire width of Rotenek from the Tupendor Gate to Lamsiter and they must avoid the actual university district where their faces might be known. At the other end, there was a long, tense wait until darkness once again gave protection against watching eyes. The woolen scholars' robes were meant to guard against drafty lecture halls, not the chill of the nighttime streets and Margerit thought she would never be warm again by the time they slipped out of the shadows to pull the bell-rope by the office and heard the tread of feet descending the stairs.

The door was opened with no light and Margerit caught the flash of LeFevre's worried face before he closed the door behind them again. His feet sounded on the wooden steps as Barbara guided her blindly to follow him up, whispering a warning in her ear where the stairs turned sharply. When they emerged into the soft glow of the parlor, LeFevre turned to gaze at them and Margerit could see tears glittering in his eyes. He dashed them away unashamedly and said, "Come here by the fire, you must be freezing! Ianni, tea please! Where's Marken? I can see you met up with him." He gestured at their clothing and for the first time all day Margerit felt embarrassed to be seen in breeches.

"We entered the city separately," Barbara explained briefly as they both huddled close to the fire.

There was a clattering of china as LeFevre's secretary brought a tray in from the next room, asking, "Shall I go out to fetch more dinner? There's nothing left in the house but half a loaf and some cheese."

"I'd rather not risk being seen to do anything out of the ordinary while they're here," LeFevre answered. "See what you can make out of nothing."

"Are you watched so closely?" Barbara asked. "We took as much care as we could."

"Not constantly, but often there are strangers poking around, asking questions of my neighbors. You can stay here tonight but I want to find a safer place in the morning."

Margerit had finally recovered enough to speak without her teeth chattering. "Safe will be when the charges are answered. Tell us everything you know. Do they have the full text of the mystery?"

LeFevre pulled a chair next to the ones they had taken by the fire. "I think, perhaps, you need to tell me what *you* know first. The accusations spoke of a mystery but there are all manner of rumors. Exactly what was the purpose of this mystery? Barbara told me a little, when she—" He looked back and forth between the two of them as if uncertain how much of that quarrel still remained. "—when she was concerned about it. But there seemed no harm in it."

And so Margerit poured out the whole story, not omitting her own folly and mistakes. "I tried to correct it—to cancel it—when we were traveling. But I don't know how well it worked. We did learn that the travelers had arrived safely. But I have reason to believe that Hennis Lutoz tried to work the full mystery at some point."

Barbara added, "Our best hope—though I doubt he'd be willing— is if Lutoz would testify that Margerit knew nothing of the ritual's deeper intent. But that would require confessing his own part."

"Mesner Lutoz won't be testifying to anything, I'm afraid," LeFevre said.

Margerit gasped. "I killed him?"

"Why would you think—" LeFevre began. "Lutoz is very much alive. But back some months ago he was struck mute. Some called it witchcraft; others say apoplexy. I'm inclined to the latter. Sometimes it takes men that way, taking away all language. He can't even write sense, they say."

"Would that have been on All Saints Day?" Barbara asked.

"I'm not sure. But shortly after, Estefen produced his proof."

Iannipirt interrupted to offer something of a soup he had produced from the bread and cheese and a few other bits of the nothing that the apartment contained. "Enough to keep body and soul together for the night," he said apologetically. "And I thought you would want me to make the bed ready for our guests."

"Ianni, you are a treasure," LeFevre said lightly as the secretary retreated once more into the back room.

Margerit was torn between the hunger for news and that of her stomach, but the latter won for a time. With the soup consumed, LeFevre sat back and asked, "Now why might you think you had something to do with Hennis Lutoz's affliction?"

She told him, with Barbara filling in the parts that an ordinary man might need explained. "It was my petition that stopped his mouth. But that means I can undo it—that is, I can ask the saints to have mercy and forgive him."

Barbara seemed less certain. "Remember what Mother Teres said about pride. Not everything happens because you arrange it."

"But it's our only chance if he's to testify."

LeFevre said cautiously, "They say he's gone mad. There may be no truth to be had from him in any case. What other plans have you made?"

"Barbara says that if we can lay a countercharge of treason against Estefen, in the presence of the prince, then our charge must be answered first. That gives us time."

He turned away from her and looked steadily at Barbara. "Only someone of noble birth can raise a charge in the royal court. Margerit can't."

"But I can," Barbara answered. "I learned a few things at Saint Orisul's."

He nodded gravely. "The debt is canceled; there's no risk to you knowing now. And, as you say, you have the right to make the charge."

"So all we need," Margerit said, "is some way to smuggle two accused traitors into the royal court at a time when Estefen is there as well."

"Arranging the time and place is the least of your problems," LeFevre said. "The succession council—they've been meeting at least twice a week since December and the wrangling seems to move no further forward. Estefen is always there among the princess's supporters and Aukust, of course, can't escape the duty. Mesner Pertinek could attend if he chose, but I think he would be suspect if he showed up with strangers in tow."

Margerit saw Barbara glance in her direction as if looking for permission. "I thought perhaps…" She reached into the neck of her shirt and pulled out the chain and the ring threaded on it. She hadn't worn it for months, Margerit knew, but she'd put it on at the start of their journey. To keep it safe while traveling, she'd said. "Can you deliver this ring to the Vicomtesse de Cherdillac? Tell her nothing else, but see what she answers."

LeFevre took the ring and examined it. "This will take some thought. Going up to the north side of town is exactly the sort of thing that attracts my watchers. And we can hardly entrust the errand to just anyone."

"Perhaps Iannipirt..." Barbara suggested.

LeFevre scowled in thought long enough that Margerit wondered aloud, "Do you doubt he—"

"I don't care to have him thrust into the middle of my intrigues!" he snapped with an uncharacteristic flash of anger. But then he passed a hand over his face and took a deep breath. "I'm sorry. This matter entangles us all and there's no way out except forward. I'll ask him."

How tired he looks. What had these last months been like for him? Treading carefully to keep her people and possessions safe from her own folly. Uncertain what the end would be or even what the beginning had been. And then as if to mock her new-wakened sympathy, a great yawn overtook her.

"Margerit, go rest," Barbara urged. "I have a few matters of law to discuss still, but there's no need for you to wait up."

CHAPTER FIFTY-SIX

Barbara

Barbara poured herself another cup of tea and nursed it while she waited until Margerit's movements in the next room quieted. LeFevre sat waiting for her to break the silence.

"I learned a few things at Saint Orisul's," she repeated at last.

"Indeed."

It was little encouragement, given that she hardly knew where to start. "I learned that my mother was Elisebet Anzeld." There was no response. "And I learned that my mother's husband was Efrans Arpik, Count Turinz."

"A curious way of phrasing the matter," LeFevre commented.

Barbara found that her hand was shaking and she set the cup down. Not even facing down an armed opponent had ever unnerved her this much. "I learned that the spring before my birth, she accompanied her old school-fellow on a pilgrimage to Saint Orisul's. But she didn't stay at the convent, she spent her nights visiting a…friend in the area."

LeFevre's silence hung heavy in the air.

"Damn it man, is there nothing you can say? Wasn't that part of why you sent us to the *Orisules*? In hopes I might learn what you couldn't tell me?" She kept her voice low. The last thing she wanted was to have this conversation with Margerit in the room. The quality of LeFevre's silence had changed. There was an expectant feel to it, as if he needed only the right word to release him. Barbara tried again. "Did the baron leave…a letter, a document? Anything? Something you were to give to me?"

LeFevre let his breath out in a long sigh. "That's close enough. Wait here."

Barbara heard his footsteps down the back stairs—not the ones to the street, but those passing directly into his offices. Long minutes passed. She would have sworn it was hours. Finally the steps returned, a door closed and LeFevre stood before her holding out a thickly folded document, bound about with ribbons and seals.

"I was to give you this only if you knew to ask for it. I don't know what it says. It was important that I not know. But I have eyes and wits and I was with the baron a very long time. I would wager that my conclusions are the same as yours."

Barbara turned the packet over in her hands. She had been wrong about the seal. It hadn't been sealed with the baron's signet ring—the ring itself was embedded in the wax, wound about with the scarlet ribbons that tied up the packet. She had assumed that ring had either been broken or buried with him. Sealing this document was the last act he had taken. And he must have written it with his own hand, since LeFevre clearly hadn't done so. That would have been a great effort for him at the end.

"Do you plan to open it?" LeFevre asked.

"I think it will carry more weight if I present it still sealed."

"You're that certain?"

"If I'm right," Barbara answered, "then everything makes sense. If I'm wrong, then nothing ever made sense. I'm willing to risk it." She tucked the packet away and stood, finally admitting how exhausted she was. "LeFevre," she said quietly. "Thank you. For everything."

He made a bow of a depth she hadn't seen from him in some time. "My pleasure, Mesnera."

* * *

Barbara woke at a soft but insistent tapping at the door and for a panicked moment couldn't remember where she was or why. Only the presence of Margerit's warmth, curled against her, reassured her that all was well. Then memory returned and she called an acknowledgment. Margerit stirred beside her sleepily. Barbara looked over at the window. The curtains were drawn, but from the angle of the light she thought it must be past noon. So late! But LeFevre would have woken them if there were any need…and then her mind came around again to the tap at the door and she pushed back the covers.

There was no help for it but to put on the same ragged scholar's garb she had worn the day before. At least there was a basin to wash in. LeFevre's apartment suited him: well-ordered and tidy, with a sufficiency of comforts but no luxuries. The home of someone who had spent his life in a great man's shadow and preferred to go unnoticed in that work.

Margerit had woken at her absence and sleepily said, "Someday you and I will spend an entire day in bed with no one coming and going about us."

Barbara crossed back to her and kissed her long and lingeringly. "I'm not so worried about the coming as the going. We have work to do."

It was Iannipirt who met them when they emerged, bringing out food and filling in the morning's events. "I saw your friend the vicomtesse," he said. "Not at first, of course, but since the ring was her own I thought there'd be no risk to sending it in to speak for me. She knew the message, right enough. I think she's been half-expecting something since you disappeared. I didn't discuss details—only that you needed help and was she willing." He poured out cups of tea for each. "René—he's gone to speak with her somewhere safe. But he said it was best if I got you ready to move, if need be."

* * *

It was evening before LeFevre returned again, carrying parcels of assorted sizes as if he'd spent the day in the market. "I thought you might like a change of clothing," he said, hurriedly laying out several of the largest on the table. "I suggested to Maisetra Pertinek that she choose something plain but suitable for a formal occasion. I haven't had a chance to see how she interpreted that."

"How is my aunt?" Margerit asked eagerly. "Does she know I'm here?"

"She knows I requested clothing for both of you, so she can guess as much as there would be to tell." He drew out another, longer bundle, wrapped up in oilcloth.

Barbara grinned appreciatively as she took it from him and felt the outline of a blade within.

"I thought it might give you some comfort," he said. "Particularly as you will be repeating your role of armin tomorrow, in the service of the Vicomtesse de Cherdillac. And you," he turned to Margerit, "will be a waiting woman. It seems the simplest approach, though one that brings her into the same risk we run if you aren't successful." Barbara frowned in concern. "The plan was all hers," he assured her. "I think, perhaps, I have misjudged your friend."

Perhaps I have too, Barbara thought. *Unless all this is simply for the thrill of the danger.*

"I was followed," he added abruptly. "I think Estefen had a watch set at Tiporsel because I didn't see them before that. You should assume he knows you're here."

"Here?" Margerit asked anxiously.

"In Rotenek. He may guess you're here in this house, but I don't think—"

"We should move elsewhere," Barbara said immediately, gathering up the bundles of clothing.

"When it gets a bit darker," LeFevre agreed. "He'd overplay his hand if he moves against you here but there may be more watchers by morning. There's a small caretaker's room in the warehouse hard by Chapil Nikule—you know the one? I'll give you the keys. The vicomtesse will attend morning services at the chapel. Three will enter; three will leave."

His estimate of Estefen's caution missed the mark. Before they could sit to dinner there came a pounding on the door below. Without a word, LeFevre led them to the back stairs as Iannipirt hurriedly cleared away the evidence of guests.

"Take the right-hand door at the bottom," he said, pressing a small ring of keys into her hand. "No lights, I'm afraid. Lock it behind you then follow the wall around to the left until you find the trap down to the river. You should be able to walk the riverwall up to the Nikuleplaiz."

* * *

That night stretched on forever. The illusion of safety that had let them rest so long the night before was gone and even the locked doors of the caretaker's office couldn't prevent every distant shout and every creak of the old walls from banishing sleep. Dawn came slowly through the cracks in the shutters and they gave up on sleep entirely, changing into the provided clothing and cleaning up as best they could. Another hour and there was enough traffic on the street to slip out and join the morning worshippers at Saint Nikule's. Another even longer hour before the right set of carriage wheels was heard outside and Jeanne arrived with her attendants. Three entered and three left.

When the carriage disgorged them at the steps of the great hall of the palace, Barbara expected at every moment to be stopped by shouts and drawn weapons. Were there more of the palace guards about than she remembered from the baron's time? Were they more watchful than their usual formal scowls? Her face had once been familiar in this place—as much as any servant's face would be noticed. The chilly weather gave them an added layer of disguise for Jeanne had thought to provide a heavy greatcoat and hat for her and a hooded cloak for Margerit. They would be well inside before anyone would find it strange that they still wore them. Barbara had fallen easily into her place and role but Margerit had to be advised in haste on how to play the waiting woman. Her attention wandered too easily as they entered the crowded assembly room and edged their way slowly through the mere hang-abouts toward the dais where the long debate played out among the titled and powerful.

Barbara scanned the ornate chairs set apart from the ordinary benches. Prince Aukust, of course, in the center, worn thinner than she remembered. At his right hand, Princess Elisebet and young Chustin. But at his left hand, in curious symmetry, sat a slightly older woman and a youth just on the edge of manhood. That would be the Austrian party: Aukust's daughter Annek, Duchess of Maunberg. She had the gravity one might expect from a prince's daughter, with dark hooded eyes that spoke of the long weight of cares but missed nothing in the room. And at her side…but which of the prince's grandsons would that be? Weren't there two? She left the thought for the moment and searched further. Perhaps back when the sessions began there had been some order among the attending nobility but it was clear that many had now sorted themselves out by allegiance. She spotted Estefen with others of like mind standing back along the walls to the princess's side, his eyes darting here and there among the crowd. That habit that had once looked arrogant now seemed anxious. So: everyone was in place and now she must act before the opening of the session…and before there was any chance they could be recognized.

She waited until Estefen had turned away to speak to someone then signaled to Jeanne. Slipping off the overcoat and hat, she strode out into the empty space before the dais, judging precisely the distance at which she would command attention but not appear a threat.

"Prince Aukust of Alpennia," she called in ringing tones that excited first a ripple of comment then a fascinated hush. "I stand before you to raise and lay a charge of conspiracy and treason against Estefen Chazillen, Baron Saveze, that he has conspired to attack the house of Atilliet and do harm to those of your blood."

A stunned silence ruled. She saw the prince turn questioningly to the clerk who stood always at his elbow and of the latter's answer she could make out only "Lumbeirt's duelist."

Estefen pushed his way to the front of the crowd, glaring furiously at her, but the charge had been made in his presence: raised and laid. She had succeeded in seizing the upper hand.

The prince rose on unsteady feet and replied in a still commanding tone, "You no longer speak in Marziel Lumbeirt's name. I don't believe your new mistress has the right of birth to lay charges in my court."

"I come in my own name and by right of my own birth." She took the sealed packet from her coat pocket and held it up.

Estefen said scornfully, "A name so disgraced by your father that it's been unspoken for twenty years. A name you never dared to claim before today. I will not stand here to be slandered by the long-lost Arpik."

"Be silent," the prince commanded. "This is not your time to answer." He gestured for her to approach and she bowed and knelt before him. At another gesture the packet was delivered. He examined the ring for what seemed like eternity before breaking the seal and unfolding the letter within. The contents may have been brief but she suspected the hand was difficult. He was a long time reading while the crowd grew restless once more. At last he looked up at her again and said, "Marziel's death came at a most inconvenient time for you."

She couldn't resist responding, "I'm sure he found it inconvenient on his own part as well." A titter of laughter ran through the room.

The prince handed the document to his clerk but Barbara noticed that he kept the ring. "Record it: Marziel Lumbeirt, late Baron Saveze acknowledges this woman as his natural daughter. Barbara Lumbeirt, you have birthright to bring suit in my court, but have you evidence?"

Barbara took a deep breath to steady her nerves. She longed to see how Margerit had taken the revelation but now was not the time. Only the first two steps were passed and a long walk still stretched before them. "I call as witness to my charge Iohennis Lutoz. And I

stand prepared to uphold the charge with my body as well, if need be."
She watched Estefen's face carefully as she spoke. At Lutoz's name he
looked startled, but at what followed there was a trace of fear. Good.
She might not be certain of victory, but if he feared to meet her it
made the rest easier.

"And you," the prince said, turning to Estefen as well. "How will
you answer?"

"Unless my dear friend Hennis has regained his wits, the charges
seem to be lacking in substance. I will gladly stand by your judgment
and forego crossing swords with a professional murderer."

He was trying to goad her but he'd moved his piece to the square
she'd intended. "Mesner Lutoz isn't mad," she hastened to respond.
"He's been touched by the saints, a punishment for his part in this
plot. But there is one who can win forgiveness for him and restore to
him the power of speech." She paused until the prince signaled her to
continue.

This was the next chasm they had to leap across. Margerit couldn't
testify to Estefen's guilt directly, but she would need to confess her own
to make sense of what needed to be done. She turned and gestured to
her to approach. The concealing cloak was shed and she came forward.
One wild glance spoke of the questions roiling in her mind. Barbara
gave her hand a hidden squeeze. "Your Grace, this is—"

Estefen broke in accusingly, "This is the real villain! That Sovitre
woman I raised the charge against!"

"Raised, but not yet laid to her face," Barbara countered quickly.
"And you cannot lay it until your own charge is settled—that's the
law."

Estefen sputtered and protested but Barbara knew her ground was
solid. For the first time in the proceedings, Princess Elisebet spoke
up. "Is there another who could lay the charge in your place, Saveze?"

As Estefen looked around, she held her breath and once again
touched Margerit's hand for reassurance. How many others in
the guild had been privy to the plot? And were any willing to risk
themselves? Estefen's game had nothing to do with the succession,
after all—it was purely his own vengeance. And there was the example
of Lutoz to urge caution.

All eyes watched as he first approached Filip Amituz, then Mihail
Salun, and was met with stony silence. He searched around for other
members of the guild's inner circle but they were suddenly absent. He
crossed at last to where Antuniet stood with their mother. The words
that passed between them were not audible but Barbara could see that

his hand had closed tightly on Antuniet's arm. It was not until a sharp word from Mesnera Chazillen that he released her and returned to his place empty-handed and trying to cover his embarrassment with bravado. "It seems that justice against this woman will need to wait. But I won't stand by while she corrupts and bewitches the witnesses brought against me. If Lutoz can testify, then let him testify. But if he cannot, then don't allow her to put words in his mouth by sorcery!"

Barbara could feel Margerit trembling. It had been many years since charges of sorcery had been taken seriously in a secular court and she doubted Estefen had meant them as an accusation. But there were ancient fears that could be stirred up.

"And what do you say to that," the prince looked to his clerk for prompting, "Maisetra Sovitre?"

Margerit remembered to drop a low curtsy before answering. "These past two months I have worked performing mysteries with the Sisters of Saint Orisul. I think they can be trusted to know the difference between the works of God and those of the devil."

He nodded. "A fair answer. And how is it that you alone know how to dispel Mesner Lutoz's afflictions?"

Then Margerit plunged into her story. There were, perhaps, more details than needed to be told but the attention of most in the hall was caught and held. Her inheritance, the university, the discovery of her talent as a *vidator*, the guild, the *castellum* and finally the extra tower whose seeds Lutoz had planted for her. "I was ignorant," she confessed contritely, "and didn't know what meaning those symbols had. And I was too full of pride in my skill to wonder why it seemed important that only we two should work on the rite. It wasn't until after…after I fled the city that I learned what I'd been a party to."

"You see?" Estefen interrupted. "She confesses her guilt." But he was silenced at a gesture from the prince.

"Continue. We have not yet come to the heart of the matter."

Then Margerit told of the new mystery she had worked and the visions on All Saints' Day. "And I prayed to them to be deaf to his words, but they—they seemed to have answered by silencing his voice instead."

"What was it you saw?" The question came from the woman Barbara assumed was Duchess Annek—she could be no one else and she had the Atilliet look about her.

Margerit answered hesitantly. "It was strange—like in a nightmare. A *phasma*, not like a regular vision. I saw leopards with glowing eyes prowling in the dark. And hedges of briar crept across the land. Then the saints stood before me, blazing like the images in the cathedral windows with swords in hand, and I thought they would cut down the thorns but then there was a great light and the leopards were edged in glory and the Virgin came in her blue mantle and spread it over the thorn and it blossomed and—" She trailed off as if suddenly self-conscious. "And then I fainted, I think."

"A pretty tale," said the princess from the other side. "Are we to spend the whole day listening to more of this?"

"She speaks the truth," Annek said. "There were strange things on the road that day. Things she couldn't know unless she were there in spirit." She turned directly to Margerit. "So it seems I owe to you both our peril and our salvation. I say you've proven your point and you should have the chance to make your witness speak. But what will that avail you? It seems he could confirm *your* guilt, but I've heard nothing to place any on Baron Saveze."

Barbara took up the answer. "Lutoz didn't plan this alone. My charge is that Estefen Chazillen set all in motion, both the guild itself and the mystery aimed at you. He worked through Lutoz and then betrayed him in turn for the sake of his own revenge. Lutoz never meant the second mystery to come to light, that was Chazillen's doing. And if not for Lutoz's affliction Chazillen's plans would have fallen short, for the evidence wasn't found at the guildhall as he meant it to be." Some of that was guesswork, but she saw nods among those who would know and knew she hadn't stumbled yet.

Estefen tried for one last bluff. Barbara could see the fear under the bravado. "It's a tale worthy of a gothic novel. All it needs is a kidnapping and a moldering ruin. Let her try her little tricks but I want no chance for plans to be made against me. Let it be done here, now, or end this farce."

"Not here," the prince said mildly, "but in the cathedral, surely, if mysteries are to be done. And to keep the peace of God on the proceedings. Let Lutoz be brought there. As gently as you may, given his madness, but bring him."

* * *

When the court reconvened in the nave of Saint Mauriz's cathedral the crowd of spectators had doubled. Within the palace assembly hall there were limits to who might enter, but as word of the spectacle ran through the *plaiz* every idler and curiosity seeker that could fit into the aisles came to watch and repeat fifth-hand stories of what was afoot.

There was time, only briefly, for a private word with Margerit in the confusion of the procession. "Can you do it? With no preparation and no experiments?"

"I think so—if I can do it at all. And nobody knows what to expect, so there's some chance to try variants in the guise of repetitions. I wish—well, it doesn't matter. This is what we get to work with. But Barbara, the baron...how did you know—"

"Not now. There's no time even to begin. Hush now, they're coming."

And then they were separated. Barbara moved to where the prince was installed on his chair of state and where Estefen stood apart, not quite under guard but close in hand, while Margerit went to the space before the altar. The archbishop had given his assent to the mystery but declined to lend his presence and the priest who remained seemed to be content to assure the seemliness of the proceedings.

Lutoz was led in. Though the guards sent to fetch him stood close by, he was supported on the arm of his father. The old man's careworn face told much of the last four months. Lutoz himself moved listlessly and his gaze focused on nothing in particular. The boyish good looks were gone and his face was thin and haunted. Only when he passed by where Estefen stood did his expression change—a brief flash of recognition, a movement quickly forestalled, his head turning over his shoulder as he was guided past. There was no emotion shown, just the glass-hard look that a hawk might give at sighting movement. He changed when he was brought to face Margerit, shrinking back against his father's shoulder and shaking his head. The old man looked embarrassed and clumsily patted his son's hand, then stepped away at a signal from the guards.

Margerit looked around and said something quietly to Lutoz. Estefen protested loudly but when Margerit looked to the prince his vague gesture gave no guidance. *Just begin*, Barbara thought.

Even with the best intent, Margerit's voice was weak as she began the preliminaries, explaining what she believed had happened and asking Lutoz's forgiveness for her part in what had befallen him. That was a nice touch, Barbara thought. There was enough in that beginning to let him know how matters stood. God only knew what he had heard or understood of what was happening—and if he had, how much temptation there might be to remain mute by choice. But he showed his assent by kneeling at the rail and bowing his head.

Barbara had seen Margerit at work often enough to know how tentative her opening was. First, the general prayers asking the blessing of God on the undertaking and for Christ's mercy on all present. Then the addresses to the saints invoked in the invasion tower. She was re-using some of the original text and Barbara saw Lutoz raise his head in recognition at some of the passages. Finally she moved into the meat of the ceremony: the petition for mercy and forgiveness. It was simpler and more repetitious than her usual work. Barbara took note of the little changes at each cycle. There were candles and a few other symbols but mostly it was only her words weaving around him: cajoling, praising, pleading. She added Saint Tirok to the roster, patron of deaf-mutes. That was a nice touch.

Margerit gave no sign of her progress but when a ripple of scattered exclamations ran through the crowd Barbara guessed that some had seen the saints respond. And then the repetitions grew more focused and more intense until at last Margerit exhorted Lutoz to join her in the *Ave*. As she drew out and repeated the opening phrases *Aaa-veee Maaa-riii-aaa, Aaa-veee…*a croaking sound—more a sigh than a word—joined her voice, growing gradually stronger until she led him through the entire prayer.

And then it was done. Lutoz still knelt, his hands covering his face and his shoulders heaving, but now the sound of wracking sobs could be heard where only silence had gripped before. His father ran to embrace him and help him to his feet. Margerit had stepped back to the edge of the crowd as if to disown her part in the cure.

A decent interval was allowed before Lutoz was brought before the prince. So he wanted a speedy conclusion, Barbara thought. Well, that was to their advantage as well. Lutoz still seemed dazed—and little wonder—as he knelt.

"Like your deliverer, you are in a delicate position," Prince Aukust admonished him. "You do not now stand accused and yet your testimony requires your confession. She gave hers freely and I have taken note of that. To you, I can promise only that if you speak the truth unstintingly I will require nothing greater than your exile."

But if he expected defiance, it seemed he hadn't accounted for the sobering effects of Lutoz's penance. "What I did," he began, "I did for Alpennia. As I have been judged in a higher court and granted mercy, I will stand by the truth."

His story, coming first haltingly as his ragged voice found its way, held few surprises. How could it? Knowing the end, knowing how everything had focused on destroying Margerit, there was only one possible beginning. But to the prince and the others who would judge, Margerit was nothing and the tale must stand on its own merits. The guild—that had been Lutoz's dream, but Estefen had urged him to realize it. And Estefen had insisted on expanding the membership to bring one particular name into play. The idea for the mystery? That, he thought, had been consensus—his memory wasn't clear. But Estefen had insisted on the invasion tower, laying out the specific symbols to use, and suggesting they keep it close until the celebration.

"And what was the purpose of that part of the ritual?" the prince asked harshly. When Lutoz faltered he added, "The truth. Unstintingly."

"To protect the interests of your true heir, Aukustin, against… against those of foreigners."

"Against my beloved daughter and my grandsons," he countered. "And did you have no thought for the consequences of raising the guardians of our land against them?"

"That, I left in the hands of God."

"And we see how God answered. Continue," the prince commanded.

The accusation, the search of the guildhall—he had been shocked at that, but mystified and grateful that only the public mystery text had been found. The treasonous *turris*? Only he and Margerit had copies. At some point Estefen had borrowed his; was that before or after? He had thought it best to let things lie but Estefen had urged completion, had arranged for a venue. Then came the disaster of All Saints' Day. And on the heels of that—when all the doctors and priests had come and gone to no avail—betrayal. Estefen had ransacked his papers and notes and carried away all trace of the ritual. And if the ritual was the foundation for the treason that was charged, then the charge belonged as much to Estefen as to any other.

Barbara watched the prince's face closely as the questioning concluded. Was it enough? Was the miracle of speech restored sufficient to give credence to that speech?

Estefen, challenged to respond, was dismissive. "My old friend Hennis lost his wits and his voice but only his voice has returned. When have I shown any interest in chanting mysteries? If I've been arranging all these secret meetings, who has seen me? If I've been dictating the details of this treasonous ceremony, who has heard me? Where is the proof? Who can produce a single document that taints me with any greater crime than a poor choice of friends?"

As the silence stretched out Barbara stole a brief glance at Margerit. Did she realize how close they were to failing? And then, like the voice of doom, two words fell into the silence.

"I can."

The stir in those around her identified the speaker. Mesnera Chazillen had no need to raise her voice to command attention. Her words, like her face, seemed chiseled from ice as she addressed her son.

"If you had betrayed a friend out of loyalty to your prince, I could forgive that," she said, stepping forward into the space where Estefen stood alone. "If you had betrayed your prince out of zeal for a cause, I might forgive that. But to betray your family, to drag our name into the gutter, to trample your honor into the mud underfoot for no better reason than petty revenge on this…this *burfro* girl? You are drowning in your own bile and now you won't be satisfied until you drag all of us under with you. It's time to make an end."

CHAPTER FIFTY-SEVEN

Margerit

And suddenly, just when it seemed they might fail, it was over. *Did she know about that too?* Margerit wondered. A crowd clustered thickly around the principals with voices raised in babble. As much as Margerit longed for the reassurance of Barbara's presence, she hung back from the press of people. This was Barbara's realm—her game to play out. But it seemed there would be no further spectacle today. Judgment would come later. She saw Estefen being led off under guard. The ordinary folk slowly began to drain away, leaving the cathedral quieter and suddenly colder.

When the crowd had thinned enough she caught Barbara's eye. After a brief conversation she came over, bringing the vicomtesse with her. "The talking is likely to go on for some time. It might be better for you to leave now. Jeanne has said she can see you safely home. I'll come when I can." But she looked worried.

"I thought it was all settled."

The vicomtesse laughed and not in amusement. "The game is only begun in earnest. One takes another's pawn—so. The other disclaims the pawn but demands a knight in return. A third player enters the board and the game changes. They will be arguing all night over moves that no one dares to make openly."

"Don't frighten her," Barbara chided. "Our part is nearly over but we've upset the balance of something larger. I need to stay to see how it plays out. At the moment, I'd rather you kept out of view as much as possible."

"But Barbara, when did you—"

"Hush. Later." Barbara laid a finger across her lips and let it linger there a moment longer than necessary. "Later."

* * *

Margerit hardly knew what to say to the vicomtesse on the brief carriage ride from the cathedral to home. The day's events were too vast to address and the past that bound them together seemed perilous territory. And she wasn't put at all at ease by the knowing smile that lingered at the corner of Jeanne de Cherdillac's mouth. But at the last, as the footmen came out to let down the steps and open the door, the vicomtesse leaned over to offer a quick embrace and whispered, "Be good to each other. I think you suit her far more than I could."

Margerit remembered little of that homecoming later: a long tearful welcome from Aunt Bertrut; careful, incisive questions from Uncle Pertinek; a constant parade of curious servants, peeking around corners until she capitulated and went understairs to show herself and share reassurances that she didn't entirely believe herself. In turn, she learned the fate of Maitelen, who had thought it wise to remain in Chalanz until sent for. Nikule too hadn't returned to the city and Margerit could only imagine what Uncle Fulpi would have to say when next they met.

And then, after a quiet supper, there was nothing left but to wait. Aunt Bertrut fussed at her to rest. "Not until Barbara returns," she responded firmly. Her aunt looked worn thin by the past months.

"But I thought…" Bertrut began. "That is, she doesn't…work for you now. That was the arrangement, wasn't it? And Charul said…" The highlights of the days' revelations had traveled faster than she had. Those of the household that had served in the baron's time found Barbara's news of far more interest than the actions of the court. No detail of that matter had escaped discussion. Bertrut finished at last, "Will she be staying here, then?"

"This is her home. Where else would she go?"

"But I should have them make up the guest room. We can't put a baron's daughter in an attic room with the servants."

Margerit forestalled her. "Tomorrow is soon enough to worry about it, Aunt Bertrut." She had a sudden thought. "We'll be up late talking. I expect Barbara will simply stay in my room tonight." But how to excuse the next night? And the night after? How did one arrange these things?

* * *

Alone, waiting in the library as so many times before, she finally had time to start turning over the puzzle pieces. The baron's daughter? Had LeFevre told her…just two nights before, it would have been? But then she thought of the charter, when she'd refused to use the name Arpik. She must have known then. How long? Had she known when she'd vowed to have no more secrets between them? And why? Why had it been secret all those years?

She hadn't meant to sleep. She would have sworn she hadn't, but the next thing she knew there was a hand on her shoulder and Barbara's whisper in her ear. "Margerit, wake up, I'm here."

Margerit blinked a moment in confusion then threw her arms around her and held her as if she never meant to let go. She could feel the other woman's body vibrating with tension. "Is it over?"

"Not entirely. But the rest will only be formalities. Estefen…Estefen will be condemned. Mesnera Chazillen had letters, documents—it wasn't just you. If it had only been the trap he laid for you he might have wriggled free. He'd kept his hands nearly clean of the mystery plot. But he owed too many debts—both in Alpennia and out—and he'd sold his honor to pay them. She'd looked the other way for too long. Even family loyalty has its limits."

"And Hennis?" Even now, Margerit found it hard to feel worse than pity for him. They'd worked so closely for so long. As callous as he'd been toward Duchess Annek and her sons, she wanted to believe he'd been ignorant of Estefen's plans for her.

"Exile, as the prince said. He stands convicted by his own words. Margerit, you haven't asked—you're safe, you're free; the charges won't be laid."

It was the relief in Barbara's voice that struck like a blow. "But I thought…when no one took up the charge…"

She was suddenly shaking and Barbara eased her down into the chair by the fire. "That only held until the case against Estefen was settled. Even condemned, he could still lay his charge against you.

That was one of the reasons I wanted you away while it was all being argued. So there would be a chance to have the charge voided before it could be laid. Princess Elisebet was looking for blood. She couldn't defend either of the men directly but she could seek to even the score. And it didn't matter to her that neither of us has any stake in the succession. She wanted your exile to match Lutoz's."

Exile. The images flashed through her mind. Wandering, homeless, a stranger…and would Barbara be willing to follow her?

"It's all right, you're safe," Barbara repeated. "Annek…I don't know what she really thought, but she suggested to Aukust that someone of your talents shouldn't be driven into the hands of foreigners. And since she was the most concerned in the plot he took her advice and pardoned you of any charges." She gave a little forced laugh. "I think you impressed a fair number of people today."

"Then it's over?" she repeated. It seemed hard to believe things had happened so fast. And then, a more practical thought, "You must be starving, it's after midnight. I'll ring to have something brought up."

"No, no, don't disturb anyone. All I want is to sleep for a week."

Margerit grinned. "I told Aunt Bertrut that we'd likely be up late talking and they shouldn't expect your bed to be slept in."

* * *

Waking was once more disorienting. A tap at the door—Iannipirt? No, this was her own bed. She disentangled herself from Barbara just as a maid came in bearing a tray with chocolate and pastries. But someone had already seen to building up the fires while they slept. If there were to be gossip, it would be started already. The maid set the tray on a table by the window and dipped a rather formal curtsy. "Welcome home, Maisetra," and after the slightest hesitation, as if to rehearse, "Mesnera Lumbeirt."

When the door had closed, Barbara rose and poured out cups for the both of them. "As Marken said, that will take some getting used to."

It seemed an invitation to the subject. "When did you know?"

"For certain? Not until Aukust opened the baron's letter. But it… fit. That night that Sister Anna died, she said some things. About my mother. And that was the one answer that would make sense."

"But…but *why?*" In a gesture, Margerit took in the whole long masquerade.

An angry look twisted Barbara's face. "Money," she said harshly. And then, as if her feelings could not be contained in stillness, she paced the room as she explained. "Do you remember that treatise on the laws of debt that LeFevre sent me? I was the child of two purses. If the baron had acknowledged me, I had a claim by right to his purse. But if Arpik failed to disclaim me, then I was tied to his purse as well—both the wealth and the debts. I was the link by which Arpik's creditors could sue the baron, even after Arpik's death."

The complexity of it began to sink in. Margerit thought it through aloud. "So if he acknowledged you after you came of age, you'd have no claim by law on his estate, but neither would there have been any bar to him making you his heir. He could have chosen any heir, just as he did me."

"Yes, that inconvenient death!"

"But then why?" Each answer brought only more questions. "Then all this was to protect you from the debts?"

"It was to protect his fortune!" Barbara seemed truly furious now. "Work the sums out. From the hour that Arpik breathed his last, the size of his debt was fixed and known. It was large—it might have taken half the baron's fortune to pay at that time—but he could have paid it if he chose." Almost as an afterthought, as if she were commenting on the weather, she said, "I hate him."

"You don't mean that," Margerit protested. Always before Barbara had defended him, excused him.

She sighed. "Margerit, to you he was kindly Saint Nikule, tossing bags of gold over your garden wall at your coming-out. But he was my father. My *father*. And he raised me in his own household as less than a servant, all for his own greed and the love of intrigue. He's mine to hate, not yours."

Those impressions she had had of the baron came back: capricious, manipulative, always with some deeper, hidden game. She ventured, "He *could* have raised you as a free woman—as his ward but with no claim on him."

"But then he would have had to put a name to me. Arpik's name. Oh, I don't really know what he was thinking, but I have to wonder if even that wasn't part of his greed—that he couldn't bear to let me belong to another even if he wouldn't claim me himself." She stood, staring out the window where the Rotein flowed silently past, like the passage of years. "Well, what's done is done." In an abrupt change of mood, she poked through her discarded garments from the day before. "I'm going to need some new clothing. I may have one or two gowns that still fit and I rather think I'll take advantage of my scandalous reputation and wear breeches when it suits my fancy. But I can't go around dressed like an armin anymore."

"Then we'll call in the dressmakers and tailors both," Margerit declared.

"You know, you aren't responsible for clothing and housing me now."

Was she teasing? Margerit wasn't certain and answered seriously, "You know this is your home for as long as it is mine."

"Ah, I had meant to tell you—" Barbara came to sit on the edge of the bed and took her hand. "Prince Aukust invited me to take rooms at the palace for now. He doesn't know about what's between us— how could he? And we need to be very discreet about that. It's an invitation that would be hard to decline in any case. Oh Margerit, it's just for a little while." She traced a hand along her cheek, forestalling the protest that came to her lips. "I think we should be very careful. Just until we've found our feet again."

It seemed as if Barbara were the only member of the household who had little trouble finding her feet. Aunt Bertrut was entirely confounded by how to say *Mesnera* to one she had learned to treat as invisible. Uncle Pertinek took refuge in stiff and utterly proper formality. But Barbara left behind the role of armin as if it were a part in a play, discarded after the show like a cast-off costume. She accepted the guest's seat at dinner with the graciousness of a visiting queen and shared the court gossip with Mesner Pertinek as if they were old friends. Where she once had commanded the servants by proxy, now she begged the loan of their assistance in packing up her things and having them carried off to the palace. At times she seemed a stranger, at others she seemed as familiar as breathing. And when she left, the house felt empty and echoing as if its very soul had gone with her. But reminders were everywhere.

Sitting in the parlor with Aunt Bertrut, waiting on the chance of visitors, a message came that Marken wished to speak with her.

"Sorry to bother you, Maisetra," he began, "but Barbara's not around to ask—Mesnera Lumbeirt, I mean. Or rather, that's the problem. Mesnera Lumbeirt may be around but Barbara isn't. I need to know if you're planning to hire another full-timer or if you want me to step up. I've always kept my own lodgings, you see, but if you want me full time, it makes more sense to live in. I asked Ponivin but he said he'd had no instructions."

It was the longest continuous speech she'd ever heard from him. The answer was easy enough. She needed someone to take Barbara's place as armin—there would be more hazards now than what a mere heiress would attract—and Marken had proven his loyalty quite thoroughly. It was time to start making her own decisions. "Yes, I'd like you to take the position. Tell Ponivin to make whatever arrangements you need." The butler would know what was required. She tried to think of what else might have changed. "Are you paid through the household or separately? I don't know what the usual arrangements are."

He shrugged. "Barbara handled it before, but armin's usually a staff position, like butler or coachman. It's only the well-born duelists get treated differently. Will you be going out today?"

"No, I don't think the invitations have caught up with my return yet." She wondered idly whether it was only that or whether she had become a social hazard. "Barbara said I should expect to be sent for when the trial is settled but I've heard nothing yet."

He ducked his head, halfway between a nod and a bow. "Then I'll see about moving my things, Maisetra."

* * *

The summons, when it came, was addressed to Mesner Pertinek, instructing him to see that Margerit Sovitre was in attendance at the court by noon of the clock on the next day. The judgment was already concluded by then. Estefen had met his end at midnight, in private, as befitted his rank. Hennis was in transit to the border under guard. When she heard that, Margerit released some of her anxiety. Whatever happened now was for the living and the remaining.

Today was not the crowded spectacle of the succession debates; business was being conducted in the smaller drawing rooms rather than the public hall. Still there were always people coming and going, whether to watch and listen or hoping for a moment of time and a willing ear. It only gradually occurred to her that among those gathering in the anteroom were several others from the ill-fated Guild of Saint Atelpirt. She saw more than one curious glance in her direction—not hostile but wary—and she felt shy of approaching them.

The doors from the audience chamber opened and several other former guild members emerged: Ainis Nantoz and Iosifin Rezik, looking variously relieved and annoyed, and—before she could step aside—Antuniet as well. Her dark eyes looked haunted and when Margerit first felt them fasten on her she knew what it was to be the prey of some great hunting hawk. But that one flash of passion faded to the same cool, distant gaze Antuniet had always affected. They both stood frozen for a long moment. Margerit could find no words to offer.

In a quiet icy voice, Antuniet said, "You once asked if I hated you and I told you it wasn't your fault that my brother was a fool. Well, I had no idea how great a fool he was but this time you have blood on your hands. This time, I do hate you." She brushed on past and out the far door without looking to left or right.

Ainis came over and with a pitying look—though whether for Antuniet or herself, Margerit wasn't sure—said, "You didn't know. Mesnera Chazillen—her mother—took poison this morning after the…after it was done."

And then they were summoned into the presence and there was no time to digest that further blow.

There was little enough to be said. The Guild of Saint Atelpirt was disbanded and banned. There would be no further pursuit of the former members and her own pardon was confirmed. She had seen Barbara watching anxiously from one side where those waiting on other business were gathered, but when she was released and Uncle Pertinek had guided her through the formal leave-taking it seemed there would be no chance for a word or a touch. They had retired nearly to the doorway when Margerit heard Barbara's name called by the usher. She pulled at her uncle's sleeve to see if they could linger.

Barbara again seemed almost a stranger, startlingly feminine in a pale blue gown, moving through the formal courtesies as if born to it. As she knelt at the prince's feet he rose unsteadily and said, "It seems the title of Saveze is vacant and there is a taint on the line that last held it. Since it falls to me to choose, I think I need look no further than a return to the house of Lumbeirt." He held his hand before her and when Barbara took it, somewhat uncertainly, he slipped a heavy old-fashioned signet onto her finger. "I think you know it's no favor I do you, Baroness Saveze, but if you're your father's daughter you'll be up to the task."

CHAPTER FIFTY-EIGHT

Barbara

Barbara stared down at the thick gold ring loosely encircling her finger. Mechanically she transferred it to her thumb where it fit more snugly. *The baron's signet.* At once it felt unreal and as if this were the natural course of her life. Thinking back, so much of her childhood could have been preparation for this moment. Had it been? Had he somehow foreseen this? Impossible. A bastard daughter would never have been considered except for Estefen's treason. She barely heard the words that accompanied the token but at the appropriate moments she kissed the prince's hand and rose and curtsied. She had gone no more than a few steps from his presence before the first of the well-wishers and interest-seekers descended. *Of course. Now I have a voice and a vote in the succession council.*

She had glimpsed Margerit briefly, lingering at the entrance to the hall, but now when she looked again the doorway was empty. And there were documents to deal with. The ring might serve as a symbol, but the title and lands required charters and deeds and official letters. It was an hour before she could think of what to do next. She would need someone to help sort through and secure the properties, to assess how dire the finances were and how she might best balance the demands of the title and the need to disencumber it.

Her thoughts turned at once to LeFevre, if he would take it on. There'd been no time to do more than send him reassuring notes in the past days. But she needed to see Margerit first. Alone, in the small chamber she'd been allotted, she worked through her options. Barbara Lumbeirt might wander the streets on foot alone, if she dared, like any common tradesman or student, but the Baroness Saveze had standards to maintain. It was the same bind she had once found amusing for Estefen. Here she was, without a single coin in her purse, dependent on the prince's charity and yet trapped by the dignity of rank. Well, if she couldn't yet hire a carriage, she might borrow a horse from the palace stables. Having no riding habit, that meant breeches. Even more than before, anything she might have worn as an armin would be completely unsuitable. She dug through one trunk and found the outfit she had used for her disguised visits to Eskamer's shop. She had no need or desire to pass for a man now, but with suitable substitutions it would do for an aristocratic Eccentric. She should take Margerit up on her offer regarding tailors and dressmakers. No doubt Margerit would provide her with a carriage and a full purse, if she asked, but that seemed…she wasn't sure what word to put to it. The thought made her strangely uncomfortable. *Like a kept mistress*, she concluded, wincing.

But when she rode at last to the doors of Tiporsel, it seemed Margerit was not at home. "Truly?" she inquired of the footman who opened the door to her. He was flustered for a moment that she behaved as a visitor.

"I swear, Mesnera, she and Mesner Pertinek haven't returned yet. The elder Maisetra is home."

No. That one day had been awkward enough when Bertrut had been adjusting to treating her as an equal. Let her hear this news from Margerit. "Tell the Maisetra—Maisetra Sovitre, that is—that I was here. I haven't a card to leave." One more petty expense that must be managed. How long might it take LeFevre to determine if some spending money might be freed up from the estate?

* * *

She found him in his office. He looked up at the door's opening and rose with a delighted cry, "Mesnera! How good to see you! We've been following all the news, of course. Is everything sorted out at last?"

She grinned at him. "There's been a new complication." She held up her hand, displaying the ring. It occurred to her wistfully that he would never again call her by her given name.

He recognized the ring, of course. He'd used it often enough to seal the baron's papers and letters. She saw his eyes go wide as he realized the significance. "Dear God!" He fell silent again, not so much at a loss for words as from the need to calculate the consequences. "He wasted no time about it. But then, there's no time to waste. Even one person might make the difference on the council. Have you…? No, never mind. And what has Maisetra Sovitre to say to all this?"

"I don't know. She was there, at the court, when it was done, but we had no chance to speak afterward." She settled into the chair opposite him at the desk and waved him to sit as well when he remained standing. "I was wondering…might you find time to do a little management and clerking for me? I have no idea what sort of salary I might be able to pay you—that would be one thing for you to discover. Or perhaps you could recommend someone?"

LeFevre made a rude noise. "If you dared ask anyone else to touch the Saveze estates I might never speak to you again. Maisetra Sovitre's affairs are light enough work at the moment—at least when she isn't stirring up trouble." He smiled to make sure she knew it for a joke. "And I handled the whole of it in the baron's time. I can't imagine there would be any conflict in handling matters for the both of you. I don't suppose you know who Estefen's business manager was?"

"No. I suppose it's possible Antuniet might know, but you—ah—have heard about the elder Mesnera Chazillen?"

He nodded soberly. "Gossip flies like the wind. No, I won't bother her at a time like this. The staff at the Chazillen house should know. Or at worst I can send off to Saveze. Is there anything you need at the moment?"

"Everything!" Barbara laughed. "But I'm lodging by invitation at the palace and Margerit has suggested she might make me a present of a new wardrobe, so at least I'm clothed and housed and fed."

"At the palace?" he asked curiously. "Not at Tiporsel?"

"Things are…complicated. Not between Margerit and me," she hastened to reassure him. "But there are deep currents flowing and I'd rather Margerit didn't get pulled under by accident. We're both under such close scrutiny at the moment. I'm not sure her good name could bear the weight of one more scandal just now."

"And what does she say to that?"

Barbara shrugged. They hadn't really had a chance to discuss it, but surely she understood.

LeFevre took a key from his pocket and unlocked a drawer behind the desk. "If you will permit, I can advance you whatever you might need for immediate expenses." He brought forth an envelope of notes and counted out a generous number. "These are my own funds, so you needn't concern yourself with the terms of repayment. I know you too well to worry that you'll spend it on gambling and vice. Consider it my part in upholding the dignity of Saveze."

* * *

On returning to her room at the palace, she was waylaid by one of the ubiquitous pages responsible for errands and messages for the in-dwellers. He handed her a small collection of cards and she sorted through them as he waited. It seemed Margerit had been busy: there were notes from one Mefro Dominique, dressmaker and Mefroi Perkin, tailor, both indicating their eagerness to wait on the baroness at her convenience. And Margerit's own card with a plea to join her for a private supper. She had underlined the word "private." The page seemed inclined to look askance at the breach of etiquette in that note but she gave him a quelling look and he thought better of commenting. Evidently they had entered a comedic farce and were destined to duck in and out of opposite doorways for a time. All it needed was for Margerit to be visiting LeFevre at this very moment. But supper, that was manageable, especially if her clothing could be forgiven.

"There was also a message from her grace the Duchess of Maunberg that she invites you to join her for a small dinner party in the blue salon this evening."

Damn. That one couldn't be ignored. But perhaps…She handed back the tradesmen's cards and said, "Let them both know that I will be at Mefro Dominique's shop tomorrow at—" She calculated quickly. "—ten in the morning." That should be early enough to avoid any social conflicts. "And bring me writing materials."

A small portable secretary box was produced and she hastily scribbled a note. *Dearest Margerit, Unavoidably detained tonight. Meet me at the dressmaker's at ten tomorrow. 'Nudus et coopervisti me—I was naked and you clothed me.' Your own Barbara.* And then, at the thought of curious eyes looking it over, she folded the paper and sealed it. Not, perhaps, the most dignified of occasions for her first use of the Saveze signet, but Margerit might be amused. "And take that to Maisetra Sovitre on the Vezenaf."

* * *

Margerit had arrived before her at the dressmaker the next morning. Barbara greeted her as warmly as the audience and propriety would allow. "I'm sorry about yesterday. Fate conspired against us—I was invited to dine by Duchess Annek and an invitation there might as well be a command. She's rather different from what I expected. Remind me to tell you about her."

And then it was off to the back room for Mefro Dominique to take all her necessary measurements and those for the waiting tailor as well. Margerit was uncharacteristically quiet so Barbara filled the space with what nothings might be heard by anyone. "Are things settled again at Tiporsel? If you send to me again at the palace, write a letter don't just send a card. The pages are incurable gossips and I don't care to have your name bandied about and your notes read by all and sundry."

"Oh," Margerit said more warmly, "was that what the seal was about? It seemed so terrifyingly formal."

"It's going to be hard to escape that. If I sneeze, there will be formalities." She shrugged. "I'll become accustomed to it, I expect. I always thought the baron rather enjoyed every little thing being a ritual but perhaps he too was just accustomed." He would always be "the baron," never "my father," she realized. He had never been her father in life and it made no sense to use the word when speaking of him now.

The measurements were done and they returned to the room where bolts of fabric were piled ready for her inspection. "And what does the Mesnera need today?" the dressmaker began.

"Everything, I'm afraid." Barbara saw the woman's eyes light up at that. "I have almost nothing suitable for my new estate. But keep to what's simple and elegant—nothing too frivolous or fashionable. I won't be wearing a new gown to every ball. Make me a few things that will last a while and do for most occasions."

"But Barbara," Margerit urged, "I want you to have what you want, not just what you need. Don't worry about the cost."

Barbara ventured a brief caress to Margerit's cheek—the sort of gesture any close friend might make. "I'm grateful for your gift, but I need a style I can maintain. It'll be a long time before the Saveze estate can keep me in the latest fashion." She smiled wryly. "At least I'm already thought odd enough to carry it off. And speaking of which—"

She beckoned the tailor over and began explaining her notion of what he should provide. Riding clothes, of course. Just because she could manage a sidesaddle and skirts didn't mean she intended to do so. And some things in a mixed style: not entirely masculine but suitable for active pursuits. Mefroi Perkin was stiff and skeptical at first but came around to the challenge.

In the end, between the two of them, an order was left for perhaps a dozen outfits, plus such incidentals as couldn't be salvaged from her previous wardrobe. A few to be delivered as soon as might be and the rest within a week.

To prolong the visit, Margerit's carriage took them back to the palace by an unhurried route. The first few minutes were given over to kisses. But then the questions could not be contained.

"But Barbara, how…why…? Did you expect any of this?"

"Of course not! I swore to you, Margerit, no more secrets. I'm sorry about the baron's letter; I know it was wrong to keep that from you. But I wasn't certain—not really—about that. But no, I was as surprised about the title as you were. And why? With no obvious heir it was Aukust's right to award it as he pleased. With the council decision coming any time now he couldn't wait. Why me? I'm closest in blood to the Lumbeirt line. There are no cousins within seven degrees. Maybe a bastard's better than a stranger. Or perhaps it was just a whim or a joke."

Margerit laughed suddenly. "Hasn't it occurred to you that he might have thought you were the best choice? After all, you'd just proven in front of the entire city that you're brave and clever, you know the law like a scholar and you're loyal both to Alpennia and to those you've given your word to."

Barbara stopped the flood of praise with another kiss. "I think your own preference is showing."

Too soon, they came into the *plaiz* and near the gates. Barbara signaled the coachman to stop. "I'll ride the rest of the way. It's better."

"When will I see you again?" Margerit asked.

"I don't know. There's so much to be done and my time isn't always my own."

"I want to help."

"I know." Another kiss. "Be patient; that will help the most. When matters are more settled we can make plans." One last kiss and a laugh. "Once I've clothed my nakedness and can start to accept invitations, no doubt we'll be at some of the same parties."

* * *

It was a tribute to the power of money and the hope of future custom that by the end of the next day she had received her riding clothes and a gown that would serve for daytime and all but the most formal of evening occasions. Also waiting when she returned from the day's errands and obligations were letters from Margerit and LeFevre. She tore open Margerit's first and found herself blushing. No, *that* was not something she wanted the pages to be viewing. LeFevre's note was more somber.

I have made initial inquiries into the state of matters. What there is good of news is that it is not worse. Whatever Estefen's personal debts may have been (and of course those are not tied to the title) he does not seem to have had the power to convince anyone to take the risk of adding to the existing mortgages. Those stand exactly as they did when he inherited. What is left to discover is the condition of the properties. That will need to wait until the Rotenek season closes, as I cannot leave my affairs here and will not trust the evaluation to another.

Well, that was no more than she expected. It would be a long road, but there would be an end to it.

In those first few days she had put off all invitations but those that were impossible to ignore. Now she sorted through the accumulation to see what could be done. It was essential to be seen but it was crucial to give no preference or appearance of preference in where she was seen and with whom. There was no telling what the future would bring and it was no time to burn any more bridges than were already in flames. Her first council meeting tomorrow, then a dinner evidently in her honor by Chozzik. He was an old friend of Marziel's—that might be awkward, but a good tie to cultivate—and like most of the old men he leaned to the *Charteires*, supporting Annek's sons on the strength of the marriage charter. Coming so soon after Duchess Annek, she would need several more on the princess's side to balance. She amused herself by describing the process to Margerit as a means to sorting out the week's schedule. *I've set out the invitations in columns by their preference in council and in rows by the day of the week. Alas, the two Atilliet cousins have both claimed me for Wednesday, but if I explain that I daren't accept either for fear of offending the other perhaps I can slip away to Tiporsel. I can make no promises. The council seems to meet at whim, announced no sooner than the day before. I'd suspect him of playing with us but perhaps it's no more than the vagaries of his health. Friday will be the opera, although I haven't yet chosen a host. Dearest, would you be willing to accept an invitation from de Cherdillac if I convince her to host something? It would allow me an evening with you free of politics.*

But it seemed impossible to steal as many moments as she wished. Life in the palace was as exposed as market day in the Plaizekil and excuses were scrutinized for significance. An unexpected hour of freedom carried no guarantee that Margerit would be home and Barbara steadfastly forbade her from sitting idle in hopes of a visit. *The council must conclude before the end of the Season,* she wrote. *Summer cannot come too soon.*

Margerit's responses carried less news and more longing. *Would that I could fold myself up in this paper and be carried to your chamber. Rotenek never seemed so vast before that we can both be here and yet so distant.*

For the opera party, it must be one of Elisebet's men and Estapez turned up at the top of the list. He'd had no connections to the guild: too old to run with Lutoz's pack and too young to have sons who had. His wife played the gracious hostess for the dozen people watching from their box and kept the conversation to inconsequential matters. But at the interval Barbara followed him down the hall to a separate room where Princess Elisebet herself held forth. She had dressed in a gown of white and crimson—the Atilliet colors—and her dark curls peeked from beneath a turban that fell just short of seeming a crown. Every detail of her appearance was meant to claim what she needed to win instead.

There were few preliminaries. "You haven't attended any of my little parties yet, Saveze. I'm disappointed."

Barbara curtsied deeply. "Your Grace, I haven't yet been invited to any of your little parties. But if I were, my schedule would suddenly be open."

"Ah, an oversight. Come here and sit beside me." Elisebet smiled in what she must have thought was an inviting manner, but it never reached her eyes. She patted the next chair and Barbara took it. "You've quite set the city on its head. The conquering heroine!"

"I hope your Grace refers to my case in law. If I may conquer in defense of the House of Atilliet, I will be content."

"A house has many rooms," she replied somewhat sharply. "So you've dined with the duchess. What did you think?"

It was crudely done. If this were how she wooed supporters for her son, he would need a miracle to prevail. "We discussed gardens, I believe. She was trying to remember the name of a flower that my father presented her at her wedding. That was well before I was born, of course, but I think it still grows in the gardens at Saveze." It was true enough, if only a brief moment from that evening's conversation.

The talk turned to other things for a time but Barbara kept her guard up. There was no mistaking this for mere pleasantries. When the topic came around again it was more pointed. "You would not be well served to fasten your hopes on the Austrian. Aukust may have forgiven your little friend, but Friedrich is unlikely to."

Every word was a fencing match. Even the choice of names was a weapon in this skirmish. Elisebet lost no opportunity to call Annek's sons foreign. Conrad, the young Duke of Maunberg, had declined the invitation to Alpennia but his brother had gone to the length of adopting an Alpennian form of his name. The *Charteires* were calling him Efriturik now and Barbara had been carefully dancing around the need to choose.

When she failed to respond, Elisebet said, "The Sovitre girl may need stronger friends than you. You don't have the influence your father had to protect his favorites."

It would have seemed a more sincere concern if it hadn't been Elisebet's partisans he'd been protecting them from. But at least she was disguising her interest as friendship rather than direct threat. Barbara affected as bored a tone as she thought would be believed. "Margerit Sovitre isn't my concern any more."

"That's not the impression I had. Wasn't it for her sake you accused poor Estefen? And I hear she's been sending you little love notes every day."

Barbara froze. She would have sworn the seals had not been tampered with—no, this wasn't even a stab in the dark, only a joke. But clearly someone had been watching her correspondence carefully. She would warn Margerit to send letters by way of LeFevre. It would be unremarkable if she had daily correspondence with her estate manager. She tried to turn her hesitation into affronted disdain. "I think you have misunderstood the nature of my relationship with Maisetra Sovitre. For the past two years she owned my services. I had no choice in the matter. That's finished. If I had a grudge against Estefen Chazillen, it was in my father's name, not the Sovitre woman's."

"Ah, my mistake. What is it she writes, then?"

Barbara forced a laugh. "This and that: 'Barbara, who should I hire to replace you? Barbara, where did you put my second-best cloak, the maid can't find it.' It might amaze you to know what falls under an armin's duties."

The answer seemed to satisfy her and she moved on to other arguments until the orchestra started again. Barbara rose and curtsied and noted that her hostess would be expecting her return, glancing expectantly at Mesner Estapez.

As they came out of the door of the box, she saw Margerit waiting for her a few steps down the corridor. Too quickly to be signaled away, she stepped forward, saying, "Barbara, I thought I saw you over here!"

With her host's suspicious glance on her, Barbara thought frantically, *No! Play the game, Margerit! Play the game!* Aloud, she replied coldly, "Maisetra Sovitre. What a surprise. And how are you enjoying the opera?" It tore her heart to see Margerit's mouth twist from an eager smile to half-open shocked dismay.

Margerit looked stunned only for a moment, then in the same coldly formal tone she answered, "I don't care for it, Mesnera. I much preferred the Vittoriani from last year."

That's better! With a stiff nod Barbara brushed on past.

"A trifle familiar for the 'nature of the relationship', don't you think?" Estapez commented.

"Old habits fade slowly." She didn't dare to look back. "No doubt there was a misplaced bonnet this time."

* * *

Before attending her first session of the succession council, Barbara had failed to understand how it was that the council could deliberate for months and fail to come any closer to a resolution. Now experience made it appallingly clear. Worse was to sit through the sessions when her feet longed to hurry down the Vezenaf.

It was laid down in law that every landed nobleman and his heir-default had the right to speak before the council on the merits of the claimants. But custom, rather than law, dictated that every point of law raised in those speeches must be pursued and verified. Every note of history must be tracked down in the annals. Every claim of contract and charter must be produced and documented. And every claimant had the right to respond to each of those points. Questions of the lineage of the claimants, of the precedents for indirect succession, of the nature of the princess Iohanna's marriage contract—these had all long been settled. And long it had been. Now the arguments turned to the questions of experience and qualifications. There was plentiful fodder for all sides and tempers were getting shorter.

Count Feniz spent half an hour granting the virtues of Duchess Annek's elder son in prelude, no doubt, to deploring the callowness of the younger one, but just as he rose to his most dramatic heights, Annek herself stood and interrupted.

"How is this to the point? Conrad doesn't enter into the matter; he is content to remain Duke of Maunberg. There was never any question that he would come to Alpennia. You might as well argue the virtues of the emperor for he won't come into the decision of this council either."

The next two hours devolved into a rehearsal of the legal basis for a direct heir removing himself from consideration, which led to an unresolved debate regarding whether the term "direct heir" applied solely to Aukustin. Barbara quickly realized that these arguments were now known by rote like a mummers' play, needing only the proper cue to be set on their own course. The first speaker returned, at last, to conclude his interrupted point.

"The world is an unsettled place; it's not so long since war flooded through our lives like the river in spate. It's not a time to be ruled by children."

He went on in that vein until even he realized there was no more to say on the topic. Barbara had adjusted her evaluation: he must be supporting one of the Atilliet cousins, though which was impossible to tell. It was a failing task, she knew. Neither could evoke sufficient passion to achieve victory. They were men of a previous age and the land hungered for youth and vigor. But how much youth?

Princess Elisebet had risen to answer the question and dwelt on the advantages of combining the promise of youth with the advice and experience of a regent in the years of apprenticeship. "A prince so trained in governing will take the reins with a steady and practiced hand, accustomed to taking counsel and well known to his ministers."

"In this, I agree with my cousin," said Annek in her own turn. Barbara could understand that she would balk at referring to a woman a decade her junior as "stepmother." "God grant my father years yet to work hand in hand with his heir. But should we not be so blessed, Efriturik will have the benefit of the six years I governed Maunberg after my beloved husband's death before Conrad's majority. I agree that wise and experienced regents can do much to bridge a brief interlude. It is only when a regency continues for long years that much harm may be done."

Barbara tried to listen with an unbiased ear, but it was hard not to see, in these debates, the character of Elisebet's long ascendency. She claimed as rights what must be earned and stumbled when she needed grace. If she had hewed to Aukustin's undeniable primacy as the prince's only living son, she might sway many of the doubters. But to emphasize her own expected role as regent was a mistake.

And the rivalry with Annek spurred her to rashness. Out of turn, she rose again and countered, "I too have experience in governing!"

"Indeed?" the duchess replied coolly. "I had always thought it was my father who rules in Alpennia. Perhaps I was mistaken."

Feeling freed from the rituals of debate by the interchange, many voices chimed in, bringing the babble to a level impossible to follow. In the end, only dismissing the council for the day restored order. For all her wariness of Elisebet, Barbara was finding herself unenthusiastic about supporting the Austrian. Whatever his virtues, he knew little about Alpennia. In his brief appearances before the council sessions she had attended, he had allowed Annek to speak for him, knowing perhaps that however fine the speeches he might make in German or French they would not endear him to his prospective subjects. In time, perhaps, that would change, but they didn't have time.

* * *

Released for the day, Barbara calculated it still early enough to call without notice and hastily changed for the short ride to Tiporsel. The footman who opened the door, on noting that he would inquire after the maisetra, disappointed her by returning with Maisetra Pertinek. She accompanied a formally correct salutation with, "My niece is not at home."

It struck Barbara as odd, for Margerit hadn't mentioned any recent excursions separate from her aunt. "Where has she gone? I'll just—"

"My niece is feeling unwell and is not at home to visitors."

Now she was all concern and glanced toward the stairs. "What's wrong? I promise I'll only be a few minutes."

Bertrut stepped to place herself in the way. "Mesnera, please don't make this awkward. My niece is not at home."

Without quite knowing how, she found herself back on the other side of the door, being handed the reins to her mount. *What was that about? Is she ill?* In a panicked moment she wondered if their encounter at the opera had been misinterpreted. She thought about going around to the servants' entrance and interrogating Mefro Charsintek. The housekeeper would know what lay behind Bertrut's sudden animosity. But she'd lost the right to behave as a member of the household. Impatiently she rode back for the palace and the cold consolation of letters.

CHAPTER FIFTY-NINE

Margerit

All morning she had waited. Her heart made excuses but her head refused to hear them and began pounding dully, driving her at last to her bed if only to escape Bertrut's prying questions. Her hopes rose when she felt the house quiver in the way only the heavy oaken entry doors could produce, but then...nothing. When her aunt came up with the tea to inquire if she were feeling better, Margerit asked, for only the third time that day, if there had been any letters.

"No—" she began. Her hesitation was suspicious.

"I thought I heard the door. Who was it?"

Bertrut drew up a chair and sat beside her bed to pour out a cup. "This isn't good for you. This waiting and moping. It will spoil your looks."

"Aunt Bertrut, did Barbara call?"

Again, the hesitation. "Yes and I told her you weren't in a state to see anyone."

"Aunt!"

"Margerit, you need to let her go her own way. All this pestering her with letters and visits—it isn't seemly. Baroness Saveze is as high above you as you were above Barbara the armin. You shouldn't seek her notice. It only makes you unhappy."

Margerit felt her anger rising and her head throbbed more sharply. "You should have told me she was here!"

"Perhaps I was wrong," Bertrut said carefully. "I don't mean to set up myself as mistress of your house. But you've done little but sit and stare out the windows ever since you returned to Rotenek. I wonder if it might not be good to go away for a little while. It's at least a month yet before the season's over and who knows when flood-tide might come, but a little trip home to Chalanz might bring a different view."

"No, I can't leave. Barbara might need me."

"And I want to talk to you about that as well," she continued. "I saw those dressmaker's bills and I don't know what else there might be that I haven't seen. You need to be careful of letting the baroness take advantage of you. She may well consider your inheritance rightfully hers but that doesn't mean that you should agree."

"But I do." Margerit pushed aside the cup that her aunt was trying to thrust on her and slipped from the bed, wrapping her dressing gown around her. She was feeling too much like a naughty child being lectured. "Everything the baron left me should have been hers. And I think one reason he left it to me was because he thought I would see the justice in that. She's refused to take anything except the clothing, though, so you needn't fear I'll end up a pauper."

Her aunt began a different tack. "I know you've had a certain fondness for her. You enjoyed playing at being students together. And see what that brought you! But—"

"A certain fondness?" Was that all she knew?

"—but it's time you started acting like a grown woman. Think about your future. Set your mind to choosing a husband. Marriage will help you forget all this."

Impatience overcame caution. "I will never marry."

"Don't be ridiculous," Bertrut said sharply. "Even after this foolishness with that guild, you're still the most eligible heiress in Rotenek. Of course you'll make a good marriage."

Her head was pounding. Why did they need to have this argument now? "I will never marry. I've already given my heart; I can't give it again."

Her aunt turned pale. "Sweet Jesus! What have you done? Who was he? Will he hold his tongue? Why didn't you—is he married already?"

Did she understand nothing? "Aunt Bertrut, Barbara and I are lovers."

There, it was said. Margerit tried to divine the thoughts behind her aunt's flustered silence. But surely she had suspected? Couldn't she see this was how it was always meant to be? She began, "Aunt Bertrut—"

"You…and Barbara?" Confusion slowly turned to scorn. "And for this you would abandon respectability? For this you'd drag your family's name in the gutter?"

"I would do anything for her," she answered with quiet intensity.

Her aunt's response was waspish. "I see. In that case you should take an example from other common-born mistresses of the nobility and avoid importuning her. Become accustomed to waiting on her convenience and give up these vapors or you'll lose her interest. Perhaps you could take lessons from the women on Chuldesmit Street."

That district was famous for elegant little houses inhabited by women who weren't invited into respectable homes. It was meant to sting and it did. Margerit lashed back, "I'll take this lesson from mistresses of the great: never, *never* deny her entrance to my house again."

But after her aunt stiffly acknowledged the command and left, Margerit curled up on the bed again, trying desperately not to cry. It was true. How could she not have seen it? The months at Saint Orisul's had been spent outside time, outside the world. Briefly they had been equals and friends and they'd planned a future side by side. Now, as Barbara had once said, she couldn't make it work. And yet she couldn't live without her. That much she knew. Could she instead learn her new role and do her duty, as Barbara once had? Could she live in the shadows of Barbara's life, never stirring the slightest whiff of scandal? Would it always be like this? Couldn't they at least live under the same roof? She could understand that the Baroness Saveze couldn't live as a guest of someone with no rank or title, but *she* might find a place in Barbara's house, when she had one some day. They'd promised each other to find a way and she, at least, would hold to her promise.

To know that there was a decision to make was to have made it.

She rose and rang for the maid, wishing she had arranged for Maitelen's return already. She longed for at least one person she could trust absolutely. If it were her role to be pleasant and charming at any time that Barbara might happen to call, then it was best to begin as she meant to go on.

There was a letter waiting when she went downstairs. She took it to the library and tore it open.

Dearest Margerit.

Her heart leapt. She was still beloved, it had all been a mistake.

Your aunt tells me you are unwell and I am desolated to think that my little charade last night might have contributed to your distress. I was in company with one who only moments before had been a party to threatening your safety in hopes of controlling my actions. The greatest protection I can offer you at the moment is to convince my enemies that I care nothing for you.

Too convincing entirely. The letter was so stiff and formal.

Our correspondence is being noted. I have sent this by way of LeFevre and must ask that you do the same. I've offered the excuse of lingering business for the letters that have gone before, but that won't last.

So. There it was. She was to keep out of sight in the future.

I can't tell who will demand my time in the coming week, but I have claimed Monday for my own. Do you think you will be well enough for an outing? I thought we might drive out of the city for the day—where we can breathe fresh air and care for no one but ourselves. Let me know and I will attend on you that morning. You, I fear, will need to supply the carriage. Your own Barbara.

An entire day to themselves. Where they needn't care who saw them together. So it must be. She penned a brief note in return and enclosed it within the misdirection. There were plans to make, instructions to give. She would play these cards the best she knew how.

Dinner might have been tense—she could see from Uncle Pertinek's glances that he had been told all. But having made her choice, she was free of his disapproval. He made one essay, beginning, "Margerit, I know it's none of my affair, but—"

She answered simply, "No, it isn't," and that was an end of it.

* * *

The day was bright and fine—all she could have asked for. Barbara needed only to give her horse to the groom and step into the waiting carriage and they were away. When they were past the city gates, Margerit folded down the windows, despite the morning chill, to let in the fresh air and the greening countryside.

Barbara began with apologies about the opera and to explain once again how her days were filled but Margerit put a finger against her lips. "None of that today. Leave it behind."

And then there was no more talking but only the small sounds of pleasure as the carriage rattled on for an hour or more. Margerit would have been content simply to drive as far as they might and then return, in order to have Barbara alone. But they weren't truly alone, of course. Outside there was the coachman and the grooms and the ever-present Marken. Some excuse had been needed to give for the trip, so their course slowed at last and the horses turned off to an old track leading up a steep stony hill. Barbara looked out the window and asked, "Chazil Lepunt?"

"We needed some destination, after all," Margerit laughed. "Verunik told me about the place and I had a mind to see it. I wore my walking shoes, you see?"

When the carriage had climbed as near to the ruins as might be, they left the horses to rest and went on foot. With Barbara's assurance to Marken, "I'll see her safe," they climbed out of sight, hand in hand—or when the path allowed, arms encircling waists—over the tumbled stones and eroded walls to find the summit of the hill.

"There," Barbara pointed, where the land fell away toward the Rotein. "You can see the old course of the river in the shape of the farms. The castle here was abandoned when it no longer commanded the passage of ships. That would have been in Domric's day, long before the rise of the Atilliets. Rotenek was just a market town then—though it had the cathedral, of course. But Domric made it his capital and built the first palace. Do you see—"

Margerit turned Barbara's face toward her and kissed her, as if they hadn't had their fill of kisses on the journey. "I didn't come here for a history lesson. I chose it because Verunik said the place had something of a reputation among lovers." She ran her fingers through Barbara's unruly hair, dislodging the pins and pulling it loose to fly about their faces in the breeze. She drowned in the pale blue of those eyes and drank them in until intoxicated.

A lifetime would have seemed too short and they had only a few hours. Then Barbara twisted her hair back up into place and fastened it haphazardly with what pins they could find. They descended to the waiting party at last, Margerit saying, "I have a surprise for you."

The bundles and baskets had been unpacked and the grooms pressed into service as footmen to set out a formal dinner, served around a small folding table. A cold ham, an assortment of fruit tarts, some plump pigeons roasted *en croute*. Until the breeze turned chill and the sun began setting low they laughed and talked of inconsequentialities. On their return, the hot blood of the morning had changed to a clinging for warmth as the dusk closed in outside.

"I wish every day could be like this," Margerit sighed.

"You'd find it lacking after a while unless you found a way to fit the library into the carriage."

Margerit laughed at that but then turned wistful. "In the fall, perhaps I'll attend lectures again?" It became a question as she spoke, wondering how it might fit with Barbara's plans.

"Of course you must!" Barbara insisted.

"I wish—" She turned what she'd meant to say into, "I wish the river would rise and give us an excuse to get away for more than just one day."

Barbara shook her head. "Until the council's done there's no escape for me. Flood-tide would just be one long debate. But I thought perhaps—" She shifted on the seat to hold Margerit closer. "When the vote is taken and the season is over, LeFevre and I need to go down to Saveze. I was hoping you might join me."

"Of course!" Margerit replied immediately. "Do you plan to spend the whole summer there? I'd need to plan what to do with the household."

"I don't know. I need to find out what condition the land is in— what might need to be done to bring it up to its best. When Marziel dug it out from under the last time, he had his trading ventures and the opportunities that the war brought. I'll need to start more slowly."

"Barbara," Margerit said impulsively, "this is silly. Why don't I just pay off the mortgages?"

Her response was immediate and vehement. "No! No, don't even think of it."

"But—"

"Please Margerit, I don't want to discuss it. I don't want your money. Let it be."

Margerit tried to keep herself still although her heart was pounding. *I don't want your money.* As if there were something tainted about it. As if anything beyond clothing and carriage rides would stain the name of Saveze. She shifted to hide her momentary discomfiture, grateful for the dark, but she didn't trust herself to speak and so she raised one of Barbara's hands to her lips to excuse the silence.

* * *

Though she'd returned from the outing with all good intentions, a long sleepless night brought back the doubts. She needed time to think. Time alone without Aunt Bertrut fraying at her nerves. Without sweet notes and brief glances eroding her resolve. Time away from anyone who knew enough to ask questions to which she didn't know the answers. Time to test whether she could not, in fact, live without her.

There was no hope for any rest, so when the girl came in silently at dawn to build up the fire she rang to be dressed and went downstairs to begin making arrangements.

"Aunt Bertrut," she announced when her aunt joined her in the morning room, "I'm going to Chalanz for a while." And then before Bertrut had a chance to express triumph or even approval she continued, "I won't be moving the household yet. I don't know how long I'll be there and there's no reason to turn everyone topsy-turvy. I won't be taking my own coach, I'll hire one for the journey, so if the floods come while I'm gone you can travel as you please."

"But you can't go alone!" Bertrut managed to slip into a moment's pause.

"I'll have Marken for protection. For propriety I thought I'd go ask at the *Orisules* school down by the university. The sisters are likely to know some respectable woman who wants to travel in that direction. When I get to Chalanz I'll have Maitelen so you needn't worry on that account."

"But when will you—"

"I don't know. There are a few affairs I need to take care of first. I'll be leaving tomorrow, if possible." And that was that. After urging her to it, there was little room for her aunt to protest.

Beyond setting things in motion for the journey, there was really only one matter to arrange. Enclosed with her daily letter to Barbara, she sent LeFevre a note that she would see him in his office on a matter of business that afternoon, if it were convenient.

Facing LeFevre across his desk, she came quickly to the point. "I would like you to arrange for me to buy the Saveze mortgages. All of them."

He seemed unsurprised, as if he'd been expecting the request. "That is certainly possible, although it can't be done instantly. I should say a week or two. We'd want to conclude things quietly, so it's best not to take too long about it. Are there any particular requirements that Barbara—"

"Barbara knows nothing about this and she isn't to know. Promise me that."

"Ah." That had startled him. "Then what do you—"

"I want to buy the mortgages and simply hold them."

He shuffled the papers on his desk in his old nervous habit. "I can't advise it. You may make your own decisions now, of course, but I would hope you still value my advice and I can't recommend this."

Margerit didn't care to argue. She wasn't sure how long she could maintain her mask. "Is it that you consider the Saveze mortgages to be a poor investment?"

"Of course not," he said hurriedly. "But Maisetra, you put me in a very difficult position. When I agreed to manage Barbara's estate I had no reason to believe your affairs would be in conflict."

"I see no conflict," Margerit said in the most matter-of-fact tone she could manage. "If it can be done, then do it. If it can't be done, then tell me so. But I believe I have enough in the Genoan account to cover the whole. There need be no delay to free up the funds on that end."

"As you wish, Maisetra. I think rather than—but you may leave the details to me, if you like."

She thanked him and rose to go. At the door he stopped her, asking, "Maisetra, is there anything further I should know?"

That was when she had to struggle the hardest for control. "Not without putting you in a very difficult position," she replied and left before her resolve could waver.

CHAPTER SIXTY

Barbara

Instead of the usual daily packet from LeFevre, the man himself was waiting for her when the day's council session broke at last for the evening. "There are a few papers I need you to review," he began. "They might have waited but I wanted your instructions on another matter. Would you like me to forward your letters to Chalanz or will you be making other arrangements?"

He held up the note she had sent for Margerit the previous day. The question made no sense. Her confusion must have been plain on her face for he explained, "The messenger brought it back from Tiporsel saying that Maisetra Sovitre had removed to Chalanz and that the note had been refused. So I wondered if I should simply send it on to Chalanz."

"Chalanz? There must be some mistake. She said nothing about... that is, we talked about where we might go after the season, but—"

"So you knew nothing about this?" It sounded as if he were confirming what he'd already guessed.

"Less than you do, evidently," Barbara returned. "Didn't she say anything to you?"

His hesitation told her that Margerit had, indeed, told him something. He only replied, "She said nothing about leaving town."

"But?"

He sighed and shook his head. "There were private business matters we discussed but I can no more share them with you than I would tell your own secrets. Maisetra Pertinek, no doubt, knows more than I do."

No doubt. But it was too late in the day for a social call and she'd already stormed that castle once and been repulsed by Bertrut's defense. Her dignity could do without shouting in courtyards after dark.

In the morning, her plans to ride out at the earliest acceptable hour were diverted when Duchess Annek accosted her on the way to the stables saying, "I wondered if you might spare me a moment of your time."

Barbara bowed in acceptance. Annek gestured the way to the palace gardens. She wondered at that. So this was not to be another formal solicitation but not a secret one either. The gardens were public enough for those who watched but not for those who listened.

"I've been taking the time to read over the ceremony for that mystery—the one that caused all the trouble. Do you know—it wasn't clear during the trial, but do you know who was most responsible for it?"

Barbara chose her answer carefully. "The prince has said that—"

"Oh nonsense, I'm not speaking of guilt or innocence. That mystery is something near to a masterpiece. And with care to tease out any other hidden surprises I think it might be well worth adding to the calendar. I had thought, from her performance that day, that your friend the Sovitre woman might be up to the task."

Was it a trap? For all that she discounted Elisebet's threats, there was no reason to think Annek had any love for Margerit's work. But the mystery *had* been a masterpiece and she wouldn't steal the credit from where it belonged. "The whole guild worked on gathering the elements, but it was Maisetra Sovitre who wrote both the framework and the details."

"Are you certain?" she asked. "She seemed barely a child and she can't have had any formal schooling in thaumaturgy. I know she said she did some work at Saint Orisul's but I know their work and this has an entirely different flavor."

Barbara hadn't realized the duchess was a connoisseur. "I'm certain because I was there. We worked together on some of the scaffolding— just the logical structures. I have no sensitivity for visions; it's Maisetra

Sovitre who's the artist." Was it wrong to take at least a little pride in her own part?

"Ah yes. A very unusual armin indeed! I had heard that…well, people say all manner of things. I should like you to introduce her to me."

And that could have been either disaster or triumph, Barbara thought. It was danger enough if Elisebet thought Margerit a useful pawn. But if Annek showed favor to her? That might give Margerit enemies in her own right. It was a relief to be able to say, "It would be my pleasure, if it were possible, but she's gone home to Chalanz at the moment. I don't know when she returns to the city."

Annek gave a little shrug. "Ah well. Perhaps there will be an opportunity if the council—well, who can say." They walked along a while in silence as Barbara waited to see if she were dismissed. "You haven't spoken at all in council, I've noticed," Annek said at last.

"I think there's no famine of speech there," Barbara replied. "I find I can do better by listening than adding to the din. And I doubt anyone cares to know my opinions."

"I'm curious to know them. If I asked, would you tell me honestly?"

Barbara weighed the chance that a truly honest answer would be valued. "Your Grace, if it were a matter simply of supporting you, there would be no question in my mind. My father held that Iohanna's charter—your mother's marriage contract—was a bond of honor for the Atilliets, however ill-advised. But Friedrich is a foreigner. In time, he might become Alpennian, but he isn't now. Your family and this land sacrificed too much and suffered too long trying to keep foreign rule at bay."

Annek looked at her speculatively. "Now there is an interesting thought."

"Pardon?"

"That you would support me yet not my son."

"I mean no slight to him," Barbara said hurriedly.

"You misunderstand me. How many of the *Charteires* do you think might feel the same?"

Barbara confessed her confusion. "I fear you've gone beyond me."

"It's no matter. This has been a very useful discussion."

* * *

The visit to Tiporsel left no one satisfied. Barbara learned only that Margerit had, indeed, left for Chalanz. When might she return?

Heaven only knew. Did she plan to remove the household there for the summer? No one could say. Had she left any letter or message? If there were any, they had been delivered. In frustration Barbara asked to speak to Ponivin or Charsintek in case they knew anything further but here Bertrut balked.

"Mesnera, I have been instructed not to deny you entrance to this house, but I was given no commands to allow you to interrogate the servants."

Mesner Pertinek had lent his silent presence to the confrontation but now he took Barbara aside and offered some carefully couched suggestions regarding keeping one's private amusements to their proper venues. It might have been meant as companionable advice. It might have been taken as offensive interference. But his fumbling efforts to discuss the poor taste of ruining the reputations of respectable young women—without actually naming Barbara's supposed offense—were, in the end, merely ludicrous. It was to spare them both embarrassment that Barbara finally gave up.

* * *

Those who had looked for an early consensus from the succession council had long since given up hope. Those who had thought that rhetoric—whether reasoned or impassioned—would win the day had not accounted for the depth of loyalties that must be moved. And those who prayed that the competing deadlines of Easter and flood-tide would force the matter failed to foresee the unwillingness of the principals to force a vote they were unsure of winning.

Only one other incident broke the endless waiting: a chance encounter in the corridor outside the council hall—a short sturdily-built man who stepped out of her path too quickly for mere courtesy. She looked more closely. He peered back nervously from under bushy brows. It was the man who had held Arpik's notes. Whose shadows had haunted her steps all through the previous winter. "Maistir Langal," she said.

The man bowed carefully. "Baroness."

"A question, if you would," Barbara said, moving to block his path. He made a gesture of welcome though his expression belied it. "Why?" she asked simply.

A man in his business didn't succeed by underestimating others. He passed over the obvious answer. "Arpik's debts wouldn't have been worth buying except that they came with one thing: the name of your true father. But knowledge isn't proof. When Lumbeirt died without acknowledging you I saw my investment slipping away. I tried to find an excuse to have that clerk of his questioned…well, that's past. But I'd been watching you. I thought there was one person in Alpennia capable of digging out the truth and as eager for it as I was. All you needed was prodding. Alas, you weren't as curious as I hoped."

"Curious enough," Barbara said, "but I had other distractions. Why not simply approach me directly?"

"I didn't know how strong the proof might be. A court would be more likely to believe you if the conclusions were all your own. It was only business. I hope you hold no grudge."

Only business. Margerit's safety, the casual threat to LeFevre… she couldn't even begin to detail what she held against him. But she only brushed the hair back from her temple to bare the scar. "I hold a grudge for that. I won't forget."

It was the last answer to her mystery and like so many of the others it mattered nothing when it came. All that mattered now was concluding the council so she could follow her heart to Chalanz.

In the last week before Easter, a shift was felt in the city. In parlors and clubs a new idea took hold, carefully planted and tended. The charter stipulated that Prince Aukust would be succeeded by his heirs through the Princess Iohanna. But Iohanna had three living descendents and one of them had been both born and bred in Alpennia. The seal was set when Ambors, the elder of the Atilliet cousins, was convinced to put the case to the council.

"There is no bar, whatever custom may dictate," he argued. "Consider this: we can fulfill the demands of honor and give our land a tried and tested ruler. And in time, when the choice comes before us again, other candidates will have gained in wisdom and experience and we will be the richer for that. I propose, for the consideration of the council, Annek Atilliet, once Duchess of Maunberg."

For two days it was as foxes in the henhouse, but on the third day, when Ambors Atilliet repeated the proposal to complete the requirements of law, Prince Aukust responded, "If this is the wish of the council, I will abide by your will," signaling the call for voting. Six hours later, the decision was sealed and the council released.

* * *

Barbara would have taken horse that moment if it weren't too late to set out without risking her neck galloping through the dark. And

LeFevre needed to know her plans first. She found him just closing his office and shared the news from the council.

"Who would have thought that such a useful decision could come from such a useless process," he wondered. "Saving your presence, of course."

"There's little enough I had to do with it," Barbara said. "I'm off to Chalanz in the morning. I'll join you at Saveze when I may but—" She frowned. "I don't know. I just don't know. She hasn't answered any of my letters. There was time for something at least to make its way here."

LeFevre took out the keys he had just pocketed and reopened the door. "Come in for a moment. There's something I need to tell you."

Barbara followed, waiting while he made a face and sighed and then fiddled with the keys again.

"I have never broken my word to someone I served. I never broke my word to the baron—you know that well enough. But I promised something to Maisetra Sovitre that I should not have promised and now I find my word is in conflict with both my duty and my heart."

At Margerit's name, Barbara was all attention.

"The day before she left Rotenek, Maisetra Sovitre requested me to purchase the Saveze mortgages in her name." He held up a hand to forestall her response. "She specifically instructed me not to tell you. I was to purchase them and hold them as I would any other of her investments. Now why would she do that?"

All she could feel was the shame. *She went behind my back. Even after we'd talked.* "I forbade her to pay them off," she said. "How dare she—"

"And by what right do you tell her what she may and may not do with her inheritance?" he countered.

Barbara was silent. There was no answer to that.

"I once told you that you two stood too closely to see each other's hearts. But now I think you keep too great a distance. What does she fear so much that she had to flee to Chalanz? Why are you so afraid of her generosity?"

"I don't want—"

He stopped her. "Don't tell me. Tell her. Give her the gift of your deepest fears and pray that it's not too late."

* * *

It was said to be possible to ride from Rotenek to Chalanz in a single day, at midsummer with enough horses. The name Saveze could command sufficient horses but not the daylight, so it was mid-morning of the next day when she slacked pace at the edge of town and made her way to Fonten Street. Perhaps the haste was unnecessary but Barbara sensed that only rumpled clothing and a lathered horse would be acceptable attendants if she were to be granted an audience.

The house was quiet and hardly seemed inhabited. That was no wonder if it had barely been opened enough for two or three residents. She banged heavily at the knocker and then, after several minutes, again, impatiently. On the fourth knock an upstairs window came open and Maitelen shouted down, "You can knock till kingdom come but the maisetra's not at home." Then she saw who it was. "Oh! Wait, I'll be there in a moment."

The window closed again before Barbara could reply but in no more than a minute the door opened.

"She's off at church, Barbara. Her uncle came by to take her hours ago. It's the first time she's left the house since she arrived."

In the distance she heard the bells chiming and realized it was Easter. She'd lost count of the days. *Barbara*, she'd called her. So that piece of news hadn't been spread yet. She envisioned Margerit sitting alone in the mansion, unspeaking, for nearly two weeks. In an instant she was back in the saddle and riding toward the sound of the bells.

Among the crowds gradually flowing from the church it was easiest to spot the Fulpis' carriage and work her way toward it. And from there, Marken's height was easy to spot, and where he was…

"Margerit!" she called, dismounting and pushing her way close.

Maistir Fulpi interposed himself, saying, "I'll thank you not to address my niece in such a familiar fashion."

Must I deal with this now? Barbara thought but Margerit roused herself to the introduction.

"Uncle, I believe you have not yet met the new Baroness Saveze."

"The…*what?*"

Barbara bowed formally as if it were a true introduction. "Barbara Lumbeirt, Baroness Saveze. Might I request a moment of Maisetra Sovitre's time?"

He gaped at her, as did the aunt and cousins, but all melted back before her.

"Margerit, please, I need to talk to you." And she certainly didn't intend to say her piece here on the church porch before everyone.

"What do we have to talk about?" Margerit asked.

"You know very well." She reached for Margerit's hand and unexpectedly found herself confronting Marken.

"Marken, don't be a fool," she said hotly. "It's me, Barbara."

"I may be a fool, Mesnera," he replied, "but I'm a fool who knows his duty. You don't take the maisetra anywhere except she says so."

"It's all right, Marken," Margerit said wearily. She turned and walked off toward the churchyard.

Barbara hurried after her, still trailing the horse, for no one had thought to take the reins from her.

When they'd gone far enough for privacy, Margerit said, "Well?" without facing her.

"Why?" Barbara asked. "LeFevre told me. Why did you do it?"

"Don't worry," she said bitterly. "I won't sully your estate with my money. I bought the mortgages and I'll keep them and that's an end of it. You needn't think you'll have to throw it back in my face again."

Barbara stood stunned, as if the horse had kicked her. "Is that what you think?"

Margerit turned on her with her fists balled at her sides. Her cheeks were flushed and her dark eyes sparkled with anger. "What am I supposed to think? When you thought you were nobody, we could plan for the future. You promised me we'd find a way—that you'd always be at my side. But now you're even too proud to accept my money—to accept your own father's money—because my hands have dirtied it."

Barbara reached out and took those hands and kissed each one in turn. How could she explain how very mistaken that was? "Margerit, I have *everything* now. I have my freedom and my name and my history. I have a title and a position that never figured anywhere in my wildest fancies. Even in rags and without a penny to my name I could go my own way now. But all you have is your inheritance. Your fortune is the only thing that stands between you and the demands of society—that opens the door to the life you were meant for. How could I be so selfish as to want to take any of that away from you, when it's the only means you have of getting what you want?"

"A fortune can't buy everything," she said hollowly. "It can't buy me you." She pulled her hands away and crossed her arms over her chest as if she were suddenly cold. "I thought we would share one heart, one life. What is a purse beside that?"

Barbara closed her eyes and thought, *My deepest fears*. She looked again at Margerit without flinching. "No secrets—I promised you. But that's what I'm afraid of: that you'll buy me. When you offered to pay my debts, I felt...that you would own me again. I couldn't bear that. I never wanted you to doubt that my love was given freely. I didn't want people to see us and say, 'There's Margerit Sovitre's kept woman.'"

She didn't understand why Margerit began laughing, at first in surprise and then more hysterically. And though she didn't understand, she put her arms around Margerit and held her tightly until the laughter passed through sobs and then at last to speech. Then Margerit too made a gift of her fears, finishing with, "And I didn't care what name people gave me—I didn't care what people like Aunt Bertrut thought. But I couldn't bear to live only on the scraps of your life. To spend all my days play-acting and pretending we meant nothing to each other."

"Perhaps it was the wrong thing to do," Barbara said slowly, "but I only meant to protect you. Until the council was finished there was no way of knowing—"

"I don't want you to protect me," Margerit interrupted. "I want you to love me!"

Barbara chuckled and traced the line of Margerit's cheek. "I'm afraid I've gotten too much in the habit of doing both to give either of them up. But that particular charade can be left behind." And she told her the news of the court. "Whatever danger might still lie in that direction, notoriety will serve us better than caution. If you're still willing, shall it be one heart, one life, one home and yes, since you will, one purse?"

The answer hardly needed to be spoken aloud. "Yes, for all my days."

Barbara looked back at the waiting cluster of people by the Fulpis' carriage. "I'm not ready to share you yet," she whispered. She lifted Margerit up into the saddle and swung up behind her, encircling her waist in a secure embrace. She lifted a hand in Marken's direction, giving their old signal that the watch had been transferred, then she urged the horse into an easy canter. It didn't much matter what direction they went. All roads were open.

CHAPTER SIXTY-ONE

Coda

Barbara Lumbeirt, Baroness Saveze, was an Eccentric. Those who had known old Marziel said it was inevitable. Those too young to have known him heard only the stories of how she had once been an armin and a duelist. She had even killed her man, they said, although in later days the tale twisted and grew until it had her dueling her predecessor in the title over a woman. Like many eccentrics, she never married, preferring the company of her own kind—and in her day that resulted in a number of very odd friendships indeed. The oddest was the one she shared lifelong with Margerit Sovitre, the scholar, who came to be called *Fil'misitir*, Daughter of Mystery.

Bella Books, Inc.

Women. Books. Even Better Together.

P.O. Box 10543
Tallahassee, FL 32302

Phone: 800-729-4992
www.bellabooks.com